# WHEN THE SILENCE IS TOO LOUD

*a novel*

VALERIE DICKINSON

This book is a work of fiction. All names, characters, businesses, organizations, places, events and incidents portrayed are the product of the author's imagination or are used fictitiously. Any resemblance to actual events, locales or persons, living or dead is entirely coincidental.

Copyright © 2015 Valerie Dickinson

ISBN-10: 1508823898
ISBN-13: 978-1508823896

# DEDICATION

*To my loving mother, Sarah Irby, from whom I've always drawn my strength and to my father, the late Virdi Lee Irby Jr.- the dreamer - from whom I inherited the gift of storytelling.*

"Our deepest fear is not that we are inadequate. Our deepest fear is that we are powerful beyond measure. It is our light, not our darkness that most frightens us. We ask ourselves, 'Who am I to be brilliant, gorgeous, talented, fabulous?' Actually, who are you not to be? You are a child of God. Your playing small does not serve the world. There is nothing enlightened about shrinking so that other people won't feel insecure around you. We are all meant to shine, as children do. We were born to make manifest the glory of God that is within us. It's not just in some of us; it's in everyone. And as we let our own light shine, we unconsciously give other people permission to do the same. As we are liberated from our own fear, our presence automatically liberates others."

Marianne Williamson

# ACKNOWLEDGMENTS

I thank God for blessing me with the gift of storytelling. I'm so thankful to finally feel comfortable enough in my own skin to share this gift. I want to thank my wonderful husband, Marvin Dickinson, for being so supportive and always making me feel like I can do absolutely anything. I want to thank my amazing children Dariel, Donovan and Devin for your support and understanding, especially when dinner was served late or when you had to endure leftovers that were left over. Thank you to my very good friends, Alma Stone and Karen Ruffin, who read and re-read the many edited versions of my manuscript; your suggestions, critiques and editing helped me immensely. I don't know what I would have done without your support and continuous words of encouragement. Thank you Alicia Redmond who designed my book cover and turned my vision into a thing of beauty. Thank you for your patience and prayers. I want to thank my editor, Karen Rodgers; your keen eye and suggestions were spot-on and I appreciate your validation of my craft. Thank you Rosalyn Alford for being apart of my reading group; your enthusiasm helped to motivate and push me into action. Thank you Amber French for helping to provide valuable insight into the foster care system. I also want to thank Dr. Daniel Black, whose Writer's Workshop was extremely insightful and just the shot in the arm I needed to help me on my WRITE JOURNEY.

# CONTENTS

# *ONE*

## *FIGHTING TO BE FREE*

---

**T**yrone's open palm smacked against Nyla's cheek with such force it made her entire body spin before crumbling to the floor. The pain was excruciating and she saw flashes of light as she attempted to crawl away and pull herself to her feet. The floorboards squeaked under Tyrone's heavy footsteps as he closed the space between them and he jerked Nyla up by her hair.

"Now, I'm gonna tell you one mo' time hand over my money!" he snarled. His permanently scowled face sported an untamed nappy beard that matched his locked hair and contributed to his menacing look. Though shorter than Nyla, his two-hundred-pound frame—and violent nature—were enough to intimidate her into submission. Twisting

Nyla's curly hair around his fat fingers, he yanked her face to within inches of his own. His heavy breathing spewed flecks of odorous drool against her cheek. The closeness of his body to hers made her stomach quiver as she struggled to steady herself. Tears spilled out of her beautiful, sad eyes while she tried not to pull away for fear he would rip her hair completely out.

"Where is it?!" he demanded, his face contorted.

"I... I don't know, Tyrone." Nyla lied. He clutched his other hand around Nyla's neck, cutting off her air supply. Nyla's eyes grew wide with panic as she pulled at his hand trying to gain some relief. Her eyes began to roll back and she knew she was losing the fight to remain conscious. "Gabby said she'd meet me and bring me her half of the money." Nyla's voice sounded small. "Please," she begged. "She'll be here ... I promise," she managed to croak out.

Tyrone snatched her head back and peered into her freckled face; he could see the fear in her eyes. It pleased him. He always got a rush whenever he forced someone into obedience.

"If that fool ain't here in the next fifteen minutes, I'm gonna take my belt off and beat the hell outta you. You got that?!" Nyla nodded feverishly. He then leaned in closer and sniffed her like he was some kind of a canine. He could smell fear oozing from her pores and it aroused him. Slowly, he slid his coarse tongue along her cheek and buried his nose behind her ear. She stiffened then shivered involuntarily. As was the norm, she mentally took herself elsewhere, praying it would all be over soon.

"You know, it don't hafta be like this... but you just can't seem to follow directions," he spoke between clinched teeth. Without warning, he threw her back onto the floor. Nyla grabbed her neck as she scampered to the nearest corner, coughing uncontrollably and sucking in precious air. She hated being such a coward, but what choice did she have? The monster she was dealing with had no qualms about ending her life—after he got his money.

"I told *you* to bring my money, not that dumb ass Gabby!"

Nyla had been with Tyrone for a year. During that time, she'd seen what he was capable of when his anger got the best of him. Rachel, the last girl who refused to service one of his clients, was beaten severely. He forced Nyla and Gabby to dump her near the emergency room. Rachel was nearly dead by the time they reached the hospital.

Nyla glanced at the clock on the wall and knew she had to get out soon or she would suffer a similar fate. She pulled her knees into her chest and lowered her throbbing head. She moaned, not believing how quickly her life had spiraled into an abyss of drugs and crime. Now here she was, trapped in a corner like a rodent; her heart ached for freedom. She sat in a fetal position, hovering and praying for a chance to correct her mistakes. Maria's face flashed behind her closed lids. Maria had been her caseworker for many years. She was the only one, other than Gabby, that Nyla considered to be a true friend. Sitting there, Nyla could actually feel her soul withering away. She remembered Maria's easy smile and the concern she always seemed to wear behind her warm, brown eyes as she sat next to her in the car.

There were many occasions, after their meetings, Maria would drive Nyla back to the group home. One night, while on their way home, they saw a young girl patrolling the streets. She couldn't have been more than fifteen or sixteen Nyla thought; not much older than she was at the time. She was thin and although she wore a smile on her face the hollowed look in her eyes told a much different story.

Suddenly Maria grabbed Nyla's hand with a sense of urgency. The softness in her eyes was gone. Her eyes bored into Nyla's as she spoke.

"Promise me something Nyla." The glassy look frightened Nyla.

"Maria? What's wrong?"

"Just promise me that you'll never allow the pursuit of prosperity to reduce you to the lowest denominator of yourself."

"What are you talking about? You mean selling myself for money? Like her?" Nyla gestured toward the girl.

"Prosperity comes in many forms Nyla. Sometimes it comes in the form of money, food or even shelter. Many times it comes in the form of a deep desire to feel loved and validated. Some people want love so badly that they'll allow themselves to be used up and then tossed aside like garbage. You need to understand that no matter what has happened to you in your past or what the future holds, you are significant and you matter."

She squeezed Nyla's hand tighter. "Never, ever forget that. Okay?"

Suddenly Nyla's head shot up.

"Okay," Nyla said to herself. The memory of Maria's words had lit a flame inside of her. She looked at the clock and realized that she had to channel every fiber of strength she had to rise up out of this pit of despair. She had allowed Tyrone to reduce her to feeling as if she didn't matter. That no one cared about her, but Nyla remembered someone was looking for her. Someone wanted her. She decided at that moment she would get out or die trying. Nyla scanned the room. *How did I get here?*

Tyrone was what most people would consider a small town pimp and he was known throughout the community for his bad temper. Nyla recalled the time he saw a dog pee on the tires of his new SUV. For weeks he searched for that dog, then once he found him, he shot it down in the middle of the street.

When their paths first crossed, Nyla had no idea how cold and ruthless Tyrone could be. He'd been kind and seemed to genuinely want to help her. He'd given her a place to sleep, with no demands and he'd fed her well. His trap of deceit was cleverly executed and Nyla, as naïve as she was, was no match for him. After a few months, he began to coax her into entertaining some of his so-called "friends." Before she knew it, he insisted that she have sex with them for money. Never in her seventeen years did Nyla see herself being prostituted. She knew she had to get out, or die trying.

From the corner Nyla could see Tyrone's head bobbing back and forth while he argued with someone on the phone. Time was running out and she had to get out before he realized that Gabby was not coming. Nyla and Gabby had agreed to meet at the bus station at seven-thirty p.m. They'd expected Tyrone to be on his way out of town. She figured he must've gotten suspicious because when Nyla returned to the house to collect a few things, he walked in on her. Nyla knew then she wouldn't be able to take many of her belongings, but she wouldn't leave without her satchel.

*Get it together, girl. You gotta go!* The voice in her head propelled her forward. Her growling stomach reminded her that it had been hours since she'd last eaten. It also gave her an idea.

Nyla leaned against the wall for support as she pushed herself up. She touched the side of her face with a trembling hand. She could taste the blood and knew the blow would leave an ugly bruise. Nyla stole another quick glance at the clock above the front door.

Tyrone had a thing about people being on time. If someone was even one minute late, there would be hell to pay. He also had his weaknesses. A big one was food. Nyla had never seen him turn down a meal. Quite frankly, she was surprised someone hadn't poisoned him by now. She cleared her throat.

"Umm mmm. Um, Tyrone?" Nyla said, as she slowly approached him. Her voice was barely audible. She looked at the clock again and spoke louder.

"Tyrone?" He jumped to his feet, and placed his

hand inside his over-sized, leather jacket.

"Whatchu' sneaking up on me for, girl? You tryin' to get yo'self killed or somethin'?"

"Uh, no I...I just wanted to know if you, uh... wanted me to fix you something to eat. I mean, you might as well eat a little somethin' while we wait on Gabby." Tyrone eyed her with suspicion, taking in all of her. He couldn't believe his luck when he ran up on this one. She was *hot*, her skin was the color of cream with a splash of coffee. Her sandy hair complimented her hazel eyes, which would sometimes change colors. He gave her a slight nod of the head.

"Make it quick. Yo, warm up some of that food ole girl cooked last night," he barked.

Nyla quickly turned toward the small, dingy kitchen. Tyrone turned his attention back to his conversation.

"Yeah, man I ain't had nothin' to eat all *day*," he said. "Running 'round with these fools, thinking they smarta'n me. I got somethin' for 'em," he said, as he dropped back down onto the worn sofa, the phone pressed firmly against his ear. Nyla pulled pans out of the refrigerator. It, like the rest of the house, was on its last leg. The motor churned and sputtered as if it could feel the despair surrounding it.

Tyrone seemed content for now but she suspected it would only last a few more minutes. She had to work fast. Nyla pulled meat from the left over hen, quickly put it between some bread and stuffed it into her pocket. Her hands trembled but she kept moving. She microwaved Tyrone's plate of

15

chicken, green beans, rice and a big piece of cornbread and set it in front of him.

"Um, can I go to the bathroom?" Nyla knew from experience that she couldn't just walk away. Tyrone waved her off as he started stuffing his mouth. She hurried to the spot in the dark, narrow hallway where she'd hidden her satchel, then dashed inside. The bathroom was drafty because of a broken window pane which had been unsuccessfully ducted taped. Like the rest of the house, the bathroom was old and dated. Nyla was sure that on the day that someone had placed the ruffled pink curtains at the window with a matching shower curtain, the dwellers had been filled with excitement and hope. Unfortunately with each passing year the house had fallen into despair and like the rest of its surroundings, the curtains were now a symbol of the depressed environment in which they hung, having faded into a sad and dusty gray. However, the shower curtain did manage to hide the rotting wood around bathtub where the bottom tiles had fallen off. Nyla shivered as the cold, February air seeped in around the window. She placed her hand underneath the towels in back of the closet and retrieved a file folder and stuffed it inside her satchel. Nyla had stolen the file from her last caseworker. She'd hoped that the information inside would be her ticket to finding her real parents and a normal life. After she secured the envelope, Nyla opened the door and ran smack into Tyrone's chest.

"Whatchu you doin' in here, Ny?" Tyrone peered passed her into the bathroom.

"I was uh... using the bathroom," she answered, shifting from one foot to the other. His large frame filled the entire doorway. Nyla had to take a step back.

"Using the bathroom, huh? Why didn't I hear the toilet flush?" Nyla had to think fast.

"I was changing my tampon." Tyrone didn't budge. He searched her face, trying to see the lie.

"You want to check?" she asked. Her knees felt like Jell-O. She knew that he was not above taking her up on her bluff. But today it didn't matter if she was on her cycle. It was her day off and since it wasn't an issue of her not being able to service his customers, he let it go.

"Get outta my way." He dragged her over the threshold and quickly shut the door behind him. Just as she'd expected, Tyrone had to go to the bathroom; he always did right after he ate.

*It's now or never*, she thought to herself. Nyla made a b-line from the hallway, toward the front door. She grabbed her book bag on her way out. As she rounded the corner, she felt the wind snatched from her lungs when she saw Jamal standing in the middle of the room, flipping through the television channels.

Jamal, Tyrone's cousin, was the complete opposite of Tyrone. He was tall and slender, with a long narrow face. Jamal was only nineteen but he looked years older. His heart was always in the right place—especially when it came to Tyrone—and he was loyal to a fault. When they were younger, it was Tyrone who used to take up for Jamal when other boys picked on him because of his stuttering.

Now Jamal was Tyrone's bodyguard of sorts. Though he was a little slow to pick up on things, he was the only one Tyrone trusted.

Nyla stood frozen. She had to get out before Tyrone came out of the bathroom.

"Oh, hey, Jamal. I...I didn't know you were here," she said, as she crossed the room. Jamal turned and saw Nyla. Smiling, he practically blinded her with his gold grill.

"Hey yo'self. Wh-wh-where did you come from?" He stood, twisting a toothpick on the side of his mouth.

"Oh, I was just in the back." Nyla made a motion toward the back room. "Tyrone asked me to get something out of his car, but I don't see the keys," she said looking around. Nyla knew Jamal had a crush on her. She also knew he was the only one who had the second set of keys to Tyrone's truck.

Jamal chuckled. "Y-y-you funny, girl. Nobody gets in Tyrone's ride alone but Tyrone or m-m-me," he said, pointing to himself.

"I'm so stupid. How could I forget? So, will you open it for me? I don't want him to be mad when he comes out."

"Oh yeah, sure. No problem." He dug his hands into his pocket as they moved toward the front door. The phone rang.

"Ho-hold on, Ny. I betta get that." Jamal took a few steps back and stood in front of the sofa as he grabbed the cordless phone, leaving Nyla standing near the door.

"He-he-hello? Who? Nah, yu-you g-g-got the wrong number. Ain't nobody here by that name."

He paused. "I said, y-you got the wrong number!"

"Who was that?" Tyrone asked, as he waddled into the room, his pants hanging well below his butt. Jamal shook his head as he clicked the phone off.

"S-some foo-fool askin' for sea-Seamore Fanny." Tyrone's face contorted even more.

"What?" Tyrone asked, impatiently.

"They was asking for s..sea...sea..."

"Forget it, man. Is Gabby here yet?" Tyrone looked around the room. "Where's Nyla?" Jamal pointed toward the door where Nyla had stood moments earlier, but she was gone. The only thing he saw was her book bag on the floor. Jamal's stomach fell to his knees.

"Uh, sh-sh-she was just right o-o-ova there."

"Well, where she at, fool?"

"Sh... she m-m-musta gone to the car to get what you told her to get," Jamal responded hopefully.

"For what *I* told her to get? You a idiot! I don't even know why I put up whit chu." Both men lunged toward the door at the same time. When they finally stood on the porch, Nyla was nowhere in sight.

Down at the bus station, Gabby hung up her new cell phone and checked the time again.

"Come on, Ny. Where are you?" Gabby whispered. She hid in the shadows toward the back of the station. She couldn't take a chance on one of Tyrone's goons spotting her. Gabrielle hoped that Nyla made it before the bus pulled away. Because with or without her, Gabby knew she had to be on that bus. After tonight, Tyrone would surely kill

them both and she had done all the dying she
intended on doing.

❧ ❧ ❧ ❧

Nyla ran the entire way. Her short stint on the
junior high school track team had come in handy.
Just as she rounded the corner and had the bus
station in sight, she spotted Tyrone's SUV. Her
breath caught in her throat as she quickly ducked
into a nearby alley. She had no way to warn Gabby.

"Oh God, please. We need your help," she
prayed.

Fearing she would be spotted, Nyla cowered
further back into the alley. Suddenly, she tripped
over something and fell to the ground. Quickly, she
scrambled to her feet and stood panting. Her breath
could be seen as it escaped into the crystalline night
air. Nyla could hear the beating of her heart as she
drew closer to inspect the body. As she rolled it
over, she immediately covered her mouth before she
allowed a scream to escape. At first, she thought the
man might've been dead. Then she saw the bottle of
Gin clutched tightly in his weathered, old hands.
She then heard snoring that sounded like a freight
train.

The bus driver finally climbed aboard and settled
into the worn, leather seat. He leaned forward and
turned the key in the ignition. The engine was loud
as it roared to life. Nyla's head jerked toward the
sound of the bus.

"I gotta get on that bus," Nyla said. She peeked
around the corner and was about to step out of the
alley when she saw Tyrone and Jamal climb onto
the bus. She froze. Nyla was frightened out of her

mind for Gabrielle as despair ran circles around her heart. *What am I going to do?*

❧❧❧❧

Gabby had literally hidden herself beneath the blanket thrown over the legs of one of the passengers and her young daughter.

"Hey, ole lady, whatchu got under that blanket?" Tyrone leaned over the lady, who sat at the back of the bus.

"What you want it to be, baby? You want some of this?" Her daughter snickered nervously as Tyrone maneuvered a toothpick around in his mouth. He studied her for a moment then shuddered as he turned and walked away.

"Let's go, man," he said, pushing Jamal ahead of him. As soon as they stepped off of the bus, the doors closed. The bus slowly lurched forward, groaning and hissing as it crushed the gravel beneath its large tires. The driver gradually steered the bus into the street.

"Now what?" Jamal asked.

"Now, we go back and look through some of their stuff. We need to find somethin' that'll give us a clue to where they may be at. And when we track 'em down, she and that big mouth Gabby gon' wish they never met me. I'm gon' be sure to make an example outta both of 'em."

Two blocks away, as the bus began to pick up speed, Gabby came up for air. Her breathing was sporadic and she felt like she was about to hyperventilate. She also couldn't contain her tears of relief and regret.

"Thank you, thank you so much," she whispered.

"That's all right, baby. You're safe now." Gabby got up and sat in the seat adjacent to Ms. Pearl and her daughter. She rocked and shook her head as tears flowed from her slanted, ebony eyes.

"Honey, he's gone. It's okay." Pearl tried her best to console the young girl. The young girl had the face of an angel. Pearl wanted to take the child, shake her and ask her what in the world she was doing with the likes of those two.

"No, it's not... My friend... my friend didn't make it. She...he's gonna *kill* her."

"Oh, my God." Pearl gasped.

Suddenly, the driver hit the brakes and the bus jerked forward. There were a few screams and several bags fell to the floor with a loud thump.

"Everybody all right?" the driver asked as he turned and scanned the dimly-lit cabin. The cataracts in his eyes made it difficult for him to see further back.

"What happened?" someone yelled from the back.

"I don't know." The driver's voice was gruff. "Looks like a grocery cart or something rolled right in front of me. I'ma go check it out. Everybody settle down," he grumbled as he unbuckled his seatbelt and opened the door. He couldn't afford to lose this job. He had eight weeks left before retirement and he needed his entire pension. His bad hip was acting up a bit so he moved cautiously as he descended the steps. Scratching at his steel-gray beard he hesitated then made his way over toward the front of the bus. It was then he saw a figure lying in the street, not far from the cart.

"Oh, my God," he said, as he quickened his pace. "Hello?" the driver called out. As he got closer, he bent slightly to get a closer look. "Hey fella you all right?"

From the way he was dressed, he suspected it was a young boy. "'Scuse me, son, can you hear me? Lord, don't let him be dead," he said, peering back over his shoulder toward the bus. Nyla moaned as she slowly rolled over and looked up from the over-sized, gray hoodie she'd taken from the man in the alley moments earlier.

"Oh!" The driver stepped back, surprised.

"I'm sorry," Nyla groaned, "but... I'm supposed to be on that bus, mister." Nyla looked up with pleading eyes. The ugly bruise along the right side of her face was now swollen and purple. One look and the driver knew she was probably the one those two thugs were looking for.

"Well, is that so?" He stood up straight and placed his hands around the belt beneath his ample belly. "So, you think running out in front of my bus and almost gettin' y' self killed is gon' get you a free ride?"

"No, sir. I... I have a ticket. I mean, my friend has my ticket and I..."

"Just as I thought! Another con job. Girl, get on outta here. I got a bus to drive and a job to keep." He turned and started limping away.

"No! Please wait!" Nyla cried out. "I'm supposed to be on that bus!" She struggled to her feet and limped behind him, pleading.

"Get on away from here, girl fo' I call the cops." The driver boarded the bus and closed the door in her face.

"Wait!" She screamed and banged on the door. "Please, just let me see my friend! Please!" she begged. She was weak but she hit the door again and again. The driver shooed her away.

"Gabby!" Nyla yelled. "Gabby! Please, can you hear me?" Nyla wouldn't budge. The driver changed gears and the bus jerked as it began to pull off. Nyla ran along the side of the bus for a moment. The bus sped up, but Nyla was too weak to keep up. She fell to her knees, sobbing. She didn't know what she was going to do.

The bus traveled only a few more feet before it came to another abrupt stop. Seconds later the doors opened and Gabby jumped off.

"Nyla!" Gabby yelled as she ran toward her friend. Nyla thought she heard her name. She looked up but her tears had blinded her. She tried to get up but she didn't have the strength. Gabby almost knocked her over when she reached her.

"Ny, I thought you were... Oh my, God!" Gabrielle noticed the purplish bruise on her friend's face. There was no question in her mind who was responsible.

"Gabby?" Nyla could hardly speak. "Is it really you?"

"Yeah. Who else but me?" They hugged briefly. Tears of relief ran down both their faces.

"Come on. Get up. The old man is already mad 'cause Ms. Pearl made him stop the bus, again."

"Let's get out of here," Gabby encouraged, as she pulled Nyla to her feet. They hurried toward the bus.

The bus driver gave them a shameful look as they climbed on board. Ms. Pearl, who had been standing at the bottom step, shot him a warning look. She moved aside to let them on, then boarded after them, but before she took her seat, she leaned over his shoulder so he would be sure to hear what she said.

"Lord only knows what those children have been through. Now, I know your heart ain't that cold that you'd leave a defenseless child on the side of the road. We're supposed to be the ones to look out for 'em. If we don't, who will?" The driver stared straight ahead, refusing to look at Pearl.

"Can I drive this bus, woman, before I lose my job?" Pearl could see his stubbornness. Before she turned and strutted back to her seat, she waved him off.

"Drive on, Mr. Bus Driver. Drive on."

# TWO

## HOMECOMING

---

Lola Devereux felt the tension in every inch of her body as the airplane started to descend. She quickly swallowed the tiny blue pill before the flight attendant collected her cup. Closing her eyes, Lola leaned back into her seat and took a deep breath. She exhaled slowly and tried to forget her last trip home. It had been a complete disaster. Lola stirred a little as she remembered what a fool she'd made of herself, stumbling into her nephews' birthday party, in a drunken state.

She questioned herself, for the hundredth time, whether it had been a good idea to come. Although her sister told her many times that all was forgiven, Lola couldn't erase the confused and painful look on Raina's face the last time she'd seen her. It had been six years and although Lola had been back to

26

Atlanta because of her job as a flight attendant, she made sure she stayed as far away from her family as possible. Now, even though she would've preferred to have stayed home in Los Angeles and taken care of her own pressing matters; coming back for her brother-in-laws' funeral was the right thing to do.

As the wheels of the airplane touched down and screeched across the runway, the Valium had not kicked in. Lola clutched the armrest and inhaled and exhaled several times, trying to regain her composure. As anxiety snaked up her spine, she contemplated taking another pill but thought better of it. Lola knew she needed to be somewhat alert when she saw Victoria again. Just thinking of her mother caused her palms to become sweaty. Beads of perspiration appeared on her upper lip, which was always a dead give-away when she was stressed. "Just keep it together, girl. You'll be in and out in no time," she whispered to herself.

When Lola first heard the news of Keenan's death, she had a complete meltdown. She had walked around dazed for the entire week, not being able to keep down even the smallest amount of food. Keenan's passing ripped at the already jagged hole in her heart; the emptiness she felt was indescribable. Had it not been for Mr. Goodman, her AA Sponsor, she wouldn't have been able to pull herself together without a drink.

Mr. Goodman, God bless him, had also questioned her decision to go back home, even for Keenan's funeral. She still had so many unresolved issues. Although now, more than ever, Lola felt hopeful about having the opportunity to perhaps heal old wounds and lay them to rest.

*Perhaps, it'll be a chance for me let go of it all,* she thought. *After all of these years, maybe Raina and I can finally have a normal relationship again.* Her brother-in-law was dead and all she knew was that her sister needed her. Lola really wanted to be there for Raina. Victoria, however, was another story altogether.

After the airplane pulled into the gate, Lola gathered her things and filed off with the rest of the impatient passengers. While everyone else seemed to be excited about reaching his or her destination, Lola felt her stomach start to churn. Walking through the airport, Lola was so deep in thought; she was startled when her phone rang.

"Hello? Oh, hi Lloyd. I'm on my way out. Where are you?"

"Hey listen, it's raining cats and dogs out here," Lloyd said, as his SUV crept through the traffic. "You need me to come in and help you with anything?"

Hearing Lloyd Higdon's deep baritone voice made Lola smile. He was one of the most reliable men she knew. If only she could find a man as loving and kind as her cousin, her love life wouldn't be such a wreck.

"No, you don't need to come in. Have you forgotten that I work for an airline? I pack light and I know this airport like the back of my hand. I'll be out in a minute."

"Okay. Hey cousin, you sound good. Glad to have you home." Lola smiled but she couldn't help the uneasiness she felt.

"Wish it was under better circumstances but thanks. See ya in a few." The voice in her head did little to help her anxiety. *Are you sure you want to do this?* "Keep walking, Lola. You'll be okay," she whispered again.

Lola was oblivious to the throng of passengers surrounding her as she waited for the train. She stared into space and fidgeted with her ring as a picture of her mother's face flashed before her eyes. She would never forget the look of disappointment on Victoria's face when she told her about the baby. It seemed as though the one mistake she'd made all those years ago took precedence over being in the Honor Society, on the Dean's List and all the awards she'd received. All Lola had ever wanted was to please her mother but none of that mattered. When she needed her mother the most, Victoria turned on her. And for that, Lola would never forgive her. Lola's phone rang again after she stepped off of the train. She answered without looking at the incoming number.

"Hey, I'm coming. You'll probably have to circle around. There was a delay with the train," Lola spoke while holding the phone between her cheek and shoulder.

"Well, I see you've landed safely," a smile swept across Lola's face as she recognized the voice on the other end. There was no mistaking Mr. Goodman's warm, fatherly voice.

He had wasted no time making contact with Lola upon her arrival. Ever since she'd met him, she found herself wishing him to be the dad she never had. Not that the Reverend hadn't been a good father and provider, because he had been.

Victoria had met and married the Reverend Joseph Devereux when Lola was five years old. A year later, Raina was born. While he'd been a great stepfather, he'd always been Raina's daddy and Lola had felt the difference.

Bernard Goodman, in her mind, was all hers. She knew from his own story that he'd lost his family to his disease of alcoholism and had limited contact with only one of his five sons. It was the story of her life; bad choices and even tougher consequences. Not to mention the multitude of guilt that never seemed to end. The fact that she'd been forced by her employer to seek treatment, Lola considered herself one of the lucky ones.

"Oh, hi Mr. Goodman. I thought you were my ride."

"I see. Well, I was just calling to touch base and to make sure you get in touch with my colleague while you're there. He's a bit unorthodox but..."

"Mr. Goodman, I already told you, I may not be here that long," Lola said, as she struggled to retrieve her luggage from the conveyor belt. "I just want to pay my respects, help my sister as much as I can and then, I'm out."

"Lola, every day you're fighting to stay sober. You need to be proactive about your recovery," he said, as he ran his hand over his thinning, salt-and-pepper hair.

Lola stopped in the middle of baggage claim, among the multitude of travelers who stepped over and around her, attempting to retrieve their own bags.

"With all due respect, you don't need to remind me about my daily struggle. I'm very aware of what I'm up against."

"It's just that being around your family, your mother..."

"Look, I appreciate the words of wisdom but I got this. Okay?" Lola threw a bag over her shoulder and began moving toward the exit.

Mr. Goodman stood up from his desk and began to pace. "Are you serious?"

He'd been a sponsor for over ten years. His own struggle with alcohol had claimed twenty years of his life and it was still a daily battle. Lola was showing the classic signs of someone attending a few sessions and thinking she had it all under control. He knew from their previous conversations that she was walking into a highly volatile situation. He also knew she was not ready.

"Lola, think about what you're saying. You've only been in the program for few months."

"I know and I hear you, okay? I really appreciate your concern but what choice do I have? I mean, I would've liked to have had more time, but death doesn't wait, Mr. Goodman, not even for me. Now, I'm trying to do the right thing and be here for my sister. So, please, don't stress me out any more than I already am."

"Hey, I'm sorry." Bernard Goodman stopped pacing and leaned against his desk. "The last thing I want to do is cause you any stress. I guess I've become somewhat of a worrier in my old age."

"Yes you have. But listen, I'm a big girl."

"Okay, okay I hear you." He threw up one of his

hands. "But promise me that if you find yourself needing support you'll give Dr. Eli a call."

"Yes, I'll call him," Lola nodded stiffly and rolled her eyes. "But only *if* I need him. I don't plan on staying that long," Lola said, as she wheeled her luggage out into the cold, damp afternoon.

"Oh. I thought since your probation period isn't up for another six months, you might plan on staying longer." She hated being reminded about her probation. Because of her drinking, she'd gotten suspended. She had to complete a stint in rehab as well as a sobriety program before her file would be eligible for review.

"I do have a life, Mr. Goodman. It may not be perfect but it's mine and I have friends that I would like to get back to very soon. Again, I'm just trying to pay my respects, okay?"

Mr. Goodman knew better. Lola was headstrong. He knew she would try to do it on her own and then she would hit a wall. He also knew when to back off. "Okay, Lola. Be blessed and please, call me if you need anything."

"Okay, I will. Goodbye," she said, with obvious agitation. Lola quickly flipped the phone closed and stuffed it into her pocket. Lifting the collar on her coat, Lola strained her neck in an attempt to spot Lloyd.

Bernard Goodman returned the cordless phone back in its cradle. He sat, thoughtfully, rubbing his hand along his graying beard. His dark eyes stared into space as he thought about Lola.

"Father, God, intervene on your daughter's behalf. She's not as strong as she needs to be, so please send her some help." Afterward, he placed another call; this time to his good friend, Dr. Jeremiah Eli.

As Lola waited underneath the covering for Lloyd, the wind began blowing the rain. The dreary weather matched her mood. She stood with her head tucked inside her coat. When she looked out again, there he was.

"That's my Lloyd, always right on time." Lloyd could always be counted on. No matter how crazy things had gotten in the past, she never felt judged by him. He was the only one in her family she kept in touch with on a regular basis. Lloyd pulled his Ford Explorer closer to the curb and hovered under the umbrella as he ran around the car to open the door, but not before giving Lola a big bear hug.

"Hey, cuz. It's so good to see you."

"Man, let me in this car. You're getting both of us soaked," she said, with a genuine smile.

"Oh, I forgot. You're like sugar. You melt in the rain," he said, flashing that million-dollar smile. Lola hit him playfully on the shoulder as he opened her door.

"You got that right," she said, as she climbed into the car.

Lloyd threw Lola's suitcase in the trunk and within minutes his large frame, filled every inch of the driver's seat. Back in the day, he'd earned a football scholarship from Clark Atlanta University. After he was injured, he decided to become a police officer. Now, after thirteen years on the force, he'd decided to get his degree in Divinity. Go figure.

"It's good to see you, Lola," he said, using a

handkerchief to wipe the rain from his forehead.

"It's good to see you too, Lloyd. How's the wife and kids?" For a moment, Lola felt light. Lloyd always did that for her.

"Jessica is fine. And the kids are eating us out of house and home. You won't recognize them," he said, as he looked back and began guiding the large vehicle into the flow of traffic.

"I'm sure I won't."

"You know the funeral was earlier today. Everyone should be on the way back from the burial site by now."

"Does anyone know I'm coming?" she asked, avoiding eye contact.

"Did you tell anyone?" Lloyd asked. "I mean, I didn't mention it."

"Oh please, Lloyd. You mean to tell me you didn't even tell Jessica?" Now Lola leaned back to get a good look.

"Well, of course I told, Jess. I mean I didn't mention it to anyone else."

"I knew you couldn't keep it to yourself."

"Listen, telling Jess is like keeping it to myself. Besides, you didn't say it was a secret."

"Well, to tell you the truth, I didn't want anyone expecting me because I wasn't sure I would be able to make it," she lied. Lola was free as a bird. However, she wasn't going to divulge that information to anyone, in case she needed an excuse to leave. It wasn't that she didn't have the time. She just wasn't sure she had the strength.

"We'll just go straight to Raina's house and be there by the time everyone arrives from the burial site."

"Sounds good." Lola nodded.

"Man, what an awful day for a burial," Lola said, as she peered up into the dark, gloomy clouds.

"Is there ever a good day to be buried?" he responded.

"Humph, I guess you're right about that," she said. I just meant it's so dreary."

"I still can't believe he's gone," Lloyd spoke with a heavy heart. "One day he was here and the next day..." Lola sat silently. She wished she could find the words that would comfort him but she could not.

"You know, he was just running an errand to the store and along came a teenager, texting his girlfriend. Man, one stupid decision and look at the devastation."

"Yeah," Lola agreed. Her eyes brimmed with tears, as she continued gazing out of the window.

"That's why it's important to get your life right with God. You know?" Lola rolled her eyes and quickly wiped the tears away.

"Mmm hmm, yes, I know."

"You do? Lola, you know?" She turned toward Lloyd and he could see that he had touched a nerve.

"Yes, Lloyd. I know. It's me, remember? The same cousin who stood in front of you in choir practice and sat beside you in Sunday school since we were five."

"Oh? That was you? I thought you looked familiar," he said, attempting to lighten the mood. Lola smirked and turned her attention back toward the window.

"I'm working on me, all right? I mean, I got a ways to go but, I'm making some progress."

"By progress you mean...?

"I'm in AA and I haven't had a drink in three months." Lloyd nodded with a big smile, while he kept his eyes on the road.

"That's good news, girl." He grabbed her hand. "I'm really glad to hear that. Raina will be happy to hear it too." They sat silent for a moment longer.

"So, when was the last time you spoke to Raina or your mother?"

"I spoke to Raina the same day I went to my first meeting. She called and we talked and cried for about an hour. Afterward, she prayed with me. When I hung up the phone, I drove to the nearest AA location. The same one I had passed many times, on my way home. We didn't speak again until I got the call about Keenan."

"Why?" He turned briefly to look at her. "Why didn't you keep her updated on your progress?"

"Well, I, uh, I really wasn't sure if I could stick it out and I didn't want to disappoint her, again."

"What about your mom?" Lola's shoulders tightened and she took a deep breath.

"It's been awhile," she said as she exhaled, looking straight ahead.

"What's a while?"

"I don't know. Maybe about a year or so."

"I see." Lloyd kept his eyes on the road.

"You see what, exactly?" Lola asked as she turned to face him.

"Well, I can see that perhaps you were just not ready." Lola nodded. "However, I also think that in order to truly be set free from this addiction, you got to let go of some of the anger you have towards Victoria. You need to be able to forgive and release yourself from whatever it is that's between you two."

"You're probably right, Lloyd, but, as they say in AA, 'one thing at a time', okay?"

"Don't you mean, one day at a time?"

"Okay, Whatever. Can we not talk about me and Victoria anymore?"

"You do know she's going to be there. At the house, I mean," Lloyd added. Lola took another deep breath.

"Of course she's going to be there. Where else would she be? But, that reminds me, I'm going to need a place to crash. I don't want to impose on Raina and you know I can't stay with Victoria. Sooo..." Lola wore the expression of a teen asking for permission but was slightly unsure of the impending answer.

"Lola, you know you're always welcome at our house."

"Thank you, Lloyd," she exhaled. "And don't worry about me and Victoria. I think I can deal with her, for a short while, anyway." Lola slipped her hand into her pocketbook and felt the bottle that contained the Valium. The cool feel of the small plastic vile seemed to calm her. She instinctively knew everyone would want to know why she had not attended the funeral. But she also knew she wasn't strong enough to see Keenan in a casket. Her heart just couldn't take it.

# THREE

## HOME GOING

---

The raindrops sounded like small pellets as they pounded against the roof of the limousine. They were purposeful in their effort to wash away the heaviness of the day. Raina's eyes were fixed on the dark, dismal clouds as she peered out of the window. She watched hypnotically as each raindrop slid slowly down the windshield. It seemed as though the world were weeping, trying to wash away the thick layer of sadness and sense of loss that permeated every pore of her body.

Her head felt heavy as it fell back against the cool, leather seat. She inhaled the scent of the car and thought that it had no particular odor, not that new car smell, not even the smell of death. The last time Raina remembered riding in the back of a funeral limousine was when her father died. It had also been the last time she, her mother and sister had felt connected. Ever since his death, their relationship had been strained, to say the least.

Even after hearing the news of Keenan's death, Lola refused to commit to coming home. Raina had hoped that Lola would be here; she missed her so much. She missed the way things used to be, before it all fell apart. Raina couldn't quite figure out why Lola had become so withdrawn. Today was confirmation that time had not healed the wounds Lola carried. Raina wasn't exactly sure what they were but she knew that it would take a miracle for there to be peace between her mother and sister.

The heaviness in Raina's chest grew as she inhaled and exhaled. The effort seemed to take every bit of energy she had. She knew she had to keep breathing, keep living and keep herself focused on something other than Keenan being gone. Her children needed her. The limousine rocked from side to side as it snaked its way through the narrow, graveled road headed away from the cemetery. The motion of the car accompanied by a week of sleepless nights, made it nearly impossible for Raina to keep her eyes open. Her eyelids finally lost the battle and she drifted off.

*She could see him now. His smiling face was illuminated as he teased and fondled her. Wasn't it just yesterday? Or could it have been last week? Yes, she could see it clearly now. The scene played itself out behind her closed lids so vividly. She could even smell him. The man she thought she'd grow old with and now.... Oh, there he was again, with that smile. Raina felt her husband's legs slowly caress hers in his effort to rouse her from her slumber. She purred and turned over, nestling her head into the crook of his neck. She smiled to herself as she inhaled his scent, reminiscing about the night before when he'd loved her with such passion it felt like their wedding night all over again.*

*"Hey sleepy head, are you awake?" Raina loved the sound of Keenan's voice. He was always so calm and self-assured. Keenan began to cover her face with small, wet kisses.*

*"Mmm... no. Not quite," Raina said, as she purred into the pillow.*

*"You know we have to check out before noon." Keenan continued kissing her.*

*"Yes, I know." Raina drew her body closer to his.*

*"That doesn't leave us much time." Keenan's words were laced with seduction. Raina tilted her head back, looking up at her husband.*

*"Time for what?" she asked, with a slight furrow of her brow, accompanied by a knowing smirk. Raina could see the mischief in his eyes as they danced with anticipation. She knew that look well.*

*"Time for me to welcome you into a brand new day, properly." He rolled his body on top of his still groggy wife.*

*"And just how do you plan on doing that, Mr. Blackman?" She loved flirting with him.*

*"The same way I said goodnight." Keenan had already buried his head into her neck, kissing her in places where he knew she would respond. He continued covering her body with small, sensual*

*kisses. When he got to the small, half moon birthmark right in the middle of her right shoulder blade, he traced it with his tongue. He knew by her body's reaction she was ready to receive him. Then came a knock at the door.*

*"Room service," a voice belted out from the other side of the door. Keenan tried to ignore it, but the second knock was louder.*

*"Room service."*

*"Room service?" Keenan stopped and looked down at his wife.*

*"Is he kidding? Isn't there a do not disturb sign on the door?" Keenan's tone was exasperated.*

*"No, because last night we ordered breakfast to be delivered, silly. Don't you remember hanging the order form on the door?" Raina said, smiling up at her husband's flustered expression.*

*"Well, I don't hear him anymore; he must've gotten the message. Now, where were we?" Another knock.*

*"Room service." Keenan dropped his head into the crook of her neck. Raina giggled.*

*"Go answer the door, man. I'm starving." Kennan looked into her mega watt smile and flawless, deep chocolate complexion. Her almond shaped, light brown eyes were full of life. Try as he might, he could never deny her.*

*"Hungry? Woman I'm about to rock your world and all you can think about is food?" Raina's laughter filled the room.*

*"Baby, you know how I get when my stomach is empty. Now, get the door before he leaves." Keenan shook his head with a grin, threw back the covers*

41

*and leaped out of the bed in one motion.*

*"Hold on I'm coming!" he yelled and grabbed for the hotel bathrobe.*

*"You're right. I do know how you get when you're hungry and it ain't pretty," he said, over his shoulder.*

*"I'm going to kill him," Keenan whispered, as he tied the white, terrycloth robe around his masculine frame. "Just a minute!"*

*Raina smiled as she watched his back. He's still got it. Even though Keenan was six years older, his body was still strong and muscular. His gait was smooth and predator - like. At six-two, many people assumed that he was an athlete but not so. Keenan's nickname was "The Brain." If he didn't have his head in a book, he was always tinkering with objects like the old cars he enjoyed restoring.*

*The tiny freckles on his back were only visible due to his café latte complexion. He wore his course, red hair, cut low and close to his head. What really made her heart do cartwheels were his eyes. They were ocean green and every time he looked at her, Raina's knees went weak.*

*"Who would've thought a woman so small could eat so much," Keenan said, as he approached the bed.*

*"Come on, get out of bed." Raina stretched her petite frame as she languidly sat up and retrieved her robe from the bottom of the bed.*

*"It smells delicious. I could eat a cow."*

*"Don't I know it." There was that Blackman sarcasm.*

*"Don't you get yourself in trouble, Mr." Raina*

42

WHEN THE SILENCE IS TOO LOUD

*shot him a warning look. They sat at the small table
on the balcony. Keenan lifted his glass of juice.*

*"To us." Raina smiled and raised her glass.*

*"Raina?"*

*"Yes?"*

*"Raina, Raina..." She couldn't understand why
he kept saying her name.*

*"Keenan? What's wrong?"*

"Raina, it's me. Wake up. We're home, honey."
Raina emerged from her wonderful dream and
found herself staring into the anxious eyes of her
mother.

The sudden realization that she'd been dreaming
and that Keenan was gone clawed at her heart.

"Oh, I must've dozed off," she said over the
lump in her throat. Raina sat up and her hand fell
across the worn, leather Bible that had belonged to
her father. She picked it up and held it to her chest.

"Come on, sweetheart, you're home," Victoria
said, as she exited the limo. Victoria was also petite
in stature, like her youngest daughter. Her caramel
complexion had started to reveal the delicate
tracings of new lines under her beautiful, onyx eyes.
She was worried about her daughter but she could
show no signs of weakness. Victoria knew she had
to be strong for Raina. Lord only knew what issues
her oldest daughter might bring home, if she
decided to show up at all. She'd already caused a
scene by not attending the funeral.

Victoria had vacated the seat beside Naomi
Blackman, Keenan's mother. She was a direct
contrast to Victoria. Her pale skin appeared ashen
and lacked its usual glow. She was tall and slender.

She wore her platinum colored hair in a short stylish cut, which accented her narrow face and slender neck. Naomi had also been widowed at a young age. Keenan was a sophomore in college, when his father became ill and passed away soon after. Although she'd had many suitors over the years, she never remarried. Naomi had fallen in love and married Keenan's father at a time when interracial marriages were not easily accepted. Even her own family had given her grief until Keenan came along. Naomi had known it would be difficult to find a man that was willing to raise a biracial child. So, instead of dealing with that, she'd chosen to focus on her only son and now, the children he'd left behind.

Naomi, Victoria and Quincy stepped out of the limousine into the driveway. Matthew didn't budge.

"Come on, Matthew, we're home," Raina said, as she reached for her youngest son. He was only nine years old and the soft roundness of his cheeks still held a baby-like quality. He recoiled from her touch.

"I don't want to go in there," he whined.

"What? What do you mean? Why don't you want to go in, Matthew?" He didn't answer. He simply hung his head and played with some invisible thing on his pant leg.

"Matthew? Are you going to tell me what's wrong?" Matthew lifted his head and Raina could see his tear-stained face. His bottom lip trembled as he tried to speak.

"Be...because Daddy's not there." His voice was barely audible. Tears fell freely now. "And he's

never going to be there, so I don't want to go in."
Oh, how her heart ached. Raina hung her head and
with trembling hands of her own reached for her
son. Her pain was physical and it held a venomous
grip at the center of her chest, making it difficult to
breathe. Raina wished a million times that somehow
she could make it go away. No child should ever
have to experience such a devastating loss.

"Dad is there." Quincy, her oldest son, had stuck
his head back inside the limo. He was almost
fourteen and she knew he was trying to be strong.
Raina watched him fight back the tears as he tried to
comfort his little brother. "He'll always be with us,
Matt. All the memories, pictures and all of his stuff
is in there. When we see them and when we're
around them, then we'll feel closer to him, right
Mom?" He looked at Raina for confirmation for
himself, as well as his brother.

"Yes, he's right, baby," she said as she lifted her
head. "His body is gone but just being in the house
where we created all of our special memories and
around all the things he loved will help us to feel
closer to him. What do you say? Let's go inside,
okay?" Matthew couldn't speak. He simply nodded.
The tears continued to roll down his small, round
face; like the trickling of a creek before it becomes
a waterfall.

As they entered the house, Raina shivered as she
felt a chill wash over her body. Even with a house
full of people, she could feel the void. Raina's legs
grew weak and just when she felt they would give
way, she saw her. The image was like a mirage at
first but as Lola drew closer, Raina had no doubt

that she was real. Raina found herself staring into her same ebony colored eyes. She blinked a couple of times before she spoke.

"Lola?" Her heart swelled in her chest. She couldn't believe it; Lola had actually come home.

"Hey Sissy," Lola said, as she opened her arms and wrapped them around her sister. Raina was in shock and at first her embrace was stiff and distant. Within minutes, the stiffness fell away, and her entire body began to tremble. A whimper escaped her and she laughed a sad little laugh. They stood for a moment longer and within Lola's embrace Raina inhaled the familiar scent of lavender and as they wept in each other's arms, time seemed to stand still. All their years apart now drifted away like a feather in the wind. Victoria, who stood weeping nearby, kept her distance.

"I, I thought you weren't coming. Your schedule…" Raina started. It had been six years since Lola had come home. She now wore her thick black hair cut in a funky, short bob. The heavy bang almost covered the right side of her face, but it did little to hide her beauty; she was still striking. When she had told Raina she may not be able to come home for Keenan's funeral, Raina was hurt but unfortunately not surprised. She knew that her sister had a lot of demons, and it seemed to Raina, Lola felt better running away from them rather than facing them head on.

"Yes, I know," Lola began as she stepped back and wiped her tear stained face. "But I rearranged some things and well, here I am," she said, with a quick, glance in Victoria's direction. "I had to be here for my family," Lola said with a practiced smile plastered on her face. "Hey, squirt," she said to Matthew as her focus of the entire family came into view. "I bet you don't remember your Auntie Lola, do you? The last time I saw you, you were riding your little bat-mobile all over the house.

Matthew couldn't stop staring at Lola.

"You're pretty," he said, with a surprised gaze.

"Thank you sweetie." She then turned her attention to Quincy. "And you! Look who's grown up! You're almost as tall as me," Lola said, awestruck. She immediately regretted the years she'd stayed away. Quincy's resemblance to Keenan was uncanny. It was like seeing a ghost. Quincy hesitantly stepped forward and gave Lola an awkward hug.

"Hello, Aunt Lola. It's good to see you." Victoria who stood nearby fidgeted with the tiny, gold cross around her neck.

"Hello, Lola. It's good to see you. I'm relieved that you could make it," Victoria said, even though Lola seemed to want to will her presence away. Lola felt the muscles in the back of her neck tighten.

"Hello, Mother. You look well." Lola moved toward her mother stiffly and they hugged briefly, barely touching.

"Well, as well as can be expected under the circumstances." Victoria spoke nervously, glancing at the others in the room.

Raina felt nauseous as she watched her mother and sister greet each other like two strangers. Thank God Lloyd and Jessica were there. Lloyd was among the few who knew the history of their volatile relationship. He and Jessica tried to head it off at the pass.

"Hey, why is everyone still standing around the door? Come on in," Lloyd's voice boomed through the room. Lloyd had always had a larger than life personality. He was the peacemaker of the family. The oldest of all the cousins, he and Keenan had become the best of friends. Both had started at the Police Academy at the same time, played golf together every Thursday and worked out at the gym every Saturday morning.

"Q, why don't you and Matt go on upstairs and get out of those clothes?" Jessica suggested. She and Lloyd had been high school sweethearts and she was aware of the fireworks that usually happened when Victoria and Lola were in the same room. Quincy glanced back at his mom before he left, his youthful face full of concern.

"Go, on Q. I know you're dying to get out of that suit," Raina said, with half a smile. Quincy seemed content with that and took off after Matthew. Raina turned nervously toward her sister.

"I'm so glad you're here. You look great, Lola."

"Well, I know that's a lie. I work too much and sleep too little. But that's just life as I know it."

"There is a better way, dear. You just seem to prefer it that way," Victoria chimed in, diverting her eyes around the room. The churning in Lola's stomach intensified as she stood with a plastic smile on her face. Before she could respond, a deaconess from the church approached them.

"Raina dear, we are all so sorry for your loss,"

she said, as she grabbed Raina's hand.

"Thank you, Sister Ina," Raina was surprised by her strong grip.

"He will certainly be missed. I never saw a more dedicated man when it came to his stewardship in the church." The tall lady looked frail and stood slightly bent forward.

"Well, that was Keenan. Whenever he committed to something, he made sure he saw it through," Raina said. Lola took the opportunity to distance herself from the small circle of women. She was en-route to the kitchen when she bumped into her aunts.

"Is that my little Lola?!" A vaguely familiar voice caught Lola by surprise as she attempted to nudge her way through the room. When she turned Lola recognized her two great Aunts, Pearlie and Sarah standing near the kitchen door.

"Oh, hey Aunt Sarah, Aunt Pearlie. How are you?" Lola asked, as she bent to give each lady a brief hug.

"Lord have mercy, child. You still just as pretty as a picture. Where's your husband?" Aunt Pearlie asked, inspecting Lola from head to toe.

"Ah, haven't quite made it down the aisle yet, Auntie," Lola grimaced.

"Yet?! Well child what are you waiting on?"

"Pearlie, leave the poor child alone. Can't you see she's grieving? You okay, honey?" Aunt Sarah asked as she looked up at Lola. She was a petite woman with flawless chocolate skin that hid her seventy plus years well. She stood back on her bowlegs and held her purse in the crook of her forearm. Her smile was kind as she searched Lola's face. "We missed you at the church and out at the burial site."

"Yes, well my plane got in late and I don't have a car here so—"

"Well, child if you need a ride we sure don't mind giving you one," Aunt Pearlie interjected.

"Oh, are you still driving, Aunt Pearlie?" Lola was surprised.

"Lord have mercy child, they took her license away last year when she almost drove the car inside one them darn drug stores."

"Well now there you *go*, bringing sand to the beach," Aunt Pearlie bristled at her sister's statement. "She didn't ask you all of that."

"I'm just trying to give the child the background since I'm now the one having to drive you all over creation."

Lola's head went back and forth between her two aunts and was reminded of the running family joke; that the reason Aunt Pearlie and her sister Sarah never married is because they were like an old married couple already. With each passing minute, Lola's stress level rose and her body ached for the comfort of her old friend, Jack Daniels. It had been her poison of choice. She'd always counted on it to calm her. However, consequences had helped Lola to realize that it would not be a practical choice, so, she tried desperately to busy herself. After listening to them for a few more minutes, Lola needed to escape.

"Well, okay. I may take you up on your offer, Auntie but right now I'm needed in the kitchen."

Lola couldn't get away fast enough. She did not need the added stress of refereeing her aunts.

"Hey, Jess. You need any help?" Lola asked, as she entered the kitchen. Jessica was preparing a plate for the youngest of their five children. She looked up and knew immediately that Lola needed a friend.

"Hey, girl. It's so good to see you, Lola." Jess hugged her with one hand while holding onto a saucer in the other.

"Who is this pretty little thing?" Lola asked excitedly, looking down into a beautiful, chocolate, china doll of a face.

"My name is Camille and I'm four!" Camille exclaimed, holding up four chubby, little fingers. Lola cut her eyes at Jessica with a pleasant smirk.

"Well, hello Camille," Lola spoke in her toddler voice. "I see that your mommy and daddy have been very busy, huh?"

"Lola, stop that." Jessica laughed.

"I'm your cousin, Lola," she said as she drew closer to Camille near the kitchen island.

"Hi, Yoya," Camille responded, in her sweet, angelic voice. They both smiled.

"Hi, baby. May I have a hug?" Camille immediately reached up her small arms and gave Lola the hug.

"Mmm, that feels so good," Lola said, as she squeezed the child.

"All right Camille; it's time to finish your dinner, okay?"

"Okay, Mommy." Jessica set the food down in front of her daughter. She and Lola took a few steps away from Camille's little ears.

"So, how's it going?" Jessica asked and motioned her head toward the family room.

"Well, besides feeling like I just walked into a room full of people who might've liked it better had I not shown up, I'm hanging in there."

"That's just your imagination. I know for a fact, Raina is overjoyed to have you here. And believe it or not, so is Victoria." Lola's head snapped back.

"Oh, now that's where you're wrong. I'm sure Victoria would like to forget that I was ever born."

"See, there you go. You need to stop that, Lola. Let me tell you something. A mother is always a mother. Even though she may not agree with her children's choices, a mother never stops loving *and* worrying. Sometimes that love means letting go."

"Well, she certainly did that. There was a time she held on so tight I felt like I was suffocating. She would never let me just be me. Victoria dictated everything. But, after the Reverend died, it seemed like she just didn't want me around and..."

"It wasn't your fault, Lola."

"Yeah, I know but we were arguing and ..." Lola looked away.

"And that still doesn't make it your fault," Jessica stepped over and wiped Camille's fingers.

"I know but it feels that way. It feels like it's *all* my fault." Lola stared straight ahead.

"You've got to let all of that go. Leave that stuff in the past where it belongs."

"So people keep telling me." Lola leaned against the kitchen counter and attempted to rub away the chill she'd just gotten. "I'm trying to change, Jess. I really am trying."

"Well, that's all you can do, right?"

"You're right. That's about all I can do right now," Lola nodded.

🌿🌿🌿🌿

Ms. Ina had walked away, leaving Raina alone with her thoughts. She stood, transfixed on the crowd when she felt the gangly, protective arms of her son Quincy, squeeze her waist.

"You okay, Mom?" He was trying so hard to be strong. He looked so much like his father.

"I'm fine, honey. I just need to sit down."

"Okay, sit right over here." Quincy walked her over toward the couch in the living room. "You want something to drink?"

"No thank you, sweetheart. I'm okay. Where's Matthew?"

"I left him playing on the Game Boy upstairs."

"I better go see if he wants anything to eat." Raina attempted to get up from the sofa.

"No, it's okay, Mom. I'll take care of Matt. You stay here and rest. Okay?"

"Okay," she said as she lightly stroked his arm.

What Raina wanted more than anything in the world, right now, was to be alone. She needed to be alone with her God. She needed the tornado raging inside of her chest to be quieted. The house was a constant flow of friends, family and neighbors coming and going. She and Keenan had just returned, three weeks prior, from celebrating their wedding anniversary. Now, here she sat, in a room full of mourners. Her best friend was gone. Her heart shattered into a million pieces. *My Lord, what am I going to do?*

"Raina, sweetheart, you really need to eat something." Naomi stood over her with a small plate of food. She set it on the table next to Raina before sitting down beside her daughter-in-law.

Raina loved Naomi. She was always the picture of sophistication and she had a heart of gold.

"Thank you, Naomi, but I'm not really hungry. I'll eat something later. I promise."

"Okay, dear." Naomi eased onto the love seat beside Raina. For a moment they were both silent, lost for words to describe their grief as they watched the ebb and flow of guest throughout the house. Raina slipped her hand inside of Naomi's.

She remembered when they'd first met. Keenan had been so nervous. He didn't know if they would hit it off. Luckily, they had an instant bond. Raina had even suggested that Naomi move in with them but she was a strong, independent woman. She would always say, jokingly, "My time has not yet come."

Raina found the soft, warmth of Naomi's hand comforting. She knew those hands had fed and helped a lot of people, including some in that very room.

"How are you doing, Mother?" Raina whispered. Naomi closed her eyes with a deep sigh.

"I don't know just yet," she said, with a sad smile. "No one ever expects to bury her child. The day Keenan made his entrance into the world I never imagined my life without him. Now...?" The knot in her throat became unbearable.

"I know." Raina said, squeezing Naomi's hand.

The two sat for a moment longer, lost in their own thoughts.

"Raina, dear. I'm so sorry for your loss."

Raina released Naomi's hand and stood to greet the condoler. Her responses were almost robotic as her mind drifted. She was growing weary. At that exact moment Lola emerged from her hiding place and discerned the need for intervention on behalf of her sister. She approached Raina with a knowing smile.

"Oh, Mrs. Crawford, this is my sister, Lola."

"Hi Mrs. Crawford, it's so nice to meet you. Raina, Jessica needs to see you in the back." Lola had just saved her from another hour of small talk.

"Oh, okay." Raina gave her sister a grateful smile. "Please excuse me, Mrs. Crawford. Thank you for coming."

"Of course dear." Raina exited the room quickly. She simply wanted to escape this horrible reality.

Raina walked down the hall and retreated to her bedroom, her refuge. She leaned against the door with her eyes closed. When she felt that her legs were strong enough to carry her across the room she opened her eyes and they immediately fell to Kennan's lucky football jersey. It was still draped over the back of the chair. She moved across the room and slowly retrieved the jersey. With trembling hands Raina raised the jersey to her nose and inhaled her husband's scent. She held the jersey to her aching body as she climbed on top of the massive bed and drew her body into a fetal position, attempting to lessen the emptiness gnawing away inside of her. The noise from the front of the house floated away as she, once again, lost the battle of consciousness.

# FOUR

## CITY LIGHTS

---

The bus heaved into the terminal slowly and deliberately. The over-crowded station was nothing like the one they'd left behind.

"So, this is what the ATL looks like," Gabby exclaimed, unable to hide her excitement as she bounced off of the bus. Nyla was still groggy. Although Ms. Pearl had given her some ice to help with the swelling, her head was pounding. Nyla squinted as she stepped off of the bus.

"It certainly is different from Saint Charles' bus station. I don't know if that's good or bad," Nyla said, as she attempted to shield her eyes from the glare of the bright lights.

"Don't start, Ny. This is exciting!" Gabby began repeatedly stepping in place on her tiptoes as her wide eyed gaze jumped from one part of the terminal to the next. Her excitement only seemed to fuel Nyla's irritation.

"Gabby, what are you so happy about?" Nyla turned to her friend. "We don't know a soul, we don't have anywhere to go and we ain't got that much money. So, please stop all that jumping."

"Why are you always looking on the negative side, Ny? You're gonna find your Dad and we have more money now than we ever had when we were with Tyrone. Besides, you were only with Tyrone for a year. I was with him for three," Gabby said, as she held up three fingers for emphasis.

"So… I don't care if I don't know anyone. We're here, Ny. We're alive and we're free! And if that ain't something to be happy about, I don't know what is."

"You girls got someone meeting you?" Ms. Pearl asked, as she slowly descended from the bus and waddled over toward them.

Ms. Pearl was short and wide, with broad shoulders. She wore her hair in a beautiful braided crown. Nyla and Gabby stole glances at one another, not wanting to let her know that no one was coming for them now or later. They were afraid she would call Child Protective Services.

"Uh...yeah, I was, uh, well my cousin is coming to meet us," Gabby lied.

"Yeah, that's right. Her cousin is going to take us to my Dad's. He should be here in a minute." The two girls began looking around as if trying to spot the mysterious cousin.

Pearl Rudolph was no fool. She knew from the scene she'd witnessed the night before, no one was meeting them. She also knew that if they didn't have the good sense to be more cautious, someone had to be. She just couldn't, in all good conscience, leave them to fall prey to the same situation from which they had barely escaped. *What's wrong with this world? These children rather live on the streets, homeless, instead of staying home. It's a shame.*

"You girls are welcome to come with me and Sophia. You can call your cousin to meet you at our place. That is, as long as he ain't anything like that fool you were running from last night."

"Oh, no, he ain't nothing at all like Tyrone, Ms. Pearl," Gabby interjected. She'd been hoping Ms. Pearl would extend them an invitation, no matter how brief. She was dying for a hot shower and a good meal. Nyla looked at Gabby as if she'd lost all of her good sense.

"Uh... Ms. Pearl? Would you excuse us for a minute?" Nyla asked.

"All right, but I don't think it's a good idea to hang around this station. It's not the best environment for young girls traveling alone."

"Okay, Ms. Pearl. Be right back." Nyla nudged Gabby inside of the noisy terminal and toward the restrooms. Inside, soon to be passengers were gathered in every corner. There were mothers sitting in chairs with swollen bags around their feet, tending to cranky, over-stimulated children. Some people sat like zombies, staring up at the flat screen television.

"Gabby? Have you lost your mind?!" Nyla exclaimed, once they were inside the restroom.

"No, Ny. I haven't lost my mind. We need help

and you're just too paranoid."

"What if she's with Child Protective Services?"

"Again, too paranoid. Do you actually think CPS would plant someone on the bus in the middle of the night with her own child, no less? Get real. Besides, she told me she was down there helping her niece who had just had a baby."

Nyla shook her head and began to pace. "I don't know."

"Well, do you know how long the money we have will last on the streets? She's offered us a place to get cleaned up and maybe a good meal. We need to take advantage of it, Ny." Gabrielle's slender frame stood in defiance. She could see the reservation in Nyla's face. They had only been friends for a short while, but together, they'd pulled each other through some rough times.

Gabby hated the idea of separating from Nyla, but she needed a break and she felt like this was it.

"Come on, Ny! Ms. P is good people. Besides, all I've ever wanted was to belong somewhere. You at least had a taste of that with your mom and dad before they died. I ain't never had that, Ny. I'm tired of being out here by myself. I grew up in the system and I've had to deal with a lot of crap. It's my turn to have some happiness."

Nyla looked at her friend and couldn't help but to think how different they both were. While she was reserved and suspicious of everyone, Gabrielle, even after all she'd been through, wore her heart on her sleeve. Gabby was trusting to a fault, which is what often got her into trouble. Nyla's eyes stung with tears.

"I can't go with you, Gabby," the words croaked out. Nyla had a difficult time identifying her own voice.

"What? No. We need to stick together, Ny."

"I gotta find my Dad. I have the address and I don't want to waste another minute. I gotta find him, Gabby." She looked at her friend, and hoped she would understand. Nyla wiped her face with the sleeve of her jacket. After Gabby got over the initial shock, she hugged her friend.

"Okay. But listen, we gotta keep in touch." Gabby opened her purse and pulled out a new cell phone. Tyrone never allowed any of his girls to have one.

"Here," she said, placing the phone in Nyla's hand.

"Where did you get this?"

"Wal-Mart, girl. You weren't the only one taking care of business back there," Gabby said, with a sad smile.

As they stood in the cramped, dirty restroom, they hugged and wept. The reality of going their separate ways took root in their hearts.

A few minutes later, Sophia burst through the restroom door.

"Hey! Ya'll coming or what? Ma said her bed is calling her name and she's ready to answer." They both laughed.

"You gonna be all right?"

"Yeah," Nyla nodded. "I'll be fine. I got you as my best friend and soon I'm gonna meet my Dad." Gabby seemed satisfied with the answer. She didn't want to keep Ms. Pearl waiting any longer, so she hugged Nyla once more.

"Okay then. Call me as soon as you get settled, okay? I already added my number to your phone."

"I'll call. I promise," Nyla said. Gabby turned reluctantly to follow Sophia out of the restroom. At the door she hesitated. She looked back at her friend, eyes brimming with tears.

"You sure?"

Nyla fought hard to contain her tears. "Yep." Her throat felt constricted as she stood under the harsh terminal lights. Gabby nodded and before she could change her mind, she opened the door and disappeared. No longer able to hold them back, Nyla's tears rushed forward like a river as she moved toward a wall of old, porcelain sinks. She stood clutching both sides of the sink as her slender frame shivered and the feeling of loneliness seemed as though it would consume her. Finally, she looked up and stared in the mirror at her reflection. The bruise, although no longer swollen, was now an ugly purple stain. She was startled when a mother burst through the restroom door with a crying child. Nyla, quickly wiped away the tears and threw water on her face. She took one more look at herself. She didn't recognize the girl that stared back at her, homeless and alone. Her life before Tyrone now seemed like a fairytale. So much had happened since her parents' death.

꩜ ꩜ ꩜ ꩜

After so many years in the foster care system, Nyla had grown accustomed to the constant chaos. But on the day an unfamiliar caseworker showed up at the group home, asking questions about her paternity, Nyla was bewildered. No one had taken the time to explain exactly what it all meant. Later, during the questioning the caseworker, swabbed Nyla's mouth for DNA testing, although she didn't know it at the time. It didn't take long for Nyla to figure out that someone was probably looking for her. She made up her mind, to meet whoever it was half way.

The day Nyla finally summoned the courage to find out what was going on, the group home attendant had dropped her off at her case-worker's office. She was disappointed but not surprised to find a different caseworker than her usual one, Maria. Nyla was escorted to a small office where she sat across from a desk stacked with files, coffee cups, and miniature ceramic frog figurines. The figurines were every size, and every shade of green, positioned all over the office. Thrown in were a few framed photos of a younger, more vibrant looking woman. Nyla noticed the woman in the photo and the one seated across from her shared a faint resemblance.

"Now, Nariah," began the frazzled, drab looking woman. Her voice was scratchy and hoarse, like there was a frog stuck in her throat.

"Excuse me?" Nyla interjected, not sure if frog lady was referring to her or not.

The woman looked at Nyla over her red rimmed glasses.

"You said, Nariah. My name is Nyla."

The frog lady took a deep breath, rolled her eyes and focused her attention back to the open folder in front of her.

"Well, now that we have *that* established, let's
try to get through this with as few interruptions as
possible, shall we?" As if on cue, the phone on her
desk rang so loud, it almost blasted them both out of
the tiny cubicle.

"Oh my god! Can't I have one moment of peace?
Lucy Foster," The frog lady answered the phone
roughly. Her face had turned a warm fuchsia; a
stark contrast to her platinum hair which looked as
if she'd placed a bowl over to cut.

"What?! That's impossible, because I took him
over there myself last week." She paused. Nyla
noticed that she was becoming more agitated with
each passing moment.

"Stop. Is Jack in his office? Okay, well put him
on the phone. No. I want to speak to him myself,"
Frog lady jumped to her feet and to Nyla's surprise,
she was only about four feet tall. Nyla wanted to
disappear. She was really missing Maria and her
soft-spoken, kind disposition right about now.

"You know what? Forget it. I'm coming up to
see him." Ms. Froggy pounded the phone down
with such force, Nyla almost leapt out of her chair.
She slammed the folder closed and jammed it into
her desk drawer. "Sit tight. This won't take long."
She grabbed another file and stormed out the door
before Nyla had a chance to ask any questions.

Ten minutes passed before Nyla stood and began
looking at the framed citations and photos on the
bookshelf. She glanced towards the door as she
moved cautiously behind the desk. Nyla noticed
that, although frog lady had locked the drawer, in
her haste, she'd left the key in the lock.

Nyla's fingers trembled as she turned the key and retrieved the file. As she began to rifle through it, that's when she saw it. The letter was from an independent laboratory, confirming paternity with a 99.9% match. Nyla's heart began to race as she stared back at the letter. Tears welled up in her eyes as she read it again. Paternity confirmed by a 99.9% match for Nyla Davis and one Keenan Blackman of Atlanta. There were so many emotions exploding within her, she didn't know what to do next. She closed the file and moved quickly back to the other side of the desk, placing the folder inside her satchel. Not sure of her next move, she sat and continued to wait. *What will happen once frog lady discovers that the folder is missing?* Her mind raced at hundred miles per minute. She realized she needed to leave. Nyla threw the satchel over her shoulder and was about to exit when the door swung open.

"Going somewhere?" Frog Lady asked, as she blocked the office threshold.

"Yes. I need to go to the restroom, if it's okay?" Frog Lady stared up at her suspiciously. Finally, she moved to the side and allowed Nyla to pass.

"Don't be long. I have another appointment," she called after Nyla. Nyla's response was simply a hand in the air, as if to acknowledge the request. What she was really saying was goodbye and good riddance.

Minutes later Nyla burst through the double doors and descended the stairs of the old World War II building. The still, humid air greeted her as she inhaled the sweet smell of freedom. She had, without any remorse or forethought, decided she had all she needed to start her own journey to find her real family and a new life.

❧ ❧ ❧ ❧

Now, a year after being tricked, abused and threatened, Nyla had finally found the courage to escape once again. Her body began to tingle all over as she realized she was only minutes from meeting the man responsible for her being in the world. Nyla adjusted her satchel and placed the hoodie over her head.

"Okay," she said to the battered image in the mirror. "This is what you said you wanted. It's too late to turn back out now." Nyla turned and started on her quest, unaware that the path she'd chosen may not be the happy ending she'd hoped for.

# *FIVE*

## *BROKEN*

---

**R**aina saw Keenan's arms reach for her but she could never get close enough. Even in the distance, she could see that he needed her. He was trying to come to her. She tried to call out to him but could not speak. Her feet felt as if they were stuck in quicksand. He turned to leave and panic rose in her chest as she struggled to free herself.

She tried again to speak but the words refused to come. He was walking away and she needed to be with him. Raina knew she couldn't lose him again. Finally, her voice burst forth like water through a broken dam.

"Keenan! Don't...don't go! Please, don't go!" She gulped air as if she were drowning.

"Keenan! Keenan!" She reached for him. Raina felt strong hands grip her shoulders, keeping her from her beloved. She struggled to free herself.

"Raina, it's me. Wake up," Lola said, shaking her sister.

Raina's eyes flew open. She saw the alarm in Lola's eyes and instantly the pang of emptiness stabbed at her chest as she remembered; Lola was here because Keenan was gone. The hollowness in her chest permeated her entire body. Raina doubled over, trying to expel herself of the pain. She wanted to be strong but she could not rid herself of the insurmountable grief. Her cries were muffled at first. Moments later the muffles became moans, like that of a wounded animal.

"It's okay, baby. Let it out. Just let it out." Lola held her sister close. She caressed Raina's hair and back as they rocked back and forth. Lola was glad she was here, allowing her sister's pain to be purged onto her. There had been many times Lola had wished Raina's perfect life were her own, but never this. Never in a million years would she have wished such a great tragedy as losing one's soul mate on anyone.

As Lola held her, Raina allowed the grief to rush out. Neither of them heard Victoria enter the room.

"Shhh, it's going to be all right, Sissy." Lola tried desperately to comfort her. It felt foreign to her now. She had allowed so many years to pass since there had been any real closeness between them. Until now, Lola hadn't realized how much she'd missed her baby sister. Nevertheless, Lola felt helpless, like a fish out of water flapping around, unable to get any footing or know how to respond.

The doctor had prescribed antidepressants and

although Raina had refused them earlier, now she allowed Lola to feed them to her. She wanted to rest. She wanted to escape and return to the place where she could be with her husband. Raina lay back down and Victoria decided to keep vigil at her bedside.

"I'll stay with her." Victoria pulled a chair closer to the bed.

"No, you don't have to. I don't mind." Lola stood and covered Raina with the large duvet.

Although Victoria was happy that Lola had finally come home, she had to admit that she also had mixed feelings. Since the Reverend's death, Victoria felt as though she had to walk on eggshells around Lola. She never knew what would set her off.

"Sweetheart, I know you don't mind, but I'm her mother," Victoria addressed Lola's back. "She and I share a common loss." Suddenly, Lola felt a jolt up her spine but she fought to maintain her composure. She pinched the bridge of her nose to rid herself of the oncoming headache.

"You know what, Victoria?" Lola turned to face her mother. "Everyone in this room has experienced a loss." Lola's eyes were transfixed on Victoria's face, as if daring her to look away. "Some of it was by the hand of God, and some was caused by people trying to *play* God." Lola's words were like daggers. Her intent was for them to pierce Victoria's cold exterior. "Either way, I think we can all relate to how it feels to lose someone we love."

"I...I only meant..." Victoria stuttered.

"I know what you meant. But it doesn't really

matter. All that matters is that Raina needs *both* of us but go ahead," she said, stepping away from the bed. "You stay, Victoria. I'm sure I can find somewhere else around here to help out." Lola turned and quickly exited the bedroom.

Victoria inhaled and exhaled and with a heavy heart, slowly she lowered herself into the nearby chair. She didn't know what to do for Raina or Lola. She wished a million times she'd done things differently where Lola was concerned. She thought about how ironic it was that it had taken Keenan's death to reunite them but life... life had had them scurrying about like leaves in the wind.

As Raina drifted off into a fitful sleep, Victoria stared out of the French doors at the winter sun as it descended. She rationalized what she'd done for Lola and for her family was the best she could've done under the circumstances. Deep down Victoria knew that Lola had never forgiven her for convincing her to put her baby up for adoption, but Lola was much too young and inexperienced to be a mother. Adoption had been the only answer. She didn't want Lola to become a statistic and be subjected to the ridicule she herself had endured. Victoria had only thought about what was best for Lola but Lola never saw it that way.

"God, how I wish I had another chance with her," Victoria whispered. Her eyes brimmed with tears. Raina stirred and Victoria stood and placed the duvet back in place. She breathed heavily as she watched her daughter wrestle with her loss, just as she'd done so many years ago. Victoria knew from experience that only time would heal this jagged wound.

As Lola entered the hallway she saw a figure move quickly toward the family room. She turned the corner and saw Quincy pick up a photo of Keenan and throw it across the room. Lola realized Quincy must've heard Raina crying. The room went silent. Everyone turned and stared in shock.

Tears ran down Quincy's angular face. He hated witnessing the devastation this had on his family. He felt helpless.

"I hate this! I hate it! Why did he have to leave us?! Lola looked in Lloyd's direction. She was at a complete loss as to what to say or do. Naomi stepped forward to try and console him but was unsuccessful.

"Hey, man, come here," Lloyd said, as he approached and pulled Quincy toward him. Quincy was rigid at first, and then he dove into his cousin's arms. His entire body trembled.

"Why did he have to die? I want my dad!" Quincy cried out. He buried his face in Lloyd's chest. Lloyd embraced him while Naomi tried to coax Matthew from the room but Matthew wouldn't budge. He stood nearby and stared at his brother with a wide eyed expression. Lloyd reached out for them both.

"Listen guys, I know this is hard. I know you have a million questions and I wish I had the answers, but I don't. All I can tell you is that it'll get easier to deal with in time." Quincy looked up at Lloyd and took a step back.

"No it won't, because he's never coming back." Quincy's face was distraught as he tried desperately to stop crying. Defiantly, he swatted the tears away. Lloyd struggled with his own emotions as he leaned forward.

"Listen, Q. We just gotta stick together and help each other, man." Lloyd's own eyes began to fill with tears. Quincy turned quickly and stormed up the stairs toward his room. Lloyd stood and breathed a heavy sigh.

"Come on, Matt; let's go take care of your brother."

Lola knew this was her cue to leave. She remembered what Mr. Goodman had said about emotions being high. He'd suggested that perhaps it would be wise to wait until she'd been sober longer. Now she thought maybe she should've listened. She had no one here to help her deal with all the drama. No Jack, no Mr. Goodman, no one. It was time for her departure; no matter how temporary she knew it was time to go.

Lola spotted Jessica talking to a group of teens who had stopped by to pay their respects.

"Excuse me, Jess." Jessica knew immediately that Lola was not fairing very well.

"Hey. What's up?"

"Lloyd had said it would be okay if I crashed with you guys while I'm in town. So, if it's okay, I'm gonna go on ahead. Can I borrow your house key?" Jessica was familiar with Lola's quick exits when things got a little messy. She just couldn't handle it.

"Sure, but I should be leaving in a few minutes because I need to get the kids settled. If you can wait for a..."

"Oh, don't worry. Aunt Pearlie and Aunt Sarah said that I can catch a ride with them."

"Oh, okay. Well just leave the door inside the garage unlocked." Jessica dropped the key into Lola's open palm.

"Okay, thanks." Lola's mad dash toward the front door caused her to collide into the young girl who was standing on the other side.

"Oh, I'm sorry, are you all right?" Lola asked, reaching out to catch the girl before she fell.

"Yeah, I'm fine," Nyla responded, as she regained her balance.

"Okay. Sorry about that," Lola spoke as she tightened the belt on her coat and continued down the front steps. Before she got to the end of the sidewalk Lola turned and looked back at the girl. She barely got another glimpse before Nyla stepped across the threshold, into the house.

Lola felt a chill deep inside. Although the February air had grown colder, she knew from experience that the chill had little to do with the weather. She pulled up the collar of her coat and trotted to the waiting car. Little did she know that tonight a long buried secret would be resurrected and would either draw them all closer together or pull them further apart.

# SIX

## NYLA MAKES AN ENTRANCE

---

**H**alf an hour earlier, Nyla had stood across the street, blowing cigarette smoke past her thin lips. She stood motionless, staring at what she knew to be her fathers' house. The rain had finally ceased but the temperature had dropped and now the frigid air seeped through to her skin and attacked her bones.

When the taxi driver pulled up to the house, Nyla hadn't expected there to be so many people. As she sat inside the taxi the constant ticking of the meter reminded her that the warmth of the taxi came at a price. It had been fifteen minutes since the taxi had pulled away and Nyla's teeth began to chatter as she contemplated her next move. Not knowing whether to go inside and surprise everyone or just try to wait it out. This was not the way she'd envisioned meeting her father for the first time. But there was no turning back now and when her toes began to throb, Nyla realized she couldn't continue standing out in the cold.

The craftsman style house was painted in different hues of Army green. Stacked stone columns and gas lanterns flanked the arched shaped entrance. Nyla only remembered seeing houses like this in magazines.

She glanced up at the dark clouds rolling across the gray sky and continued to study the house. She saw people leaving but minutes later, more would show up. Suddenly, a strong wind blew and Nyla made up her mind. If she stayed she would freeze to death. She took one last drag of her cigarette before she dropped it onto the ground and smashed it with her half-laced combat boot. "It's now or never," she mumbled. Nyla tucked in her chin and drew tightly within herself as she darted across the street.

Once on the porch, her nerves got the best of her. Nyla paced in front of the door. When she'd finally mustered enough courage to reach out and ring the doorbell, the front door flew open and a lady collided into her, almost knocking her to the ground. After she regained her footing, Nyla looked up into the face of one of the most beautiful women she'd ever seen. When she asked Nyla if she was okay, Nyla's voice tore at her throat making it difficult to speak. Nyla simply nodded, and as quickly as she'd appeared, with a brief apology and a quick smile the lady jetted off and disappeared into a waiting car. Nyla turned her attention back to the now open door, hesitating for a moment longer.

The warmth of the house wrapped itself around her body and drew her in. Nyla took a deep breath and stepped over the threshold into her very uncertain future.

Although the crowd had thinned out, there were still a lot of mourners inside. With all the commotion, no one noticed the slender, freckle faced girl enter the house.

Once inside, Nyla stiffened. Her feet felt as though they were nailed to the floor. She clutched her satchel and waited for someone to greet her, but no one came. Her eyes darted nervously from room to room, desperately seeking a glimpse of the man she had dreamed about for so long. Moments later the aroma floating from the dining room forced her feet to move in its direction. When she turned the corner and saw the magnificent display of food, it took her breath away. Nyla, quickly moved toward the table and began piling food onto a small plate; while secretly slipping napkins of food into her pocket.

Jessica was the first to notice Nyla hunched over the buffet. She couldn't place the young girl but she assumed that she was with a friend of the family. Ten minutes later, Jessica noticed the same girl who had moved only a few feet from the table and now stood in a corner of the dining room. Jessica also noticed the girl didn't appear to be with anyone else. She watched her for a moment longer and when she saw her sneaking food into her pockets, she decided to approach her.

"Hello." Jessica spoke as she approached the young lady. Nyla jumped at the sound of Jessica's voice. Jessica was also startled when she noticed the ugly, purple bruise on the right side of Nyla's face.

"I'm sorry. I didn't mean to startle you."

Nyla swallowed her food, as the tall, friendly looking lady stood only a few feet away. Her shoulder length brown hair was pulled back into a ponytail. Her light brown eyes were soft and her smile seemed genuine. *Could this be my dad's wife?*

"Oh no, it's cool. I was just looking around." She didn't know what else to say. *Oh my God, I hope she doesn't throw me out before I get a chance to see my dad.* Nyla grew nervous.

"Oh, okay. Are you here with anyone?" Jessica asked concerned. She detected a certain level of anxiety in the girl's demeanor.

"I was just, uh... I was looking for my fa..." Suddenly, Nyla became defensive. Still holding the small plate she straightened her posture and tried to sound more like an adult. "I'm here to see Mr. Blackman."

"Mr. Blackman?" Jessica repeated, with a perplexed look. *She couldn't be referring to Keenan, could she?* All the kids Keenan mentored throughout the community had heard about his untimely death, many had even attended the funeral earlier today.

"Um... which Mr. Blackman sweetheart?"

"Ke..." Nyla's voice cracked. "Umh hmmm," she cleared her throat. "Keenan Blackman," she answered, avoiding direct eye contact. "Is he here?" Nyla asked, peering around Jessica into other parts of the house.

"Wow," Jessica said, mostly to herself. Seeing

Jessica's reaction, Nyla became even more apprehensive. She set her plate on a nearby tray table.

"Listen, I didn't mean to crash your party or anything, it's just that I really need to see him. It's important." Jessica shook her head to clear her thoughts. *How am I going to tell this girl about Keenan?*

"Hey, honey," Lloyd walked up and stood beside Jessica. Nyla's heart leapt into her throat. She could feel the rhythmic beating of her pulse as it quickened. *Oh my God, it's him!*

"Oh hey, baby. How's Quincy?" Jessica asked, not taking all of her attention away from Nyla. She was still puzzled.

"He'll be fine. It's just going take some time."

"Uh, honey? This young lady..." Jessica gestured toward Nyla. "I'm sorry, sweetheart, what's your name?" Nyla's palms began to sweat. Her body temperature was rising and she felt nauseous. Her throat felt constricted when she attempted to speak.

"Nyla," she said, with a croak.

"Yes. Well, Nyla is here to see, Keenan," Jessica said, as she looked up at Lloyd. She attempted to hide the look of bewilderment on her face. "She says it's really important that she speaks to him." Jessica spoke in hushed tones. Lloyd's left eyebrow shot up.

"Oh. You're not Keenan Blackman?" Nyla looked disappointed.

"No, I'm not," Lloyd responded slowly, and shot his wife a questioning look. "I'm his cousin, Lloyd, and this is my wife Jessica." Nyla shoved her hands in her pockets and looked away. She was embarrassed.

"Oh. Well is he here?" she asked, clearly agitated. Her discomfort was growing and she felt like they were stalling.

"Umm hmm." Lloyd cleared his throat. "Um, are you here with anyone?"

"No." Nyla was abrupt. She could feel the ground shifting beneath her feet. She felt unsteady and the suffocating desire to escape had begun to travel up her body.

"Okay. Well, uh, how do you know Mr. Blackman, if you don't mind me asking?"

"Well, Mr. Lloyd, I kinda do mind you asking. I mean, I know he might be real busy with the party and all but this is urgent." Nyla was only seconds from running back out the front door. *Maybe this wasn't such a good idea. I shoulda listened to Gabby.* Lloyd began sizing her up. By her appearance she looked like a runaway. And whoever put that nasty bruise on her face was maybe the reason why she was looking for Keenan. Keenan had helped many teens get their lives back on track. When Lloyd looked at her again, something about her slowly came into to focus. First, it was the green of her eyes, then the freckles and the slight tilt in her chin. *Oh my god!* Lloyd felt as if the wind had been knocked out of him once he realized who this child might be.

"You know what? Why don't you come over here and have a seat in Keenan's office. I'll get him for you."

"What?" Jessica's head jerked towards her

husband. She stared at Lloyd, as if he'd just grown two heads. Nyla hesitantly followed Lloyd into Keenan's office. A large oak desk sat in the middle of the room, flanked by bookshelves displaying pictures, awards, and certificates that Keenan had acquired over the years. Lloyd pulled out one of the over-sized chairs and motioned for Nyla to sit.

"Okay, you wait here and I'll be right back." Nyla pulled her satchel closer as she lowered herself into the chair. Jessica stood near the office door, still not believing what Lloyd had just done. After Nyla was settled in the office, Lloyd walked out pulling the French doors closed behind him.

"What is wrong with you?!" Jessica asked, in a loud whisper. They moved only steps away from the office.

"Why did you tell that poor child that you were going to get Keenan? Have you lost your mind?!" Her tone was incredulous.

"I have my reasons, Jess."

"Well, why don't you fill me in, because I can't imagine why you would do something so cruel."

"Just tell me what she said when you first spoke to her."

"What? Why? And what does that have to do with why you have her thinking she's about to see Keenan?"

"Jess, please. Just tell me."

She began, exasperated. "She just said she was here to see Mr. Blackman. I asked her which Mr. Blackman and she said, Keenan." Lloyd began rubbing his goatee. Jessica knew that look well. She could see the wheels turning in his head. There was something going on. Something she didn't know about, and that was unfamiliar ground for her.

Jessica and Lloyd had been high school sweethearts and they shared everything.

"What is it, Lloyd? Who is she?" Before Lloyd had a chance to respond the doors to the office swung open and Nyla stood in the doorway, trembling with a pained expression. Both Lloyd and Jessica were taken aback by the stricken look on her face.

"Nyla, what's wrong, hon...?" Jessica stopped suddenly when she noticed what Nyla held in her hand. Slowly, Nyla held up the funeral program and both Lloyd and Jessica stood frozen. Neither knew how to respond.

Nyla could barely see past the fat tears that brimmed her eyes. She swatted them away as quickly as they formed.

"Is it true?" Her voice quivered as her steel green eyes bore into Lloyd's bewildered expression. The color had drained from her face as she stood in shocked disbelief. Lloyd was a big man at 6'2, but at that moment, he felt very small and very sad. He was at a loss for words so he simply nodded.

Nyla was overcome by grief. Her small body began to cave into itself and her legs could no longer support her. She stumbled backwards and before she fell to the floor, Lloyd moved quickly and caught her. Jessica also moved in and helped Nyla back into the office, as Lloyd lowered her into a chair. Jessica knelt beside her, wishing she knew what was going on, as she attempted to comfort her.

Nyla was silent. Now she allowed the tears to

stream down her ashen face.

"Why?" she asked as she buried her face in her hands, shaking her head from side to side. "Why? Why?" she repeated as the monumental feeling of loss began to swell inside of her. She didn't know where she would go. All of her hope was gone.

"Nyla, why were you looking for Keenan? Jessica asked. "What was so important?" Nyla couldn't answer. Her shoulders shook as the tears ran from her beautiful eyes. Keenan's eyes.

"She's his daughter," Lloyd answered. Jessica looked up at Lloyd in utter shock.

"What?"

"Am I right, Nyla? Were you looking for Keenan because he's your father?"

Nyla couldn't believe what she was hearing. She could only nod. Jessica finally stood.

"Keenan had a daughter and you knew about it?!"

Lloyd nodded. "Yes."

"But, how? When? I mean, Lloyd what's going on?" She looked to Lloyd for the answers but she could see he was at a loss. His eyes filled with tears as he stood there, unable to comfort his wife or Nyla.

"Does Raina know?" Jessica asked, still bewildered. Lloyd pinched the bridge of his nose and wiped his tired eyes.

"No. No, she doesn't know, but it looks like I'm going to have to break the news sooner than I had expected to."

"You don't have to tell her anything." Nyla stood up from the chair and started toward the door.

"I'm out." Lloyd caught her by the arm.

"Don't touch me!" Both he and Jessica jumped at Nyla's outburst.

"Hey, I'm sorry, okay?" Lloyd held both palms in the air, an attempt to calm her down.

"What in the world is going on in here?" Naomi asked, as she entered the room.

The day was coming to an end and Naomi, tired and experiencing her own inner turmoil, had decided it was time to head home. She stood regally, looking from Lloyd to Jessica and then at the young lady who was obviously upset with them both.

"Is anyone going to tell me what's going on?" she asked, again.

"Nyla, this is Keenan's mother." Jessica, quickly made the introductions, and hoped it would intrigue Nyla enough to keep her from fleeing.

Nyla couldn't bring herself to make eye contact and Naomi could see that she was distraught. She cautiously stepped closer and extended her hand.

"Hello, I'm Naomi Blackman." Nyla didn't respond. Naomi stole a quick glance toward Jessica.

"You know, this is usually when most people would say, it's nice to meet you, my name is..."

Naomi still stood with her hand extended. Nyla finally looked up into her face. The mere fact that she could possibly be her grandmother was lost on Nyla. It didn't register and she was too exhausted to care. There had been so many times she'd dreamed of finding her real family, only to have her hopes and dreams dashed. The fact that Keenan Blackman was dead meant she would probably never have a chance to have a normal family.

"Well, I'm not most people." Nyla stepped around Naomi and was out of the office and the front door before anyone had chance to stop her.

The bitter February air snatched the breath from her young lungs, almost making her retreat back into the warmth of the house. Nyla pressed forward and picked up speed as she ran to escape the heart-wrenching truth. She didn't know where she was going but she knew, without a doubt, where she didn't belong. When Nyla got to the end of the street, she made a left and ran as fast as she could. The cold wind rushed through her hair and the howling in her ears only made her run even faster. She needed to get as far away from that house and those people as fast as she possibly could. She ran until she saw a baseball field and decided to seek shelter in the dugout. As she neared the field, Nyla threw her satchel over a chain linked fence and climbed over. Once over, under the cloak of darkness, she made her way to the dugout. She slid back into the far corner and pulled the hoodie over her head. Moments later, her fingers felt like icicles as she struggled to light a cigarette. She shivered and inhaled, allowing the smoke to slowly fill her lungs. As she exhaled, and allowed the thin, white smoke to escape and rise into the darkness; Nyla felt as though shattered pieces of glass were floating around in her chest, cutting away at the smallest seed of hope she had. She lowered her head again, and drew her knees into her torso. Sitting in the damp, musty dugout she began to rock. All that could be seen was the small red tip of the cigarette as she took another drag. Alone in the darkness, Nyla allowed herself to grieve. She cried silently until no more tears would come.

"Why was I even born? No one should have to live like this." Nyla continued to rock, a futile attempt to warm her body. Moments passed and her head fell back against the thin, narrow wall. She had no more fight left, no plan B or thoughts for tomorrow. Nyla stared up into the blackness of the sky. She could see the wispy, translucent cloud from her breath as it escaped her mouth and floated into the night air. *I can't do this, anymore. I want to die just like my dad. You hear that, God! I'm sick and tired of this life! Please, just let this be over.* Nyla closed her eyes and allowed one last tear to escape as she surrendered to a defeated spirit.

# SEVEN

## BLINDSIDED

---

Lola tossed and turned as the dreadful image played itself over and over again. Repeatedly, she saw her father fall to the floor and the vacant look in Victoria's eyes after he was pronounced dead.

Lola's breath caught in her throat as her eyes flew open and there it was—the ever-present, relentless weight of guilt. It felt as though the guilt had manifested into a physical presence and stood guard over her, making sure she would never forget, even as she slept. The T-shirt she'd worn to bed now clung to her sweaty body like a second skin. Her mouth felt like cotton so she felt around on the floor for the bottle of water she'd brought to bed. After she took a sip, Lola fell back and ran her hands through her hair. She continued to lie in a semi-conscious state allowing her breathing to return to normal, while contemplating what method she would use to rid herself of the thunderbolt of a headache she now had.

The muffled sounds beyond her door became louder as Lola drifted in and out of consciousness. The house had started to come alive as Lloyd and Jessica's children tumbled about. She could hear them as they played and argued about things children argue about. Lola rolled over and reached down around her feet until she found another pillow to bury her head.

The fact that the guest room was really the kids' playroom, and her bed was actually a lumpy, overused futon, contributed to her night of discomfort. She started to drift off again when she heard a light knock at the door. She didn't answer. Another knock came and then the door eased open.

"Hey, you up?" Lola kept her head buried and hoped that he would go away.

"Mmm...," was the only sound that came from beneath the pillow. Lloyd slid into the room. He was a big man and he seemed to fill up the entire space.

"Lola, get up and get dressed. I need you to take a ride with me." There was no response.

"Lola. I know you can hear me. Listen, I really need to talk to you about something important." Lola peeked from beneath the pillow and grudgingly pulled herself up, sitting Indian style. Even with her hair mashed and sleep in her eyes, she was still very striking.

"Lloyd?" she started, still with her eyes closed. Her voice was raspy and hoarse. "First of all, it is

freezing outside. Second—and no offense—'cuz I
don't know what ungodly hour it is but I do know
it's too early for whatever boot camp ya'll got going
on in this house. Can't we just talk right here where
it's nice and warm, so I can go back to sleep."

Before he could get another word in, his two
oldest children, Serena and Simone, burst through
the door.

"Auntie Cuz, are you gonna sleep all day? Come
on, get up and tell us some of your funny flight
attendant stories!" Simone begged, trying to pull
Lola up from the futon.

"You sleep like a bear, girl," Serena, always the
leader of the group, spoke in a tone much older than
her twelve years.

"Serena?! Who are you calling, girl?" Lloyd's
tone did not hide his disapproval. "Lola is an adult
and you will address her as an adult. You got it?"
The two girls hung their heads.

"Sorry, Daddy," they both said. "It's just that
Mommy said sometimes Cousin Lola acts just like
she's our age, so..." Serena tried to explain.

"That's enough." Lloyd's embarrassment was
obvious. Lola leaned back with a smirk. Her right
eyebrow shot up as she looked up at her cousin.

"Well, you can both tell your mommy that
Auntie Cuz said you're as young as you feel. And
quite frankly, I like feeling like I'm twelve
sometimes." The girls giggled as Lola began to
tickle them.

"You all go on and help your mom with lunch.
Give Lola some space," Lloyd said, as he stuffed
his hands into his pockets.

"Okay, Daddy," they said in unison, as they hopped off the futon.

"Lunch?" Lola was known for sleeping in, but she had no idea she'd slept past noon. She looked around at the small Mickey Mouse clock on the side table.

"Yes, it's the ungodly hour of twelve-thirty," Lloyd said, as he grabbed Lola's robe and threw it on top of her.

"Now, get dressed. This is important, and no, we can't talk here." Lloyd closed the door behind him, waited a few minutes and opened the door again. He caught Lola curled back up on the futon.

"Lola!" She jumped as if she'd heard a gun shot.

"Okay, okay. Dang, you're going to give me a heart attack."

"Lola, this is really important and I don't have much time before I have to go back to work. So, get your butt up."

"I'm up." She stood and rubbed her lower back as she stretched.

"It's not like these are the most comfortable accommodations, anyway," she mumbled. *Man, what I wouldn't give to be in my own bed.* A sharp pain shot down Lola's back as she continued to stretch.

"That's more like it." Lloyd closed the door. He turned and started down the hallway and was almost sideswiped by his second set of twins: two rambunctious boys, on their way to see their cousin.

"Whoa... where's the fire?" Lloyd asked, as he caught them mid-air.

"We want to see Cousin Lola," Joshua, the

youngest of the eight -year-old twins said. He tried
to wiggle from his dad's embrace.

"You know what? She wants to see the both of
you too, but she can't right now because she's
getting dressed."

"Awww.... but Dad, we didn't get a chance to
talk to her yesterday," Jacob whined.

"Come on, guys." Lloyd put them down. "Let's
go see what Mom's making for lunch. You'll get a
chance to see Lola later." Lloyd smiled as he
watched them race each other back down the
narrow hallway. Had someone told him that he and
Jess would be the parents of five children, he never
would have believed it. He loved his family and that
was why he and Keenan had hit it off from the start.
Lloyd wasn't exactly sure what role he would play
in helping his cousins accept Nyla, but he knew he
had to try to do the right thing by Keenan.

❧ ❧ ❧ ❧

Lloyd sat at a table near one of the many
fireplaces at The Coffee Cat Café. It was a one
hundred-year-old house that had been renovated and
converted into an eclectic, neighborhood bookstore
and coffee shop. The arched, double oak doors hung
heavily and held beautifully beveled glass windows.
A large ornate counter greeted patrons as they
entered. Four over-sized chalkboards hung behind
the counter, displaying the many different delicacies
in which customers could indulge. The frigid
February temperature had done its job and driven in
many cold and hungry customers. The place was
buzzing. Lloyd sat patiently and watched Lola as
she ordered her pastry and coffee.

The atmosphere had a lot of rustic charm and the smell of Kona coffee and fresh baked pastries floated through the air, adding to the warm, cozy vibe. Lloyd drank his herbal tea, and hoped that Lola would be strong enough to help her sister deal with Nyla and all her baggage.

After Nyla ran off, Lloyd contacted his unit and had them search the area. They found her, unconscious and half frozen, at a nearby ballpark. Lloyd had been up practically all night. He was exhausted. Burying his best friend and sitting at the hospital half the night with Nyla had made for a difficult end to a very long week. Operating on only a few hours of sleep, Lloyd was now trying to figure out if he could convince Lola to extend her stay to help Raina.

Lola's boots clicked on the old hardwood floors as she crossed the room and sat down across from her cousin. She smiled as she sipped her caramel latte.

"Mmm, this is just what I needed; nothing like a little caffeine to start the day." She took another sip.

"Okay, now that you have me all alone, what's so important that we couldn't discuss it at your house? Although, I do love what they've done with this place," Lola said looking around. Lloyd took a deep breath and rubbed his goatee as he stared into the fireplace.

"Earth to Lloyd," Lola waved her hand in front of his face. "Come on now. You're scaring me. What's up?" she asked, her voice laced with concern. Lloyd gave her a half smile and sat up. His throat had become dry so he reached for his cup and sipped his beverage.

"Lola, last night after you left a young girl showed up at the house."

"Oh, yeah. I saw her."

"You did?" Lloyd's head shot back. Lola sat back in her chair.

"Yes. I was moving like a rocket trying to get out of there, I almost knocked the poor child down." Lola took another sip of her drink before she continued. "I have to tell you, I had to get the he...uh, I mean, the heck out of there." She remembered Lloyd was working on his degree in Divinity, and didn't want to be disrespectful. "You know how Victoria can work my nerves."

"Yeah, I remember. But back to what I need to tell you, the girl at the door… she was looking for someone."

"Okay… so do you want me to guess who she was looking for?"

"She was looking for her father," Lloyd said. Lola nodded and continued drinking. "Did she find him?"

"Lola." Lloyd took another sip of his now lukewarm tea. Beads of sweat started to pop out on his forehead. "Keenan was her father." Lola stared at him like a deer in headlights. Lloyd continued.

"Her name is Nyla." Still, Lola sat completely frozen. She watched Lloyd, and his words and movement now came out in slow motion. Lola tried to focus on the rest of what he was saying but after he told her Nyla's name, her brain would not compute. All the noise of the café, along with Lloyd's voice, seemed far away. Lloyd noticed the distant look on her face and could see the death grip she had on her coffee mug. Lola shook her head slightly, as if it would help to clear her thoughts.

"I'm sorry, Lloyd, but what? I mean, what did you say?"

"The girl that you almost knocked down last night is Keenan's daughter." Lola held up her hand, an attempt to stop the onslaught of too much information.

"Excuse my French, Lloyd, but what in the hell have you been smoking?!" Lola spoke, in a loud whisper. "I mean, are you crazy? No, wait a minute." She sat up straighter and leaned forward. "You're not on that stuff are you? Because I know with Keenan's passing and the stress of your job, some cops have a tendency to...

"Lola! Don't be ridiculous. I *know* she's his daughter and I've known about her for a while now." Lola's right eyebrow shot up. The sirens in her head were now so loud she could barely hear herself think.

"Listen. About a year ago Keenan got an anonymous tip, telling him that he had a daughter.

"Anonymous?"

"Yes." Lola's hands began to sweat and her stomach was doing somersaults.

"Why would someone, *anonymously* tell him something like that? It doesn't make sense." Suddenly, her face lit up. "I know." Lola snapped her copper colored nails. "Someone was probably trying to extort money!" Lloyd shook his head.

"No."

"What do you mean no? Of course someone tried

to get money! After Keenan was promoted to captain, people tried to discredit him." Lloyd looked bewildered.

"What?"

"My sister does still confide in me from time to time, you know."

"Yeah? Well that may be, but no one came after him for money. One day, he received a letter that told him he had a daughter." Lola felt as though she was about to pass out. Her hands began to tremble.

"What else did the letter say?"

"I'm not sure about everything, but I do remember that it gave details like the date and location of birth..." Lola didn't feel the mug slip from her hand. Not until Lloyd jumped from the table, as he tried to avoid the spill.

"Whoa..."

"Oh my gosh! I'm sorry, Lloyd," she said, frantically reaching for napkins. "Did any get on you?"

"It's no big deal." Lloyd grabbed the napkins Lola pulled from a nearby canister and wiped his pants. "Listen, are you all right? Why are you so upset?"

"Well, of course I'm upset. I mean, this is Keenan we're talking about. To know that someone is trying to damage his reputation..." She continued cleaning the spill. Lloyd stopped her.

"Lola, didn't you hear me? No one is trying to damage his reputation. It's the truth."

"How in the world do you know that, Lloyd? I mean how can any of this be confirmed? Did he have some kind of DNA test or something?"

"As a matter of fact, he did." With a dazed expression, Lola lowered herself back into her chair.

"It took six months for him to narrow the scope of potential matches, but you know Keenan. He was a great detective and he used that to his advantage. Keenan was able to get copies of the case records for each girl. There were four that had the same birth place and date. Two had been adopted and the others had been in the system almost their entire lives. He was really sick at the thought of any child of his growing up in foster care. That thought alone drove him to find her. Two out of the three left had their parental rights terminated."

"Wait. *Both* parents had terminated their rights?"

"No. The records showed that one of the girls who'd been adopted had the mother's consent for adoption while the father's rights were terminated. The strange thing was that five years after the adoption she was placed into foster care in South Carolina. After a year, when no one came forth to claim her, she was considered abandoned and all parental rights were terminated."

"That's crazy. What about the biological mother? She's the one who put her up for adoption! Why didn't they notify her if the baby was placed in foster care?"

"Unfortunately, it was a closed adoption."

"What? What does that mean?"

"It means that information about the biological parents was sealed. There was no way to find out anything about the mother; therefore, the courts moved to terminate the parental rights in hopes of having the child available for another adoption."

"Oh my god," Lola said, in complete shock.

"Keenan called in a few favors and was able to get two of the girls tested. He wanted to be one hundred percent sure before he told Raina. Nyla's test came back 99.9% positive. By the time he tried to make contact, he was told she'd run away. He continued his search but unfortunately, he died before he could do anything about it."

Lola's eyes focused on Lloyd as if he'd just levitated.

"Does Raina know?"

"No. Well, I don't think so."

"What do you mean you don't think so?"

"Well, he'd planned to tell her while they were on their trip. But I don't know if he did or not." Lola exhaled. She hadn't realized that she'd been holding her breath.

"I gotta tell Raina but first I need you to—"

"Lloyd, I've gotta go." Lola's head was spinning; she felt as though she was about to be sick.

"Lola, what's wrong? Are you okay?"

"Yes, that's it. I mean no. I'm uh, I'm not feeling very well." Lola began to collect her coat and purse.

Lloyd stood up. "Okay. Well, I'll take you back to the house."

"No!"

Lloyd was taken aback by her abrupt reply and Lola looked around shyly. "I'm sorry, Lloyd. I didn't mean to startle you. It's just that I'm having a friend meet me at the restaurant down the street and I think the fresh air will do me some good."

"You're serious?" Lloyd looked at her suspiciously. "I thought you didn't feel well. Besides that, you're the same person who complains that the frozen food section of the grocery store is too cold. You're not really going to walk around in this weather are you?"

"Yeah, I know. But maybe the cold air will do me some good." Lola had already taken a few steps backward toward the door. "I'll see you at the house later, okay?" This was not the reaction Lloyd had expected. He was completely baffled. Before she reached the door, Lola collided into what felt like a brick wall. When she looked up, she had caused another spill. This time it was all over another customer's sweater.

"Oh, I'm so sorry. I'm..." tears welled up in her eyes and she could barely see. Lola felt as though the walls were closing in on her. She had to get outside and allow the cold air to penetrate her lungs. She didn't want to feel. She didn't want to think. Lola turned quickly and made a mad dash through the door. How could this be happening? Just when she thought her life was about to come together, her past had come out of nowhere like a blazing fire, threatening to destroy what little stability she'd finally pulled together. She was completely blindsided.

*What am I going to do? What if...?* Once outside the doors Lola stopped and fumbled through her purse. Her hands shook as she pulled out a cigarette. Holding the cigarette loosely between her fingers, she made her way to the bottom of the steps.

"Excuse me. Excuse me, miss?" Lola did not

hear the footsteps quickly approach her from
behind. She nearly jumped out of her skin when she
felt a strong hand bear down on her shoulder.

"What?!" she said, as she pulled away from the
stranger's grip and spun around.

"I'm sorry. I didn't mean to frighten you."

"What do you want?" Lola asked, looking
alarmed and confused.

"You dropped your scarf back there, when we
collided and I..."

Only then did Lola notice that the stranger was
holding her scarf out toward her. He stood a little
over six feet tall. His teeth were almost blinding, a
stark contrast against his beautiful ebony skin and
his eyes shone like pieces of black glass.

"Oh, thank you," she said, absentmindedly. As
Lola took the scarf from his outstretched hand she
noticed the dark coffee stain on his sweater.

"I'm sorry about that," Lola pointed at the stain
on what appeared to be a cashmere sweater.

"That's quite all right. Accidents happen." He
spoke with a slight British accent, as he waved off
the incident. He couldn't take his eyes off of her.
He'd noticed her when she and her gentleman friend
first entered the café. She was absolutely gorgeous,
but he could tell that she seemed upset.

"I could get it cleaned for you, if..."

"No, no. That won't be necessary," he said as he
shook his head. "I'll tell you what. The next time,
I'll let you buy me another cup of coffee."

"Next time?" she repeated, confused. He simply
smiled with those perfect teeth.

"Yes." He blew into his hands, an attempt to

warm them. "There's always a next time." He then turned and trotted back toward the café. Lola stood dumbfounded for a moment longer.

An arctic rush of cold air brought her back to herself. *Just my luck to meet a gorgeous creature like that on a day like this.* She quickly wrapped the scarf around her neck. *This is why I live in L.A.* Lola turned and started walking. She didn't know where she was going, but she knew she had to put as much distance between herself and Lloyd as possible.

Ten minutes later Lola was still walking. By now her feet were numb from the cold and she realized she needed to seek some kind of shelter. When she looked up there it was. The Thirsty Squirrel, the neighborhood bar.

Lola stared at the neon sign, which seemed to mock and beckon her at the same time. She felt the pull but she walked past it. She continued to pace back and forth, up and down the sidewalk until the temperature and temptation got the best of her.

As soon as she stepped through the door, the rank aroma of spilled liquor insulted her nostrils. The dankness and smell of the dimly lit bar was so very familiar, like a hundred bars in a hundred other cities. Her mouth began to water as she made her way to the bar. Lola's head and heart told her to turn around and run in the other direction, but the anticipation of the familiar sting hitting the back of her throat would not go away. Her world was spinning out of control and this was the only way she knew how to cope. *One drink is all I need— just a little something to help me think straight.* Even as the thoughts came to her, she knew them for the lies they were. But at this point, she didn't care. She kept hearing Lloyd's voice repeat the girl's name. 'Nyla, Nyla is Keenan's child'. Lola shook her head. She needed to forget. No guilt, no regret. Her old friend beckoned.

"Jack and coke, light on the coke," Lola said, to the bartender as she climbed onto the barstool. Her hands shook as she unwrapped her scarf. She stole a glance around the bar and hoped she wouldn't run into anyone who recognized Reverend Devereux's daughter. It never seemed to matter how old she got, she was still a preacher's kid, especially here in the Bible belt.

Lola jumped when the bartender abruptly set the glass down in front of her.

"You want to open a tab?" His voice was rough.

"Sure. Why not?" She stared at the deep bronze liquid for a few minutes before raising the glass. The bourbon's pungent aroma was intoxicating, even before she took the first sip. Her hands still shook as she lifted the glass to her lips. At first she drank it slowly and then she gulped the rest down as though she was dying of thirst. The stinging sensation became a warm, slow burn as it snaked its way down her throat. She could feel the alcohol racing through her body. Lola felt instant remorse and she hated herself for not being strong enough to resist, but the more contempt she felt, the more she needed to drink. She raised her hand to the bartender, indicating that she wanted another. Before the night was over, three months of sobriety had been washed down the drain.

Hours passed and she didn't stop drinking until

she finally ran out of money. Unable to gather herself, Lola laid her head on top of the bar.

"Hey. Hey, lady. You need me to call you a taxi or something?" the bartender asked. He retrieved her glass and poured the ice cubes down the sink.

Lola raised her head slowly and looked at him. "Who you gonna call, Ghost Busters?" She laughed at her own pitiful joke. The laughter soon turned to tears.

"Yo, sista you a'ight?" Lola wiped her face and waved him off. She attempted to stand up from the barstool.

"I got this," she said and sat back down before she tried again. "Okay, girl, get it together." Lola gave herself a little pep talk.

"Look, lady. Let me call somebody for you. This ain't no place to be alone in your condition." Lola laughed to herself. He had no idea some of the holes she'd awakened in, not remembering how she'd gotten there.

"I'm not alone, Mr. I am *never* alone." She slurred her words. "You want to know why?" Lola tapped her temple, "I've got my memories, you know? And no matter where I go or what I do, they're always right here." Again, tapping her temple. She then laid her head back on top of the bar and finally passed out.

"Man, what a waste," the bartender said, shaking his head. He pulled out his cell phone and placed a call.

༻ ༻ ༻ ༻

The glacial wind hit Lola's face with such force she felt as though she'd been slapped. Someone was

moving her and she was helpless to fight off
whoever it was because, in her usual fashion, she'd
gotten wasted. Lola made an attempt to fight off
whoever was trying to take advantage of her. She
tried to yell, to muster some kind of fighting spirit,
but her efforts only trickled out as a small, meager
moan. She didn't know what was happening. Her
last thought before she passed out completely was,
*Who would ever want me for a mother?*

# *EIGHT*

## *KEENAN'S SECRET REVEALED*

---

It had been almost one week since the funeral and today Raina was determined to find the strength to get out of bed. Naomi and her mother had been such a big help caring for the boys. She lay on her back and stared at the ceiling, wondering how she would continue to live without Keenan. With each breath she took, her entire body felt weighted down, as if the weight of the world were sitting on her chest. She was sure that the world had simply stopped spinning; that everyone, everywhere, felt the void that was now in the universe. Sadly, with each passing day, Raina realized that it had not. Keenan's senseless death didn't stop the merry-go-round of life. It still went round and round, without the slightest indication of slowing down. Raina turned onto her side and stared out of the French doors which led to the balcony. This had been their favorite room in the house—their sanctuary. The view of the lake from the balcony was always so beautiful and serene. Now, with the grayness of the day, even the trees outside her window appeared to grieve. Bare and skeletal, the branches reached toward the sky as though begging for some great reprieve. Raina hugged a pillow into her body as she contorted into the fetal position.

"My God, my God, where are you my Jehovah?" Her prayer was barely a whisper.

"I need your strength, Father. I need your peace. This pain is too much." Tears slid across the bridge of her nose and down her heart shaped face.

"Help me this day. Help me, even this hour." Raina prayed and waited for the peace that she knew only God could bring. She heard the creak of her bedroom door. She didn't turn to see her mother entering with a tray of food.

"Raina? Baby? Are you awake?" Victoria asked, as she padded across the thick carpet in her stocking feet.

"Yes," Raina responded, using the sheets to dry her tears. She turned over and gradually pulled herself up into a sitting position. She was tired of crying but the mere thought of living without her best friend always sent her spiraling.

"Hey, sweetheart." Victoria set the tray on the bedside table. "Now, I know you haven't had much of an appetite but you've got to eat sometime." Victoria spoke as she proceeded to fluff Raina's pillows. Not because it needed to be done but because she needed to keep busy.

"Mom, you don't need to do this."

"Child, don't tell me what I don't need to do. I'm your mother and no matter how old you get, I'm still going to mother you." Raina smiled a knowing smile.

"It smells delicious." Raina inhaled the aroma of a vegetable omelet, and a slice of whole grain toast. A small bowl of fruit and a glass of orange juice completed the meal. "Wow, did you cook this yourself?"

"Well, now, I don't cook much these days since it's just me at the house, but I can still do a little somethin', somethin' in the kitchen." Even Raina's sad smile was a delight to Victoria.

It pained her to see either of her girls in distress. She wished she could change things. If only she could bring Keenan back to Raina and undo all the mistakes she'd made with Lola, things would be better. It seemed that no matter how she tried to help Lola, it always blew up in her face. But she didn't have time to rehash all that had gone wrong between her and her eldest daughter now. Victoria decided to put her energy into making sure Raina got through this difficult time. She couldn't bring Keenan back, but as long as she was alive, she'd try her best to make sure his family was taken care of.

"Here we go." Victoria unfolded the napkin and lay it across Raina's stomach.

"Well, it sure looks good, Mom." Raina's stomach growled. She couldn't remember the last time she'd actually eaten a full meal.

"How are the boys?"

"The boys are as well as can be expected."

Victoria sat down in the chair next to the bed. "They miss you both."

"I know," Raina sipped her juice. "That's why today when they get off of the bus I'm going to be there to greet them."

"That's wonderful, Raina, but are you sure you're ready?"

"Ready to live without Keenan? No. But what choice do I have? I am ready to get out of this bed." Victoria got up and moved closer to her daughter. She held both of Raina's hands.

"I know what you're going through, baby. It's hard to lose your husband, but time heals and the pain dulls a little each day. You're stronger than even you know, Raina. And you have all of us here praying for you." Raina could feel her emotions swelling inside of her. She didn't want to cry anymore. She blinked back the tears.

"I know, Mama. I know." She closed her eyes and lay her head back against the headboard.

"Hey, have you talked to Lola?" Victoria let go of Raina's hands and walked around the bed, fussing with the duvet and pillows. Raina knew, all too well, that the subject of Lola was not high on her mother's favorite list for conversation.

"No, I haven't. She's staying with Lloyd and Jessica and we really haven't gotten around to visiting."

"Oh. I really want to talk to her. She looks good, huh?"

"I think she looks too skinny. And she needs to stop that smoking."

"Mom, when are you going to learn to accept

106

that Lola has her own way of doing things?"

"Oh, I know that all too well. I tell you, no matter how I tried to steer that child in the right direction, she has never listened to anything I've said. If I say go left to avoid a cliff, she'll purposefully go right and jump *off* of the cliff just to spite me."

"Mom." Victoria turned around and held up both hands.

"I know what you're going to say. It's just that when she was younger, she had such promise." She walked toward the French doors. "I don't know where I went wrong," Victoria said, almost to herself. She looked out of the window and wondered if she and Lola would ever make amends.

"She's not a child anymore, Mom. You've got to learn to accept her just the way she is. I think she feels judged and that's not good for anyone." Raina took a small bite of the omelet.

"I'm not judging her, Raina." Victoria turned her attention back to her newly widowed daughter. "I love her and I only want the best for her. But anytime I mention something about going back to medical school or if I try to introduce her to an eligible young man, she bolts." Raina finished half of the breakfast and placed the tray on the other side of the king-sized bed. She threw back the covers and slid out. Raina walked over and wrapped her arms around her mother. They held each other for a few minutes.

"You've got to let her live her life her way, Mom. Maybe one day, she'll understand what it means to be a mother. God has a way of teaching us by allowing us to get tired of our own mess. When she gets tired, she'll make the changes she needs to make." Victoria shrugged her shoulders and inhaled.

"I certainly hope so."

"It'll happen for Lola, Mama. It will." Victoria patted Raina's back.

"How did you get to be so wise?"

"Oh, I had a pretty good teacher." There was a light knock on the bedroom door. They were both startled. Victoria and Raina looked at each other, puzzled.

"Who in the world could that be?" Victoria asked, as she quickly made her way toward the door. "I know one of your nosy church members has not taken leave of her senses and let herself into your house!" Victoria cracked the door and was relieved to look up and see Lloyd.

"Hey, Aunt Tori. I hope I didn't scare you. When there was no answer at the front door, I just let myself in. Is everything all right?"

"Yes, honey," Victoria said, holding her hand to her chest. "But you shouldn't scare an old woman like that. I thought I was going to have a heart attack."

"I'm sorry. I just came to check on you all and talk to Rae, if I could." Victoria looked back at Raina who nodded.

"She'll be out in a few minutes. Go on in the den and make yourself comfortable." Victoria crossed the room and retrieved the tray. "Are you sure you're up for it?" Raina inhaled deeply. She wanted to scream a big, fat, "NO!" She wanted to crawl back under the covers and not think about living without her husband, but Raina knew she had to go on living.

"Yes. I'll be out in a few minutes."

※ ※ ※ ※

Moments later, Raina walked into the sunken family room, feeling a bit stronger than she'd felt earlier.

"Hey, Lloyd."

"Hey, beautiful." Lloyd bent down and gave his cousin a peck on the cheek.

"How are you doing?" he asked, his voice laced with concern.

"I'm doing, I guess." Raina sat on the sofa.

"Yeah. Well, I really hate to bother you but there's something very important that we need to discuss. As a matter of fact, I need to talk to both of you."

"Okay, Lloyd. What's going on? You're making me nervous," Raina said with a perplexed expression.

"Lloyd, if this is about Keenan's pension or insurance, we can take care of all of that later," Victoria said in a huff. She didn't like the idea of upsetting Raina unnecessarily.

"This is not about Keenan's pension." Lloyd cleared his throat.

"Is it Lola? Has something happened to my sister?!" Lloyd saw the panic in Raina's eyes.

"No. Lola's fine."

"Well what in the world is it, Lloyd?" Victoria was becoming impatient. Although it was thirty degrees outside, beads of sweat that formed on

Lloyd's forehead made him look as though he were sitting in a sauna. "Okay. Last week during the repast, a young girl showed up here to the house.

"Okay?" Raina waited patiently. She remembered many of the kids Keenan had mentored had come to pay their respects.

"Lord, don't tell me someone has claimed to be Keenan's other wife or something ridiculous. You know people run all kinds of scams nowadays. They think they're going to get some big payoff. I can't believe that someone would have the nerve to show up on the day of—"

"That's not it, Aunt Tori," Lloyd tried to reel her back in. "Well, not exactly."

"Well, what *exactly* is it?" Victoria asked, curtly.

"I'm getting to that. The young lady's name is Nyla and she's..." Lloyd pulled his handkerchief from his back pocket and wiped his brow.

"Go on," Raina said.

"Nyla showed up looking for her father." Raina's expression did not change. She was a little confused.

"Lloyd, why would she be looking for her father he—" Before she completed her question, the light bulb came on.

"What are you telling me, Lloyd?" Lloyd wished a million times that Keenan had told her. It pained him to be the bearer of this news.

"Raina, she was looking for Keenan. Nyla is Keenan's daughter."

"Oh my, God!" Victoria clapped her hand over her mouth. Raina was shocked into silence.

"But... but… how can you be sure? I mean, did

she have papers or something?" Victoria asked incredulously, moving closer to Raina. "Are you telling us that Keenan had an affair and has an illegitimate daughter?"

Raina's entire body began to shake. Lloyd was really not equipped to handle this sort of thing. He wished he'd brought Jessica along.

"No, no, no. This was before... I mean, I think she's around seventeen years old," Lloyd sputtered out.

"I see. So, this is something that happened before they were married," Victoria clarified. Raina's breathing slowed, relieved that her memories of the man she married would not be tarnished by infidelity. She didn't think she was strong enough to handle that. "Keenan has another child?" Raina whispered to herself.

"Where's the child's mother?" Victoria asked, crossing her arms.

"I don't know."

"What do you mean you don't know? You must know that the girl's mother probably put her up to this!" Victoria placed a protective hand on her daughter's shoulder.

"I don't think that's the case, Aunt Tori. She's been in foster care most of her life and because her adoption was closed, I doubt if even she knows who her biological mother is." Raina took a deep breath to steady herself. Lloyd pulled an envelope from the breast pocket of his blazer. "This is a copy of the DNA test Kennan received before you all left on your trip. I thought you should have it." Raina hesitated for a moment before taking the envelope from Lloyd.

"What does she want?" Raina finally asked.

"Nothing." Lloyd shook his head as he stood towering over her. "When she came here, she had no idea that Keenan had passed away. She found out that Keenan was looking for her so she came to find him."

"I just can't believe that Keenan didn't tell me about any of this. He was searching for her and didn't tell me?" Raina stared down at her hands.

"He just wanted to be sure, Raina." Lloyd wished he could soften the blow. His face was full of compassion. "He didn't want to put you through any unnecessary stress if he didn't have to. You know how he was when it came to you and the boys." Lloyd wiped his forehead again as Raina stood and began to pace the floor.

"Well, it's rather unfortunate, but I guess she'll have to go back where she came from," said Victoria resignedly.

"Mom!" Raina looked at her mother, shocked. "I'm surprised at you! Didn't you hear Lloyd say that she grew up in foster care? I can't imagine that life. *Her* loss is probably much greater than ours. At least we had him and we have our memories of him. She doesn't." Raina began to tear up. She'd always had a compassionate heart. Lloyd exhaled; relief flooded his body and he knew he'd done the right thing by telling her. He had promised Keenan.

"Okay, calm down. Well, Lloyd, where is she?" Victoria asked.

"She's at Hopkins Hospital."

"Hospital?!" Raina exclaimed. "Why?! What's

wrong with her?"

It was not his intention to cause Raina any unnecessary grief. He quickly explained what happened after Nyla found out about Keenan's accident. Raina's heart was heavy.

"She must be devastated," Raina said to no one in particular.

"Oh, no. No, no, Raina. I know that look. You can't possibly be thinking of bringing that girl into this house. Not with all that you're already dealing with," Victoria spoke up. She knew her daughter too well. While Lola was the first one to run away from problems, Raina was the child who was always bringing home a stray puppy, friend, or anything else she felt needed saving. She was always trying to fix someone else's problems. Raina turned to her mother.

"Mom, if she is Keenan's daughter, I have no choice."

"Of course you do!" Victoria looked bewildered. "I'm not saying not to help the girl. I'm just saying you don't have to have her staying under your roof to do so."

"Mom, she's a teenager with no place to go. If she wants to stay, I'm not going to turn her away."

"What about Quincy and Matthew? What will you tell them?"

"The truth. Besides, I was thinking about asking Lola if she would stay here with me and the boys. You know, to help me out a little. She's still at your place, right Lloyd?"

"Um, yes." He didn't want to tell them that she was MIA since her last text saying she had hooked up with an old friend. Knowing Lola, she would show up eventually.

"Well, if Lola agrees to stay for a while longer, I see no reason why the both of us can't try to help her." Even as she was saying it, the thought of looking into the face of Keenan's daughter, made her anxious. A child, who didn't belong to both of them. Raina knew deep down that she had no choice. She knew the kind of man Kennan was and she knew if he had been looking for Nyla, he intended to do everything in his power to make up for the last seventeen years. Raina decided to honor her husband's memory by making sure *all* of his children were properly cared for.

"Then it's settled," Lloyd said, with a sigh of relief.

"Yes, it is settled," Raina repeated to reassure herself more than anyone else. She gave Lloyd a half smile and avoided eye contact with her mother. *Lord, I hope I'm doing the right thing. Please let this be the right thing.*

# NINE

## RAINA MEETS NYLA

---

**N**aomi stared at the young girl as she lay in the hospital bed. She reflected on all that Lloyd had told her. For the life of her, Naomi couldn't believe that Keenan had a child that he knew nothing about. *Who was the mother? Where has she been all of this time? Why now?* At first Naomi thought that it was all a colossal mistake. However, Lloyd had confirmed that it was indeed true. The paternity test had come back positive. Keenan Blackman was the father of a girl that he would never get the opportunity to know. A million questions still buzzed around Naomi's head.

She watched Nyla sleep and could see Keenan's features in her delicate face: the color of her skin, the small freckles on the bridge of her nose and those eyes. She remembered those eyes from their brief meeting during the repast. They were definitely Keenan's eyes. Nyla shifted a little and turned her head away from Naomi. That's when Naomi noticed the bluish, half moon birthmark just behind her left ear. She'd seen that mark before, but she couldn't remember where.

Nyla's eyelids fluttered. They felt weighted down as she attempted to open them. At first the sunlight, filtering in through the hospital blinds, assaulted her eyes. Slowly, Nyla raised her forearm in an attempt to block out the light. A small groan escaped her, and alerted Naomi, who had closed her eyes to pray. Naomi's eyes flew open at the sound of Nyla's discomfort and she moved in closer. Naomi wanted to make sure that when Nyla awoke, she would see that she wasn't alone.

"Good morning," Naomi greeted her and stood to pour Nyla a glass of water. She thought her mouth must've felt like the Sahara desert.

"I'm not dead?" Nyla asked, still with her forearm over her face.

"Not quite, but you almost succeeded. You gave us quite a scare. You know, you could've frozen to death out there," Naomi chided gently, as she handed Nyla the water. "Here, drink this."

Nyla was clearly agitated. She squinted and looked up at Naomi. When Nyla tried to reposition herself into a more upright position, her skin felt all prickly. It felt as though a million pins had penetrated her body. She took the water and gulped the entire glass. Nyla handed the glass back, as she eyed Naomi suspiciously. *She can't be a nurse, dressed like that!*

"Who are you?" Nyla asked. She didn't take her eyes off of the tall, elegant lady.

"You don't remember meeting me?"

"No. Should I?" Her tone was sharp.

"I guess not, but we met at my son's house last week."

"Your son?" Nyla's voice was laced with skepticism. "Look lady, I don't know your son. I'm not even from around here and—"

"No, no." Naomi interrupted. "You came to his house. You were looking for him."

Nyla took a closer look at the lady. Suddenly, there she was, standing face to face with this woman in Keenan's office. The vision came through like a raging flood. Her head fell back against the pillow.

"Oh yeah, I remember." Her head shot back up. "Wait. Did you say a week?" Naomi nodded.

"I've been here for a week?!" Naomi nodded again.

"Almost."

Nyla's head began to pound like someone was trying to pry it open from the inside. She closed her eyes and massaged her temples. "I gotta get out of here." With effort, she threw the covers back and attempted to climb out of bed. Naomi stopped her.

"And go where?" Naomi stood directly in front of Nyla. Naomi's voice was laced with panic and apprehension. She didn't believe Nyla had anywhere else to go. She'd seen so many programs and had heard so many horror stories about what happens to runaways. Just looking at the faded bruise on Nyla's cheek sent chills down her spine.

"Why does it matter to you?" Even though Nyla put on a tough front, Naomi knew she had to be frightened out of her mind. She sat lightly on the edge of Nyla's bed and turned to face her newfound granddaughter. Just rolling that word around in her brain made filled Naomi's heart with joy.

"Nyla, my name is Naomi Blackman. If you are indeed Keenan's daughter, which I believe you are, then that would make you my granddaughter."

"But....but you're...."

"White? Yes, yes I was shocked when I realized it myself but I've dealt with it the best I can." Naomi's attempt to lighten the mood seemed to work, given the brief smile on Nyla's face. "Over the years I've tried to come to terms with this old pasty skin. I hope you won't hold it against me."

"Wow," Nyla said. Laying her head back onto the pillow. "You got jokes."

"Are you hungry?" Naomi asked with a smile as she stood up from the bed. Nyla shook her head in response. "You should eat something, Nyla. You're going to need your strength."

"What do I need to be strong for? I came all this way to find my dad and look where it's gotten me; here in a hospital bed that I can't pay for." Nyla stared down at her feet.

"I know it was a horrible blow finding out about Keenan the way you did, but you can't give up. Even though he's gone, you do have a family that would like to get to know you."

"Does his wife know about me?"

"Well, yes, I believe Lloyd has told her."

"If she wants to get to know me then why she

ain't here?" The room went silent. Naomi had no idea how to respond.

Nyla stared out of the window. *What am I going to do now?* Moments later the doctor entered her room.

"Well now, I see the princess has finally awakened," Dr. Irby announced as she entered the room. Her skin was a deep cocoa brown and her hair was a crown of silver locks that framed her perfectly round face. Her big smile brightened the room as soon as she entered.

"Good afternoon, Dr. Irby," Naomi welcomed the interruption.

"Good afternoon to you both. And how are we feeling?" The doctor, asked as she looked over Nyla's chart.

"I don't know how *we're* feeling but *my* skin hurts. I feel like it's on fire." Dr. Irby closed the chart quickly, pulled out a small flashlight and proceeded to inspect Nyla's pupils.

"Yes well, that's normal. We had to initiate a re-warming process to reestablish blood flow so you'll probably experience that aching, throbbing sensation for a few more days." Dr. Irby clicked off the flashlight. "You're a very lucky young lady. Your frostbite was superficial and therefore didn't cause any major tissue damage. However, the throbbing sensation could last for weeks, maybe longer. It's going to take some time, but we can expect a complete recovery," she said as she placed the chart inside the holder at the foot of Nyla's bed.

Dr. Irby turned to Naomi. "We'll keep her for observation for a while longer and if everything checks out, you'll be able to take her home soon. Nyla, you're lucky you weren't out there any longer than you were. Many patients who suffer frostbite wind up losing a limb.

*Wonder why I don't feel so lucky right now? Nyla thought, as she stared at the tips of her wrapped fingers.*

"I've prescribed some Ibuprofen to help with any discomfort and I'll be back later this evening. If everything looks good, you'll be free to go." She directed the next statement to Naomi. "She'll probably need a little rehabilitation to help strengthen her muscles and get back up to full speed. Do you have any questions for me?" the doctor asked, looking back and forth between the two of them. Nyla shook her head, and focused her attention on a small piece of thread that lay on top of the hospital blanket.

"When does the rehab start?" Naomi asked.

"Well, if everything goes as planned and she's released tonight, I recommend she starts as soon as possible. The sooner she starts, the faster the recovery. Do you play any sports?"

"No. Not anymore."

"What did you play?"

"I ran track." Naomi's heart leapt in her chest. Keenan had attended college on a track scholarship.

"I could tell you were athletic when I examined you. Hopefully, you can be back out on the track in no time."

"Thank you," Naomi said, as Dr. Irby left the room.

"So, you're a track star huh?"

"Nobody said anything about being no star. I ran track on and off, no big deal."

"Hey, how are you ladies doing?" Lloyd asked, easing the tension slightly as he entered the room. "Glad to see that beautiful face." The room filled with the sound of his robust voice.

"We're fine, Lloyd. You just missed the doctor. She said that Nyla may be ready to go home tonight," Naomi said, nervously.

"Well that's good because that's just what I came by to talk to her about." Nyla looked at Lloyd with suspicion. After he lied to her about her dad, she didn't trust him.

"Talk to me about what?" she asked, sharply. Lloyd pulled a chair closer to her bed and sat down.

"Well, seeing that your father is deceased and you're still a ward of the State of Florida—"

"I'm not going back there!" Nyla interjected, as she pulled herself up straighter. "Even if you send me back, I'll run away! I'm almost eighteen. That's the legal age to be on my own. You can't make me go back!" She was on the verge of hysteria. Her eyes welled up with tears as she shook her head in defiance.

"Whoa! Calm down and hold on before you bite my head off, will you? I was just trying to explain that if you didn't have a guardian, the State would require that you be sent back. However, you do have someone who has agreed to be your legal guardian." Both Nyla and Naomi looked at him, surprised.

"Really?" He had Nyla's full attention. She was unable to imagine who would do such a thing for her.

"Who?" Naomi asked, not being able to imagine who other than herself would do such a thing.

"Me." All heads turned toward Raina, who stood in the doorway. She entered the room and slowly walked toward Nyla.

"Hello, Nyla. I'm Raina Blackman." She extended her hand. The room stood still for what seemed like an eternity. Nyla finally shook Raina's hand with the one hand that wasn't bandaged all the way.

"Hi," she responded, unable to look Raina in the eye. Raina looked at Naomi, who tried, unsuccessfully, to keep the tears at bay.

"Ms. Naomi, how would you like a cup of hot tea?" Lloyd asked.

"Some tea would be lovely, dear."

"Then what are we waiting for?" I'm sure you ladies have a lot to discuss. We'll be back shortly." Lloyd extended his arm to Naomi and they walked out, leaving Raina and Nyla alone.

The silence was awkward. Raina stood tensely; she began to realize the effect being back in the hospital had on her. She was still not quite herself. She was still struggling to gauge her own emotions; nevertheless, she knew this was right.

"So… Nyla, where are you from?" Raina desperately wanted to know her story. She wanted to know about this part of her husband's life that she was not a part of.

"St. James County. It's a small town in Florida. Nyla was reluctant to give too much information about herself. It was just too soon.

"Why did you agree to do this?" Nyla continued to stare down at her fingers.

"Do what?"

"You know what. Agree to be my guardian. You don't even know me. You being my guardian means I'll have to live with you." Nyla still didn't look directly at Raina so Raina took the opportunity to dissect her features. She could clearly see Keenan.

"Would you object to living with us?"

"Us?"

"Yes. My two sons, Quincy and Matthew and me. Oh, and my sister, Lola. Although she'll only be there temporarily."

"Sounds like you already have a house full. You sure you have room for one more?" Nyla had a quaking in the pit of her stomach. She wasn't sure if she wanted this or not. Nevertheless, she didn't want to ruin her chances at something better. "I mean, I'm seventeen but I'll be eighteen soon. I'll only be there for a little while."

Raina nodded her head as she listened. She could hear the uncertainty in her voice.

"Okay then. If you'd like, when you turn eighteen you'll be free to go."

Raina saw Nyla twist uncomfortably. "But the choice will be yours," she added, to make sure that Nyla understood that she was welcome as long as she wanted to stay. Raina cautiously moved closer to the bed.

"Nyla, I'm sorry you didn't have a chance to meet your father." Raina's throat tightened. "I know he would've loved to have known you." Nyla nodded, and angrily swatted away the tear that ran down her cheek. She was overwhelmed.

"And what do you get out of it?"

Raina sensed Nyla's mistrust and understood that she probably had good reason. She couldn't imagine the life Nyla she had endured in her 17 years. Raina hoped she could make Nyla see that she was genuine in her offer to help. Keenan wouldn't have had it any other way.

"Well, for one thing, my sons, *your* brothers, will get to know their sister." Nyla's heart leapt in her chest at the thought of having brothers. For many years she had not been connected or felt connected to anyone, except for maybe Gabby, but that was different. She'd never had a brother or sister, not even a cousin. Now she had two brothers.

"And it'll give you a chance to learn about the kind of man your father was." Nyla nodded. All of those things sounded good, but she wasn't convinced that this wasn't some kind of pity party.

"You still didn't answer my question. You mentioned your sons but what do *you* get out of it?" Raina knew that she'd been vague; perhaps because she was still grappling with the idea of having Keenan's daughter under her roof. She was a reminder that there were parts of his life that she was not a part of and that made her miss him even more. She moved to the end of the bed.

"Well, some may say my reasons are selfish."

"Selfish? I don't get it." Nyla finally looked up at Raina.

"You see, having you with us will hopefully keep us from focusing so much on what we've lost, but instead on what we've gained." They were both silent for a few minutes. Nyla was the first to break the silence.

"Okay." Nyla's voice was barely a whisper.

"Okay?" Raina repeated, with a slight smile. Nyla gave a slow but definite nod.

"Yep."

"Then it's settled." They both breathed a sigh of relief. As if on cue, Lloyd and Naomi entered the room. Nyla searched the faces of these strangers who were her family. She couldn't quite put her feelings into words but if she were pressed, she would describe them as undecided. For so long, she'd dreamed of her perfect family. However, a stepmom, brothers, an uncle and a grandmother was not how she'd imagined it would be.

# TEN

## FALLING OFF THE WAGON

---

**G**raham Billingsley walked down the hotel corridor with a purposeful stride. She wore her charcoal-gray power suit that fit her size six frame like a glove. A duffel bag hung over her left shoulder while she balanced a cup holder with two cups of coffee in one hand and the room key in the other. As Graham entered the room she dropped the duffel bag onto one of the double beds, placed the coffee on the nearby desk and marched over to the window where she snatched the curtains open.

"Rise and shine, sleeping beauty!" Graham sang out over Lola's limp body as she moved to pull back the covers. Even though it was cloudy outside, the pale sunlight was an unwelcome intrusion. With as little effort as possible, Lola attempted to shield her eyes from the light.

"Come on, Lola, get up. I don't have all day," Graham repeated, standing over her.

Graham was five-two, one hundred and twenty-five pounds of attitude. Her tongue was sharper than any switchblade and she used it to her advantage. She'd seen many drunks but she was both saddened and disappointed when she was called to pick up Lola Devereux, who had passed out in her cousin's bar. She'd known Lola since high school, but the person she saw passed out at the bar was a far cry from the scholar she'd known before. However, Graham was not one to judge. Lord knows she'd had her own troubled past.

"Come on, Ms. Thang. Get up!" Lola grimaced and reached blindly for the covers unsuccessfully. She then reached over, grabbed a pillow and buried her head underneath.

"Lola, get up!" Graham commanded.

"Could you please stop yelling?" Lola's muffled voice begged from beneath the pillow.

"Okay, I'll stop but you asked for it." Graham had come prepared. She crossed the room, retrieved a pot and a wooden spoon from her duffel bag. She stood over Lola and banged the pot, non-stop. Lola tightened her grip on the pillow and rocked back and forth. She tried blocking out the sound but Graham continued. Finally, Lola sat up abruptly. The sudden movement intensified the pounding and weight of her head. The room started to spin.

"Oh god." Lola attempted to steady herself by holding her head. She spoke to Graham in a steely, raspy whisper and gave her a death stare.

"If you don't stop banging on that pot, I'm gonna

take that spoon and shove it—"

"Where?!" Graham's short natural haircut made her facial features more pronounced. Her large brown eyes were stretched wide as she straightened her back and waited for Lola's reply. Lola was not in any condition to challenge the crazy lady who had the stance of a cheetah that was about to pounce.

"Just please, stop." Lola held up a hand. She closed her eyes and massaged her throbbing temples. Graham threw the items on the adjacent bed and walked over to retrieve the coffee.

"Here." Graham handed Lola the now lukewarm cup of black coffee. Lola cautiously accepted. Her mouth felt like cotton and had a foul taste. The bitterness of the black liquid was a welcome treat.

"May I ask you a question?" Lola finally asked.

"Sure." Graham leaned back against the desk and sipped her coffee.

"Who are you? Where are we? And why are we here?"

"First, that was more than one question. Second, I can understand why you may not remember me, but you and I have history." Graham took a seat on the opposite bed.

"What?" Lola asked, absentmindedly. The throbbing of her temples was almost audible.

"You and I were quite close once upon a time. But you have no clue who I am, do you?" Lola peered at Graham through squinted eyes. She had no clue who this lunatic was nor did she care.

"No. I can't say that I do." Graham took a deep breath, got up and walked over toward the dresser.

"I can't really blame you. It's been a long time and I look very different than I did in high school. Wow, and you? Never in a million years did I think I would see you, of all people, in this state." Lola stopped drinking her coffee. She peered at the stranger who seemed to be inspecting her.

"Don't you dare judge me. You don't know me. You know nothing about my life," Lola snarled.

"Lola. It's me! Graham Billingsley. Remember, the chubby girl from your tenth grade Algebra class?"

"Huh?"

Graham drew closer and sat at the opposite end of Lola's bed.

"You were the one who helped me face that school bully. She'd terrified me since the beginning of school. Not only did you help me face her, you helped me come out of my shell. Girl, you even gave me my very first makeover." Lola stared back with a blank expression. Graham could see that Lola still didn't remember.

"I've never forgotten how you helped me. You made me believe in myself and not be afraid. You have no idea how much your encouragement changed my life." Graham was beaming. Her eyes were bright with gratitude but Lola was still a puddle of confusion.

"Well, um... I'm glad I could help." Lola placed the half empty cup on the nightstand. "But could you please tell me where my clothes are because I have somewhere I have to be." Graham continued as though Lola hadn't said anything at all.

"You know, what you did helped me to realize

my true calling. It made such an impact, now I do that for a living. I help people like you realize their potential and get their lives back on track." There was an awkward silence before Lola cleared her throat.

"Well, I'm uh, I'm really happy for you, Graham. But to tell you the truth, I really don't remember the bully incident or you for that matter. And as far as helping me "realize my potential"— Lola made air quotes with her fingers—"I don't need any help. I already know my capabilities." Lola's tone dripped with sarcasm. Graham raised her eyebrows.

"Well honey, falling down drunk in a bar sounds like someone screaming out for help to me," Graham fired back, with a bit of her own sarcasm. Lola nodded her throbbing head.

"Okay, little miss sunshine," Graham started, "I've had about enough of memory lane and your snide comments. Your clothes are in the closet. You're free to go, but I'm sure we'll see each other again real soon."

"Don't hold your breath," Lola responded, careful not to make any sudden moves as she stood up from the bed.

"Oh, don't worry, sweetheart. Most of the bartenders in town have me on speed dial. I'll give you 48… no, make that 24 hours, before I'm called to pick you up again. Lola turned toward Graham and despite her weak knees and pounding head, charged toward her.

"How dare you stand there and judge me! You don't *know* me or what I'm dealing with. So take your psychoanalyst bull and work it on someone else!" Graham's petite frame rose up like a viper. Her nostrils flared as she steadied her gaze to address the disheveled Lola Devereux.

"Do you honestly think you're the only person dealing with pain? The truth is you haven't dealt with anything. Every time trouble comes your way you try to leave it at the bottom of a bottle, or whatever crutch you use to escape reality. And at the end of the day, the very thing that you're trying so hard to forget is still here, sweetheart. You call that dealing? Well, it ain't!"

Lola looked at the pint-sized woman and decided she was in no shape to continue this altercation. "Why are you doing this?" Lola asked, in a state of confusion. "What's in this for you?"

"I know you've forgotten me, Lola, but I do remember you. I know your family and your stepdad preached at my childhood church Lily Baptist, before he died. You know, I was even at your twelfth birthday party when your biological father showed up and made a scene."

"You were at that party?" Lola was taken aback. She'd forgotten about that party. About how embarrassed she'd been when Henry Jackson had shown up out of the blue. She had no idea who he was when she first saw him. He'd made a complete spectacle of himself and had ruined her party.

"Yes I was there, and I understand that you've got baggage, but so do I and the rest of the millions of people in the world. We've all experienced disappointments, lost dreams, loved ones who've passed away. But whatever it is that's haunting you,

you can*not* drink it away." For a moment Lola was at a loss for words. She turned and sat back down on the bed.

"If only it was that easy," she said, rubbing her temples again.

"Look, I don't know how long you've been drinking, but in the words of Dr. Phil, 'how's it working for you?'" Lola was unresponsive. She sat and stared at a spot in the middle of the floor.

The look of embarrassment on her face pained Graham. She heard Dr. Eli's voice in her head, "Go easy, you can get more with sugar than you can with salt." But Graham's way was different from his. She was definitely a bit more salty. However, the last thing she wanted to do was to hurt Lola. She'd come to help, so she tried again.

"Listen, I'm sorry I lashed out at you." Graham sat next to Lola. "I told you I knew you from school. I've always looked up to you and your family. But I know from my own experience that appearances are not easy to live up to." Tears brimmed Lola's eyes.

"Look, my cousin, Benny owns the bar you were in." Graham pulled tissues out of the box on the nightstand and handed them to Lola. "My entire family used to attend your Dad's church. Benny knew who you were the moment you sat down at the bar." Graham touched Lola's arm. "I work for a non-profit organization that helps treat teens with addictions. When Benny saw that you were in no condition to drive, he called me."

Lola wiped away the tears. "Well I'm no teen; so now what?"

"Well, now it's all up to you. We can only help you if you want to be helped."

"I do want it. It's just that..." The knot in her throat made it difficult for her to speak. "Before this happened, I'd been sober for three months and now..."

"And now, you start again."

"But how?" she asked, staring at a worn spot in the carpet. "If I run for a drink at the first sign of trouble, I may not be capable—"

"That's nonsense," Graham interrupted and tightened her grip on Lola's arm. "You just have to realize that you've got to face your problems, because no matter how drunk you get, when you sober up, they'll still be there." Lola shook her head and blew her nose.

"Okay?" Graham's heart was filled with compassion.

"Okay," Lola whispered. She was tired of waging this war alone. She'd tried to convince herself and Mr. Goodman that she could do it on her own terms. Clearly, this thing was bigger than she was.

"You know I came here for Keenan's funeral, but that's not the only reason," Lola said, not quite able to look Graham in the face. "I've been suspended from my job and I was evicted from my apartment." She released a thin, sarcastic chuckle. "So, while everyone thinks that I'm jet setting around the country, living the dream, what they don't know is that I'm on the verge of losing everything."

"What happened?" Graham's brows furrowed.

"Well, in my usual fashion I'd been out drinking all night and was scheduled for a trip the next morning. I couldn't call in sick again for obvious reasons, so I convinced myself that everything would be okay."

"And?"

"And that was mistake number one. One of my co-workers saw that I was in no condition to work so she reported me. After which I was pulled off of the trip and sent home. I was given a choice to resign or go to rehab. I went to rehab but..." Lola covered her face with her hands. "How did I let my life get so messed up?" Graham, who had been stroking her back, sprang up from the bed.

"Girl, we've got to get you in to see Dr. Eli, ASAP!" Graham marched into the bathroom and turned on the shower. Lola didn't budge.

"Dr. Eli? That wouldn't be Jeremiah Eli, would it?" she asked Graham.

"As a matter of fact, it is. You know him?" She looked surprised. Lola told her about her counselor in L.A. and how he'd strongly recommended she schedule a meeting with this Jeremiah Eli.

"Wow. That's more than a coincidence," Graham replied.

"Yeah, I have to agree with you on that." Suddenly Lola remembered Lloyd. "Oh my gosh! I haven't called Lloyd. He must have a SWAT team searching for me by now." Lola frantically searched for her phone.

"Don't worry. I replied to one of his texts from your phone. He was asking when you would be home. I told him you ran into an old friend and that

134

you were going to hang out for the next day or so. I didn't know how long it would take for you to sleep it off." Lola was stunned.

"Well, I guess you thought of everything. But I've got another question for you."

"Shoot."

"You gotta job up in that bag?" Lola tilted her head toward what seemed to be Graham's bag of tricks. Graham thought for a minute.

"No. Your job is to work on getting well."

"My job is to be able to feed myself without mooching off of my sister."

"Okay. What do you know how to do?"

"I don't know. I've been a flight attendant for the past fifteen years. I don't know if I can do anything else."

"Don't sell yourself short. I'll contact some of my people and see if we can find you something, but first things first. We've got to get you in to see Dr. Eli. You up for it?" Graham held out her almond colored hand.

Lola was slow to take it, not completely sure if this was something she really wanted to do.

"All right then. Let's get you cleaned up." Graham pulled out a fluffy, pink towel set out of her duffel bag and handed it Lola. The one raised eyebrow on Lola's face spoke volumes.

"What? I just got a thing about hotel towels so I brought you some from home."

"Oh, thanks," Lola said, taking the towels from Graham as she moved toward the bathroom. "But um... are you sure that I'm the only one that needs to see the doctor?" Graham did a double take and saw the smirk on Lola's face before she closed the door.

"Humph, okay. The next time I'll just let your behind catch cooties!"

# ELEVEN

## NYLA MOVES IN

---

The following week was a whirlwind. Lola had finally gotten herself cleaned up and Graham, true to her word, had gotten her an appointment with Dr. Eli. She also used her contacts and had gotten Lola an interview with the county's Department of Education to become a substitute teacher. All Lola could think about was those poor kids.

When Lola finally checked in with Lloyd, she was shocked to find out that not only had Raina visited Nyla at the hospital, but she had invited Nyla to live with her. So when Raina asked Lola to stay at the house to help everyone adjust to the new living arrangement, Lola's loss for words was taken as a yes.

Lola packed up the few things she'd had at Lloyd's and moved into Raina's basement. She'd vacillated over whether or not it was the right thing to do, wondered if she was, in fact, strong enough to handle being under the same roof, given the circumstances. But she'd come to Atlanta because she knew Raina would need her. She just had no idea what kind of help she would need. To say she was a little more than apprehensive was an understatement, but she knew it was time to step up to the plate. Besides, trading in that lumpy futon for a real mattress was a major incentive.

Now here she was in her sister's kitchen playing Suzy Homemaker and doing her best to keep the butterflies in her stomach at bay. She and the boys waited anxiously for Raina and Nyla to walk through the door.

"Aunt Lola, when are they going to get here?" Matthew asked for the fourth time. He paced back and forth, stopping every few minutes to peek out of the kitchen window. Lola was a nervous wreck.

"Come on, Matthew," she pleaded, "you're driving me nuts, dude." Lola wished she'd had more time to process everything that was happening. It was all coming at her so fast. She should've been with Raina to help bring Nyla home from the hospital. She wondered how many times Nyla had looked to another woman for the help she should've received from her own mother. It broke her heart.

"Aunt Lola? Did you hear me?" Lola shook her head. "I'm sorry, honey, what did you say?"

"I said, what *time* did she say they would be here?" Matthew asked in his very mature little voice.

"Your mom called about a half hour ago, so they

should be pulling up in a few minutes." Lola wiped the counter that hadn't needed to be wiped the last time couple of times she did it and peered at the clock on the wall. Matthew dropped his chin into his chest and walked out of the kitchen. He swung his arms from side to side as though they weighed a ton. "Ugh. I can't take it!" he said, throwing his small body onto the nearby sofa. "I'm going crazy!"

"You're driving *us* crazy!" Quincy barked at his little brother. Matthew ignored him.

"I wonder what she looks like," Matthew said to no one in particular. Quincy, who was obviously in a bad mood and had been brooding at the kitchen table, stood abruptly.

"Who cares?!"

Lola stopped wiping the counter and both she and Matthew stared at Quincy. Lola realized that she'd been so wrapped up in her own anguish and how all of this was affecting her, she'd neglected to consider how Nyla's living here was affecting everyone else.

"Hey Q, what's with the attitude?" Lola moved toward her nephew.

"I ain't got no attitude. I'm just tired of everyone talking about this girl likes she's really going to be a part of our family."

"But she *is* a part of our family. Didn't you hear what Mom said?" Matthew asked his brother.

"Yeah? So?"

"So, she's our sister."

"Um, Matt, weren't you working on a card for Nyla?" Lola asked, as she wrapped the dishtowel around her hand.

"Yeah. I'm almost finished with it."

"Well they're going to be walking through that door any minute, so why don't you go up and finish it, okay?"

"Aunt Lola, are you trying to get rid of me?" Matthew asked. Lola smiled and stood, shaking her head.

"I don't know why I thought I could get anything over on you, Matt. If you don't mind, I would like a few minutes to speak with Quincy alone."

"Be my guest." Matthew gave a slight shrug of the shoulders before he sprang from the sofa and dashed up the stairs.

Lola sat on one of the bar stools at the island and pulled out the other one. She patted the seat, motioning for Quincy to join her.

"Hey, you. Take a load off for a few minutes, okay?" Quincy sighed heavily and dragged his feet reluctantly across the kitchen before plopping down on the barstool.

"So, what's up? Do I detect a little resentment about Nyla moving in?" she asked. Quincy shrugged. "Is it because you don't want her here?" Another shrug.

"I don't know. I mean… no, not really. She's a perfect stranger. We don't even know where she came from."

"You know your mom already explained everything to you."

"And that's another thing. Where's *her* mom? And why does she have to stay here?"

"Well Q, from what little I know, she wasn't as fortunate as you." Lola leaned in closer toward her nephew. "She grew up in foster care, going from one home to the next." Even as Lola spoke the words, the weight of guilt was almost unbearable. A tsunami of emotions swirled inside of her chest and her stomach was in knots.

"When your dad found out that he might be her father, he started searching for her. You know, that was the kind of man your daddy was. He never would've allowed you, Matt, or any child of his to be anywhere but right here." Lola pointed at the floor. "He wanted to protect and take care of each of you. He wanted to make sure *all* of his children had the best that he could offer. And that each of you would know that you're loved *and* wanted. Sounds like she hasn't had much of that, Q." Lola choked the words out. "So I believe your dad would want you to make sure she feels welcome. Whaddaya say?" Lola held her breath.

Quincy shrugged again. She tried again.

"Tell ya what, every time you feel yourself getting angry, just think about how your dad would want you to treat her, okay?" Before Quincy had a chance to answer, the door swung open and in walked Raina and Nyla, with Lloyd not far behind.

"They're here! They're here!" Matthew shouted, as he ran down the staircase. He jumped down the last three steps, ran into the kitchen and almost collided into Raina.

"Hey, slow down, kid," Raina said, as she reached out to stop him. Despite the cold weather, Lola was sweating like a horse. She looked as though she'd seen a ghost.

"Nyla *this* is Matthew, the welcoming

committee." Raina turned her youngest child toward, Nyla. Matthew beamed as he extended his hand.

"Hi, glad to meet you."

"Hey," was all Nyla could say. Her discomfort was obvious.

"And *this* is Quincy." Raina motioned for him to come closer, but he didn't budge.

"What's up?" Quincy said, with an upward nod of his head. Raina was perplexed at his uncharacteristic sullenness, but she realized this was all probably too much for him to process.

There was an awkward silence for a few minutes, but Lloyd in his usual fashion, picked up where Raina left off.

"Nyla, this is Lola, Raina's sister." Lola was staring so hard she hadn't even noticed that Lloyd had walked in. Her skin felt prickly and a small line of perspiration formed at the top of her lip.

"Lola, this is Nyla. Lola? Lola!" Lloyd's voice finally got her attention.

"Huh?" Lola responded, with a jerk and quick shake of her head.

"This is Nyla."

Lola smiled nervously and walked closer with an extended hand. She tried hard to stop staring, but she couldn't help herself.

"Hi, I'm Lola." She spoke almost trance-like. Lola held Nyla's hand and took in every inch of her, from her toes to the top of her beautiful head. Matthew snickered.

"Aunt Lola, Cousin Lloyd just said that." Thank God for Matthew. He was definitely the only lighthearted person in the room. His excitement about having a big sister helped to put everyone else at ease.

"Right," she said as she released Nyla's hand. "Well, um... are you hungry? I'm no Paula Deen, but I make a mean spaghetti." Lola tried to recover from the awkwardness.

Nyla felt like a statue on display. She hated everyone staring at her like she was some kind of freak.

"Uh, no. I'm still kind of tired," she said, avoiding any eye contact as she pulled her jacket around her.

"Of course," Raina said. "Let me show you to your room." Matthew moved to pick up the small bag at Nyla's feet, but she quickly grabbed it.

"I was just going to help you with your bag," Matthew said, apologetically.

"That's okay. I got it," Nyla responded nervously, with a brief smile.

"Well, okay. I'll show you to your room. Okay, Mom?" he asked, looking back at Raina.

"Sure, honey. That's fine."

"Follow me," he said, with a big grin. He seemed to be handling the situation with ease.

"Well, is anyone else hungry? I cooked enough to feed an army," Lola said, with a nervous laugh.

"May I be excused?" Quincy asked, solemnly. Raina glanced at Lloyd and Lola.

"Sure, you can be excused," Raina responded. Quincy jumped up from the barstool and quickly exited the kitchen. Raina could see the pain and confusion on her child's face, but she knew he needed time to adjust to all that had happened.

"You want me to talk to him?" Lloyd asked.

"No, Lloyd." Raina pinched the bridge of her nose. "It's just going to take some time. We're all still adjusting to Keenan not being here and now this. It's not an easy thing."

"Yeah, I know. But it is the *right* thing, Raina," he said, placing his hand on her shoulders.

"I certainly hope so." Raina looked hopefully at her cousin. "I certainly hope so."

"You're strong, Raina but just remember, even strong people need help. Please remember that we're here for you." Lloyd tilted his head in Lola's direction.

"Thank you, Lloyd. It's just that it seems that this girl has been through so much. I don't know how to be anything to her."

"Just be her friend," Lloyd said.

"That's right." Lola chimed in.

"And we'll all do our best to let her know that she's wanted. Lord knows she's probably had a lot of disappointment in that area of her life," he added, looking at his cell phone for the third time since they'd arrived. "Listen, ladies, I'm going to have to get home before Jess decides to disown me. I'll call to check on y'all later." Lloyd kissed each of them on the cheek.

"Thank you so much for everything. I mean it." Raina gave him a big hug.

"Yeah, Lloyd. Thanks," Lola added.

"You're more than welcome, cuz," he said, returning the hug. "Call me and let me know if you need anything before I get back over here." Lloyd left and Raina looked at her sister and took a deep breath.

"I'm so glad you're here."

Lola crossed the room and embraced her.

"So am I."

They let the silence fall around them, each lost in their own thoughts. It was Raina, who broke the silence.

"Well, I guess I'm the only brave soul left to try your spaghetti." Lola pulled away abruptly and saw the smile on her sister's face.

"Uhn uhn... I *know* you're not trying to go there." She shoved Raina away and turned toward the stove. "There are plenty of things I don't cook, but I can throw down on some spaghetti and you know it. Girl, I've perfected my recipe over the years. You better recognize." Lola said, as she presented Raina with a spoonful of sauce.

"Taste this."

"Okay, but first I'm going to need to take a little Pepto Bismol before—"

"Shut up and taste it."

"Okay!" Raina stuck out her tongue reluctantly and took a small amount of the sauce into her mouth. Suddenly her eyes widened.

"Oh, it *is* good."

"See, you know you need to stop." Lola swung the kitchen towel over her shoulder.

"You know I'm just kidding."

"Shut up and let's eat." Lola took out a couple of plates from the kitchen cabinet and Raina saluted.

"Yes, ma'am."

It felt good to see the lighter side of her sister

again, even though Lola knew Raina was putting on a brave face so she wouldn't worry. Lola was glad to be there; although, having Nyla under the same roof was surreal. She wanted to help Raina, even if it was simply to distract her for a little while. Lola knew there would come a time when this moment would be a distant memory, but right now, she decided to just enjoy it and relish in the possibilities of a brighter future.

Later that evening as Raina was about to climb into bed, she was startled to find Matthew's small body there underneath the covers. She smiled to herself and welcomed the intrusion. *The bed is far too large for one person anyway,* she thought.

She moved over to the chaise beside her bed and began her nightly ritual of dousing her feet with Vaseline, an old home remedy her grandmother had taught her. Raina sat for a moment, staring at nothing in particular as she thought about Quincy. She knew she'd done the right thing by Nyla. She just hoped that it would be the right thing for her own child as well. Even though Quincy tried to be tough, Raina understood that he was hurt and confused. The loss of his father had affected him deeply but she knew that his healing would come in its own time.

Something out of the corner of her eye caught Raina's attention. She looked up and there he was, staring at her like a lost puppy. He didn't speak. The swell of tears fell from his eyes and his footsteps were heavy and robotic as he walked across the room and fell into her arms. Quincy didn't try to be strong or tough. He was just her child, who needed to be comforted. Raina whispered words of love softly in his ear and rocked him.

"It's going to be okay, sweetheart. *We're* going to be okay," she emphasized as she drew him in closer.

"I miss him so much." Quincy could hardly speak past the lump in his throat.

"I know. I miss him too."

They held each other and cried for what seemed like hours. Quincy finally fell asleep and Raina peeled herself from his embrace and covered him with a blanket. Before she climbed into bed Raina knelt to pray. Her grief and pain hung heavy in the center of her chest. All during her childhood she'd been taught about the power of prayer. She searched her heart for the right words to say but found none. Her sense of loss was raw and unforgiving. After a few more minutes passed, Raina whispered only one word: "Help." She pulled herself up and climbed into bed and as she lay on her back staring into the blackness, she could hear the soft breathing of her children as tears gradually slid down her face. She couldn't allow them to see her fall apart, so she closed her eyes and willed her brain to stop thinking. Moments later, she was asleep.

※ ※ ※ ※

Down the hall in the guest room, Nyla awakened with a jolt. She'd fallen asleep fully clothed on top of the bed. At first she couldn't remember where she was. She pulled herself up and a photo of Keenan fell from underneath her. Nyla drew her legs in Indian style in the middle of the bed. She studied the photograph for a long time. She traced his features with her finger.

"So, what do I do, now?" Nyla directed her question toward the picture as though it would speak to her. "I don't belong here." Nyla looked around the room. "You started all of this. You were supposed to be here." She looked back down at the photo. "Now what?"

❧ ❧ ❧ ❧

In the basement Lola lay in bed, gazing at the ceiling. The entire situation was all so unbelievable. If it weren't for the fact that she was awake, she would gladly believe that it was all a bad dream— worse yet a nightmare. *How could this be? Keenan dies and Nyla shows up.*

"God…" She stopped. It had been so long since she'd prayed she hesitated, questioning whether or not her prayers carried any weight at all. She decided to continue. "I know it's been a long time since you've heard from me," Lola continued. "You do remember me, don't you? I want to help them but how can I? My own life being such a wreck, I don't know what to do." She was exhausted from the emotional roller coaster she'd been on all day. "They're going to hate me," she muttered tearfully to herself. Her eyes became heavy with sleep as her mind pondered her next move.

"Where do we go from here? Help us Father," Lola petitioned, before she too slipped into a restless sleep.

# TWELVE

## REACHING BACK AND MOVING FORWARD

---

The next morning Nyla lay in bed and appeared to be resting peacefully. However, upon closer inspection small twitches became apparent. The twitches turned into reflexes as she attempted to fight off whatever was attacking her. It was only a matter of minutes before the reflexes became full fist jabs. Nyla tossed and turned until she became entangled in the sheets and awakened, gasping for air.

"No!" She sat straight up and for a moment she was still, allowing her eyes to focus and her heartbeat to return to its normal rhythm. Her hair was a tangled mess and the large t-shirt that Raina had given her to sleep in was now damp with perspiration.

"Gabby," she whispered before she threw the covers aside and searched her bag for the cell phone Gabrielle had given her. She turned it on and hoped that the phone had enough battery life for her to make a call.

"Yes," Nyla said excitedly when the phone came on fully charged. Immediately, Nyla saw that she had several messages. *Probably all from Gabby,* she thought. She didn't bother to listen to any of them, but quickly dialed Gabby's number and waited anxiously.

"Hello?" Nyla smiled when she heard her friend's voice on the other end.

"Hey."

"Hey. Who is this?" Gabby fired back with an attitude.

"Dang, how many people did you give your number to?"

"Nyla? Is that you?!" Where in the world have you been? I've been calling you like crazy! Did you find your Dad? Was he surprised to see you? Do you—?

"Whoa, girl! Come up for air."

"Don't whoa me. I thought I was your girl." Gabby paced back and forth in the small room she now shared with Simone. She was in full on drama mode. There was a hand gesture for every word she spoke. "What? You find your long lost daddy and you just throw me out with the bath water, huh? Is that how friends are supposed to treat each other? After all we've been through?"

"I'm calling you now, ain't I?" Nyla leaned forward and rubbed her forehead. She could feel a headache coming on. Like a small crack spreading through a wine glass. "Besides, I've been kinda out of it for the last few days."

"A few days?! Try a week and half. Wait." Gabby stopped pacing. "Out of it? What does that mean?" Nyla sat up and her eyes fell to her father's photograph.

"Well, I found out where my Dad lives, but he doesn't live here anymore."

"Well, that's okay. We'll just keep looking. I'll help you."

Nyla didn't want to say it. She didn't want say the actual words that would validate the horrible truth. Her father was dead and she would never have a chance to know him. Nyla pressed her eyes together tightly and inhaled. "He's dead, Gabby." She released her breath and those three words filled all of the empty spaces in the room. She could feel herself crumbling.

"What?!" Gabrielle's breath caught in her throat. "Oh my god, Ny." With widened eyes, Gabrielle stumbled backward and plopped on top of one of the twin beds. She shook her head; *it is all so unfair,* she thought. "I'm so sorry."

"Yeah. So am I." Nyla tried to be strong but she was hurt beyond measure.

"So what happened?! How?"

"Some idiot was texting and driving. It's only been a couple of weeks."

"Oh my god, Ny. I'm so, so sorry." Gabby's hand slid from her forehead through her short hair.

"That makes two of us."

"So what are you gonna do?" Gabby sat on the

151

edge of the bed staring at the cell phone as she spoke.

"I don't know. His wife offered to let me stay here at their house, but I don't know."

"Ny, that's good. I think that might be for the best."

"You do? Why?"

"Well, you know that fool Tyrone is probably out there looking for us. This will give you some time for things to cool off. Besides that, where else you gonna go? You don't want to be out on the streets again, do you?"

"No, but I don't know if I can do this, Gabby. She has two sons and one has made it clear that he doesn't want me here."

"Oh my gosh, Ny, you have two brothers? That's awesome!" Gabby was excited again. "I say stay… just for a little while so you can plan your next move."

"I don't know, I'll think about it." Nyla didn't know what her next move would be and she was tired of thinking about it. She wanted to change the subject. "So what's up with you and Ms. Pearl?"

"Oh, Ny they're so nice. Her husband's name is Pete and they have a son too, but he's in some Military school somewhere. They have a little store on the corner and they sell everything from snow boots to grandma's draws, girl. Simone and I take turns helping out at the store, and get this… they said they would help me get my GED. Can you believe it? They're really into education. I share a room with Simone, but she doesn't seem to mind. I like it here. As long as they'll have me, I plan to stay. At least until I've finished the GED program."

"Wow, sounds like you got yourself a real home."

"Sounds like you do too. They did ask you to stay, right?"

"Yeah, but...."

"But what, Ny? Don't you think your dad would've wanted you to stay?"

"You don't understand."

"What is there to understand? You don't have anywhere else to go. You got people... excuse me, a stepmom and two brothers to stay with. What more do you want?"

"I don't need or want a stepmom. She has her own kids. I want...," Nyla stopped. She was frustrated for allowing Gabby to goad her into saying too much about how she felt. It wasn't that she didn't appreciate Raina's offer. With Keenan gone, it just wasn't the same as she'd imagined and she couldn't begin to explain it, because she didn't quite understand it herself. All Nyla knew was that she still felt like she didn't belong. "Hey listen, I gotta go, but I'll call you later. Okay?"

"Ny, listen to me. I'm not trying to pretend I know how you feel, but I think I have a pretty good idea."

"Not really." Nyla said dryly.

"Well, I do know how it feels to not have a place to belong in the world. Call me crazy to jump at the first act of kindness, but I don't want to be out on those streets alone anymore, Ny. I want a warm, safe bed to sleep in. I want someone to genuinely care about me without having to do sexual favors.

Aren't you tired of running?"

Nyla blinked back her tears. She didn't answer.

"Ny, why don't you stay and use your dad's information to see if that will help you find your birth mom. That way when you decide to leave, you'll know where you're going and won't just be out there still trying to figure things out."

Nyla lifted her head. She could see a sliver of the sun peeking through the bedroom blinds. The rays danced across the floor and climbed along the bed, falling on the picture of Keenan. Her heart ached for him. Her mood quickly changed to anger. She felt that it was a cruel joke to have come so close, only to find that she was a week late. *Maybe finding my birth mom should be my next move. The least she can do is explain herself.*

"Ny? You still there?"

"Yeah, I'm here." Nyla breathed deeply. "I was just… I was thinking about what you said about finding out more about my birth mom. I might try that."

Gabby breathed a sigh of relief. She knew Nyla didn't trust easily. She had always kept everyone at a distance. But Nyla also knew that there was a lot of truth to what Gabby was saying; the streets were very mean. At least when they were out there together, they had each other's back. Gabby couldn't stand the thought of Nyla being out there alone.

"So does that mean you're gonna hang out there for a while?"

"Yeah, I guess. Like you said, where am I gonna go?"

"Sounds good," Gabby said with a smile. "Hey, I can help you. I mean, you know I'm a straight tech-head girl. Maybe I could come over and we could get on the computer and start our own little investigation."

A small knock came at the bedroom door; Nyla's head jerked to attention.

"Well, I'll call and let you know. Okay?"

"Okay. Keep me posted. I mean it, Nyla."

"I will. I gotta go. Talk to you later," she said, scrambling off the bed.

"Okay, take care. Love you, Ny."

"You're a trip. Bye, girl." Nyla loved Gabby, too. She was the closest thing she had to a sister but to say things like that made her uncomfortable. The knock came again as Nyla's feet hit the floor. She went and stood near the door.

"Yeah?"

"Nyla, it's me, Raina. May I come in?" No one had ever asked her for permission to enter a room before. Even if the room was supposed to be hers. Nyla cracked the door and peeked out with a confused expression.

"This is your house, right?"

"Yes."

"So why you asking me if you can come into a room in your own house?" Nyla opened the door wider and stepped back. As Raina entered, Nyla again noticed her beauty. Her smile was warm and kind.

"Good morning. How'd you sleep?" Raina noticed that Nyla had actually worn the t-shirt she'd given her to sleep in.

"I kinda fell asleep on top of the bed. I hope you don't mind." Nyla looked sheepishly at the rumpled pile of covers in the middle of the bed.

"No. Why would I mind?" she asked, looking around. Raina noticed Keenan's photo on the bed. She turned to face Nyla and could see her discomfort.

"Listen, Lloyd is coming by to take the boys out today, so I figured you and I could maybe do brunch and a little shopping." Nyla looked back at Raina with a blank stare.

"Uh… okay. That sounds cool, I guess."

"Really? Do you feel up to it?" Raina tilted her head with a slight smile.

"Yeah, sure. I mean I could eat."

"Great. Then I'll leave you to take a shower and get dressed." Raina checked the time. "What do you say we head out in about an hour, okay?"

"Sure." Nyla shrugged.

"Okay, then. There are towels in the bathroom and there should be some soap underneath the sink." Raina started to move toward the bathroom, but Nyla quickly interjected, "I think I can find everything." Raina stopped in the middle of the room and turned around.

"I mean… thanks." Nyla hoped that she didn't sound ungrateful.

"I'm sorry. I'm treating you like you're four aren't I? Of course you can find everything."

"Yeah, I can handle it."

"Okay then, I'll leave you to get ready. If you need anything I'm just down the hall," she said, pointing over her shoulder as she turned to leave.

"What about your sister?"

"Excuse me?" Raina turned back to face Nyla.

"Is she coming too?"

"Oh Lola? No. She's already off this morning doing her thing. She got out early, and to tell you the truth I was kind of surprised; that's not like her at all."

"Oh, okay. So it'll just be me and you?"

"Yep. Just the two of us. Is that okay?"

Another shrug. "Yeah. Sure."

"Okay, see ya in a few." Raina closed the door and headed down the hall. Her heart was beating in her chest so loudly, she hoped that Nyla couldn't hear it.

*Dang, what in the world am I gonna talk about with this woman?* Nyla thought as stood biting her nails. She knew Raina would ask her a million questions that she didn't want to answer. Nyla had absolutely no intentions of ever letting Raina find out the kind of life she'd been living. Nyla knew she would have to make up a story to satisfy Raina's curiosity, but right now, her body was craving a shower. Nyla pulled her hair into a ponytail, grabbed her bag from the chair and headed for the bathroom. Her stomach was telling her, even if she didn't really want to hang with Raina, it was past time for a good meal.

# THIRTEEN

## JEREMIAH ELI

---

Lola felt good. She'd gone to the Board of Education and completed all the necessary paperwork to become a substitute teacher. After an unusually good night's sleep, she rose early for her appointment with Dr. Eli. Although Lola usually never scheduled herself to be *anywhere* before ten a.m., she rose at what she considered the ridiculous hour of five o'clock, making sure she wouldn't be late for her first appointment.

It was early March and there was still a chill in the air, Lola sported her brown tweed Anne Klein slacks with a caramel-colored turtleneck and cashmere sweater, loosely tied around the waist. She wore her favorite gold, tear-drop earrings and a beautiful gold pendant necklace. Her hand-sewn, brown, leather boots were the perfect compliment.

She didn't know what Graham had told the doctor, but she didn't want to be perceived as some falling-down drunk who was completely out of control. She adjusted herself several times trying to appear comfortable, as she sat waiting in the reception area. It was Saturday, and most of the staff was off. The receptionist busied herself with phone calls and files as Lola anxiously nursed a cup of coffee.

She glanced at her watch and noticed that the doctor was late. When she looked up, she caught the rosy cheeked receptionist watching her over her red-rimmed glasses. Moments later the door swung open and in walked Dr. Jeremiah Eli. He was not at all what she'd expected.

"Good morning, Hazel." The tall, ebony skin-toned man spoke with a velvet, British accent. "You're looking quite lovely this morning." He smiled as Hazel handed over several phone messages and a file folder.

"Good morning, Dr. Eli," Hazel responded curtly, while blushing at the same time. "You're late."

"I most certainly am not," he said as he consulted his watch. "I had to take Greta for a run this morning. You have no idea how cranky she can be when she doesn't get her exercise."

"Well, too bad that Greta is a dog and can't remind you to check your schedule. Your next appointment has been waiting for fifteen minutes," Hazel said, with a slight nod in Lola's direction. The doctor glanced over his shoulder not quite seeing who was in the waiting area, and looked closely at Hazel with a slight grimace. He'd

159

forgotten all about the last minute appointment and was embarrassed at his tardiness. He didn't turn to greet his waiting client but leaned in closer to Hazel.

"How long has he been waiting?" he whispered.

"Since seven," Hazel whispered back.

"Okay, send him back in two minutes." He placed the folder under his arm and started toward his office.

"Her."

"Excuse me?" Dr. Eli stopped and stared back at Hazel for clarity.

"I'll send *her* in, in two minutes," she said, continuing to stare at the computer screen in front of her.

"Oh, I see." The doctor stood a little straighter. "And you said Graham scheduled the appointment?" he asked, seeming a little unnerved.

"Yes," Hazel responded looking up from the screen and over the glasses perched on her nose.

"Okay. Two minutes." Dr. Eli held up two fingers and quickly disappeared down the hall.

Hazel didn't have a good feeling about this. She didn't know whether it was intentional or just by accident, but Dr. Eli rarely treated female patients. After she'd worked there for about a year, she'd felt comfortable enough to share her observation. The doctor simply smiled that gorgeous smile and told her that helping men was what he was best suited for. He said he knew what made them tick. "Women? Not so much," he'd explained. After that, it was business as usual, but today, Hazel smelled trouble.

"The doctor will see you now," Hazel spoke over the desk in Lola's direction. Lola stood quickly. She was clearly agitated.

"Thank you," Lola said curtly as she moved swiftly past Hazel's desk. She didn't bother to knock before she walked into Dr. Eli's office. When Jeremiah looked up from his desk, he recognized her immediately. She was the reason he had to toss his favorite cashmere sweater. The cleaners had been unsuccessful in removing the coffee stain. And the name. Lola Devereux. *Could this be the same woman that his good friend and colleague, Bernard Goodman had phoned him about a couple of weeks ago?* Jeremiah was now intrigued and disappointed. Before, when he saw her at the Cafe, he'd contemplated getting to know the mystery woman, but if he took her on as a patient that would never happen.

"Hello, Ms. Devereux." He looked down at the folder to make certain of his pronunciation. "Please, come in and have a seat." He rose and came around his desk to greet her. As Lola drew closer her agitation evaporated.

There it was, that prickly feeling on her skin. She knew that feeling and she knew she should turn and run, but the smooth baritone of his voice, laced with that accent had her feet nailed to the floor.

"Please forgive me for my tardiness, but the appointment completely slipped my mind." Lola was entranced.

"Ms. Devereux? Are you okay?" Dr. Eli waved his hand in front of her face. She jumped a little and knew had she been a couple of shades lighter, her entire face would've been red.

"Yes, of course. I'm fine, except for the fact that you've kept me waiting and thrown me completely off schedule." Her tone was abrupt as she tried to hide her embarrassment. His left eyebrow rose, surprised at the tartness of her voice, given the dreamy way she'd looked at him.

"Well, let's get right to work, shall we?" Jeremiah walked back around his desk and took a seat. Lola sat in one of the art deco chairs adjacent to his desk, but not before taking a peek at his backside.

"Stop it." Lola shook her head but spoke in too loud of a whisper.

"Excuse me?" he turned.

"Oh, nothing." Lola stared back with a blank expression.

"No. I thought I heard you say stop it."

"Oh, uh… no. I said, drop it. We can just drop it and get it on. No. I mean, get down to business. Wait. That's not what I meant. What I meant to say..." Jeremiah held up his hand.

"Ms. Devereux, please. I understand what you meant. Let's just get to work on why you're here, okay?" Now, it was Lola's turn to grimace.

"Yes, let's."

"Very well," he said, as he began to peruse her file folder. The silence was killing her. He glanced up at her and Lola wanted to crawl under the floor. Suddenly, he closed the folder and sat upright in the large, leather chair.

"So why don't we start out by you telling me a little about yourself and what you wish to gain if I take you on as a patient?" Lola was taken aback. She didn't know what she'd expected but this wasn't it. She shouldn't be here. She wanted to dive into the depths of his dark eyes and never think about why she was here. *I should just go. I need someone older, fatter, shorter even. Anyone but this Adonis sitting here, asking me to describe the grim details of my life.*

"Well, um, let's see. First, I came to town for my brother-in-law's funeral."

"Oh, I'm sorry to hear that."

"Yes, well, we all have to go." Another raised eyebrow. *What? Why did I say that?* "Anyway, the entire experience has been completely overwhelming and one night I had a little too much to drink. That's when I made the acquaintance of your lovely colleague, Graham Billingsley. She insisted that I come here, but to tell you the truth, I'm beginning to think that it was a mistake."

"Oh, you do? So do you think that coming to see me was a mistake or was coming for help a mistake?"

"Well...," she started with a nervous laugh, "I think that, perhaps, someone with a little more experience under his belt would be more beneficial." The doctor stopped writing and sat back in his chair. He studied Lola for a few minutes before he took a deep breath and closed the folder.

"Well I can assure you, Ms. Devereux, that I have all the necessary credentials and qualifications that are required. Not to mention over fifteen years of experience. However, I'm a firm believer in not wasting time. So you're free to go."

Lola was stunned. She sat with her mouth partially opened a moment longer before his words registered to her. "What?"

Dr. Eli picked up the phone and had begun to dial Hazel to inquire about his next appointment. He looked up at Lola again.

"Is there something wrong, Ms. Devereux?"

"Yes, Dr. Eli. There is something very wrong." Lola could feel her blood start to boil. Dr. Eli slowly placed the receiver back into its cradle.

"And what would that be?"

"Is this your idea of professionalism? You show up late and when I disapprove of your tardiness, which also makes me question your qualifications, you simply dismiss me?! You're rude and arrogant and I don't appreciate being tossed aside like some, some insignificant piece of furniture!"

Jeremiah continued to observe Lola's meltdown. As he watched her, he took in all of her. She was striking, but he made a note to self—she was a potential patient. The makeup and the clothes did their part to conceal the jagged edges, but he recognized a cry for help when he saw it. However, he would not play the interpreter. She would have to ask for the help she needed, straight out.

After she'd given the doctor a piece of her mind, he did not respond immediately. After a moment or two, Jeremiah stood quickly and walked around his desk. He was at least six feet with a lean, muscular frame. He sat in the chair adjacent to Lola's.

"Ms. Devereux, may I be frank?

"You can be anybody you want to be, but *please* stop calling me Ms. Devereux. That's my mother's name," she said, in a huff.

"Okay, Lola. Let me be perfectly clear. I am a doctor who treats people with a disease called addiction. I can't afford to waste my time on anyone who's not ready to be real with me or with themselves. Now if you got tipsy at a bar and you don't have any other issues, then I agree, you don't need to be here. However, if you have an addiction problem, and you're ready to admit it and try to work through whatever it is that's keeping you bound to this terrible disease, then you've come to the right place. But I am not here to convince you of that or to play mind games. Either you want help or you don't."

Lola was mortified. He'd shocked her once more with his candidness. She began to shake with anger. Dr. Eli had called her bluff and she was pissed off. Lola knew she needed to be there. She wanted to get help for all the right reasons, but she was frightened because she always seemed to come up short. This man had seen right through her act. He'd called her out and now she would have to decide if she would swallow her pride and stay or save face and run, like she always did.

"So what is it going to be?" He leaned back, intertwining his fingers while resting his elbows on the narrow arms of the chair. Lola stood and walked toward the door. Dr. Eli didn't move. He'd learned many years ago that the only one that could save a person from an addiction is the addict. He hoped that this disease wouldn't totally consume her before she would seek help again.

Once at the door, Lola stood with her hand on

the knob. The coolness of the knob against her sweaty palm seemed to have grounded her, as she stood staring into the frosted glass. Suddenly she turned and moved across the thick carpet and stopped directly in front of Jeremiah. Lola extended her hand.

"Hello. My name is Lola Devereux and I'm an alcoholic."

Eli stood and enclosed her delicate hand within his own. A bolt of electricity went from the top of her head down to her pinky toe. "It's a pleasure to meet you, Ms. Dev... Lola. I'm Dr. Jeremiah Eli; let's get started, shall we?"

With an awkward smile Lola breathed a sigh of relief and for the first time in a long, she felt hopeful.

# FOURTEEN

## BRUNCH

---

**R**aina had spent the better part of the week searching through Keenan's papers, trying to find information that would help lead them to Nyla's biological mother. Her search came up empty. Even though Raina dreaded probing her for information, she knew that Nyla was her best resource. It couldn't be avoided.

Just as they were about to leave for the restaurant, Victoria popped over. Now the three of them sat tensely in Raina's SUV on their way to brunch.

As they rode through the city, Raina's stomach felt queasy as she thought about how to get Nyla to open up. *Lord, please help me with this endeavor, Amen,* she whispered under her breath. Raina knew that in order for her and Nyla to work together, she would first have to gain Nyla's trust. She hoped her plan wouldn't backfire.

"I hope you like quiche," Raina spoke over her shoulder as she maneuvered the car through the streets. "Milford's has the best."

"I never really had it," Nyla said, studying the landscape as it passed her window. "They didn't cook a lot of quiche in the foster homes."

Raina and Victoria gave each other a quick glance.

"Oh. I'm sorry... I guess I wasn't thinking about..." Raina's voice trailed off. Now Victoria took a turn to try to engage Nyla in conversation.

"So, Nyla, where did you live before you came here?" Still facing the window, Nyla cut her eyes up toward the front of the car.

"Here and there. Mostly with friends."

"I see. Well how did you get here? Did you fly in or take the train?"

"Uh… no." Nyla raised her eyebrows as she shook her head, indicating how out of touch she thought this woman was. "An airplane ticket wasn't in the budget so I just hopped on the hound."

"Oh that's nice. Wait. Did you say the hound?"

"Yeah."

"What in the world is that?" Victoria's brow furrowed.

"You never heard of the Greyhound Bus?"

"Oh. Well, yes. Of course I've heard of Greyhound, I've just never heard it referred to in that way before," Victoria said, with a nervous laugh. "Where did you say you caught the bus from dear?" They hadn't even gotten to the restaurant yet and things where turning out just as Nyla had feared. She had no intention of allowing her life story to be the appetizer for today's brunch. All the questions made her anxious, so she decided it was time to turn the tables.

"How long have y'all lived in Atlanta?" Nyla asked.

"Oh, pretty much all of my life," Victoria announced proudly. "My mother moved here when I was a toddler and I attended school not too far from here. Both of my girls were born in Atlanta and quite frankly, I've never seen any reason to leave." Victoria's words were prideful.

Nyla nodded thoughtfully. She sat with her fist pressed down inside the pockets of her hoodie.

"Look, that's the first church Daddy pastored." Raina pointed to the small, white church they were passing.

"Oh, now I see," Nyla said from the backseat.

"What do you see?" Raina asked looking at Nyla through her rearview mirror.

"Why y'all are being so nice."

"You think the reason I'm being nice to you is because my father was a preacher?"

"Isn't it?"

Raina pondered the thought for a moment. She turned the car into the parking lot of the café and parked it before she turned to face Nyla.

"I guess you could say that's true, in a sense. I mean, he did teach us how to treat people. But that isn't the only reason."

"No?"

"No, it isn't. Nyla, you're Keenan's daughter and

I loved him very much. What kind of person would I be to turn you away in your time of need? As I said before, you're welcome in your father's house and I mean it. As long as there is respect and regard for others, you are welcome. Okay?"

Nyla nodded.

"That's cool."

"So, is anyone hungry?" Raina asked with a smile.

"Oh yes. I'm starving." Victoria chimed in, relieved that some of the tension had been lifted.

"Didn't you hear my stomach from all the way back here? I hope this quiche stuff is as good as you say," Nyla added.

"Trust me, it is." They all got out of the car and walked toward the already crowded restaurant.

That's when Victoria noticed something oddly familiar about Nyla. She watched her mannerisms as she and Raina walked side by side toward the entrance. Was it her walk? The way she held her head? There was something about this child that was a bit unsettling, but Victoria couldn't put her finger on what it was.

❧ ❧ ❧ ❧

Across town, Gabby stepped off of the city bus with Beyoncé's newest release blasting from the earphones she had stuck firmly in her ears. She didn't even see the black Cadillac SUV pull up beside her, until it was too late. When Gabby realized who it was, she had no time to react before Jamal jumped out and forced her inside the vehicle, leaving her book bag and cell phone sprawled across the street.

Jamal threw her across the back seat where she came face to face with her worst nightmare. Her heart was beating so hard it felt as though it was about to jump out of her chest. Gabby's breathing became erratic as she struggled to make sense of what was happening. Her entire body trembled as she sat staring at the floor. Before she raised her eyes to see him, Gabby smelled his musky sent. A million thoughts ran through her mind, but before she could speak or try to talk her way out of trouble, Gabby heard what sounded like a firecracker in her ear. A piercing pain followed and traveled through her entire head, afterwards there was darkness. The serenity of the darkness was brief. Gabby's return to a conscious state was abrupt and painful. First, there was yelling, followed by more blows.

"Hey, Gabrielle! Remember me? Huh? You remember me, ho?!" Tyrone repeated the questioning through clinched teeth, as he hit her over and over again. Where's my money, huh?! Where is it?!" He yelled and beat her, relentlessly. Gabby gasped for air as her breath caught in her throat. She had no time to respond, no time to hatch a plan of escape. Tyrone threw her around the car like a rag doll. Her attempts at blocking the blows were futile. *I'm going to die,* Gabby thought as she felt the power behind each angry blow. She began to drift in and out of consciousness, which seemed to make Tyrone even angrier. Finally, the car came to a stop and so did the beating.

"You and yo' lil friend thought you could outsmart a dumb, country hick like me, huh? Yeah, but you the dumb one. Got yo'self all ova'

Facebook; bragging 'bout how you got a new life."
Tyrone, spat the words at her as she lay shriveled
and bleeding on his car floor. "Hey, listen to this
Jamal, she even goin' to school."

"You eva' seen somebody this stupid goin' to
school, Jamal?"

"Nah cuz, ain't neva' seen this much
stu...stu...stupid."

Tyrone had broken Gabby's nose. Her bottom lip
was split and thick clots of blood oozed out onto the
floor. Both of her eyes had begun to swell shut. She
didn't know it, but he'd also broken a couple of her
ribs. Her breathing grew increasingly shallow. She
could hear their muffled voices as she lay gasping
for air. She thought that this was the end for her, but
she didn't regret running away. The sheer
experience of living freely had been worth the cost.
Tyrone sneered at her, as he looked down with
disgust.

"You and Ny cost me a lot of money, not to
mention embarrassin' me. Ya'll got folks thinkin'
I'm soft but I got news for ya'll. I'ma use both of
you as an example. I'ma let *everybody* see what
happens to hos, who thank they smarta than me."
He balled his fist again.

"Don't be scared, Gabby, 'cause I'm not gon'
kill you yet. It'll take me too long to find my
money. So...," he said, pulling her limp body up
from the floor. Gabby's body shivered involuntarily
with the awful expectation of what was about to
happen. The only sound that escaped her was a
garbled, inaudible whimper. He drew her closer and
she could feel the moisture from his breath on her

face.

"I want you to tell Ny that she betta get me my damn money or she betta *neva* stop looking ova her shoulda." He slammed his fist into Gabby's face and there was no more sound. A half-a-mile away from Grady Hospital, Tyrone opened the door and rolled Gabby's lifeless body onto the cold, hard concrete. "You betta not die, ho!" He then signaled Jamal to drive off.

≈ ≈ ≈ ≈

Milford's Café was one of Raina's favorite places to eat. They sat in her favorite section, which was the covered patio near a wall of windows. This allowed them to people watch, one of Raina's quirky little pastimes. The sky was clear and the sun was high and although its rays felt good beaming through the window, there was still a little nip in the air. The outside heaters created the perfect atmosphere.

The restaurant was busy, as usual. Waiters darted back and forth as they attempted to stay ahead of the brunch rush. Raina, Victoria and Nyla were surrounded by restaurant sounds of constant chatter, glasses clinking and silverware hitting china, as they settled in. The delicious aromas that floated through the air only added to the warmth of the Café. That's why Raina loved it so much.

The next hour passed quickly and the small talk had grown sporadic, to say the least. However, Raina knew she needed to get to the business at hand.

"I see the quiche was a big hit." Raina smiled and wiped her mouth. She noticed Nyla had finished her second slice.

"Sorry," Nyla spoke, realizing that she'd probably eaten more than her share.

"Don't be sorry. If I had your figure, I would eat with abandon as well. Mom, wouldn't it be great to be seventeen again and not have to worry about weight gain?"

"Yes, ma'am. When I was seventeen, I never worried about what I ate," Victoria chimed in.

Nyla stuck another slice of cantaloupe in her mouth. "I'm almost eighteen." Raina leaned in closer to the table.

"Really? When's your birthday?"

"July 26."

"Wow. That's not too far off but it's not close enough either."

"What do you mean?"

"Well, I have something I'd like to give you. I thought it would make a good birthday present, but July seems too far away." Raina didn't look at her mother. She didn't want to be influenced by a look of disapproval. This was something that God had placed on her heart and she wanted to share it with Nyla.

Victoria could sense Raina's uncertainty about whatever it was she was going to say or do, so she decided to give them a little privacy.

"Raina, honey, if you'll both excuse me, I need to find the ladies room."

"Oh, okay, sure." Relieved, Raina smiled as her mother walked away.

"Well now, where was I?"

Nyla sipped her sweet tea and looked at Raina

with anticipation. "You said you had something you wanted to give me."

"Oh yes." Raina reached into her purse and pulled out a small, black leather box. She slid it across the table in front of Nyla. "This belonged to your father."

All the air seemed to leave Nyla's lungs. She stared at the black box without any response. Her hands became sweaty as she slowly lifted the box from the table and opened it. It was a high school track and field, state championship metal. Nyla ran her fingers over the engravings and felt the coolness and weight of it. Raina continued to explain the gift and tried not to become overly emotional. She didn't want to make Nyla uneasy.

"Your dad had many different awards and trophies but there were a few that were special to him. This is one he truly treasured and I know he would want you to have it."

Nyla pulled the box closer, took the medal out of the box and held it like it was a fragile piece of glass.

Something gripped her heart as she imagined him actually touching this very thing and wearing it with pride.

"He always said when he ran he could taste freedom." Nyla looked up at Raina and saw her quickly wipe away a tear.

"Freedom? Freedom from what? It ain't like he was some kind of slave or something." They both laughed nervously. Raina continued, "He was corny like that, sometimes. He told me that running helped him sort things out. His father got very sick when he was young, so having to deal with his dad's illness and the probability of his death really weighed him down. I remember him telling me about when he had to make the decision to transfer colleges to be closer to his parents. That was the last year of his father's life."

"Wow." Nyla didn't know how to feel about it all.

"I believe we all go through things like that. Not really being certain about what lies ahead, you know?" Raina gave a slight shrug of her shoulders.

Nyla's insides were exploding. She closed her eyes and held the medal to her chest.

"Wow. I don't know what to say. Thank you. This means... ah man, it really means a lot." Raina reached across the table and Nyla reached back. They held hands. "I miss him," Nyla said, as she shook her head a little and wiped her eyes. She'd been caught off guard. "I mean... I know it sounds crazy to miss someone you never really met but... I can't explain it. I just miss him."

"No need to explain. Just know he loved you, Nyla. Even though he never met you, he was determined to find you and try and make up for the time you both lost. I can't be your parent, but I can be your friend. I want you to know that I'm here for you and I'll help you any way I can, okay?"

Nyla nodded. She didn't trust herself to speak. She fought to hold it all together. She wasn't used to openly displaying her emotions.

Raina studied her for a few minutes before she spoke again. She looked out of the window of the café and could see the signs of spring just around the corner. Spring was Keenan's favorite time of year. He always said it reminded him of new beginnings. A glare from the sun came through the window and caused Raina to furrow her brow a little.

"Nyla, do you mind if I ask you a few questions about your parents?"

"It depends." There. The moment was gone. The tone of Nyla's voice told Raina that the invisible armor she wore had been raised again.

"On what?" Raina asked.

"On if I have the answers," Nyla answered tensely as she began to tap her fork on the table.

"Fair enough."

"Do you have any papers that may help us locate your biological mother?"

Nyla thought about the question for a few minutes as she continued tapping the fork. Finally, she stopped and placed the medal back in the black case and for the very first time, looked Raina directly in the eye.

"No. If there were any papers, I never saw them. Mom and Dad were both only children. It had always been just the three of us." Nyla peered out of the window. "Like the three musketeers. When they died, it was... well, just me," she said, and took another sip of tea.

"I'm so, sorry," Raina said as Nyla shrugged her shoulders.

"How old were you?"

Nyla took a deep breath. "I don't really remember. Around five, maybe six."

"What was mother's maiden name?"

"Why?" Nyla felt as though she was being interrogated.

"Well, I looked through some documents Keenan collected while he searched for you. Your parents might've had information that would help us locate your biological mother. I would like to help you find her."

"Raina, you'll never guess who I ran into over there," Victoria said, on her return to the table. "It was Grace Ruffin. She told me her youngest daughter is expecting twins! You remember Morgan, don't you? You used to babysit her."

Raina kept her eyes fixed on Nyla. Nyla thought about Raina's proposal. She knew she was trying to help, but she really didn't know how she felt about finding her birth mother. She had given her away and didn't even have the decency to tell her dad about her. Not to mention covering her tracks so she couldn't be found. The more she thought about it, the more Nyla knew she had no desire to find her at all. She couldn't risk any more rejection. Nyla looked at Victoria and slid the box off of the table. She held it tightly between her sweaty palms.

"I'll think about it," she said to Raina.

"Okay. Great." Raina said, hopeful.

Victoria looked at them both and tried to decipher what had just transpired. She continued her rant about the young lady having the twins as Raina smiled and nodded, all the time wondering what kind of woman could've given up a child without telling the father. Keenan would've raised her on his own, had he only known.

Nyla looked out of the window at a tall, bronze

colored woman walking across the street. For a
moment, she allowed herself to wonder, *What if this
lady is my mom?* She knew it was ridiculous, but it
had some validity. For all she knew, her mother
could be the next woman who walked into the
restaurant, the one at the next table, or one of the
waitresses.

"So how do you feel about dessert?" Raina asked
to lighten the mood.

"Oh yes, by all means," Victoria added. "The
desserts here are wonderful."

Nyla shrugged her shoulders again. "Got any
suggestions?"

"One word: chocolate," Raina said cheerfully.

"Now you talkin'." Nyla smiled, albeit, briefly.
She opened the dessert menu and perused the
selections and for the first time that day she exhaled
as she held on to her father's medal. Slowly the
anxiety she'd felt earlier started to roll away like
raindrops dripping off the end of a leaf.

# FIFTEEN

## A NEW FRIEND

---

Naomi sat at the kitchen table and scanned the newspaper while Quincy sulked nearby. Across the room, Nyla and Matthew played another game of Wii boxing. Try as he might, Quincy found it difficult to ignore this stranger that looked so much like him, right down to the same eyes and chin. Nyla resembled him even more than his own brother. When she first arrived, Matthew said to their mother, "She's Quincy but with more hair." Quincy wouldn't admit it, but it kind of freaked him out. He didn't know if he would ever get used to it.

"Umph. Take that!" Matthew yelled and landed another virtual left hook to Nyla's cheek. They were in the middle of a boxing match when the doorbell rang. Raina was busy in Keenan's office so Naomi answered the door.

"Hey, Ms. Naomi. Um...how are you?" The tall, lanky teen asked hesitantly.

"I'm fine, Isaias. Come in." Naomi stepped backward, as Isaias entered the foyer.

She had not been prepared for the onslaught of emotions that clutched at her chest when she saw Isaias. She remembered the first time Keenan had introduced them. He'd been a wide-eyed, shy little boy. She looked at him now, a handsome seventeen year old with caramel skin and dark brown, almond-shaped eyes. He had been abandoned as a toddler and Keenan had been instrumental in helping to get him adopted. Over the years, Keenan had mentored him and Isaias had always felt like family. Now Naomi saw him growing into the young man Keenan had always known he'd be. She also saw the hurt in his eyes as he peered around the corner, probably still hoping Keenan would turn the corner with one of his grand hellos. Isaias leaned in for a quick hug.

"Is Ms. Raina here?"

"Yes, she's in the office," Naomi said as she turned back toward the family room. Isaias followed.

When Quincy saw Isaias, he shot up from his seat.

"Hey, Isaias. What's up? Where've you been?"

"What's up, Q?" he said with a slight tilt of his head. I just got back from a soccer tournament." He turned to Naomi. "Mom needed me to go to the store so she sent me over to see if y'all needed anything."

"Ha! Told you. I'm the king!" Matthew shouted,

after he'd beaten Nyla for the third time. All heads turned toward the noise.

"Okay, I'm done." Nyla stood and tossed the controller onto the sofa.

"Noooo. One more game, please? I promise not to beat you so bad the next time," Matthew whined.

Nyla had already started texting as she made her way from the family room into the kitchen. She hadn't heard from Gabby and had started to worry.

"Who's that?" Isaias asked Quincy.

Quincy turned slightly and saw Nyla open the fridge, then turned back to face Isaias.

"Nobody. Hey, you want to go out and practice some moves?" Naomi knew Quincy was having difficulty adjusting to Nyla, but she was taken aback at how easily he dismissed her. Raina finally emerged from the office.

"Hey, Isaias. I thought I heard someone at the door. How are you and your mom and dad?" Raina gave Isaias a quick hug.

"Everyone is fine. I just came by to see if y'all needed anything from the grocery store," he said, as he stole another look toward the kitchen. Both Naomi and Raina picked up on the stolen glances. Naomi tilted her head toward the kitchen and Raina quickly picked up the signal.

"Well, let's see," Raina pondered. She took a few steps into the kitchen. Nyla stood at the island drinking a bottle of water. Now it was Naomi's turn to interject.

"Isaias, you haven't had the opportunity to meet Nyla, have you? Nyla, this is Isaias, he lives a couple of houses down. Isaias, this is Nyla Davis,

Keenan's daughter." Isaias' eyes widened.

"Daughter?" He paused and looked at both of the ladies. "Nah... really?" he said with a non-believing chuckle. "I mean, really? Like, how? Uh... no, I'm sorry." He shook his head. "That was inappropriate. What I meant to say was that I didn't know Mr. B had a, uh, daughter." He looked back and forth at all three of them. Quincy let out a sigh as he turned and dashed up the staircase to his room.

"Yes, well Nyla is going to be with us for a while and she attends the same school as you," Raina added.

Nyla slowly screwed the top back on her water. "I do?"

"Yes. You do," Raina said. Nyla and Isaias made brief eye contact.

"Hi," they both said simultaneously.

"I haven't seen you around," Isaias said. He was still trying to figure out how Mr. B had a daughter that he knew nothing about.

"Yeah, well I've been there. And I ride the bus every day."

"Oh, I don't ride the bus. This is the first year my parents let me drive to school. They said it'll teach me to be more responsible."

"Oh." Nyla turned her attention to picking over the fruit in the fruit bowl.

"Yes, well I'm sure you'll both notice each other a little more now that you've been introduced," Raina said, while she made a short grocery list. Afterward, she handed the list to Nyla. "Nyla, would you go to the store with Isaias and pick up these items for me?"

Nyla looked at Raina with a bit of surprise. She really didn't want to go anywhere with this boy. She didn't like that Isaias stared at her like she was some kind of alien. She also didn't like having to explain the what, who, and how of being Keenan Blackman's daughter; besides, he looked like a geek with those dark rimmed glasses he wore. Nyla made a mental note to have a talk with Raina when she got back.

Nyla slid the water bottle back onto the island and hesitated before she took the list from Raina's hand. She wore such a look of discomfort it made Raina feel sorry for her. But Raina thought it was a good idea for her to get to know other kids nearby, especially someone as sweet as Isaias. After Isaias and Nyla walked out, Raina and Naomi smiled at one another, both wishing that Keenan had been there to witness it all.

"You know, he could barely put two sentences together when he laid eyes on Nyla," Naomi said, with a chuckle.

"I know. And did you see the look she gave me?"

"Yes. She was not happy," Naomi chuckled.

"Yes, but it's good for her to meet kids her own age," Raina said. "Besides, they've both been through a lot in their short lives. Getting to know someone else who can relate to some of the stuff she's had to deal with may help her more than even she realizes." Naomi nodded her head.

As Isaias and Nyla drew closer to the car, Isaias quickened his pace and moved ahead to open the door for her.

"What are you doing?" Nyla snapped as she stood a few feet from the car and stared at him.

"I was just opening the door for you."

"I can open the door for *myself.* I ain't weak."

"Oh, I know. It's just that my moms always told me to open the door for a lady."

"Well, I can open my own door, thank you." As she approached the car, Isaias held his hands up in the air and stepped back.

"A'ight. Cool." He turned and walked around to the driver's side. After he slid in and turned the key in the ignition, music blasted from the radio and almost blew both of them into the back seat.

"Sorry about that." Isaias took another quick glance at Nyla and adjusted the volume.

"You mind if I have a smoke?" Nyla asked as she pulled the cigarette carton out of her purse.

"Uh, yeah. I kinda do." Isaias was disappointed when he saw that Nyla smoked. It was such a nasty habit for someone so pretty, he thought.

"Oh. *Sorry,*" she said, with an attitude to hide her embarrassment. Nyla shoved the cigarettes back into her purse. They rode the rest of the way in silence. On the way back, he finally got the nerve to try to start a conversation.

"So where you from?" Nyla didn't answer. Isaias gripped the wheel a little tighter, and looked out of his left view mirror as he tried to think of another way to engage her in conversation.

"What do you think about Ferrell High? We got the number one—"

"Listen," Nyla interrupted, "I don't mean to be

rude, but I'm not good at small talk. Let's just get back to the house."

"You could've fooled me."

"What?" she asked, curtly.

"The part about you not trying to be rude? You may not be trying, but you're doing a good job."

"Whatever." Nyla rolled her eyes and continued staring out of the window. She was more than a little surprised. She hadn't expected geek boy to come back at her like that.

"Yeah, whatever is right." Isaias pressed down on the accelerator in an attempt to hurry and get Nyla home.

Once they arrived back at the house, Isaias pulled into the driveway. Normally, he would've done what his mother had taught him and gotten out to open the door. However, tonight he simply drove into the driveway and waited for Nyla to climb out. He was not going to get burned twice.

Nyla jumped out, grabbed the bags from the back seat and slammed the door. Isaias watched to make sure she got inside safely. Once Nyla was in the house, he turned and backed out of the driveway.

*I told mama girls don't appreciate that stuff,* he thought to himself.

When Nyla returned to the house the first person she saw was Quincy, who grimaced and turned his attention back to the television. Nyla placed the items on the kitchen island and headed down the hall toward her room. She desperately wanted to talk to Gabby. She had not heard from Gabby all week nor had she responded to any of Nyla's text messages. *If I don't hear from her soon, I'm gonna have to pay Ms. Pearl a visit.* She had no idea what terrible discovery she was about to make.

# SIXTEEN

## *VICTORIA PLANS TO HELP*

---

Victoria Devereux was out of breath as she walked into La'Rue. The once abandoned cathedral had been refurbished into an eclectic, ultra-chic restaurant. Victoria loved the regal feel of the place, with its beautiful stained glass windows and architectural details. The piéce de résistance was the antique organ. It had been restored to its former glory and used as the magnificent backdrop to enhance the dramatic décor.

The maî·tre d' greeted her by name. Victoria had held many private luncheons for several clubs and organizations at La'Rue as the First Lady of Lily Baptist Church.

"Good evening, Ms. Devereux. Your party is waiting." He led Victoria through the throng of patrons. It was dinner-time and as usual, very busy.

A quartet played soft jazz in a corner of the dining room. The music was accompanied by laughter floating through the air. The delicate tinkling of glasses mixed with the soft hum of conversation and decadent smells, only added to the elegant atmosphere. It was one of Victoria's favorite places.

As Victoria approached the table, she saw her childhood friend checking out the waiters as they whizzed about. The maî·tre d' pulled out one of the velvet, fuchsia chairs and placed a napkin in Victoria's lap before he handed her a menu.

"Ladies, your server will be with you momentarily." He spoke with a thick, French accent. "If you need anything, please do not hesitate to bring it to my attention."

"I'll bring something to your attention all right," Ramona said, as she licked her lips and blew the ebony skinned Frenchmen a kiss.

"Ramona, stop it!" Victoria glanced around to make sure no one saw her friend's public display of lust.

"Girl, please. Loosen up. Nobody saw me and to tell you the truth, that was PG. Nowadays that wouldn't even raise an eyebrow."

Victoria nodded her head. "Yes, sad but true."

"Ooo, Vicki I'm so glad you chose this place. I've wanted to come here ever since they opened." Ramona marveled at the richness of the purple, velvet drapes that hung from the ten-foot windows. "It's so...chi, chi, as my granddaughter would say." When Victoria didn't respond, Ramona knew something was wrong. They had been friends since they were children, before Victoria became first lady and started keeping company with what Ramona considered "stiff necked" women, who liked to pass judgment on everyone. Nevertheless, their friendship had remained intact, so much so that Ramona could always tell when something was bothering her. Like now… one look at Victoria confirmed Ramona's suspicions. She reached across the table and held Victoria's hand.

"Want to talk about it?" Victoria closed her eyes and took a deep breath.

"Lola's back."

"She is?" Ramona sat straight up, releasing Victoria's hand. "I mean, I thought she would come for the funeral, but when I didn't see her there I assumed she'd decided not to come."

"Yes, well she's here and I think she may stay for a while. You know, ever since Reverend's funeral, she avoids the actual ceremony like the plague."

"Mmm, yes, I remember," Ramona replied, sitting with her hand propped under her chin.

"She was at Raina's house when we arrived from the cemetery," Victoria added.

"So how are things going?" Ramona knew about all the drama that had transpired over the years between Victoria and her oldest daughter.

"Well, she stayed with Lloyd and Jessica for a while, and now she's staying with Raina. We haven't really spent much time together."

"Okay. That's a good thing, right?"

"Hello." Both Victoria and Ramona looked up into a fresh-faced young waitress.

"My name is Monica and I'll be your server this

evening. Would you ladies like to start your order with a drink?"

"Yes, and we would also like to go ahead and place our entrée order." The two of them ordered quickly, handed the menus back to the waitress and she quickly disappeared.

"Okay, so let's go back. If the two of you haven't had any run-ins yet, what's the problem? And how is Raina holding up?"

Victoria cleared her throat and stole a quick glance around the room before she spoke. "Well to tell you the truth, Raina is doing well, considering the recent chain of events."

"What events? What's going on?" Ramona took another sip of her now half-empty glass of wine.

"Well it appears that Keenan has a daughter."

"What?!" Ramona almost choked.

"Yes. She showed up at the house during the repast."

"Come again?" Ramona was shaking her head to make certain that she'd heard Victoria correctly.

"After we'd all gotten back from the burial site, this young girl showed up at the house looking for Keenan. She had no idea that Keenan was dead."

"What did she want?"

"Aren't you listening? She was looking for her father. And Lloyd confirmed that Keenan had also been looking for her. She's Keenan's daughter, Ramona."

"Oh my God, Vicky!" Ramona gasped. "What in the world?! I mean, where did she come from? Who's her mother? How did she find out about him?" Victoria held up both hands.

"I don't know. I haven't gotten all the details but..."

"Excuse me, ladies. I have your salads." This waiter was different from the first.

He set the salads in front of each of them. Both women stared at each other.

"Pepper?" The waiter asked.

"No. No thank you," Victoria responded, as she smoothed the napkin that lay across her lap.

"Is there anything else I can get you all?"

"Yes. Bring us a bottle of this honey," Ramona replied, as she gulped the last of her wine.

"With pleasure," the waiter said as he retreated.

"The girl has been in foster care for most of her life," Victoria continued. "She said she was taken there after her adopted parents were killed in a car accident."

"Oh my gosh." Ramona leaned back in her seat, then, suddenly leaned forward again. "So how in the world do y'all know for sure that she's Keenan's daughter? I mean, don't they have to do a blood test to determine that?" Ramona asked.

"Yes. The test has already been done. I told you Lloyd confirmed everything. Apparently, Keenan got an anonymous tip that he'd fathered a daughter and he'd been searching for her for the past year."

"What!" Ramona said, as she held a forkful of her salad in mid-air, inches away from her mouth. She shook her head, trying to make sense of it all. "Wait a minute." Ramona sat upright again. "Who in the world would have sent him an anonymous tip? I mean, the only other person that would know would have to be... the mother!" They said in unison.

"So where is she? She obviously wanted Keenan to find the child. She probably figured that a detective would have the means to do it."

"Yes. But no one has come forward to claim her."

"Where's the girl staying?"

"You know my child, the one that's always out to save everyone in the universe, took her in." Victoria stabbed at her salad.

"She's staying with Raina? Are you kidding me?"

"I know, I know. I told Raina that I didn't think it was a good idea. Especially with all she has to deal with."

"And, let me guess. She said that that's what Keenan would've wanted."

"You hit the nail on the head," Victoria said, and took a small bite of her food.

"All right, ladies, here are your entrees." A third server said as he stood over them with the steaming plates. Since they had barely finished their salads, he allowed them time to make room before he placed the plates down in front of each of them.

"Is there anything else you require?" he asked.

"Wine." Ramona spoke up. "We really need that wine, I ordered it a while ago."

"My apologies, mademoiselle. I will have that to you right away." He disappeared and was back within a matter of minutes pouring their wine.

"Thank you. I think that will be all," Victoria spoke making a quick appraisal of the table. The server bowed slightly before stepping away.

Ramona took a sip of wine before she continued.

"Okay. Didn't you say that Lola was also staying at Raina's?"

"Yes. Which is why I really feel like it's just too much."

"Well, maybe that's a good thing. At least Lola can help Raina with the kids."

"I don't know, Ramona. Having Nyla there may just send Lola into a tailspin."

"Really? Why? Oh... You mean because of the..."

"Exactly. It'll just bring up old memories about the baby. That issue has been long buried and I don't want to have to deal with it ever again." Victoria took a sip of wine.

"I hear you. Has she said anything to you about it?"

"No, not directly, but even though she puts up a tough front, I can see the longing in her. It breaks my heart. Sometimes I find myself wondering if we did the right thing."

"Listen to me, Victoria. You can't do that to yourself. We both know that you did what you thought was best. If you start to question yourself now, you'll drive yourself crazy."

"I know. But...."

"But what?"

"Afterward, she was never the same."

"No one ever is after bringing another life into the world. Giving a child up is a difficult decision, at best. And when you're not one hundred percent certain about it, it can haunt you. Trust me. I know what I'm talking about." Ramona took another sip of her wine. "A mother never forgets," Ramona said, mostly to herself as she stared into her glass.

"Well, I've got to find some way to help ease the pain for both of my daughters."

"What are you going to do?" Ramona asked, back from wherever she had gone moments before.

"I don't know. Maybe I'll try to locate the biological mother. Then if I can get them reunited, Raina can concentrate on her own family and Lola won't start dwelling on the past."

"Whoa! Slow down Vicky. Don't do anything foolish. Maybe you shouldn't get involved."

"How can you say that? How can I not? What kind of mother would I be if I didn't try to help my children?"

"But that's just it, Vicky. They're not children anymore. They're grown women."

Victoria didn't hear her friend. She had barely touched her dinner. A million thoughts ran through her mind.

"I gotta go, Ramona. I'm sorry. I just..."

"Hold on for a minute. You need to calm down. I of all people understand that you want to help and that you mean well, but this is a very delicate situation."

"Don't you think I'm aware of that," Victoria bristled.

"Okay, okay don't shoot the messenger. All I'm saying, Victoria, is please be careful. I'll be praying for you and the girls."

"Thank you." Victoria dug into her purse and withdrew money to take care of the check. She placed it on the table along with her napkin. "I'll call you later, okay?"

"Okay," Ramona said as she reached up and hugged her friend. "Remember what I said."

"I will." Victoria made her way back outside into the blistering wind. March had come in like a lion. The wind whipped under her skirt and through her perfectly coiffed hair. Victoria was so distracted she barely felt the cold.

She was determined to help her girls. What she didn't realize was that her efforts would, once again, take the family on a journey from which they might never recover.

# SEVENTEEN

## SHE'S A SURVIVOR

Another week had passed and Nyla still hadn't heard from Gabby. She knew something was wrong; she could feel it. She was determined to get over to Ms. Pearl's to find out what was going on. Nyla stood at the kitchen sink and stared into space as she dried the dinner dishes. Moments later Lola swept into the kitchen from the garage and noticed Nyla's blank expression.

"Oh, hi Nyla. Look who I found in the driveway," Lola said, followed closely by Lloyd.

Nyla gave them a small smile.

"Hello," she said, her voice barely audible.

"Hello. I see they got you on kitchen duty," Lloyd said, as he stood by the door.

"Yeah, we all have a chore list." Nyla looked down into the sink. She still felt uneasy around

Lloyd. Lola sat on one of the barstools to remove her boots.

"So Lloyd, what's going on in the criminal system?"

"You mean the Justice system."

"No, no," Lola held up her index finger. "I mean, criminal system because we all know..."

"Don't start, Lola."

Raina walked into the kitchen from upstairs.

"Hey. I thought I heard voices down here."

"And where have you been, stranger?" Raina asked her sister as she gave her a hug.

"I've been working on a few things. Oh by the way, thanks for letting me borrow your car."

"No problem. But inquiring minds would like to know, are the things you're working on top secret?"

"No. It's nothing like that. You know how I am about stuff. I'll let you know when I iron out some of the kinks."

"Hey, it's mighty quiet around here. Where are the boys?" Lloyd asked, looking around.

"Quincy caught a ride with one of his teammates, so he should be here in a few minutes and Naomi volunteered to take Matthew to soccer practice, which I gladly accepted."

"I see you've got a good helper here," Lloyd nodded toward Nyla.

"Yes, I certainly do. She's been wonderful. So don't feel like you need to stop by every other day to check on us, Lloyd. We know that you and Jess are already outnumbered over there."

"You know you got a point, but y'all are my family too. Besides, I feel better when I can see for myself that you guys are okay. Especially with what I've been dealing with this week down at the station."

"What's going on?" Lola asked, as she picked over the fruit in the fruit bowl to keep her nervous energy from being suspicious.

"I was called in on a case about a young woman who'd been severely beaten and left for dead."

"Oh no," Raina said, covering her mouth.

"Yeah. And what's weird is that her guardian doesn't seem to want to cooperate. I mean, she's been at the hospital every day but when we ask her specific questions about the young lady she draws a blank. Either she doesn't know or she's afraid to answer."

"Maybe she's the one who beat her," Lola added, cutting her eyes in Nyla's direction.

"No. Not likely. Ms. Pearl is as genuine as..."

Suddenly, Nyla felt the air in the room evaporate and the glass picture she'd been drying slipped through her fingers and smashed into tiny pieces all over the kitchen floor. Everyone jumped at the sound. They turned and saw Nyla who stood stricken in the middle of broken glass. Raina and Lola jumped to their feet simultaneously and raced toward her.

"Are you all right?! Don't move," Lola said. Nyla didn't appear to hear her.

"Nyla? What's wrong?" Raina asked, as she reached for the broom and gave it to Lola.

"Huh?" Nyla began to blink back tears. They all busied themselves around her. The words, "beaten severely, left for dead," circled her head like fireflies. *Is the Ms. Pearl that Lloyd just mentioned Gabby's Ms. Pearl?* Nyla wanted to disappear. She wanted to scream and escape the horrible possibility of Gabby being the person Lloyd had just described. Nyla gradually emerged from her trance.

"Oh my gosh." She looked around at the floor, still sounding somewhat dazed. "I'm so sorry, Raina."

"Don't worry about it, honey. Accidents happen," Lola said.

"What happened? You look like you saw a ghost," Lloyd said.

"I do?" She looked blankly at Lloyd. "No... I just, um... I picked up the pitcher and it just slipped. I'm really sorry."

"Don't be. Like my sister said accidents happen," Raina said trying to console her, she rubbed Nyla's arm. "Listen, don't worry about it. You go on upstairs, we'll clean this up."

Nyla nodded and carefully stepped over the glass. She could hear her heart beating in her ears. *No wonder I haven't been able to reach Gabby. No! There's got to be another reason. Gabby could be pretty flaky. She probably just lost her phone.*

*Yeah, that's it.* She held her arm around her stomach in an effort to calm herself, as she walked toward her room. She didn't know what was going on, but she knew she would surely find out tomorrow.

Nyla remembered Gabby had mentioned that Ms. Pearl and her husband owned The Little Corner Store. She sat down at the laptop she had in her room and Googled it. She got the exact location and address. Now all she had to do was figure out how and when she could disappear without anyone noticing.

❧ ❧ ❧ ❧

The next morning, when the school bus stopped at its last stop in the neighborhood, Nyla went into action, rushing to the front of the bus.

"Excuse me. I left my homework, I gotta go back home and get it."

"I'm sorry, but if you get off, I can't wait for you." The large lady with what appeared to be permanent red splotches on her pale cheeks responded flatly.

"Okay. I'll just get my mom to take me." Nyla quickly exited the bus, threw her book bag on her back and pretended to head toward her house. After the bus passed Nyla turned and walked through a patch of nearby trees. She didn't see Isaias in the car behind the school bus as she headed for the city bus stop, but he saw her.

"Where is she going?" Isaias knew that this couldn't be good. But no matter how rude she'd been to him, he owed it to Mr. B to look out for her. So against his better judgment, he followed the city bus.

Nyla stepped off the bus at the Little Five Points station and walked the rest of the way. She pulled a cigarette out of her backpack, lit it, and inhaled deeply, allowing the smoke to course through her lungs. Although spring was in the air, there was still crispness in the early morning breeze. Nyla pulled her brand new, red hoodie over her head and continued down the brick sidewalk.

As she made her way down the street, Nyla admired all the funky clothing stores and coffee shops.

*I really like this vibe. I'm stuck in boring suburbia while Gabby is living the life over here.* She made a note that it would be a cool place for her and Gabby to hang out once she found her and gave her a piece of her mind.

Nyla took another deep drag of her cigarette, read the street numbers and continued down the block. As soon as she rounded the corner, she saw it. The Little Corner Store, exactly as Gabby had described. It was a one-story, brick building and the closer Nyla moved toward the store, the more anxious she became.

Over the last twenty-four hours, Nyla had convinced herself that Gabby was not the badly beaten girl Lloyd had spoken of yesterday. *Gabby's probably studying. As soon as I find Ms. Pearl, I'll find her and give her a piece of my mind.* Before she smashed the cigarette into the ground, Nyla stood staring at the storefront. She felt butterflies in the pit of her stomach as she pulled the door, and a large cow-bell rang, announcing her. At first Nyla stood near the door and took in the contents of the space. The store had a little bit of everything and everything, except the groceries, was second-hand.

"I'll be right there!" A voice called out from the back of the store.

Nyla began to leisurely walk through the aisles and she could see why Gabby loved it so. To take something old and turn it into something new was so Gabby. Ms. Pearl walked out of the back room.

"Whew! I hope I didn't keep you waiting too long." Ms. Pearl said as she waddled toward Nyla, wiping her hands on a towel. "I was taking some cookies outta the oven. Now, how can I help you?"

Pearl had been speaking to Nyla's back, as she stood frozen. *Man, did I do the right thing by coming here? What if she don't even remember me?* And just as quickly as the doubt materialized, Nyla realized that none of that mattered. She needed to find out about her friend.

"Hello? Can I help you find something?" Nyla turned around and removed her hoodie. Pearl gasped.

"Oh, my God. It's you!" Nyla gave her a nervous smile and before she knew it, Pearl had swept her up into a bear hug.

"Peter! Come here! Look who's here!" she hugged and rocked Nyla like she was a long-lost relative.

A tall, tan man with salt-and-pepper hair and mustache hurried through the back curtain.

"What is it?!" he looked around for the cause of his wife's excitement.

"Look! It's her! It's Gabby's friend."

Now he rocked back on his heels and gave a relieved nod as he peered down at the two of them. After Ms. Pearl released Nyla, she saw tears well up in her eyes. Nyla knew, instinctively, that there was cause for concern. Nyla's legs began to tremble.

"Ms. Pearl? Where's Gabby? Is she all right?"

"Child, we've been trying to find you."

"Why?" Nyla started to panic. Pearl got choked up and her husband answered.

"Gabby's in the hospital. Someone beat her up pretty bad."

Nyla felt as if someone had thrown a brick into the center of her chest.

"Is she still..." Nyla couldn't bring herself to say it.

"Yes. She's alive, but like I said, she's in pretty bad shape."

"I gotta see her. Where is she?"

The cow bell rang again. Nyla's entire body began to shake. Gabby was the girl Lloyd had talked about. Nyla's mind raced with thoughts of how this could've happened. *Has Tyrone really found out where we are? That's impossible! We left no traces.*

"Just a minute. We'll be right with you," Pearl called out as she wiped her eyes.

"Here, Peter. Take her to the kitchen." Just as Pearl handed Nyla off to Peter, Isaias rounded the aisle and became alarmed by what he saw. By the looks of things, his earlier premonition had become a reality.

"Hey! Leave her alone." Isaias rushed toward the three of them.

"Excuse me?" Pearl asked, confused.

"Take your hands off of her or I'll... I'll call the cops!" Isaias yelled at Peter.

Peter looked at his wife.

"Sweetheart, is she a friend of yours?" Ms. Pearl asked.

Isaias hadn't really considered them friends but he guessed that at the moment, he was the closest thing she had to one.

"Yes. So leave her alone!"

Nyla regained her composure. When she turned and saw Isaias, she became angry.

"What are you doing here?"

"I uh... saw you get off of the bus and I followed you. What are *you* doing here? Does Ms. Raina know you..." Nyla broke away from Mr. Peter and grabbed Isaias by his jacket. She pulled him a few feet away from Ms. Pearl and her husband.

"Listen. I don't know why you followed me, but you need to leave. I can handle myself."

"It doesn't look like it to me. Why were you crying? Did they do something to you?"

"Not that it's any of your business, but no." Nyla peered back over her shoulder.

"I really could use some space right now, so if you could please just go I—

"I can't. I can't leave you here. What if something happens and they ask me why I left, huh?"

"Are you kidding me? We barely know each other."

"Yeah. But I knew your dad." He pushed his glasses up higher on his nose. "And I gotta feeling that he wouldn't want me to leave you."

Isaias stood a few inches taller than Nyla. His complexion was pecan-tan and he wore his coarse, black hair at least three inches long. He would often twist the ends; his attempt to lock his hair. He was slender with an athletic build and if you looked close, you could see the remnants of a mustache, sprouting on his upper lip.

Nyla rolled her eyes. *I can't believe the nerve of*

*this guy.*

"Okay. Fine. If you want to be a hero, I need you to take me to the hospital to see my sister."

"Who? You have a sister?"

"She's hurt and she needs me," Nyla turned toward Ms. Pearl.

"Where is she?"

"She's at Grady Hospital. I've been going down there every night after we close shop but if y'all are driving, we could just catch a ride together."

Nyla turned to Isaias again. "You said you wanted to help me? *This* is how you can help."

Isaias knew he should call his parents but there was no time. He also knew, from the few encounters he'd had with Nyla that she was a pretty strong-willed person. If he didn't take her, she was going anyway. He nixed the idea to call his parents, for the moment, and agreed to take them to the hospital.

"Okay. Let's go," he said, sounding a bit uncertain.

"Okay. Peter, honey, will you get my jacket please?" Peter was already half way down the hall before she finished her request.

"I'll be there after I close the shop," he said, helping his wife into her jacket. Minutes later Isaias, Nyla and Ms. Pearl were seated in Isaias' Jeep headed down I-20.

※ ※ ※ ※

The ride to the hospital was quiet. Nyla sat in the front seat. She leaned her head against the window and watched the highway slip past as they drove. The coolness from the glass against her forehead had a calming effect. Ms. Pearl directed Isaias from the back seat.

They parked the car and Ms. Pearl led them to the ICU, where Gabby had been for the past week and a half. Isaias took a seat in the waiting area as Nyla and Ms. Pearl made their way back towards Gabby's room. Nyla almost fainted at the first sight of Gabby. She was hooked up to so many tubes and machinery Nyla had to take a step back. She was completely unprepared. She held her hand over her mouth to keep from screaming as tears streamed down her cheeks.

"No, no, no." She shook her head and turned away; she didn't want to face the reality of how and why this happened. Ms. Pearl grabbed her and held her until she calmed down.

"Listen baby, she's going to be all right," Ms. Pearl whispered in Nyla's ear. "She's a fighter, just like you. And right now, you have to be strong for her. You understand?" Nyla couldn't speak she simply squeezed her eyes closed and nodded.

"Now, pull yourself together and let her know you're here for her."

Nyla wiped her tears, although it seemed like a futile effort. The more she swatted them away, the faster they came. She took a deep breath.

"Oh god, Gabby," Nyla started, as she cautiously approached the bed.

"Is this her sister?" A short, round nurse who was there recording Gabby's vitals, asked Ms. Pearl. Both Nyla and Ms. Pearl nodded yes.

"She's been in and out of consciousness, but every time she wakes up, she's saying something like, by or sky. Can't really make much of it at all."

It was almost too much. Nyla's breathing became erratic and she had to be led to a nearby chair before she hit the floor. She sat and tried to catch her breath. She held on to Ms. Pearl's hand for dear life.

Finally when she had regained her composure she rose and moved timidly toward her friend.

"Gabby, I'm here, okay?" she said, as she searched to recognize her friend beyond all the swelling and bruises.

"Hey, Gab." She gently lifted Gabby's hand into her own. "It's Ny. I've uh, been trying to reach you, so when you didn't answer I decided to come and see what was up."

She looked over her shoulder at Ms. Pearl and the nurse. Ms. Pearl motioned for her to continue.

"I saw these um... really crazy clothing stores and some cool places for us to hang out when you get outta here."

There was no response. Nyla didn't know what to do. She was scared and confused. She knew it had to have been Tyrone who did this. But how could he have found her? And if he found Gabby then she was next. She became overwhelmed with fear. Still holding Gabby's hand, Nyla lowered her head; her small frame shook. Just as she was about to pull her hand away, she felt it. Gabby squeezed her hand. It took Nyla's breath away.

"Oh, my gosh. She squeezed my hand! She did! She squeezed it!"

"I'm here Gabby!" she said excitedly. "Can you do it again?"

208

It took a few minutes but once again, there it was; a small squeezing of the hand. Just enough to let them all know that she was fighting her way back.

≈≈≈≈

Isaias had been sitting in the waiting area and checked the time on his cell phone for what felt like the hundredth time. School would be out soon and his parents would be notified that he had not been in attendance. He had to think of something that would minimize his punishment for doing the wrong thing for the right reasons.

Ms. Pearl emerged from Gabby's room to see her husband sitting in the waiting room along with Isaias. Nyla soon followed. Time was ticking by quickly but Nyla didn't want to leave Gabby. She approached Isaias and tilted her head, letting him know she wanted to talk to him privately. Isaias rose and wiped his sweaty palms on his pant leg. They walked to the other side of the room.

"Hey, listen. You should probably head on back home now. I need to hang out around here for a while."

"So, is your sister okay? Did she tell you what happened?" Nyla looked confused.

"Sister?"

"Yeah, you said she was your sister, right?" Isaias asked, with a hint of suspicion.

"Of course she's my sister," Nyla responded defensively. "And no, she's not in any condition to talk. She's in pretty bad shape and that's exactly why I don't want to leave her. And if you could just do me a favor and not mention this to Raina, I would appreciate it." She knew if he told Raina, the questions would come. Nyla didn't want to deal with that right now.

"So I know you can't imagine me having any kind of street smarts but something just isn't adding up. Q told me the whole story about you and his dad. He said you came into town alone, but... now you have a sister that stays right across town. I thought you didn't have any relatives." Nyla's eyes became narrow slits.

"Why is it any concern of yours? I don't have to answer to you." She spat the words out.

"That's true. I just thought it would make you feel better to have someone to talk to. To really talk to and not have to try to cover your tracks. Nyla, I'm no dummy and I know from experience, the more lies you tell now, the more lies you're gonna have to tell. And even though I know you're not being a hundred percent honest, I can't leave you here with people I don't know."

"What difference does it make if you know them or not? You barely know me and I don't need a babysitter."

"And what am I suppose to tell Ms. Raina?" Isaias leaned back and shoved both of his hands into his front pockets.

Nyla continued to try and convince Isaias to go home without her when Lloyd walked in. She was more than taken aback, but she quickly guessed that Isaias had phoned him.

Lloyd walked over to where they stood. "Hey, guys. I got here as fast as I could." They both fell silent.

"Okay. What's this all about?" He looked from Isaias to Nyla and back again. Neither one of them said a word. Lloyd waited for a response.

"Hey listen, what's up? You call and ask me to come to the hospital, tell me it's an emergency and when I get here, you become mute? Come on... tell me what's going on?"

"Nyla's sis—"

"Friend!" Nyla interjected. Isaias was stunned as Nyla proceeded to explain to Lloyd about her "friend."

"Yeah... well, I hadn't heard from her in a while so I went to her house and that's when Ms. Pearl told me that she was in the hospital." Nyla avoided eye contact with Isaias.

"Wait a minute. Ms. Pearl? Is your friend the same young lady I told Raina and Lola about yesterday?" Lloyd asked, perplexed.

"Oh, I don't... uh, know. I didn't hear what you said to Lola and Raina. I just hadn't heard from her so—"

"You didn't hear? You were standing right there when I told them." Nyla shrugged.

"I don't know. I guess. I wasn't really listening to your conversation." Lloyd nodded. He didn't believe a word she said.

"Mmm-hmm... Okay. Tell me how you know this girl, Nyla."

Nyla didn't answer at first. She hated that Lloyd was there and she hated that she had to answer to him—or anyone for that matter.

"She's just a friend. Someone I met on the bus and we said we'd keep in touch. When I found out what happened, I came to see her."

"Okay. Ms. Pearl told me that she also met Gabrielle on the bus and that she was with another girl. Was that you?"

"Yeah, I guess. I mean, I didn't know her before that. We just kinda hit it off. So I guess that's why Ms. Pearl thought we were together." Isaias couldn't believe what he was hearing. Not only had Nyla told him something completely different, she said it all with a straight face.

"Did you see her with anyone else on the bus or at the bus terminal? A boyfriend or a father figure perhaps? Anyone?"

Nyla shook her head. "No."

"Well, did she mention who she was coming to see?"

"She may have said something about coming to see a boyfriend or something, but I can't really remember," Nyla lied. Lloyd was totally perplexed and agitated.

"Well I guess we're just going to have to wait until she regains consciousness before we can get more answers." Lloyd had almost forgotten Isaias was there. He looked at Isaias. "Okay, and how is it that you're here?"

"Well, I drove her. She was really concerned and I didn't think she was that familiar with the city so, I offered to drive her."

"Do your parents know that you're here?"
"No sir."
"Does Raina know you're here?" he asked Nyla.
Nyla gave Isaias a death stare.
"Well, does she?"

212

"No," she mumbled.

"I see. Come over here and let me talk to you for a minute." Lloyd placed his hand on Nyla's shoulder and led her a few steps away from Isaias. "Now, I know you're not use to answering to anyone, Nyla. You've probably been coming and going as you please for some time now. But things are different now. You have people who are concerned about you. You can't just take off without asking permission."

"I'm not a little kid."

"In the state of Georgia, that's exactly what you are. Besides that, it's a matter of respect. No one is saying that you can't come see your friend, but when Raina gets an email from the school that you weren't there today, what do you think is going to happen?"

There was no response.

"She's going to go into panic mode. Now is that fair to her?"

"Nobody asked her to ask me to live with her."

"Come on, Nyla. No one asked and no one had to ask. She did it because of the kind of person she is. Still, is it fair that you would disregard her by not informing her of your plans?"

"I thought she might say no and I really wasn't tryin' to hear that."

"But she may have said yes. She may have said, 'Sure, I'll take you myself '."

"But I don't need her to take me anywhere. I can get around on my own."

Lloyd took a deep breath. "It's not about what you need or don't need. She's responsible for you.

And I know that's probably hard for you to wrap you head around but, you've got to know that this ain't cool."

Nyla's response was a shrug of the shoulders as she looked off down the hospital corridor.

"Listen, it's an adjustment, I know. But it's an adjustment for everyone involved. You're not the only one who has to change the way you do things, okay?"

Now, it was Nyla's turn to take a deep breath.

"Yeah, okay. I guess I should've asked."

"There you go." Lloyd placed his hand on the back on her shoulders and turned her toward Isaias.

"Let's go say goodbye to your friend and I'll take you home." Nyla stopped in her tracks.

"Uh, if you don't mind, I'd rather say goodbye alone." Lloyd was a little surprised but not much. He knew there was something she wasn't telling him.

"Okay, sure."

Nyla made her way back down the hall and quietly entered Gabby's room. The machines were humming and the monitors were beeping to their own rhythm. A chill ran down her spine as she approached Ms. Pearl, who had her head bent as she prayed.

"Hey," she whispered.

"Oh, hey baby," she said as she raised her head.

"Anymore progress?" Nyla asked, looking on at her friend.

"No, nothing," Pearl responded, grimly. Minutes passed as they sat, each lost in her own thoughts.

"Nyla?"

"Yes, Ms. Pearl?"

"Do you think the man y'all ran away from did this to Gabrielle?" Nyla pulled her jacket tighter around her body. She didn't know how to answer.

"I hope not, Ms. Pearl. I certainly hope not." She didn't want her to worry.

"Well, if he did, he must be the devil himself. Now I see why y'all were so desperate to escape. You did the right thing. But why would he come here and do something like this?" Nyla thought about the two thousand dollars that she and Gabby had split when they left. But her only response was another shrug of the shoulders.

"Maybe it *wasn't* him. Maybe she was just in the wrong place at the wrong time." Even as her mouth formed the words, Nyla knew better. She knew Tyrone's M.O. He let Gabby live just to send Nyla a message.

❧ ❧ ❧ ❧

On the drive home, Nyla realized it was time for her to leave. She didn't want to go. Even with all the rules, she loved being in her father's house. She loved being around the things she was sure he'd once touched and that had been a part of his everyday life. But now she would have to run again because she was sure if Tyrone caught her, she might not fare as well as Gabby. He would probably kill her.

Seeing Gabby had changed her plans. At first she had balked at the idea of finding her biological mother. But now she thought that perhaps it wasn't a bad idea. She would need somewhere to hide out until it was safe. Nyla made up her mind she would leave as soon as Gabby was better. Until then, she would just have to lay low.

# EIGHTEEN

## OIL & WATER

---

The next evening Raina sat at Keenan's desk with several file folders in front of her. She'd studied them for days, trying to piece together her shattered life. Although she was still a little groggy from the sleeping pills, Raina knew she needed to sort through some of his papers.

As she scanned the documents, Raina felt her anxiety intensify. *How in the world am I going to handle all of this alone? And what about helping Nyla? Lord, what have I gotten myself into?* Raina's head began to pound. She massaged her temples and then reached for her purse and began searching for relief. When she felt the small, plastic bottle, her shoulders became less tense almost immediately. She quickly popped one of the small pills into her mouth. Her doctor had prescribed the Prozac to help

217

with her anxiety and depression. He had also prescribed sleeping pills. For the past few weeks Raina had taken them both with regularity. She told herself that it was just to get her through the next few days. As each day rolled into the next, Raina became more dependent on the calm that both the Prozac and sleeping pills provided. She decided that until she could cope on her own, she would use the help she was given.

Raina looked up when she heard a light knock. She saw Lola through the French glass door and motioned for her to enter.

"Hey you. Whatchu' doing?" Lola asked as she entered.

"Oh, just trying to get my life in order."

"Oh yeah?"

"Yes. And girl I thank God that Keenan was so meticulous with all of our family papers. I've been able to pick up where he left off with the bills. Now all I have to worry about is how I'm going to make enough money, in this economy, to pay them all."

"He had insurance, right?"

"Yes. He also had a pension, which I'll receive payments from, but I need to make that last as long as possible. And while I would love to keep this house," she said, looking around the office at all the memories, "I don't know how I'll do that and keep up with everything else."

"So you're thinking of selling? You don't really want to do that do you?" Lola stood with her arms crossed in front of her.

Raina exhaled forcefully and leaned back against the soft leather of the chair. "Well, yes and no. I don't know what to do. I don't want to make another drastic change in the boys' lives. And I know it might sound silly, but sometimes I can feel Keenan's spirit here.

Lola's heart was heavy. She saw the pain etched in her sister's face and wished she could take it away. She wished she had the words that would make it all better. "That doesn't sound silly at all. I mean, you both created something very special here."

"But... I'm afraid if I stay, I won't be able to...um....I don't know, Lola. I just don't know." Lola came around the desk and put her arms around her sister.

"Well there's no rush to make any decisions now. Eventually, the time will come and you'll know what to do."

"Yes," Raina said as she patted Lola's arm. "I hope you're right." She wiped her eyes. "Besides, by the time that happens, maybe the real estate market will have come back around."

"So will you list it yourself?" Lola asked. Raina raised her brows.

"Of course. Who could sell my house any better than me?"

"I don't know, I mean, I know you've been selling real estate off-and-on for a while, but I just thought it would be hard to you know, sell *this* house. You said it was you and Keenan's forever home." Raina looked around again.

"Yes well, there were two parts to that equation and now there's only one. It'll be hard, but no harder than what I've already had to face." They were both silent for a few minutes then Lola glanced down and saw a file with Nyla's name on it.

"What's that?" she nodded toward the file.

"What?" Raina looked down. "Oh, I thought I would try to find out more about Nyla. I was just trying to figure out how I can help her."

Lola's heart pounded in her chest. "Oh? What've you found out so far?"

"Not much of anything," Raina picked up an envelope and placed it on top of the desk. She pulled out the anonymous letter that Kennan had received over a year ago. Lola froze.

"This is the letter that Keenan received that started his search for Nyla. You know, when I read it, it felt like whoever sent this had firsthand knowledge."

"Really? What makes you think that?" Lola asked, as she reached for the letter.

"Well, because it has details that only someone close to the situation would have. I think...."

"What? What do you think?"

"I think this was sent by Nyla's birth mother. I mean, who else would do something like this?" Lola felt the room shift so she steadied herself and sat on the edge of the desk.

"You really think the *birth* mother sent this letter?" Lola asked.

"Yes."

"But why?"

"I don't know. Maybe the guilt was getting to her. Or maybe she was dying and wanted to clear her conscience. I mean, who would put a child up for adoption and not tell the father? I didn't even know that was legal."

"Well Raina, you don't know the situation."

"Yes. I agree," Raina added. "I don't know the situation, but I do know that it was wrong. No matter what, Keenan had a right to know. He had a right to agree or disagree with whether to put the child up for adoption. The fact that neither he nor Nyla were given that option is just wrong. Whoever she is, she was very selfish."

Beads of sweat started to break out on Lola's top lip and forehead as she listened to her sister's harsh words.

"Hey, you okay?" Raina noticed the perspiration and uneasy look on her sister's face.

"Huh? Oh, yeah, I'm fine," Lola waved off Raina's concern. "It's just that, um, I don't know. It may have been something I ate."

"You need me to get you something?" Raina closed the folder as she stood up from the desk.

"No, I'll be okay. Where are the kids, anyway? Shouldn't they be home by now?"

"Actually, Nyla asked me if she could stay after school and go out for the track team."

"Oh yeah?"

"Yes. I got a call from the track and field coach the other day. He asked if I would give Nyla permission to try out for the team. He said she's a natural. And I think that being part of a team will help her adjust to living here. What do you think?"

"Me?"

"Yes you."

"Well I say she's her father's child. I remember

---

when Kenny won the state track championship. Boy, he sure was fast." Lola spoke dreamily. Raina looked confused.

"How did you know he won state?"

"Huh?" Lola asked, as she slowly came out of her trance.

"You said you remembered how Kennan won the State Championship. How did you know that and why did you call him Kenny?"

"Oh." Lola became jittery. "I'm sure you told me," she said, and moved away from the desk.

"No. I don't think I did because it happened way before he and I met."

"Girl, don't be ridiculous." She waved her sister off. "If you didn't mention it, I'm pretty sure I've seen one the gazillion plaques or trophies y'all have around here." Lola motioned around the room. Raina looked around and had to agree.

"Yes. There are quite a few. I've wondered if I should start taking some of them down but..." She inhaled and exhaled slowly. "It feels like I'm erasing him and I just..."

"Nonsense. You could never erase what you and Keenan had. Besides, there's plenty of time to decide what to do about his things, Raina. You gotta stop putting so much stress on yourself."

"I know, but I just don't know if I'm making the right decisions. Like with Nyla."

"Oh, sissy. Now you know I know about making wrong decisions, *okay*?"

Lola had been avoiding Nyla like the plague. She'd made several unsuccessful attempts to try to get closer but each time, she simply froze or made herself look like a complete idiot. She didn't know what to say to her. Besides, she wanted Nyla to know the new and improved Lola Devereux, not the homeless drunk she was.

"But listen, I'm here to help. So, if there..."

"Oh no!" Raina looked at her watch.

"What?! Where's the fire?" Lola looked around as Raina jumped up from behind the desk.

"I forgot that I have to meet with my broker. Listen, Quincy stayed after school with Nyla, but Matthew should be home in a few minutes," Raina said, as she ran around the office, gathering folders and stuffing them into her briefcase. "Could you please do me a huge favor and stay here with Matt until I get back?"

"Not a problem. That's what I'm here for."

"Thanks." She stuffed the last of the paperwork, including Nyla's folder, into her briefcase. Raina was headed out of the office door when she turned to her sister.

"Hey, I'm really glad you're here, but I know you have a job and a life to get back to. So let me know when you need to stop babysitting your little sister, okay?"

"I was going to talk to you about that."

Raina looked at Lola inquisitively.

"Before I left L.A., I put in a request for a sixty-day leave of absence and I found out it was approved. So if you'll have me, I'm yours for a while longer. I even got a gig lined up to sub at the high school."

"Are you serious? *You*, a teacher?" Raina looked at her sister in amazement.

223

"A *substitute.* Let's not get crazy," Lola corrected Raina. "It's only temporary and it'll give me a chance to help you out more with the kids. So… you up for me hanging around here a little while longer?"

"Are you kidding? Having you here is what's going to keep me sane." Raina gave Lola a big hug.

"Okay, gotta run. Take some of that Mylanta for your stomach; it's a miracle worker," Raina said, before she rushed out the door.

"Okay." Lola waved to her sister's retreating back. "Because a miracle is exactly what I need."

🍂🍂🍂🍂

Lola had her head stuck in the refrigerator when she heard the backdoor open and close. "Hey, squirt! Do you want some cookies or ice cream for your after school snack? A little bird told me..."

She stopped dead when she looked up and saw her mother.

"Oh, hi. I thought you were Matthew." Lola's anxiety prickled her spine like a dozen little spiders.

"So I gathered," Victoria placed her purse and keys on the kitchen counter. "You can't really think it's a good idea to give him all of that sugar this early in the day, especially before he sits down to do homework."

"Mother, please don't start," Lola said, as she forcefully closed the refrigerator. Lola could feel her pulse quickening as her body temperature began to rise. Victoria always had that effect on her. No matter how far away she was or how briefly they spoke, any kind of contact with her always made Lola feel small and tense.

Victoria instantly regretted starting off on a bad note. "I'm sorry, Lola. I didn't mean to—"

"Didn't you? If you ask me, you always mean to." She turned her back to Victoria and closed her eyes. She fought to control her temper, but with everything that had been going on, it had become increasingly difficult to quiet the volcano that was about to erupt.

"I mean to what?"

"To belittle me!" Lola turned to face Victoria. "As if I can never do anything right."

"That's not true. It's just that I often disagree with the choices you make."

"But they're *my* choices and they have nothing to do with you."

Victoria crossed her arms. "How can you be as old as you are and still be so naive? Of course your choices affect me. They affect everyone who loves and cares about you."

"You don't love me, Mother. You love the idea of what you want me to be. You want me to be the *perfect* daughter, married to the *perfect* man in your *perfect* little fantasy world."

"Is that what you think? You think that my life is some fantasy? It doesn't feel like any fantasy. I spend most of my time over in that big, old house alone. The only joy I get is to come over here and be with my grandchildren."

"Oh, and I guess the fact that you're alone is also my fault."

"I didn't say that, Lola."

"You didn't have to say it, but you meant it!" Lola slammed the cookie dough down on the counter. Victoria became flustered.

"You're putting words in my mouth and I don't appreciate it."

"You know what I don't appreciate, Mother?" Lola narrowed her eyes as they bore into Victoria. "I don't appreciate us walking around pretending that we like each other. You've made it very clear that you don't approve of the way I've chosen to live my life and that's why I stay away." Lola started to pace.

"Why do you make the kind of decisions you make, Lola? Was I that bad of a mother?"

"It's not about you!"

"Well then who is it about?! Why do you try so hard to keep me at a distance and to make a mess of everything?"

"Oh, now we're getting somewhere!" Lola was completely enraged. "Why don't you just go ahead and say it! It's because of *me* that he's dead!" She stopped pacing and pointed at herself. "We both know that you've felt that way since the day he died! So here's your chance. Let's just clear the air!" Victoria shook her head.

"That's not true."

"It *is* true. If Dad and I had not been arguing then he wouldn't have had the heart attack and died, and you wouldn't be over there in that big house all by yourself." Lola spread her arms for emphasis.

"Is that how you think I feel?"

"Oh come on, Victoria. You don't have to play this game anymore. We both know that you blame me." Before she knew it, Victoria slapped Lola across the face. For a moment, they were both in shock.

"I hope that made you feel better." Lola's voice was laced with venom as she lifted her hand and massaged the side of her face.

"Don't you *ever* disrespect me like that again, Lola Devereux. After all I've done to try and protect you and give you a good life."

"Who are you trying to convince, me or yourself? All you really ever cared about was what other people thought. You didn't do it for me. You did it for the family image." Victoria ignored Lola's statement. Tears welled up in her eyes.

"I'm not perfect, but I tried my best." Her voice cracked. "You don't know what a mother goes through when she tries to shield her children from pain."

"And whose fault is that?" Lola spat the words as if they were a foul taste in her mouth.

"Why don't I know how a mother feels? Did you ever consider that had you given me the chance to raise my own child, I would've known?! Or maybe I wouldn't have been pleading with Dad to tell me where she was? Maybe, just maybe, had you left well enough alone, Dad would still be here and I would know what it feels like to *be* a mother!" Lola's tears fell freely now. She no longer tried to hide her pain. Victoria wanted to reach out to her, to turn back the clock and correct her mistake, but she didn't move. It was all happening just as she'd feared. Nyla's presence had become a reminder of the baby Lola had given up.

Neither noticed Matthew in the doorway until it was too late. Suddenly the air in the room became

thick with regret. They didn't know how long he'd
been standing there or just how much of the
argument he'd heard, but he was clearly upset.
Tears brimmed in his bright, brown eyes, as he
looked at them both.

Lola quickly wiped the tears from her own face
and moved toward her nephew.

"Hey, Matt. I'm sorry you had to see that but you
know, sometimes grown-ups have disagreements.
It's nothing for you to worry about. Right, Mother?"

Victoria nodded in agreement. "Yes. Just a little
disagreement." The words scraped passed the knot
in her throat. "Nothing to be worried about." She
gave an unconvincing smile and Matthew nodded
his head.

"Where's my mom?" he finally asked.

"She had a meeting to go to. I was about to make
you a snack. You want some cookies?" Lola
purposefully avoided looking in her mother's
direction.

"No thanks. I'm just gonna go to my room and
start on my homework, if it's okay." They both
nodded.

"Yes, of course. That's fine, Matt. Just let me
know if you need anything, okay?" Lola said, as
embarrassment and guilt started to set in.

"Okay." Matthew dashed up the back staircase,
leaving both ladies to reflect on the scene that had
just taken place.

Victoria felt horrible. She had no idea that Lola
thought she blamed her for the Reverend's death.
And as for the adoption, at the time, Victoria had
pushed for the adoption but they had all agreed that

it was for Lola's own good. She was so young and had barely known the young man that impregnated her. It was for the best. However, right now, Victoria felt heaviness in her spirit. It felt as if someone had placed a large boulder around her neck.

"I'm sorry," she whispered. "I never meant to... I'm so, sorry." It was all Victoria could say before she fumbled for her keys and stumbled out of the door. Her purse dangled from her hand as she walked to her car. Lola watched her mother's retreat. From the window she could see her with her body slightly tilted forward. She looked as if she was about to tip over. Lola watched until Victoria backed out of the driveway and pulled away.

"You're not the only one who's sorry, Mother. You're not the only one."

# NINETEEN

## JUST WHAT THE DOCTOR ORDERED

---

Lola pushed through the large glass doors to Dr. Eli's office with unexpected urgency. Hazel had just thrown her purse over her shoulder, as Sara, the new associate, placed yet another file folder onto the already staggering pile atop Hazel's desk.

"Is he in?" Lola asked, in a huff as she approached Hazel's desk.

"Excuse me?" Hazel was surprised by Lola's sudden appearance.

"Is Doctor Eli here? I really need to see him."

"Did you have an appointment?" Hazel asked, already knowing the answer. Lola looked at the plump receptionist and fought to maintain her composure. After the run-in with her mother, Lola had driven around the city for hours. When she finally stopped, Lola found herself in front of Dr.

Eli's office.

"Hazel? It is Hazel, right?" She asked with a furrowed brow.

"Yes." Hazel answered as she surveyed Lola's tousled appearance.

"Hazel, you and I both know that I don't have an appointment. But I've just been through some very heavy *shit* and before I do something I'll regret, I need to speak with Doctor Eli. So I'll ask you again. Is. He. Here?!" Lola's eyes bore into Hazel's with one brow raised. Hazel stole a quick glance at Sara, hoping for some intervention.

"Um, yes, hi, Ms. Devereux. I believe Dr. Eli has another appointment," Sara said as she made her way around the receptionist desk and stood directly in front of Lola. But if you really need to speak with someone, I'd be more than happy to lend my ear." Lola had not even noticed her before now.

"I'm sorry. Do I know you?"

"Oh, my name is Dr. Sara Carter," she said extending her hand towards Lola. Lola scanned the fiery red headed beauty while Sara continued. "I'm an associate here and I can see that you're upset; I'd like to help if I could." Lola hesitated before taking Sara's hand.

"Well, Doctor Carter, it's a long story and since he's already familiar with my situation, I would feel more comfortable talking to Dr. Eli."

"Yes, I understand; but while he is currently here in the office, he's just about to leave for another appointment. We can just go down the hall to my office and talk, if you'd like." Sara motioned toward the opposite end of the corridor. Lola hesitated for the second time. She had only seen Sara in passing, but she reasoned since she was a part of Dr. Eli's staff she couldn't be too bad. Besides, this couldn't wait.

"Okay, sure." Lola was still shaken from her earlier confrontation. Just as they were about to head down the hall, Dr. Eli's office door swung open.

"Oh good. You're still here. Listen, before you leave, I need you to fax these papers over to the recovery center and—"

He stopped when he noticed Lola, Sara, and Hazel staring back at him. Lola looked as though she'd just been in a fight.

"Lola? I mean, Ms. Devereux? Did I... did we have an appointment?" He looked over at Hazel.

"Not to worry, Doctor. Lola and I were just about to have a little chat." Sara spoke before Lola or Hazel could respond.

"With all due respect, Dr. Carter, Ms. Devereux is my client. I'll take it from here."

Sara was taken aback. She hadn't been with the practice very long and didn't want to appear unprofessional. Sara admired Dr. Eli's passion, not to mention his rugged good looks. She knew he was passionate about each of his clients, but she was beginning to wonder if this particular one wanted more from him than even *he* realized. Lola didn't notice the stunned look on Sara's face before she turned and left both ladies standing in the reception area.

"Have a good evening, ladies," Jeremiah said, as he held the door open so that Lola could enter.

The hairs on the back of Sara's neck stood at attention when she saw the way he looked at Lola, as if he wanted to breathe life back into her. *But at what cost?* Sara needed to make sure he wouldn't cross the line. She had her own plans for Jeremiah Eli.

"Doctor. What about your other appointment?" Hazel asked before he had a chance to disappear behind the office door.

"Yes. Please call with my apologies. Tell them I've had an emergency come up and reschedule the meeting." Afterward, he turned and followed Lola into his office. Sara attempted, unsuccessfully, to hide her embarrassment. Her pale skin was still three shades of red after Dr. Eli had closed his office door.

Hazel shook her head as she considered whether it had been wise for Graham to bring this wilting flower into the doctor's healing rays. He was one of the best at what he did, but he was also a man.

"Well, okay. I guess he can handle it from here. Goodnight, Hazel." Sara wore an awkward smile as she straightened her back, tossed her hair over her shoulder and headed to her office.

"Goodnight, Dr. Carter," Hazel said, with a little smirk. She'd suspected that Sara's admiration for Dr. Eli was a bit more personal than professional. Now she was sure of it.

꽃 꽃 꽃 꽃

It had been almost a month since Lola had had a drink but after the scene with Victoria, she wasn't sure if she could hold it together without one.

"This is just too hard," Lola spoke, as she paced

the floor. "I don't know if I can do this. I don't know if I can handle all of this. She thinks that she can still control me, but she can't. I'm not sixteen anymore." She stopped and pointed at her chest. "Do I look like I'm a child?"

"No. You most certainly do not," he replied with raised brows.

"I don't give a damn about what she thinks of me or how I live my life. I don't care!"

Jeremiah sat down at his desk, and allowed Lola to continue her rant. She'd been coming to him for a few weeks now and this was the first time he saw beneath her shield.

"Now, may I assume that the *she* to whom you're referring is your mother?" Lola stopped pacing.

"Of course she's my mother. The great Victoria Devereux." Lola threw up her hands. "Who else?"

"I take it the two of you had an altercation."

"Very good deduction, Doctor. What gave it away?" Lola plopped down in a chair across from his desk. "I need a cigarette."

He didn't take offense nor was he surprised by her sarcasm. From the first day they'd met, Jeremiah had been intrigued by her quick wit and sharp tongue.

Lola leapt back out of the chair and began to pace the floor again.

"I mean, we all know she blames me for his death. I don't know why she just won't admit it."

"Your brother-in-law's death?" He looked confused.

"No!" She stopped and looked at the doctor, her

face not hiding her frustration. "Why would my mother blame me for my brother-in-law's death? Keep up, Doctor. I'm talking about my father."

"Okay. And why do you think she blames you?"

"I don't think it. I *know* it." Lola walked over and stood in front of the large picture window. She stared out at the winter sun as it began its slow descent behind the trees. Beyond the trees, she could see cars lined up as they crept through the parking lot, heading home for the day. While she stood watching, she felt stuck, reliving a nightmare that she so desperately wanted to escape.

"Not a moment goes by that I don't regret that day," she spoke in almost a trance-like state. Lola had never admitted her shame or guilt to anyone, not even herself. But with the beginning of each new day, for the past sixteen years, Lola remembered that horrible day and her part in it. She turned to face Jeremiah, but she dared not move, for fear her legs would give way.

"He always told me that I was as stubborn as a mule. Said I was just like her. And that day, I was determined to find out where they had sent my daughter. They told me it was for the best, that I should give her to a loving family who could afford to give her a good home. I was so scared, and I was sorry for having disappointed them. I wanted to do the right thing, but from the moment she left my arms, I regretted it. Every single day of my pitiful life, I've regretted it."

Jeremiah waited patiently for her to continue. Lola wrapped her arms around herself and closed her eyes.

"At first, we got pictures of her. Even though I missed her, I saw that she was happy and well cared for. But one day, the pictures just stopped coming and they couldn't tell me why. I decided right then that I wanted her back. I begged and pleaded with him to tell me where she was. My mother had orchestrated the entire adoption. Every time I would bring it up to her all she would say was that I needed to move on. I knew Dad had to have some information. I kept after him and accused him of playing God."

Lola's breaths became shorter. "I saw how that hurt him, but I didn't care. I knew I was wearing him down. Even when he walked away and said he didn't feel well, I didn't let up. We were still arguing when Mom and Raina came home and as soon as they walked through the door, he... he collapsed." She stood with outstretched hands. "Right there on the kitchen floor." Lola stared into nothing as if seeing the entire scene unfolding right in front of her. She looked up at Jeremiah; her eyes pleaded for forgiveness. "I wouldn't stop and he... he died."

Lola collapsed to the floor. There was no more sarcasm, no more pretending to have it all together. She had allowed him to see her battle scars and it was not Jeremiah the doctor but, Jeremiah the man whose heart was crumbling in his chest as he crossed the room and lifted her from the floor. They settled on the sofa and he held her while she purged all of the guilt and pain that she'd carried around for so long. Finally Lola drifted off to sleep.

Hours later Lola awoke with a jolt. At first she

couldn't remember where she was. As soon as she was able to focus, she saw Jeremiah. He was sitting at his desk, working quietly. The warm glow of the lamp washed over his ebony skin. He looked like African royalty. Lola lowered her feet to the floor and sat up slowly.

"Wow. How long was I out?" Jeremiah looked up from his writing and removed his glasses.

"Only a couple of hours."

"Hours?! Oh, I'm so sorry, Dr. Eli." Lola stood clumsily and began to search for her shoes. "I didn't mean to monopolize so much of your personal time." Jeremiah stood and walked over. He lightly touched Lola's shoulder.

"Listen, don't worry about it. That's why I'm here." He felt hypnotized as he stared down into the amber depths of her eyes.

Lola was feeling embarrassed for having come completely unglued.

"You must think I'm bipolar or something."

"In my line of work, you tend to hope the coming undone, as we call it, will happen sooner rather than later."

"Really?" Lola asked, unconvinced. "Tell me about it."

Jeremiah noticed how delicate her hands were when she placed her hair behind her ear. He inspected the soft outline of her cheek and the suppleness of her lips. Her beauty was almost hypnotic. It was a cruel fate that such a mesmerizing woman would come to him so very vulnerable and so damaged. Ever since he first laid eyes on Lola Devereux Jeremiah started imagining 'what if'. What if, she wasn't his patient? What if they'd met under different circumstances? What if she was healed from her addiction? This was dangerous territory and a mindset Jeremiah knew could lead to danger. Lola had no idea the effect she had on him and he would do his best to keep it that way.

"I have an idea. Why don't we finish discussing it over a bite to eat? There's a great place that's not too far from here."

"Oh no. It's late and I probably should be going. Besides, wouldn't that be considered... unethical?"

"What? Eating? Nah, I don't think the powers that be would frown too harshly on me getting in my three meals a day."

She smiled at his joke. Lola wasn't very hungry, but she didn't want to be alone.

"Well, since you put it that way, sure. Why not? But I need to freshen up a little first."

"I don't know why you feel the need to do that. The disheveled look kind of suits you."

"Ha, ha." She gave Jeremiah her infamous raised brow as she made her way to the restroom. Lola was horrified when she saw her reflection in the mirror.

"Oh, my goodness! I look like I've been on a three-day binge." She rummaged through her purse for a comb. After she whipped her hair into shape Lola wiped under her eyes and doused her face with cold water. Once she was able to recognize herself again, she smiled at the image in the mirror. She was proud of herself for the first time in a long time. She'd finally confronted her mother and said things that she'd shoved down for years—and the world didn't stop. And she did it all without taking a drink.

Lola smiled again, dabbed on a little lipstick. Then with one more glance, she walked out with her back a little straighter.

❀❀❀❀

The Library was a small restaurant and bar near the Atlanta University Center, the epicenter of the historical black colleges and universities in Atlanta. During the day the restaurant was frequented by students, faculty and other staff members. In the evening, the locals and professionals alike went there to have a good meal and catch a football game or boxing match. It had an old-school, jazzy vibe. There was deep mahogany wood throughout, heavy leather chairs and large flat screen televisions on the walls. Photographs of famous alumni along with paraphernalia from all the nearby colleges, fraternities and sororities adorned the walls. It reminded Lola of a pub she'd eaten in while on layover in Ireland.

Jeremiah slid into a booth by the window. The delicious aromas floating through the air had awakened Lola's taste buds. She was now famished. Lola watched Jeremiah as he removed his jacket inside the booth.

"The food here is outstanding." Somehow, his British accent seemed more pronounced in this place. A hostess promptly placed their menus and a basket of bread on the table.

"Good evening, Dr. Eli. Your server will be with you shortly." Lola couldn't help but notice the seductive smile she gave Jeremiah. And surprisingly she found herself irritated by the girl's familiar exchange.

"Ah, thank you, Laila," he responded with a warm smile. The girl seemed pleased as she almost skipped off to tend to other patrons.

"So," Lola said, ready to resume their previous conversation. "You were about to tell me what happens when people come undone."

"Yes. Well you see, it's the holding back that gets people into trouble. To come undone is quite cathartic. It's a way to release the thing that has caused so much angst. Not letting go," he said, while smearing butter on one of the warm rolls, "for fear of being judged or ridiculed is the thing that keeps most people bound to the shame. And what do you think happens when one can no longer stand oneself?" Jeremiah popped a piece of bread in his mouth and looked at Lola, as if waiting for her to answer. Lola's raised eyebrow made it evident that she didn't know where he was going. He leaned in a little closer.

"They self-medicate."

"Ah..." she nodded. "And so goes the alcoholic," Lola added.

"Exactly." He narrowed his eyes. "Alcoholic, workaholic, shopaholic, sexaholic, you name it. People will use anything to help push down the pain or keep themselves from facing the ugly truth, if you will."

"Then what happens?" Lola asked, as she toyed with the necklace she was wearing.

"Well, eventually they self destruct. Some call it

hitting rock bottom." Jeremiah leaned his elbows onto the edge of the table and watched her, closely.

"So instead of giving that pain a voice, we just kind of keep... unraveling?" Lola asked.

Jeremiah nodded. "Yes, and what most people fail to realize is that pain is never silent. Pain is loud. It's loud in a way that manipulates one's heart and even one's thoughts." He tapped his temple. "It says 'don't trust.' You'll wake up every morning and pull it on like an over-worn coat that weighs you down with fear and mistrust. Pain shows itself as anger and aggression without reasoning. Some people become despondent or confrontational. Gradually your life becomes one big lie of pretending—pretending not to care about anyone or anything and before you know it, you've accomplished something that you really didn't intend. You look up one day and you're alone. Perhaps not physically but within yourself," he points at his chest. "You're alone. And loneliness will cry out for whatever remedies will make it go away. Until there is no more pretending, no more sound, only silence; that my dear, is when the silence becomes too loud."

"Humph." Lola sat back thoughtfully and allowed the full impact of Dr. Eli's words to sink in.

"So... what are you thinking?" he asked with concern. Lola sat back and looked out of the window. She continued to play with her necklace, moving it back and forth. *Man, what a day, first mother and now this?* It was all too much to process right now. She was feeling lost and she needed time: time that she didn't have. She looked back at

Jeremiah.

"I'm thinking that... that's deep enough for me for one night," Lola said, with an awkward smile as she picked up the menu.

"What's good here?" she asked as she pretended to focus on the menu. Jeremiah knew that it was not a good idea to push, but to allow the healing process to be as organic as possible.

"Okay. Agreed," he said with a quick nod. "That's enough shop talk for tonight. Let's see," Jeremiah picked up the menu. "Are you adventurous?"

Lola peeked over the menu, and tried to gauge whether or not he was flirting. She knew better than to be here, in this place, with this man. Jeremiah Eli's presence in her life would either be a catalyst in the positive outcome of her recovery or derail everything she was trying to achieve. *Why couldn't we have met under different circumstances? Just my luck, he had to be who he is and I had to be the drunk who desperately needs his help.* Lola knew deep down, that she would never have a chance to be anything other than a patient to the doctor, so she decided she would not resort to her old ways of flirting shamelessly. She would maintain some decorum. She cleared her throat and gave him the best answer she could.

"No. Can't say that I am," she lied, and continued to study the menu intently. It was her spirit for adventure that had gotten her into many precarious situations, which she usually later regretted.

"Well, my favorite is the sushi lobster roll."

Jeremiah had already made up his mind what he was going to eat.

"Can't say that I'm a sushi kinda girl," Lola responded, still perusing the menu.

"What kind of girl are you?" he asked, focusing on the fullness of her lips as she formed her response. She had unknowingly cast a spell on him.

There it was again. *Was that a.... Is he....?* Lola decided to ignore the question.

"You know what? I think I'll just have a burger." She closed the menu and placed it back on the table. "No sushi for this girl."

"Very good," Jeremiah replied and signaled the waitress who appeared to be eyeing their table. She took their orders, barely acknowledging Lola, and disappeared.

"So... is this one of your hangouts?" Lola sipped her water and took in the scene.

"Well, I guess you could say it's a spot I tend to frequent." Lola nodded.

"I can see why. It has that man cave kind of feel."

"Do I look like the type of man that would have a man cave?"

"I don't know. Why don't you tell me what kind of man you are? But first," Lola held up a finger. "Tell me how a black man from the UK got the name *Jeremiah Eli*." They both laughed.

"Yeah. I get that a lot."

"Really?"

"My mum's parents named me and helped to raise both me and my brother. They were devout Christians, originally from Jamaica."

"Jamaica? Okay now I'm really confused."

"Yes, well they were Jamaican, but my grandfather was a well known chef. When I was six years old, he received an offer to be a member of the cooking staff for a small university in the UK. Both he and my grandmother thought it would be a good move and took us with them."

"What about your parents?" Lola asked, while pulling apart a piece of bread and placing it in her mouth.

"My parents were young when they had us and were not ready for the trappings of parenthood. My father, unfortunately, was a violent drunk. So when my grandparents decided to leave, we all moved, including my mum. Everyone knew it was for the best."

"And was it?"

Their waitress returned with their drinks and a fresh bread basket.

"To tell you the truth, at first," he said, blowing the steam that swirled around the surface of his hot tea, "it felt like we had been exiled. It always seemed to be so gray and cold. I missed my friends, the warm climate and the ocean. Man, I longed for it. Still do, at times," he said, finally taking a sip of his drink.

"For the ocean?"

"Yes. I craved the sound of the waves crashing against the rocks and the sand flowing under my feet. I missed the smell of the salt in the air and warm wind against my skin."

"Well what did you do? I mean, what saved you? That had to be hard for someone so young."

"Yes, it was. But my grandfather was, and still is, a very wise man. He saw my longing and he understood it as well."

"So what did he do?" Lola asked, taking a sip of her own drink.

"Well true to most islanders, we had a love for futbol. And being in a country that thrived on futbol didn't hurt. However, my grandfather was a man of many talents. He was a fantastic storyteller and he enticed us with the most fascinating stories. Later he introduced us to books that held still more amazing stories. It wasn't long before we were both hooked. My brother, he always seemed to have the ability to see the stories unfold visually and now he's a film maker. I, on the other hand, was intrigued by the human psyche."

"Really?"

"Yes. I would always wonder *why* a character would do whatever it was he was doing. I needed to know the reasoning behind the actions. So between books and futbol and school, our little minds were kept very busy."

"Okay. I have one sushi lobster roll," a second waiter said, as he approached the table. Jeremiah reached for the plate. The waitress set the burger down in front of Lola. "Is there anything else I can get you?" she asked, as she practically drooled over Jeremiah. Lola was not amused at how desperate the young lady acted. She opened the napkin near her plate and shook her head.

"No. I think we're good," Jeremiah informed the waitress.

"This looks delicious," Lola said, as her stomach

rumbled.

"Trust me. It is," he said, before he bowed his head to bless his food. Lola watched him before she did the same. They attacked the food and a few minutes passed before they came up for air. Lola couldn't help but to laugh a little as she thought what they must've looked like. He caught her eye and shook his head as he wiped his mouth with a smile.

"People must think we haven't eaten in ages."

"I know, right?" she said, and wiped her mouth as well. "So tell me about your grandmother?"

"Oh, she was the disciplinarian. We could never get away with anything with her. She could see right through our tricks and fake tears."

"Oh, you all tried to fake her out, huh?

"Of course we did. What kid doesn't?" They both laughed. And it continued that way for over an hour. The conversation was easy and comfortable.

"And what about you?" Jeremiah asked.

"What *about* me? You already know so much."

"Well, let's see. What kind of kid were you? What did you grow up loving to do? What are your passions?"

"Wow." Her brow furrowed. "I, um... I haven't thought about anything like that in a long time." Lola looked up at the copper ceiling. "Let's see..." Finally she had to admit it, "I don't know."

"Think about it. What did you like to do?"

"Wow. You're serious, huh? I don't know. I mean, I can't remember what I liked." She sipped her iced tea and squirmed a little, noticing how intently he watched her. "Okay, okay. Um...I guess

I liked doodling."

"What?"

"You know, doodling. Putting pencil to paper. Creating an image from nothing in particular. It used to calm me."

"I see. So you're an artist."

"I wouldn't call it that."

"What would you call it then? Someone who creates images from nothing."

"I don't know."

"Did you ever get any feedback from your parents about this doodling?"

"Yes. My dad was my biggest fan. He told me that one day I could be a famous artist. He used to say stuff like that all the time. No matter how ridiculous it was."

"Now why do you say that? Sometimes, other people can see our gifts long before we can. Your father sounds like my papa."

"Maybe." Lola's shoulders became tense. She didn't really want to talk about her father.

"Yes. I guess you could say that." She inhaled. "He was very accomplished." Lola desperately wanted to change the subject.

"So where exactly did your grandparents relocate to?" Lola asked. He already knew much more about her than she could've dreamed possible. But she didn't want to be the topic of discussion anymore tonight.

"London. Actually, Wembley, which is a borough northwest of London," he answered, in his very relaxed way.

"Are you always this laid back?" Lola crossed

her arms leaned back in her seat. Jeremiah's left eyebrow went up.

"I mean, you must see a lot of craziness, right? How do you, I don't know.... how do you keep yourself sane after dealing with other people's baggage all day?"

"To be honest, there are times it gets to me. Like when I see so much promise in someone but they can't see if for themselves. The world can be very cruel and unforgiving, but it's when we lose our spirit of hope that the battle can be lost."

"The battle, but not the war," Lola added with a pointed finger.

"Touché. I stand corrected."

Lola was beginning to feel less uneasy about being there with him. She decided she wanted to know more about Jeremiah Eli, the man behind the doctor.

"May I ask you a question?" she queried.

"By all means." He dipped the last of his sushi into some soy sauce.

"Being intrigued by the characters in the stories your grandfather read, is that why you chose to go into this line of work?"

A sarcastic chuckle escaped him. "It wasn't so much of me choosing it, it was more like it chose me."

"And how's that?" Lola asked, taking another sip of her tea.

"My father was an alcoholic, as well as his father before him. When you grow up seeing someone you love self-destruct like that, two things can come out of it." He held up two fingers. "Either you succumb to the same generational curse or you fight to keep from going down the same path. I chose the latter."

"Wow. That's incredible."

"What's incredible? That I chose not to emulate my father?"

"No. That even though you were exposed to that you rose above it. While someone like me, who had everything growing up... well...I just...let life beat me down."

"What helped me is that I finally decided to forgive him."

"Forgive?" Lola fidgeted with her necklace again.

"Yes. You see, most of us hold on to the pain of being hurt, disappointed or rejected and it becomes this, this sort of virus."

"You know you're beginning to sound like an Oprah re-run with all that forgiveness talk."

"Oh yeah?"

"Yes. And how would someone do that anyway? What? Do they make a call say, "Hello, I've thought about what you did to me all those years ago and even though you may not have given it another thought, it affected my entire life. But I'm just calling to let you know I forgive you?"

"Why would that be so difficult?"

"Why should anyone be let off the hook just like that?" She snapped her fingers.

"The question is do people even know they're on the hook? You just said they've probably been living their lives and have not given the situation much thought. While you, on the other hand, have kept it so close, you've probably relived it every time you heard a certain song, or smelled a certain scent. They're not being let off of the hook. Forgiving them will, however, let *you* off the hook. It will allow you to leave it behind, where it belongs. Sometimes it can even mean forgiving yourself."

Lola sat and stared at the condensation slowly sliding down her tea glass. She didn't respond.

"Forgiveness of self is just as important, as forgiving others." Jeremiah looked around and signaled the waitress for a refill of his hot tea. Lola looked up at him with a fading smile. For a moment, neither one of them spoke. The waitress came over and set down another cup of hot water and attempted to refill Lola's iced tea when Lola sat up and held her hand over the glass.

"No thank you," she said. After the waitress left, Lola looked over at Jeremiah with a weak smile.

"I should be going," she said and placed her napkin on top of the table. She felt weighted down. "I have a job lined up for tomorrow and I need to rest my brain before I have to deal with those teenagers." Lola pulled out her wallet.

"Please, allow me." He motioned for Lola to put her wallet away. "And I hope you'll forgive me. I didn't mean to keep going on and on about this stuff. I mean, we came here to wind down and—"

"No, no. There's no need to apologize. It's apparent that you love what you do. You were just trying to help," she said, as she began to slide out of the booth. Jeremiah grabbed her hand.

"Ms. Devereux, please call me whenever you need to talk."

"You know what's funny? I've felt this way for so long, I don't know how to feel any differently."

"Everything takes time. The process is not an easy one and anyone who says that it is, is lying to himself. Just make up your mind that you're going to move forward."

Lola smiled and nodded before sliding completely out of the booth. "Good night, Dr. Eli."

"Good night, Lola Devereux."

Lola stepped outside onto the cobblestone street. The high winds from earlier had subsided. Now nothing more than an inconsistent breeze brushed against her cheek. As she crossed the narrow street her heels clicked against the sidewalk. *Is it realistic to think that the thing that has kept me from making a full recovery was my inability to forgive myself?* It sounded so easy but it was such a hard thing to do. But Lola Devereux was known for trying anything once. She made up her mind it was time to at least try.

# TWENTY

## SIBLING RIVALRY

---

**Q**uincy twirled his basketball on the tips of his fingers as he walked into the family room. Nyla sat at the kitchen table and glanced up from her cell phone as he entered the room.

"Hey," Quincy said, as he looked around the room as if expecting to see someone else. He began bouncing the basketball as he walked into the kitchen. Although Nyla tried to ignore it, the bouncing made her want to scream.

"You know your mom said for you not to bounce that ball in the house," she said, nonchalantly.

"Well, my mom's not here and if you don't like it, you should just leave."

"Why should I leave? I was in here first."

Quincy stopped bouncing and held his hand to his ear. "What's that?"

"I *said*, I was in here first," she repeated.

"Yeah, that's what I thought you said. So let me correct you because you're clearly mistaken. *We*"— Quincy pointed back and forth between him and a photo of his brother—"were here first. This is *my* house." He stood with the basketball under one arm and pointed at the floor. "And I can do what *I* want in *my* house." Quincy bounced the ball again, but this time even harder.

"Whatever," Nyla rolled her eyes. She would never admit it but it hurt to have him dislike her so much. She didn't know what she'd expected. She'd been in and out of many foster homes and had encountered more than her share of territorial children.

"Whatever," Quincy repeated, mocking her. Nyla stood quickly and started out of the room.

"Yeah, that's a good idea. Leave."

Nyla stopped dead in her tracks and turned around.

"What's your problem?" She walked toward him with a purposeful stride. Even though he was younger Quincy had at least an inch on Nyla.

"I ain't got no problem." Quincy twirled the basketball again and walked away.

"Obviously, you *do* have a problem. What have I done to you?" Quincy stopped twirling and turned to face her. He stared back at her and without a word began bouncing the basketball again. The noise drove Nyla crazy. She turned once again to walk away.

"What do you want?!" Quincy stopped bouncing and yelled at her back.

"What?" Nyla turned back to face him again.

"What do you want? I mean, you came here to find your dad and he's not here. So why are you still here?"

"Not that I have to answer to you, but your mom asked me to stay."

"She was just doing that because she felt sorry for you."

"Well, I don't need her pity!" To her surprise, Quincy's words stung. Nyla attempted to blink back the tears before she turned to leave.

He pretended that he didn't care, but Quincy was immediately sorry for his harsh words as soon as he saw her tear up. Matthew jumped down the last three stairs and almost plowed right into Nyla. She didn't stop. She headed straight to her room. She would never let him see her cry.

"Hey Q, show me that trick you did with the ball the other night," Matthew requested when he saw his brother with the basketball.

Nyla entered her room and fell onto the bed. She closed her eyes and thought about what Quincy had said. *Did Raina ask me to stay because she felt sorry for me? How long is she going to let me to stay?* Nyla closed her eyes for a few minutes and tried to think. Minutes later she opened her eyes and slid to the floor. She pulled her satchel out from beneath the bed and slowly unrolled a sketch. Staring back at her were several small, laughing faces. These were some of the children she'd met at her first foster home. She'd lived with the Martins for four years and they had begun to feel like a real family. She ran her fingers over the drawing and smiled when she remembered the day she'd discovered her gift for sketching. Since that day, Nyla sketched anything that would stand still long enough. She climbed on top of the desk and began to tack the drawing on the wall. Just before she put in the last tack, she heard a loud crash. She jumped down from the desk and rushed back into the family room.

As soon as she turned the corner, Nyla saw pieces of Raina's crystal vase shattered, all over the kitchen floor. Both Quincy and Matthew stood frozen with their mouths open. Not a second later Raina walked into the house with her cell phone pressed against her ear, carrying three bags of groceries.

"Yes, Ms. Alphonso. I'm aware of that. We won't be able to close on the property until the title search has been completed and—" she stopped when she saw the broken vase.

"What in the world?!" All three kids still stood, bug-eyed, as Raina tried to get over her initial shock.

"Oh no. That wasn't for you, Ms. Alphonso. Yes, please forgive me, yes. I'm sorry but I have a situation here. May I call you back? Yes, I'll be sure to do that. Okay. Goodbye."

Raina stood in the doorway speechless. The vase had been the last gift Keenan had given her before they'd left on their couples' retreat.

"Quincy! What happened?" No one responded.

"Well?" Raina noticed the ball in the middle of the floor.

"Well, I uh... I was uh... we..." Quincy

stammered.

"Did you do this?! After I've told you a million times not to play with that ball in the house? Are you kidding me?!" Quincy felt terrible. He knew what the vase meant to his mom.

"Uh, Mom, I'm so..."

"I'm so sorry, Raina." Nyla spoke up. "Quincy was telling me what a super star he was on the court so I decided to show him how I could handle the ball and it got away from me. I'm really sorry." Quincy and Matthew were dumbstruck. But no one was more surprised than Nyla. *I can't believe I'm doing this. I must be getting soft.*

"*You* did this, Nyla?" Raina asked, incredulously.

"Um, yeah. I didn't mean to break anything. I really am sorry, Raina."

Raina shook her head and tried to keep the tears at bay. It had been a terrible day and until a few minutes ago, she was glad to be home. She pinched the bridge of her nose.

"I can't believe this. Nyla, you're old enough to know better than to do something that irresponsible." Raina was hurt but she tried to refrain from going off too harshly on Nyla.

"Yes. I know. Listen, I have a little money saved. I'll pay you for it or get you another one."

"No. That won't be necessary. Just make sure you don't let it happen again. Quincy, don't just stand there, help get this mess cleaned up!" Nyla stepped closer and took the bags from Raina. Matthew walked over and hugged her.

"Sorry, Mom."

"Hey, baby. How was your day?" Raina drew him close and patted him on his back.

"It was good. How was yours?" He looked up into her tired eyes.

"Well, let's just say if I can get one more hug, it'll make everything better."

With a big smile, Matthew was happy to oblige. While Quincy and Nyla moved around the kitchen cleaning the broken glass, Nyla noticed tears brimming in Quincy's eyes as he swept up the glass. It dawned on her that he wasn't so tough, especially when it came to his mom.

Nyla held the dustpan as Quincy swept the big chunks of glass into it. Matthew's voice trailed off as he and Raina walked toward her bedroom. After they were out of earshot, Quincy made an attempt to make a truce.

"Um, hey..." Quincy started.

Nyla stood up and looked up at him. "Save it." She shoved the empty dustpan into his chest, turned and walked back down the hall, leaving Quincy to ponder what had just happened. Nyla had saved him even though he'd treated her so awful. *Man, how am I going to fix this?*"

🍃🍃🍃🍃

Lola let herself in through the basement door. She quietly slid out of her jacket and dropped onto the large sofa. Her tired body melted into the softness of the cushions. She threw her forearm across her face and allowed herself a moment to fantasize about Dr. Eli.

Sometime over into the night she awoke to the sound of a steady clicking noise. Lola sat up and was momentarily at a loss for where she was. "I must've drifted off," she said to herself, as she ran her fingers through her hair. She felt around on the floor for her shoes and once again there was that sound. Slowly she rose from the sofa, rubbed the sleep from her eyes and stumbled toward the noise. As she rounded the corner, she saw Nyla in front of the computer.

Lola gasped and quickly stepped back out of the room. She hadn't expected to have an encounter with Nyla. She'd made sure to keep her distance. Now the inevitable was upon her and she felt her stomach start to flutter. Before Lola could decide her next move, the noise stopped and Nyla almost collided into her as she came around the corner.

"Oh, hey," Lola said, stunned.

"Whoa! Sorry. I didn't know anyone else was down here."

"Ah, yeah. I was uh... I must've taken a little snooze on the couch," Lola pointed backward toward the sofa. A few moments of awkward silence passed before either of them said anything else. "So what are you working on?" Lola asked.

"Nothing really."

"Oh. Top secret, huh?" Lola laughed nervously.

"No, it's not. I just have a school project due and I had to do some last minute research."

"Oh, hey, that's cool. I mean... school is good. I'm actually going to be subbing over there this week."

"Over where? *My* school?" Nyla asked, anxiously.

"Yeah. Looks like I'm going to be here longer

than expected so a friend lined up this... Hey, are you okay?" Lola couldn't help but notice the unsettled look on Nyla's face.

"Yeah. I'm cool."

"What is it? Would you rather I not work at the school?"

"Nah....I mean, whatever. If that's your thing, you know. I just don't know why someone who's finished with school would ever want to go back. When I'm done, I'm never going back."

"Well, sometimes you gotta do what you gotta do, you know?"

"Yeah, sure." Nyla nodded.

"You know, if you need a ride to school, I could...."

"Nah... I'm good."

"Oh, forgive me. How could I have forgotten how un-cool that would be?" Lola said, with a slight smile. Nyla watched her closely. *Wow, she's so beautiful. Raina is pretty too, but Lola, she's got a different thing going on. She doesn't even act like she knows how pretty she is either.* A few more minutes of awkward silence passed before Nyla spoke again.

"Well, I better get ready for tomorrow," she said, taking a few steps toward the stairs.

Lola had been enjoying the brief conversation and didn't want it to end.

"So... what uh... what subject is your project on?"

Nyla became tense. She'd been online trying to map out an exit plan. She wanted to get as far away from Georgia as possible, but she couldn't let

Raina's flaky sister know that.

"Um... history. Yeah. I was working on a history project."

"Oh, yeah? Hmm. I used to be pretty good at history."

Nyla suddenly felt the need to flee. "Well, I better get to bed," Nyla pointed at the staircase behind her. "You know, gotta get up early and all," she said, with an uncomfortable smile.

"Oh yeah, sure. I'll see you around school then." Nyla had already turned in the direction of the stairs but stopped.

"Yeah, about that."

"What?"

"Seeing me at school. When you do, I hope you won't feel bad if I don't stop and talk to you or nothin' like that." Lola faked a sad look as Nyla waited for her to acknowledge that she understood.

"Really? You mean, no sitting together at lunch? You know we can have girl time and..." By the expression on Nyla's face Lola could see that she was not amused.

"You're joking, right?"

"To tell you the truth, I'm kind of hurt. Tell you what. How about a slight tilt of the head? You know what I mean? Like a "what's up" kinda thing." Lola demonstrated and Nyla laughed. Lola couldn't begin to explain it, but at that moment, Nyla's laughter was like rays of sunlight spreading throughout her entire body.

"Nyla, before you go can I ask you a personal question?"

The hairs on the back of Nyla's neck stood at

attention. What little interaction she and Lola had was always brief and awkward. Now, she wanted personal information? It made her very uncomfortable.

"How personal?"

"Well, it's um… it's about your parents, more specifically, your mother."

"She's dead," Nyla responded with a stoic expression.

"I know your adopted mother is deceased, but I was talking about your—"

"The only mother I ever had is dead," Nyla said abruptly. "The woman who gave birth to me and gave me away is not anyone I want to talk about."

"Oh, really? Well um... okay." Lola's heart sank.

"Yes, really."

"It's just that I know Raina was thinking that perhaps she could help you find her and—"

"I don't want to find her. Why would I want to find someone who didn't want me? Who never cared to know whether I was dead or alive?"

Lola's heart raced and her emotions became an internal tsunami, but she couldn't allow Nyla to see that.

"But what if you found out she didn't have a choice?" Lola's question was barely audible.

"She may not have had a choice then, but it's been seventeen years. What about now, huh? My dad started looking for me as soon as he found out about me. That means he wanted me. He wanted for me to be a part of his life. But now he's dead and I'll never get the chance to know him. So no, I don't want to meet her. All she's ever done for me is cause me pain. Why would I want a person like that in my life?" She stared into Lola's sunken expression.

"Oh. Well, yeah, I see what you..." Lola's throat felt constricted; as if a noose had been tightened around her neck, making it difficult for any other sound to escape.

"Well, I guess you should get to bed then, huh?"

"Goodnight," Nyla said, and jetted up the staircase taking two at a time.

After she heard the door close, Lola allowed the air from her lungs to escape slowly as she exhaled. She hadn't realized that she'd been holding her breath. She placed her hand on her upper torso, sat on the arm of the couch and took several deep breaths. The realization that Nyla hated her was almost unbearable. Lola knew that sooner or later, the truth would come out. She wanted to make sure that when it did, she would be able to handle the repercussions without resorting to her old ways. Lola's knees felt weak as she attempted to stand. She wiped her sweaty palms on her jeans and carefully walked toward her room. She didn't turn on the light, but sat on her bed in the darkness, with just the moonlight streaming through the blinds. She wondered what would become of her family when the truth was revealed. "The truth shall set you free," is what the Reverend used to say. She didn't feel free. She felt trapped, like an insect in a spider's web and she needed someone to talk to, someone who wouldn't judge or condemn. Finally, she found the strength to kneel and as the soft glow of the moon spilled into the darkness, Lola prayed.

"God? I know I've been inconsistent but here's the deal. In my usual fashion, I seem to have made a mess of things down here. This life... well, it hasn't turned out quite like I imagined it would. I really don't know what to do. I have sinned and I pray that Raina and Nyla will be able to forgive me. I don't know how this is all going to work out, but I know we'll all need you to get us through it."

≈ ≈ ≈ ≈

When Nyla got back to her room, Quincy was there.

"What do you want?" she asked, as leaned against the door frame, crossed her arms over her chest and waited.

Quincy turned around quickly when he heard Nyla's voice. He was embarrassed.

"What? Can't a guy come by to check on his own sister?" Both Quincy and Nyla were surprised by his words. Her left eyebrow shot up as she studied him. Nyla walked to the middle of the room where they stood, almost nose-to-nose.

"What's your game?"

"What? I'm not playing no game," Quincy said, as he drew back.

"Yeah. You playin' a game, alright. You told me I should leave. Now all of a sudden, you're calling me your *sister*?"

"Look. I know I've made it hard for you, but after what you did—"

"Whoa, hold up. I know you don't think I did that for you." Quincy was quiet.

"I did that because I saw the hurt on Raina's face. She's already dealing with a lot, but you

263

wouldn't know that 'cause you're an over-privileged butt-head who can't think of anyone else but himself."

"Wait a minute."

"No. *You* wait." Nyla's could feel her heart racing. She hadn't planned this confrontation, but she couldn't hold her tongue any longer.

"You have no idea what I've gone through to get here. And you don't need to try to pretend you care now. All of your life you had him. You had him right here!" She pointed to the floor.

As Nyla continued, the words flew from her mouth like daggers being hurtled through the air. "He was here taking care of you. Making sure you had food to eat and a nice house to live in. Asking you how was your day when you got home from school. He made sure the bills were paid, so you would have lights and nice clothes to wear. You had him the whole time and all I had was a dream of who he might've been."

"I'm sorry, Nyla. I really am. I didn't realize how much I hurt you. I didn't mean to be like that. It's just that... I don't know. I'm mad that he had to die and I guess I needed somebody to take it out on."

"Why blame me?" She patted her chest. "I didn't kill him."

"I know that. I can't explain it. I know that I acted stupid and selfish and I really am sorry if I hurt you."

"You didn't hurt me," she said defiantly.

"Well, I'm sorry for trying to hurt you and not thinking about what you might've been going through."

They both stood silently facing each other, not knowing what else to say. Quincy noticed the drawing on the wall.

"Did you do that?" he asked, with a tilt of his head. Nyla cut her eyes at the drawing and responded with a nod.

"You're really good!" Quincy shoved both of his hands into his pockets and cocked his head to one side.

"It's just a stupid picture I drew a long time ago."

"Who are they?" he asked, still staring at the drawing. Nyla didn't want to get into a long explanation of who they were or how she knew them.

"Just some people I saw in a magazine once."

"You should think about entering the art competition at school." Nyla wasn't interested in any art competition, but she was pleased by Quincy's compliment.

"Maybe," she said.

"Well, okay. I'm gonna get outta your hair now. Since it looks like you need to do something with it before school tomorrow."

Quincy stood at the door and made motions with his hands all around his head.

"Oh, you got jokes?" Nyla threw a pillow, but Quincy closed the door just in time. Then she tried to smooth down her wild mane and realized he was right. Nyla took one look in the mirror and knew she'd better try to tame that beast before tomorrow, because she was going to see Gabby again and she wanted to look good.

# *TWENTY-ONE*

## *NO WAY OUT*

---

The hospital hummed with activity as Nyla sat next to Gabrielle's bed and stared at the television.

"So, what are you gonna do?" Gabby whispered. She had been moved out of ICU and into a shared room. Unfortunately, Gabby's roommate was a mother of two, who had been in car accident.

The young mother's friends and family had been coming and going with regularity all day. Both Nyla and Gabby made a conscious effort not to have others overhear their conversation.

"Talk to me, Ny. I know what I did was stupid, but I didn't think Tyrone had enough brains to look for us on the Internet."

"How could you not know that, Gabby?" Nyla rolled her eyes in the direction of her friend.

"I don't know. I wasn't thinking. Ms. Pearl and

her husband had just given Simone a new computer. We were both so excited and when she showed me her Facebook account she asked if I wanted her to start one for me. I guess I just got caught up. It was all just so, I don't know, normal. Not like the life we'd been living."

Nyla's shoulders slumped forward. "I know what you mean. Living with Raina and her family, it's a trip, you know. I mean, they have breakfast and dinner together and stuff. It's kinda cool."

"Yeah." They both were quiet for a moment.

"Ny, you scared?"

Nyla didn't want her friend to worry. "Nah, not really. I mean, you didn't tell him where I lived did you?"

"Oh no," Gabby said, shaking her head.

"So that's good. I mean, Atlanta is a big place and I'm *not* on the Internet, so I'll just continue to lay low."

"Yeah, that's a good idea." Gabby nodded; her expression was trance like.

"Tell me what else he said."

Gabby lowered her head. She didn't want to remember anything about the night she almost lost her life. "I don't know, Ny. All I can remember is how mad he was and if Jamal hadn't stopped him, I probably wouldn't be here."

"Don't say that, Gabby."

"I'm scared he's gonna come back, but I don't have nowhere else to go. I don't want to put Ms. Pearl and her family in danger."

Again they sat quietly, each trying to think of a way out. "I'm leaving, Gabby." Nyla looked at

Gabby with sad eyes. Gabby gasped.

"What?! Whadda you mean leaving? Where you going?"

"I don't know." She shrugged. "Maybe California."

"California?! What's out there and how in the world are you going to get there?"

"Nobody is out there. That's the point. I can make a new start." Nyla sat up straighter in the chair. The look of shock had not left Gabby's face.

"What's wrong with being connected to people, Ny? I mean, you got a whole family over there who love you and—"

"They don't love me, Gabby. They're just putting up with me because of who my daddy was. But he's no longer around and I can't let them find out about..."

"About what?" Gabby stared back at her friend.

"Nothing. I just want a new start. I'm gonna re-invent myself. Shoot, I may even change my name."

"You scared they gonna find out what Tyrone made you do? That wasn't yo' fault, Ny. You didn't have a choice."

"You think they're gonna see it like that? They won't. I mean, they go to church every Sunday and I see Raina reading the Bible and praying, but that doesn't matter. What do you think she's gonna say when she finds out that not only was I a stripper, but now her family is in danger 'cause of me?"

"If she the Christian you say she is, she'll understand." Nyla was silent. She wished things had been different. *Why couldn't my dad have been here when I got here? Why does everything always have to turn out so bad?* Nyla shook her head in defiance.

"I don't want her to have to understand. I don't want any of them to ever have to know anything about that stuff. So I gotta go."

"You gonna let 'em know you're leaving?"

"No. They'll just try to talk me out of it. I'm just gonna go."

"Well, as much as I want to go with you, I'm tired of running, Ny. I wanna belong to someone. I want someone to be looking for me, worried about me, excited to see me. I'm still scared, but I'm not gonna let Tyrone, or anybody else, cheat me outta having a good life."

"Yeah. I feel you, Gabby. We both gotta fight for what we want, but it's okay if we choose to do it a different way, right?"

They both pondered the situation for a few more minutes, but before the mood became any more somber, Nyla, in her usual fashion, proceeded to sweep all their concerns back under the rug and acted like everything was okay.

"Hey, listen. I gotta head back. I told Raina I was staying after school for track practice, so..."

"Track? Girl, you joined the track team?" Gabby smiled.

"Well kinda but not really. The coach asked me to consider it and I told him I'd think about it. Raina thinks I'm at practice now, so I gotta go so she won't get suspicious.

"You know, if you're gonna be a track star"— Gabby placed her fingers in quotation marks— "you might want to put down those cigarettes."

"Yeah, well I said I would *think* about it." Nyla stood and gave her friend a hug. "Not that I'm actually gonna do it.

"But you should. You're fast, Nyla and who knows, this could open up a whole new life for you," Gabby said, with a little too much optimism.

"Like I said, I'll think about it. It'll definitely be a way to pass the time while I'm here."

"Now *that's* what I'm talkin' about!" Gabby said, excitedly. She really didn't want to see her only friend leave. Nyla looked at the time on cell her phone.

"Yeah, I'm gonna need for you to bring it down a notch. And I really gotta get outta here before I miss the bus."

"Okay, chica, be safe," Gabby said, as they hugged again.

"I'll touch base with you later in the week," Nyla said, as she stood upright.

"Cool. Talk to you later. Oh, and Nyla, watch your back, okay?"

"I will." She said to her friend with a reassuring smile as she slipped through the curtain that separated the beds and hurried out of the room.

Nyla stuck her headphone in her ears and began surfing the internet as she rode the elevator to the hospital lobby. Her visit with Gabby had been good and the news that she would get out tomorrow was even better. With Gabby's confirmation that it was Tyrone who had done this to her, Nyla knew her plan to leave would have to happen sooner rather than later. She'd had a feeling that time was running out.

As she exited the elevator into the dimly lit parking lot, peering into her cell phone, Nyla walked right into what felt like a brick wall. She looked up into Jamal's snarled face and took one step back and turned to run. Before she could escape, Jamal grabbed her. Nyla winced at the pain and pressure of his large hand as it closed around her arm.

"Hey, Ny. Long time n...n...no see." His grip became tighter as she attempted to pull away.

Nyla looked around frantically. She tried to call out for help, but her throat closed up. Before she knew it Jamal quickly forced her toward the waiting SUV and threw her into the back seat. Nyla looked around frantically and saw Tyrone sitting against the soft, black leather seat. He stared out of the window as if nothing else was happening. Nyla shrank back against the door and tried to put as much distance between the two of them as possible.

"How's Gabby these days, Nyla?" he asked, still not looking in her direction.

"She took a pretty bad fall into my fist a few weeks back. We been wondering if she was gon' make a full recovery 'cause uh, I'm gon' need her to work off the debt she owes me."

"You gonna beat me too?" Nyla tried to be tough, but her voice quivered. She hated that her voice gave way to the fear and even worse that Tyrone knew that she was afraid. "I got people who'll be looking for me," she said as her heartbeat quickened.

"Oh, I know that. I done seen yo' lil' family. Yo' brothas, yo' stepmama with her fine self. She fine, ain't she Jamal?" He yelled forward with a chuckle. "Yeah, that's right. I had her show me and Jamal a couple of houses we thanking 'bout buyin'."

Nyla was beyond shocked.

"What? You think I'm just some dumb country hick who ain't got enough sense to track you down and make you pay for stealing from me?" Tyrone leaned forward. "How could you do me like that, Ny? I gave you a home. I fed you. And this is how you repay me?! I know you didn't think I was gon' let you get away with trying to make a fool outta me, did you?"

"Tyrone, I... I'll pay you back." Suddenly there was no air. Nyla almost blacked out as Tyrone drove his fist into her stomach. Afterward, he slapped her on the right side of her temple with such force it drove her back up against the door. He grabbed the front of her shirt and pulled her so close that she could smell the pungent odor of tobacco. She almost vomited in his face.

"Girl, you ain't got enough money in the world to repay me for what you did." He spoke through clinched teeth. "If I wasn't a business man, I would kill you right now." They were nose to nose.

"You think you so damn smart. I got yo' smart," he said, as he threw her back across the seat. Tyrone wiped his face with his large hands and took a deep breath.

"Girl, I don't why you make me do the things I do. You lucky, I like you. So here's what I'ma do. I gotta few deals going down in the next couple of weeks and I need you to deliver some packages for me. I know you wouldn't want anything to happen to yo' precious lil' family, so, uh, I'ma assume that you on board with this little arrangement. Am I right?" He asked, already knowing the answer. Nyla couldn't speak; she simply nodded. She now realized that there was no way out. Gabby had almost died at the hands of Tyrone and Nyla knew these were not empty threats.

"Yeah. That's what I figured. Here." He shoved a cell phone into her hand. "Take this and when it rings, you betta answer. I'll be callin' to let you know when and where to meet for the deliveries. And you betta *not* be late. You got that?"

"Yeah." Nyla's voice was finally able to croak out a response accompanied with a nod of her head. "Yeah, I got it. Anything else?"

"Anything else like what?" he asked, clearly agitated.

"I just want to know how many deliveries I gotta make before I'm done?"

Tyrone's gold grill caught the light from the outside lantern as a wide grin spread across his face.

"You know what? You stupid." He pointed at her and gave a small chuckle. "Brave but stupid. You want to know when you're done huh? Okay, hear you go, you're done when they throw the dirt on your coffin, you understand? Besides, I feel like I'ma like it here in the A. Who knows, I just might let mommy dearest sell me that house after all. Ain't that right, Jamal?!" Jamal chuckled in agreement.

"Ye... ye... yeah, cuz; w...w...we just might make this our new ho...ho...home base."

Nyla wanted to scream. *Why is this happening?*

The only family she had was in danger and it was all because of her. The car came to a sudden stop.

"Get out." Nyla opened the door and as she started to climb down from the back seat, Tyrone put his size ten foot in her back and pushed her out of the vehicle. Nyla landed still holding her stomach. Before they drove off, he stuck his head out of the window.

"Remember, when that phone rings you betta be on the other line—pronto!" The car sped off, and Nyla was left in the dark, both literally and figuratively.

She gradually stood to her feet; her entire body trembled as she walked unhurriedly toward the bus stop. She was terrified and wanted to run back upstairs and tell Gabby what had just happened. Her worst nightmare had come true. Tyrone knew where she lived and about her family. She would have to find some way out of this mess. But she had missed the last bus, and right now, she needed to find a ride home.

# TWENTY-TWO

## FIRST DAY OF SCHOOL

---

Lola made it halfway through her first day at the high school without screwing up or running into Nyla. It was a beautiful day. For lunch she decided to sit on the campus yard instead of staying inside the stuffy teachers' lounge. Luckily, she found a vacant bench, sat down, and began digging into her brown paper bag for the turkey sandwich she'd made that morning.

Lola bit into her sandwich and looked around the yard at all the young, exuberant faces. She watched them all as they passed by. *So young and so stupid,* she thought. Lola thought about when she'd been their age. She had fought so hard to race ahead and leave her childhood behind. Now she would give anything for the simpler, carefree days of being a kid. It felt surreal to be back in this place. Lola felt

276

as if she'd traveled back in time. With a quick shake of her head, Lola took another bite of her sandwich.

The campus was bustling with activity when Lola thought she caught a glimpse of Nyla, but wasn't sure until the man who stood talking to her turned in such a way that she could see Nyla's face clearly. Lola's heart swelled with emotion as she watched her. As the man spoke, Nyla nodded her head. *Who is that guy and why does Nyla have that fake smile plastered all over her face?*

Lola had just taken the last bite of her sandwich and was sipping her mango tea when the same man, passed within a few feet of her. Lola grabbed the brown bag, hopped up from the bench and fell in stride alongside him.

"Hi," she said, as he examined what seemed to be some kind of memo.

"Hi," he responded, distractedly.

"Uh, I'm kind of new here. I'm actually subbing today and I noticed you talking to my niece, Nyla." He stopped abruptly.

"Nyla Davis is your niece?"

"Yes," Lola said, a little winded. She noticed the Athletic Department logo on his shirt. "You're the track and field coach, right?"

"Yes, I am." The man with thinning blond hair and hazel eyes responded excitedly. Even though there was a breeze in the air, his face was flushed.

"I'm Lola Devereux." She extended her hand with a slight squint of her eyes because of the sun shining directly in her face.

"Ken Collins." He gave her a brief handshake. "I'm glad she's finally feeling better." He clipped the memo to a clipboard.

"Who?" Lola asked.

"Nyla. She told me that she'd been battling a stomach virus and that's why she's missed so many practices, and last week's track meet."

"Oh, yeah, that." Lola now stood with one hand over her eyes, as she attempted to block the sun. "Yes, it really hit her hard but we're all glad she's back on her feet."

"Yes. Well, I hope she won't miss any more practices because she's very gifted. I've not seen anyone with her natural ability in a long time. It would be a shame if she doesn't use her talent."

"Really? She's that good huh?"

"Yes. I think she could go all the way to the State Championship but it'll take a lot of work on her part."

"Well, you've got my promise that my sister and I will do our part to help her get there."

"Good," he said, with a brief nod. "Now, if you'll excuse me, I have a meeting to get to."

"Oh, of course. Nice to have met you," Lola said, as he sped off. Lola looked at her cell phone and noticed that she was due back in class in less than ten minutes, but something was fishy. Nyla had told Raina that she'd been at practice, when it fact, she hadn't. *Just what has Nyla been up to and where has been spending her time?* Lola made a mental note to make sure Nyla didn't blow this opportunity, whether she liked it or not.

WHEN THE SILENCE IS TOO LOUD

# TWENTY-THREE

## *A WEIGHT LIFTED*

---

Lloyd stood over the grill and made sure that the burgers and chicken didn't overcook. He'd been grilling since early afternoon and he wanted to make sure everything was just right. He'd thought twice about having all three Devereux women under one roof at the same time, but it couldn't be avoided. He was deep in thought about Nyla and her friend at the hospital when Jessica came out with more meat to put on the grill.

"Here you go, baby," she said, as she handed him a plate full of ribs. "This is the last of the meat," she said looking around. Jessica saw the two other trays of barbecue. "Uh, honey. I really think you overdid it with the meat."

"What? Aren't your sisters bringing their husbands and crew?

"Yes."

"I'm thinking we might not have enough."
Jessica hit him on his shoulder.

"You are wrong for that," she said with a
chuckle.

"I'm just kidding, baby. It's just been so long
since we've had a family gathering for a *happy*
occasion. Besides, this isn't only for the kids, it's
for the entire family."

"Speaking of family, I hope you know what
you're doing by having the three Devereux Divas
here at the same time." Lloyd nodded his head
knowingly.

"Yes. I understand what you're saying. In the
past it's been a challenge, but Lola is trying really
hard to get her life back on track. And you know
mama is expecting Aunt Victoria to be here.

"I know. I just don't want them to turn our girls'
birthday party into their own little reality show."

"I'll do my best to keep them focused on the
kids. Besides, this will be Nyla's first time being
around everyone in the family. It's time we
celebrated instead of focusing on our loss."

"Okay. I hear you," Jessica eased up on tiptoe
and kissed her husband. He was such an optimist,
and he loved his family, which was one of the
reasons she fell in love with him. Jessica knew it
killed him to see the discord between Lola and
Victoria. Both Lola and Raina had been like sisters
to him, growing up. It was natural that he wanted
there to be peace between them. She just hoped that
today would be a good starting point.

※※※※

Victoria was the first to arrive. "My, my, my. It's only May and we're already feeling the wrath of the Georgia heat," Victoria said, as she entered the front door. Jessica greeted her with a hug and took the gifts she'd brought to place on the gift table.

"Aunt Victoria, you didn't have to get them anything. They already have too much stuff."

"Oh, hush now. It was no bother. I saw these cute little dresses and thought they would look adorable in them." Jessica kissed her on the cheek and noticed Victoria peering around the room.

"Raina and the kids should be here shortly," Jessica said, anticipating her curiosity.

"Oh, okay," Victoria responded with a nervous smile. "What about Lola? Will she be stopping by?" she asked nonchalantly, patting her face with a handkerchief.

"Yes, I think she said she would be stopping by." Jessica placed the gifts on a nearby table and turned back to face Victoria. "Hey, Mom is in the kitchen."

"Oh yes. I knew that's where I would find my sister. What is she cooking up now?" Victoria asked, as she made her way through the house while dodging toys and children.

※※※※

The birthday party was in full swing by the time Lola and Dr. Eli pulled up in front of Lloyd's house.

"Wow. Looks like half the neighborhood is here," Jeremiah said, as he looked around the cul-de-sac at the parked cars, bicycles and water toys scattered over the front lawn. Lola sat quietly, watching each guest as they entered the house.

"Yes. Lloyd and Jess have always known how to throw a good party."

"Do you feel up for this?" Jeremiah asked. He sensed her apprehension. Lola nodded and gave him a half smile.

"Will I ever?" Lola looked over at him with a slight frown and swatted at something invisible. "You know what? Don't pay me any attention. I'm sure I'll be fine."

"You don't seem fine." Lola looked back up at the house. "You know, you have to face her sometime," he added with concern. Lola inhaled a little and closed her eyes briefly.

"Yes. I know." She exhaled forcefully. "It's just that the last time we were all got together like this was at Quincy's birthday party a few years back. I got sloppy drunk and made a complete fool out of myself."

"Listen," Jeremiah placed his hand on top of hers. "That was then. You've got to stop living in the past. You're a work in progress, Lola and you're changing every day."

"You're right. It's just that ever since Dad's death, I've let my nerves get the best of me. I feel like everyone's judging me. Sometimes it's easier to run in the opposite direction."

"Well, today there will be no running. And it just may be that the judging is coming from you and not them. Now stop beating yourself up and go have fun with your family." Lola looked at him as if he'd just grown two heads.

"It is possible you know."

"If you say so," she said, doubtfully.

"I say so. Now go." Lola took in another deep breath and released her seatbelt. "Okay. Thank you for meeting with me on your day off and for the ride."

"Hey, that's what I do. Now stop stalling and go," he said, pushing her slightly toward the car door.

"Okay, okay. I'm going." Lola opened the door, stepped out and walked around to the drivers' side. With the house looming in the background, she could feel her anxiety moving over her body.

"I was um... Would you like to come inside? I mean, being from London, I wasn't sure if you eat barbecue." Jeremiah chuckled and gave her one of his brilliant smiles.

"Yes, as a matter of fact, I do eat barbecue. But I don't think it would be wise right now. Listen," he grabbed her hand again. "You're stronger than you think. You can do this." This time, his touch sent lightning bolts through her body. Lola quickly pulled away and instinctively knew she had overreacted.

"I'm sorry," he began, "I didn't mean to..."

"No, no. You didn't, I mean, it's just me being... me, you know?"

"No. I didn't mean to take advantage of your need for a friend and..."

"Please don't think that I took offense. I'm just jumpy and I'm trying to get my head together and you're right. You're absolutely right. I am strong and I'm going to be okay." She took another breath and gave him her best soldier boy smile as she turned to go.

"Go," he encouraged.

"Okay, I'm going. Thanks again." Lola walked toward the house and started up the steps, toward the front door. As she got closer her knees felt weak. Out of nowhere, Lola was almost bowled over by three rambunctious boys as they ran toward the front door.

"Hey!" Jeremiah called out, "Don't forget to call me if you need to talk." Lola nodded, continued up the walkway and disappeared through the door.

As Jeremiah watched her go through the door he felt vexed. He knew he was getting in too deep. His feelings for Lola had grown and as much as he tried to keep it strictly professional, he was losing the battle. The reaction she had to his touch was one he had not anticipated. Lola had been carrying around an incredible amount of guilt, along with just as many scars, and had turned to alcohol to escape. Now, she was learning to face her demons head on while he was allowing his feelings for her to cloud his judgment. Jeremiah knew that anything other than professional counseling was unacceptable. As he pulled away from the curb, Jeremiah decided that he would do everything in his power to see her succeed, even if it meant he had to walk away.

Lola stepped through the door and the smoky smell of barbecue greeted her like an old friend. Lloyd came in through the patio doors with more food and spotted his cousin.

"Hey! It's about time you got here," his voice boomed through the house. "Where've you been?!"

"Oh, I had some errands to take care of. Man, I didn't know y'all were feeding the entire neighborhood." Lola smiled and looked around at all the activity.

"Well, we invited their friends from their soccer team, swim team and a few of their classmates. Some of the parents decided to hang around too. So.... you gonna stick around for a while?"

"Of course."

"Raina was asking for you earlier."

"Where is she?"

"She's sitting out on the porch along with Mama and Aunt Vicky."

"Oh. Okay."

"Hey, fix yourself a plate first and go join 'em."

"You don't have to tell me twice. I'm so hungry my stomach is talking to my back."

"Well, there's plenty here to take care of that," Lloyd said, with a hearty smile.

"Is Nyla here?"

"Yeah. She's in the pool with the rest of the kids."

"Okay." Lola prepared her plate and made small talk with some of the parents before making her way to the porch.

"Hey everybody," she said, as she entered.

"Oh good. You finally made it," Raina said.

"Yep. Hey, Aunt Louise. How are you?" Lola said, as she greeted Victoria's twin sister.

"Girl, come here and give me a hug. I ain't seen you in a month of Sundays." Lola put her plate on the small table and moved toward her aunt and gave her a hug.

"Ooh wee. You still just as pretty as ever. How've you been, baby?"

"I've been well." Lola answered as Victoria sat

quietly in the corner.

"Hey Mom," Lola added quickly. She didn't want to appear disrespectful.

"Hello sweetheart, glad you made it." Victoria was truly happy to see Lola. Ever since their confrontation, Victoria had done a lot of thinking. She wanted things to be better between them. She finally realized that Lola's double loss of her father and the baby had been something that Lola had not gotten over. And Victoria knew her own actions had only made it worse.

Lola looked out in the yard and saw Nyla sitting on the side of the pool. While all the other kids were kicking and screaming at the top of their lungs, Nyla sat and observed. Victoria noticed Lola watching, but she dared not say anything.

🌀 🌀 🌀 🌀

As day turned into evening guests continued to filter in and out of the house. 'Happy birthday' had been sung, the cake had been cut, and kids throughout the house could be heard crying as they balked at the suggestion of leaving. The birthday party was winding down, and Lola, Raina, Victoria and Louise had moved into the kitchen to help Jessica clean up. Raina was carrying a tray of leftover cupcakes when suddenly the tray slipped from her hands and fell all over the kitchen floor.

"Lord, have mercy!" Louise exclaimed.

"Oh my gosh. I...I don't know what happened. I'm so sorry, Jess."

Jessica grabbed a broom. "Don't worry about it, girl. If I went a day without something being dropped, dismantled, or broken, I would think something was terribly wrong with the Universe."

"Are you okay, Raina? You seem a little dazed," Louise said.

"Yes. I'm fine," she said, reaching down to retrieve a couple of the cupcakes from the floor.

"You do look a little tired, sweetheart. Have been getting enough rest?" Victoria asked.

"Okay already. Everybody, give her a break." Lola was a little agitated. "She said she's fine. It was an accident. Let it go." Raina was thankful to have her sister there. Ever since they were kids Lola always had her back. She wished she knew what had come between them.

"To answer your question, Mom, I've been sleeping fine," Raina answered. "It's just that we all got started really early this morning so it's been a long day. Excuse me for a second." Raina grabbed her purse and headed to the bathroom.

"Hey, where's my mom?" Quincy asked, as he and Nyla entered the kitchen.

"She just went into the bathroom," Lola answered, as she began wiping down the kitchen counter. "So, Nyla how do you like being on the track team?" Lola asked. Nyla was taken aback.

"How'd you know I was on the track team?"

"Well we do live in the same house." Nyla relaxed. "Not to mention, I ran into your coach the other day on campus." Lola watched for Nyla's reaction. "He had nothing but good things to say about you." Nyla gave an awarkward smile.

"Oh yeah?" Nyla said, nervously.

"I didn't know you were on the track team, Nyla," Jessica chimed in.

"According to Coach Collins, she's pretty fast," Lola bragged.

"Well I'm not surprised. From what I can remember, Lloyd told me that Keenan was a pretty fast runner too," Jessica added.

"Sweetheart, how did you get that bruise?" Victoria asked. Even though Nyla attempted to cover it with her bang, she couldn't completely hide the purplish bruise right above her eye.

"Oh. I, um, bumped into the wall going to the bathroom the other night," Nyla lied, and pulled her bang further over the bruise.

"I can't deal with all that running out in the hot sun, myself," Quincy added. "It's boring. Everybody knows that basketball is the number one sport."

🌀🌀🌀🌀

The voices from the kitchen were muffled beyond the bathroom door. Once inside the restroom, Raina saw her reflection and knew her mother hadn't lied. She looked exhausted. She dug into her purse and retrieved a small bottle of pills. She took one, splashed water on her face and reapplied her lip gloss. "There, that's as good as it gets," she said, to her reflection. Raina rotated her head to try and ease the tension in her shoulders. No matter how many pills she took to shake her feelings of apprehension or to help her sleep, nothing worked one hundred percent. *In due time, Raina. In due time.* She took a deep breath and stepped out of the bathroom and walked back into the kitchen.

"Hey Mom. Can Nyla and I walk down to the

basketball court at the park? We're getting tired of babysitting all these kids," Quincy said, grabbing his third burger of the day.

"Sure, but don't be too long. We'll be leaving in about an hour."

"Okay. Thanks," he said, as they turned to leave.

"Hey, Nyla, thank you for helping out with the kids," Jessica said, "I didn't realize we were going to need a lifeguard."

"No problem. I enjoyed it," Nyla replied, as she kept moving toward the door. She was ready to be out of the kitchen and out from under the Devereux telescope.

"What am I, chopped liver? I helped too," Quincy added, and held his arms open as he inquired with a mouth full of food.

"Boy, all I saw was you getting your grub on, as usual," Lola interjected. They all laughed.

"A brotha's gotta eat, right?"

"That's right. So, thank you also, Quincy," Jessica said, as she placed what was left of the burgers and potato salad into the fridge.

Quincy followed Nyla out the door and they headed to the park.

"So what really happened to her head? That sure is an ugly bruise," Lola asked Raina.

"Like she said, she ran into the bathroom door."

"Well, she must've been going fifty miles an hour," Lola said under her breath. Lola hated to admit it but she was all too familiar with the bathroom door story. She had a strong suspicion that the bruise didn't come from a door. Lola thought about what the coach had said about Nyla missing practice.

"You sure she's not involved with some little knuckle-head?" Aunt Louise queried. "You know, I saw on the news how these young folk start stalking one another and getting all physical."

"Yes. I heard about that but not to worry," Raina added. "Nyla goes to school and comes right home when she's not at practice. The only people she hangs out with are Q, Matt and Isaias."

"How is she adjusting?" Jessica asked.

"She's still a little distant sometimes but it's to be expected, she's been through a lot." Jessica nodded in agreement. "I think she's okay living with us, but Keenan isn't there and..." Raina's voice trailed off.

"Mm, mm, mm, that would be tough for anybody. I can't get over how much she and Q resemble," Louise said.

"Yes. They both have Keenan's strong features. But you know, we were talking the other day and I asked Nyla the names of her adoptive parents. It's strange, but the names sounded vaguely familiar."

"Oh yeah, what were they?" Lola tried to sound nonchalant.

"Candace and Steven Davis. Candace Davis. That name sounds so familiar."

The wine glass Victoria held slipped out of her hand and fell onto the table. She began coughing profusely. Raina jumped to her feet and patted Victoria's back while Lola wiped up the spilled wine.

"Mom, are you okay?" Raina asked.

"Yes dear. I'm fine," Victoria responded, still

spurting coughs with a nervous laugh. "The wine just went down the wrong pipe. I guess I've reached my limit."

"You sure you're okay?" Lola asked, suspiciously.

"Yes. I'm fine."

"Lord have mercy," Louise said, with a small frown. "Victoria you know you shouldn't be drinking that stuff, anyway."

"Does that name sound familiar to you, Aunt V?" Jessica asked, while she dried a large bowl.

"Huh? What? What are you asking me, dear?" Victoria said, fanning herself.

"Candace and Steven Davis," Jessica repeated. "Do they sound familiar?"

"I can't get it out of my head," Raina added.

"No. Absolutely not. It doesn't sound familiar to me at all." Victoria's abrupt response raised a few eyebrows.

Lola and Jess stood and watched the exchange and thought it strange. Raina's left eyebrow went up.

"Okay. I was just asking," Jessica said.

Victoria looked around the room and realized her tone was inappropriate.

"Well, I think it's important to have some kind of connection to someone. So I tried to research the names online. I thought maybe Nyla could meet some of her adoptive parents' relatives. Afterward, maybe I can also help find her biological mother. The room went silent. Raina looked up and stared back at all four perplexed faces.

"What?" she asked.

Victoria was the first to speak. "Raina. I think it's commendable that you want to help Nyla, but you already have a great deal to contend with."

"That's right. Just the other night you were struggling with the idea of whether or not to sell your house. You shouldn't be adding anything else to your plate right now," Lola said.

Now it was Raina's turn to look perplexed. She looked from Lola to Victoria and back again. She couldn't remember the last time those two had agreed on anything. Now on something as important as helping Nyla locate her biological mother, they both disagreed with her.

"Wow." Raina looked at Jess. "Can you believe this? Mom, haven't you always taught us that charity starts at home? Nyla is hurting. She's been through a lot. I just want to help her find her mother."

"What if you're wrong? What if the mother doesn't want to be found?" Victoria asked. "I've heard of that happening. People search to find their biological parents and once found, the parent doesn't want to reconnect."

"Are you serious? I can't believe that. I understand people make mistakes when they're young but I think at some point they would want to know their own flesh and blood," Jessica added.

"Not necessarily. What if the person was raped and became pregnant? They probably wouldn't want to be reminded of that." Victoria asked Raina the question but she was looking directly at Lola.

"Raina, I don't think you need to rock the boat right now," Lola said. "Nyla seems to be adjusting well. If you open up this whole can of worms you may do more harm than good." Lola could feel her heart in her throat.

"What if she's rejected by this woman?" Jessica asked.

"Well, what about the letter?" Raina asked.

"What letter?" It was Victoria.

"The letter that started Keenan's search in the first place. *Someone* sent him that letter with all the details of Nyla's birth. Who would do that or know all of that information other than her birth mother?"

"It could've been anybody." Lola was beginning to panic. "It could've been a caregiver or something; I don't know."

"I don't know either, but I do know that there's someone out there who wanted him to find her. That someone could be the person that Nyla needs in her life right now," Raina said in defiance.

Victoria felt distressed. "I... um, I'm not feeling too well." She pinched the bridge of her nose.

"Mom? What's wrong? Do you need me to call the doctor?" Raina asked, alarmed.

"No. It's probably just something I ate that didn't agree with me. Lola, would you please bring my car around to the front for me, dear?" Lola was stupefied.

"Me?" she asked, almost choking on the bottle of water she'd been sipping. "Um...okay, sure," Lola said, as she retrieved the keys from her mother.

"Victoria, you just need to go home and get some rest. You're not a spring chicken anymore," Louise chastised.

"Perhaps you're right," Victoria rose from the

table.

"You sure you're okay to drive?" Raina asked, taking a step closer.

"Yes, dear. I'm fine, just a little weary. We'll talk tomorrow. Louise, I'll call you later this week to discuss our shopping trip," Victoria called back, as she started out of the kitchen.

"All right," Louise replied. "I'll talk to you later."

"I'll walk you out," Raina said.

"No. I'm not an invalid, Raina. I can walk myself out just fine. You continue helping Jessica. Oh, and Jessica, please tell Lloyd it was a fine party, as usual." Victoria turned again to start out of the kitchen.

"Okay. And thanks again for the gifts."

"Get some rest, Mom," Raina spoke to her mother's back. Victoria simply waved.

As Victoria descended the front steps, Lola got out of the car and walked hesitantly toward her mother. Lola noticed how much older she seemed. Victoria had somehow shrunken in size and moved slower than what Lola remembered.

"Here you go." Lola handed over the car keys. To her surprise Victoria quickly grabbed her wrist and held it with such force, Lola stumbled toward her.

"Why didn't you tell me?" Victoria asked with a look of stunned concern.

"What?!" Lola was alarmed. "What's wrong? What do you mean tell you?!"

"How can this be? How can she be Keenan's daughter and *yours*?" Lola's breath caught in her

294

throat.

"What are you talking abo—"

"I'm talking about Nyla's adopted parents! Candace and Steven Davis. Candace was your father's secretary for many years. She and her husband couldn't conceive so when Nyla was born, we agreed that they would take her." Lola tried to pull free, but Victoria was stronger than she seemed only moments before.

"Did he rape you? Did Keenan force himself on you? Is that why you became so distant and angry?"

"What? No! He would've never done anything like that. Besides, don't you realize how old she is? I met Keenan long before he met and married Raina. After I left school I never saw or heard from him again until the night of the wedding rehearsal dinner." Victoria loosened her grip.

"Lola, I don't understand. How did this happen? Why didn't you tell someone? "

"Mother, did you really want to know? What would I have said? The entire wedding would've been destroyed and you never would've forgiven me. No matter what you may think of me, I couldn't do that to Raina.

"Did Keenan know? Did he know you gave birth to his child?"

"No." Lola said, as she lowered her head. "No one knew. We met a couple of months before I came home for Thanksgiving break. He was a sophomore and I couldn't believe he was interested in me. I mean, I was just a freshman. But he didn't care about that."

"I told your father you were too young to go

away. But he fought me on it. He said if you were smart enough to graduate a year early, you were smart enough to maneuver your way through college.

"Well, that made two of us who felt that way." Lola added.

"What happened, Lola?"

"I told you. We met. We were attracted to each other and we had sex." Victoria gasped.

"It wasn't like that, Mother. He was kind and he was patient. He never forced me and I wanted to be with him. It was serious, or so I thought, but when he didn't return to school after Thanksgiving, I realized that I didn't really know that much about him. He was introduced to me as Ken and that's what I called him. All I knew was that I was happy to be with him, but after he didn't come back to school, I couldn't find out anything. Now I know that he didn't return because his father was sick. It was all so complicated. By the time I came home for Christmas, I knew I was pregnant. And... well, we both know the rest of the story. Victoria's breathing became shallow.

"Oh my god. So you never told him?" Lola shook her head as Victoria stared back at her, in shock.

"But what about the letter? Did *you* send Keenan that letter? Lloyd and Raina think that it came from the biological mother," Victoria asked, confused.

Tears rolled down Lola's cheeks so fast she couldn't wipe them away fast enough. She couldn't speak. She simply nodded.

The scene unfolded in her head as if someone

had hit the rewind button to a movie. Lola saw herself kicking and screaming as she tried breaking down the door that led into the mailroom at the rehab center.

"I was trying to get myself together," her words finally choked out. "I was so tired and ready to let go of it all. So I tried this thing, to… I don't know, to cleanse myself I guess. You know… all that stuff you hear about the truth setting you free and letting go of the past?" Lola asked, as she took a tissue from her mother. "I got caught up and for a moment I believed it. I wanted to free myself of all the guilt and shame I'd carried around for so long. So I wrote the letter and mailed it before I lost my nerve. Afterward, I got really scared and decided to try and get it back. But the mailroom had closed and I became desperate. I tried to break in."

"What?"

"Yeah. Can you believe it? Needless to say I was caught and thrown out. I left there, went out and got pissy drunk. A week later I joined AA." They were both silenced by Lola's admission.

"You know, when I first arrived at the rehab center, one of the counselors asked me what was my passion. Even in the pitiful state I was in, they wanted to know if I could see my life beyond the drunkenness. It was difficult but there was a glimpse from time to time. I never told a soul but the entire time I was there, all I wanted was to find her. The more sober I became, the more I ached for her. All I ever wanted was to know her and I knew Keenan could do that. I knew he could find her. So I wrote the letter. Afterwards," Lola paused, covering her mouth, "I started thinking about Raina and her family and how this might destroy them. So I panicked."

"Oh, my god." Victoria looked at her daughter with such compassion and sadness. She closed what little space there was between them and placed both of her hands on Lola's wet cheeks.

"You've carried this burden around for seventeen years. I'm so sorry and I'm ashamed that I haven't been there for you. I never completely understood." Victoria tried to draw Lola closer and she became rigid.

"I wasn't there for you then, but I'm here now. Let me help you." Lola crossed her arms in front of her and dropped her head.

"I don't want your help."

"Why Lola? Why won't you let me help you?" Lola found the courage to look into her mother's face. "When it was just the two of us, I felt like it was you and me against the world. I felt that there was nothing that I could do wrong in your eyes. You were my love and my protector. When you married the Reverend and gave birth to Raina, things changed. It seemed that there was nothing that I could do right, no matter how hard I tried. And I tried with everything I had in me.

"Lola, my feelings never changed for you, I—" Lola held up one hand.

"But I didn't feel that. I felt that you had what you always wanted; your perfect little family. I was just a constant reminder of your past. That's why I tried so hard in school.

"I was proud of you. Of everything you ever

did."

"Everything but come home pregnant, huh?"

Victoria looked away but when she peered back into Lola's face, she knew she had to be truthful.

"I was afraid. I was afraid for you and for me. Afraid to see you go through the same shame and judgment that I experienced. Your father and I never married. When I became pregnant, my mother put me out on the street and I was only a child. I was homeless and jobless with barely a high school education. I had no skills and no way to feed myself, let alone a baby. I was scared Lola, and even after I met and married the Reverend, I was still scared. That's why I pushed you. It's true. I wanted the perfect family."

"But we weren't perfect Mother! And all your efforts to make it perfect made me feel more and more like a failure. And after I became pregnant..."

"I wanted to protect you."

"But taking my child away was not your decision to make!"

"Lola, you were barely seventeen! You were my baby, and at the time, I thought it was for the best. I'm sorry. I never meant to allow my insecurities to make you feel like a failure. I love you, Lola." Victoria looked up into her daughter's face. Lola looked past the tiny lines that were now etched into her mother's beautiful skin. Victoria's eyes pleaded with her.

Victoria stepped toward Lola. "I'm sorry. Please forgive me?" Victoria reached out and gradually embraced her child, something she hadn't done for many years.

"What are we going to do?" Lola asked, finally allowing her head to rest atop her mother's petite shoulder. Little by little Lola felt the hardness surrounding her heart begin to melt away. At first she wasn't sure if she wanted to allow herself to be so vulnerable. The shell had been her protection. At the same time, it had been many years since someone had held her out of love and not lust. It felt good. She wouldn't admit it but she was happy to have Victoria for an ally.

"I don't know, but we'll figure something out."

"They're going to hate me." Lola looked back at Victoria with a tear-stained face.

"No. You've only tried to protect them. Eventually, they'll see that."

"Nyla won't. She already told me that she couldn't care less about the idea of finding her biological mother." Victoria felt overwhelmed but she knew she couldn't let Lola down again.

"She's speaking from a place of pain. Someday that pain will be replaced with love. And love heals, Lola. Love heals. We're going to figure this out together. We have to," Victoria said, as she stood with her emotions swirling throughout her body while holding Lola in her arms. Oh, how she had missed her.

As the sun began to descend from the multi-colored sky, Victoria and her daughter had finally allowed the healing power of forgiveness to begin. Neither of them noticed Raina as she stood peering out of the front window.

# TWENTY-FOUR

## AN UNLIKELY ALLY

---

It was dusk but the neighborhood was still filled with activity. Spring in Atlanta had its residents shedding their winter skin and coming out of hibernation. Nyla and Quincy strolled down the street toward the basketball court amid the sound of children playing and the smell of barbecue filling the air. As they drew closer, they heard the guys on the court trash talking among themselves.

"Did you have a good time today?" Quincy asked his sister. "I mean, I know it was a silly kids' party but at least they had some good food."

Nyla tilted her head and took a minute to think about his question. She knew everyone had tried to make her feel like she belonged and that she was a part of the family. She hadn't been able to come to terms with it until Tyrone's threat. Before she had felt like an intruder, but now she only wanted to protect them.

"Yeah. I actually did have a good time. It was kinda weird meeting all these people who I'm supposed to be related to when most of my life I've felt like I didn't have a connection to anybody."

"You know you're pretty good with kids. You should maybe think about becoming a teacher or something when you go to college." Nyla frowned.

"College? Me? And a teacher?" She had never given much thought to college. She'd always been in survival mode. Even now, with Tyrone hounding her every move, she still couldn't focus on the future until she could fully escape her past.

"Yeah. I mean, you seem pretty patient with all that running, crying and screaming." Nyla shrugged her shoulders.

"I guess I got good at it from taking care of a lot of the younger foster kids. When the social workers would drop them off, I saw how scared they were, you know? I knew how that felt, not knowing if the person in charge would be a friend or enemy. After a while, you just considered everyone an enemy until they proved otherwise. And even then, you still had to be careful.

Quincy listened intently. He'd never considered the ugliness that Nyla had experienced. It was all so foreign to him.

"Man, I'm really sorry you had to go through that."

Nyla shrugged again. "It is what it is, you know?"

"Yeah. I guess." A basketball bounced toward

them and Quincy stooped down and grabbed it. Moments later, Isaias trotted toward them to retrieve the ball.

"Hey Q. What's up?"

"Hey, what's up, Isaias? I didn't know you'd be over this way today," Quincy said, as they leaned toward one another, and engaged in what appeared to be some kind of secret handshake.

"Oh, yeah. I had to come by and cut my grandmother's grass. Thought I'd shoot a little hoop before I headed home," he said, looking at Nyla. Quincy may have been a few years younger, but he was old enough to pick up on the look Isaias gave his sister.

"Yo. You mind if I shoot a few hoops?" Quincy asked, as he bounced the ball.

"Nah man. Go ahead. You can take my spot for the next round."

"A'ight." Quincy said, already headed for the court of waiting teens. Suddenly he stopped and turned back toward Nyla.

"You okay?" Nyla couldn't help but smile at his attempt to be protective.

She nodded her head to assure him that she was fine.

"I'm cool."

"A'ight, I don't want no trouble, now," he said, half warning, half joking as he pointed at Isaias.

"We cool, man," Isaias said, as he threw his t-shirt over his shoulder. With that, Quincy took off.

"Hey," Isaias said nervously as he turned his attention back toward Nyla.

"Hey yourself," Nyla responded.

"You still not gonna tell me who did that to you?" Isaias asked, as he eyed the bruise on her forehead.

"I told you the other night that I ran into—"

"Into the wall, yeah, I know. And I'm Honey Boo Boo."

"Whatever," Nyla rolled her eyes. "Why do you even care?"

"Are you kidding me? You call me and ask me to sneak out of the house *again* to come pick you up and when I get there, looks like you've been beaten up just like your friend. Are you going to tell me what's going on or—"

"Or what? You gonna go run to Lloyd again?"

"Maybe I should. You won't talk to me. Maybe *he* can get some information out of you, because I sure can't help you if you won't be honest enough to tell me the truth."

Nyla stood in silent defiance. Isaias wrapped his t-shirt around the back of his neck and waited a few minutes. Nyla said nothing.

"So it's like that, huh? A'ight. Keep your secrets. It's just sad that you've finally got people around who want to help but you won't even let 'em. Good luck with that. I'm out." Frustrated, he started back toward the courts.

Isaias was halfway up the block when he heard Nyla's steps coming up fast behind him.

"Isaias, wait." He surprised her when he turned abruptly.

"For what, Nyla? You want to play all hard and not talk to anybody. I don't have time for this. You're in trouble, that's obvious, but I can't help you like this."

"It's not that... I mean, I want to tell you but... I just..."

He could see the uncertainty in her expression. "What is it, Ny?"

"I don't want anyone else to get hurt."

"Get hurt? Wait a minute. What is this about?"

"Okay, listen. When I first ran from the foster home I kinda got mixed up with this guy who was really nice to me at first. After a while he started making demands on me... making me work at this club. I'd never seen anything like it and it was exciting at first but after a while, Tyrone wanted me to give some of his friends special attention, if you know what I mean. I wasn't down with that so me and Gabby took some of the money we earned and split. We caught a bus to Atlanta and now he's here."

"Whoa... that's some crazy... wait a minute. How did he find out where you were?"

"Gabby and her stupid Facebook page. He's here and he's..." Nyla almost broke down.

"He's the one that beat your friend like that?!"

"Yeah." Nyla was barely able to get the word past her lips.

"And he'll do the same to me, or worse, if I don't make some deliveries for him, to pay back what we took."

"Hold up. You stole from your pimp?!" As soon as he said it, Isaias was sorry.

"He wasn't my pimp! And we had to get outta there! We needed that money. Besides, we earned it."

"Look. Just tell Lloyd. He's a detective."

"See, now there you go. I can't tell Lloyd. Tyrone knows where I live. He's already had Raina show him some houses just to show me he's serious about hurting my family if I don't do what he says."

Isaias shook his head in disbelief. Although there was a slight breeze, sweat still poured from his head. He wiped his entire face and head with his t-shirt, not believing what he was hearing. "Oh my god. This can't be real."

"Trust me, it's real."

"So when are you supposed to make the first delivery?"

"I don't know," she said, with a shrug of her shoulders. "He said he would be in contact."

"Nyla. Listen to me. You've got to go to the police. He's never going to let you stop."

"Okay. I already told you he'll kill me, Raina, Q and Matt. Are you listening?"

"Are you listening to *yourself*? He's never gonna to let you off the hook. People like that just use you until they have no more use for you and then they kill you anyway. You're in a no-win situation."

"You know what? I knew I shouldn't have told you. I got this." She turned and began to storm off. Isaias grabbed her forearm.

"Hey wait. Stop." He attempted to slow her down. Nyla pulled away.

"Don't touch me!"

"Listen, I'll do it. I'll help you, okay? Just calm down." From a few feet away, Quincy noticed the commotion and came up behind them.

"What's going on? You okay, Ny?"

"Yeah. I'm fine. We gotta go," she said to Quincy before she turned and headed back toward Lloyd's house.

"Ny! Call me, okay?" Isaias called after her.

Nyla walked as fast as she could. She wanted to get as far away from Isaias as possible. She was sorry that she'd confided in him. Isaias words still rang in her ears. *He's never going to let you stop.* In her gut, she knew it was true. Nyla rationalized that the only way out was to bring Tyrone down. She would just have to take matters into her own hands and deal with him the only way she knew how.

That night, Nyla placed a called to Nathan, the cousin of one of her track and field teammates. She needed protection and she knew Nate was just the one to get it for her.

# TWENTY-FIVE

## LOLA & GRAHAM MEET FOR LUNCH

---

Lola sat near the window at The Taste Bud, waiting. The gourmet sandwich shop was located near Grant Park, an eclectically artsy side of town. It sat nestled among the trees, bungalows, and specialty boutiques that lined either side of the street. Lola looked around, and took in all the colorful décor. For a moment she stared unseeing at a Mexican mask that hung on the far wall. She checked her cell phone again for the third time and sipped her latte while she waited for Graham. Finally, she saw Graham's silver and blue convertible Volkswagen Bug swerve into the parking lot.

It was another gorgeous day in Atlanta. The buds had blossomed on the dogwood trees and a soft breeze stirred the petals as they danced through the air and across the ground. It looked like a springtime snowfall. Lola smiled and waved at Graham through the window, as she popped out of the car and made her way into the sandwich shop. Graham knew the owners. The manager had been one of the teens she'd helped get back on track. He was clearly in his mid twenties now. He was a tall, lanky-looking fellow with large holes in his earlobes and tattoos down both of his arms.

"Hey Graham," he greeted her as she entered the shop.

"What's up, Josh. I'll have the usual." He nodded knowingly as she headed toward Lola.

"What's up? How's life, chica?" Graham asked, reaching over for a quick hug.

"I don't know. You tell me," Lola responded. Graham took a deep breath as she removed her jacket and smiled at Lola.

"Well, I must say, sobriety certainly agrees with you. You look great!"

"Thank you. It's only been three months, four days, twelve hours and fifteen minutes, but who's counting?" They both laughed.

"Dang, girl! It's like that, huh?" Graham asked lightly, but her voice was still laced with a bit of concern.

"Yes. I can't lie. Some days are just like that." Graham reached across the table and grabbed Lola's hand. There were no words that could make it all better. They both knew it would just take time.

Josh came over with Graham's order and after a brief introduction he disappeared as Graham dug in.

"Oh, this is so... good. I've been thinking about

this sandwich all day." Lola took another sip of her coffee and watched in amazement as the tiny woman attacked the not-so-small sandwich. She seemed to have inhaled the entire thing in only a few minutes.

"How in the world do you eat like that and stay a size, what... two?" Lola asked, her voice laced with envy.

"Well, actually I'm a six and well... I don't know. I guess I've just been blessed with a high metabolism." Graham washed down the sandwich with a bottle of water.

"Speaking of blessings, I just want to say thank you for what you did in helping me get in to see Dr. Eli. He's been a godsend."

"Yeah. And he's not bad on the eyes, either," Graham added, as she sat back.

"I ain't gonna lie, now. You're right about that, but"—Lola held up her hand—"I'm trying to stay focused and just work on me."

"That's good to hear. Because a little birdie told me that you two may be getting a little too close for comfort."

"What? Who would say something like that?"

"Oh, someone who just may have the hots for the doctor herself."

"Who? Hazel?!" Graham almost sprayed Lola with the water she'd just drank.

"Girl, no. Hazel's old enough to be his mother."

"Humph, that doesn't matter these days. Haven't heard the term cougar?"

"Yes, but Hazel is not a concern for you. Besides, do you really think Dr. Eli would look at her twice?" Graham shuddered at the thought.

"Well, who?"

"Sara."

"Really? She has a thing for Dr. Eli?"

"Well, can you blame her? Working in the same office with that tall chunk of dark chocolate, with those dimples... and those beautiful full lips that frame those perfectly white teeth like..." Graham spoke in a dreamlike state.

"Uh... earth to Graham." Lola waved her hand in front of Graham's face. "Yeah, come on back, honey."

"Oh yeah, where was I?"

"You were talking about Sara having a thing for Doctor Eli."

"Yes, well, she called and expressed that she felt you all were getting a little too familiar. And considering the professional ramifications, as your friend, I just wanted to tell you to be careful."

"So, you're telling me as a friend or do you have an ulterior motive?" Graham who had been reapplying her lipstick, stopped suddenly.

"Okay, now you're about to piss me off. I've known Dr. Eli since grad school. He was one of my professors and although I will admit that I've had my share of fantasies, my *fiancé* wouldn't be too thrilled with the idea of us hooking up. Graham tossed her left hand in front of Lola's face so she could inspect the perfectly round, one-and-a-half carat diamond for herself.

"Oh, my gosh, Graham! It's beautiful! Congratulations!"

"Thank you. All I can say is it's about time." She

looked at the diamond again for the fiftieth time that day. "But, let's not get off track. We're talking about you."

Lola waved her off. "Let's not go there. I'm not stupid. I'm not going to lie. I could sense some chemistry between us. I mean, the man is fine but the last thing I want to do is jeopardize what he has going on. I certainly don't want to risk successfully completing this recovery program. I need to do this for the people I care about."

"Okay. Good. I'm glad to hear that. By the way, how's the subbing going?

"Girl, don't get me started on those hard-headed kids. I never thought I would say I miss flying, but dealing with passengers for a few hours is better than being trapped in a classroom full of over-privileged, disrespectful children all day.

"Ah... and what about your sister and her kids?"

"Oh, they're all doing well. Here, check this out. I took this the other day when they were headed out to school. Lola showed Graham a photo on her cell phone of all three kids.

"Wow. They're older than I thought they were. I didn't know she had three kids."

"Oh, no. Only two. The girl is her, uh...her step-daughter." Lola found it difficult to explain Nyla. Every time she tried, the truth caused her stomach to do flips.

"Let me see that again." Graham reached for Lola's phone. "I've seen this girl before. Yes, she's been down to the center a couple of times."

"Really? What center?"

"The youth center. I work there part-time. Yes, I

saw her hanging out with one of the guys. What's his name?" Graham snapped her fingers. "Nate! Yes, that's it."

Lola wondered if Nate was the one who left the bruise on Nyla's face.

"I've been trying to get him off the streets for a while. You might want to keep a close eye on her. Make sure she doesn't get into any trouble," Graham said, as she handed Lola back her phone.

Lola nodded, absentmindedly. She'd been so consumed with getting better so she would be able to handle what she knew would one day come that she hadn't considered how immediate Nyla's need was for her, even in her present state.

"Yes. I'll definitely keep an eye out."

"Well, chica, I gotta get out of here. Benny and I are meeting to pick out his wedding band."

"Okay. I'd better get an invite to this wedding," Lola said, as they both got up from the table.

"But of course."

Graham paid the tab and with another brief hug she was out the door, leaving Lola to ponder it all. *Boy, you just never know what curve balls life is going to throw at you.* Lola had always been somewhat of a magician when it came to dodging those curve balls. Now she needed to be the one at bat to face the incoming head on. She wrapped her scarf loosely around her neck, covering the half-moon shape birthmark right below her collar-bone and headed toward the train station.

৯৯৯৯

Raina had just taken another pill and jumped as she turned and saw Lola watching her.

"Oh my gosh, Lola! You scared me to death. I didn't hear you come in."

"Oh yeah? What's that?" Lola asked, tilting her head toward the bottle that Raina quickly placed inside her purse.

"Oh nothing. I'm just trying to rid myself of this headache." Lola approached her sister.

"Have you been having headaches on a regular basis?" she asked, now standing only a few feet from Raina.

"No. Not really."

"May I see what you're taking?" Lola asked, with an outstretched hand. Raina was caught off guard.

"What? No. What for?"

"Raina. Please tell me you're not still taking those anti-depressants." Lola reached for the purse and Raina pulled it back at the same time.

"Lola," Raina said, warningly. "Don't. What I do is my business and if I need a little help to get through the day it is none of your concern." They both pulled at the purse again and when the contents fell to the floor, Lola's suspicions were confirmed.

"What's this?!" Lola asked as she snatched the plastic container of pills. Raina reached for the bottle but Lola was faster. "Anti-depressants? Sleeping pills, Raina? I thought you weren't going to take these."

"Well, you thought wrong." Raina bent down to pick up the rest of the contents. She didn't see the letter that had slid underneath the chair.

"You don't need these pills, Raina. This can become a dangerous habit." Raina stood quickly.

She was clearly flustered.

"Look, Lola. I'm not a child." She snatched the pills from Lola's hand. "In case you haven't noticed or perhaps you've forgotten, I'm a grown woman with children of my own. I don't need you to preach to me."

"Somebody needs to tell you. You can become dependent on those pills without even realizing it."

"Lola, I know you mean well, but I'm not like..." Raina stopped.

"You're not like who? Like *me*?" Lola stared back at her sister. Raina couldn't bring herself to finish her sentence. "Isn't that what you were about to say? You're nowhere near falling into an addiction like your pitiful sister?"

"I didn't mean it like that. It's just that I got this, okay? You don't have to come to my rescue like you did when we were kids. We're not kids anymore and..."

"And you've got this. Okay. I get it. I mean, what was I thinking? You're all holier-than-thou. Always telling me to rely on God's strength to get me through. Well, why aren't you taking your own advice, huh?"

"Lola. This is different. It's not like I'm smoking pot or doing some hard drugs. I just need—"

"You need? You need what? Some comfort? You need to forget? Oh, I know, you need to rest and clear your head. That's how it all starts, Raina. You can tell yourself those lies if you want to but when you need a substance to get through the day, you're well on your way to becoming *just... like... me.*"

315

"You don't get it! You've never lost someone that you loved so much that the pain is actually physical. You'll never understand what I'm going through! This is just until I can deal with it all." Raina drew her purse to her body. "Please. Just try to understand." Lola's heart went out to her sister, but she wanted to get through to her.

"And how are you going to learn to deal with it if you're numbing yourself?" Lola asked as she bent down, picked up the envelope and turned it around.

"You know what? I can't talk to you about this," Raina snapped. "Don't talk to me about numbing myself. You of all people. You run as fast as you can when you don't want to face something! You don't know what it's like."

"Who's Michael O'Reilly?" Lola asked.

Raina froze. She approached Lola and held out her hand. "Please give that back."

Lola was confused by the pained expression on Raina's face.

"Sissy, what's wrong? Who is this?"

Raina grabbed the envelope and quickly stuffed it in her purse.

"Nobody."

"Well that's certainly not true. Who is he and why has he gotten you so upset?"

Raina was quiet and reflective for a moment. Tears welled in the corners of her eyes.

"Come on, sis. Talk to me," Lola pleaded.

"It's...um... the boy that crashed into Keenan's car."

"Oh. Okay. Well, what does he want?"

Raina inhaled. "It's an apology. He started

sending them a few weeks ago. He wants me to know how sorry he is."

"What are you going to do?"

"Do? I'm not going to *do* anything."

"Well, I mean, it sounds like he's asking for forgiveness. Are you at least going to—"

"I'm not interested in forgiving. He took my husband from me! He took my children's father and all I can think about is how is it that he's still walking around and Keenan is gone!" Raina's tears were coming fast. Lola walked over and embraced her sister. She was at a loss for words. She thought about what Dr. Eli had said about forgiveness.

"I'm so sorry, sissy. I'm so sorry." They stood in the stillness of the grief for a moment longer. Lola wanted so badly to help.

"Raina," she said as she stroked her sister's hair. "Maybe you should try hear him out. It might help to..." Raina's sudden movement stunned Lola. She quickly withdrew from Lola's embrace and glared at her in disbelief.

"What? You of all people are telling me that I need to forgive and forget!" Lola was taken aback.

"Am I too ungodly that you can't take advice from me?" Raina laughed sarcastically and shook her head.

"You're a trip. *You,* Lola Devereux, the only woman I know who can disappear in the blink of an eye, when things go south. Now, you're actually advising me on forgiving someone?"

"Isn't that what the Bible says?"

"Don't tell me what the Bible says. I know what it says!"

"Then act like it! Stop taking those pills and—"
Raina held up her hand.

"Stop. Just stop. Do you think you're the only
one who gets a pass on not being perfect? Yes, I'm
a Christian, but I'm not perfect. I hurt too." Raina
pressed her hand to her chest. "I'm angry, okay?
I'm frustrated and disappointed! It wasn't supposed
to be this way."

"I know but—"

"No you don't. You have no idea what I'm going
through. I know what God says about forgiveness
and I never would've believed that I would feel so
unforgiving. So please stop saying you understand
because I don't even understand it."

"I know more than you realize, little sister. But I
tell you what, I didn't come in here to fight with
you." Lola snatched her jacket and purse from the
barstool and as she did she noticed Raina's Bible.
"But the next time you reach for something to help
you *get through it all*, why don't you reach for
this." Lola tossed the Bible which Raina caught
clumsily. The sisters parted without uttering another
word. Lola left the kitchen feeling that she'd made a
colossal mistake as Raina drew the Bible closer to
her bosom; each woman caught up in her own
feelings of senseless loss.

# TWENTY-SIX

## ARMED & DANGEROUS

---

Nyla's hands shook uncontrollably, as she pulled a sandwich bag filled with flour out of her backpack. Never before had she been so bold as to open one of the packages she delivered. A week ago, she'd devised a plan, a plan that she thought would surely free her from her double life and have Tyrone taken care of for good.

Nyla had begun mixing flour in with some of the cocaine. She knew the word would eventually get out that Tyrone's stuff was bad, but she had no idea the news had already begun to spread like wildfire. She was also too naïve to realize that she could be caught smack in the middle of the same web she was weaving for her tormentor.

After mixing the flour and cocaine she resealed the bags and made her way around to the side of an abandoned house, where she'd been instructed to make the drop.

The skyline was a mixture of orange and lavender as the sun began to melt behind the horizon. A warm breeze teased the few loose curls that escaped from underneath her ball cap. It did very little to cool the inferno which swirled in the pit of her stomach. The neighborhood looked as if, once upon a time, it had been bustling with new families and a spirit of hope. Now, it just looked tired and forgotten. Nyla shifted from her left foot to her right. She peeked around the corner, and tried to spot the vehicle she'd been instructed to look for.

She had mixed feelings about the fading sun. While the darkness would assist in keeping her anonymity, it also put her in greater danger. Nyla wore the same oversized, shabby hoodie she'd worn when she first arrived in Atlanta. She also wore oversized, loose-fitting jeans and tried to blend in with surroundings. This was no place for a young female to be alone but what choice did she have? Tyrone didn't seem to care how dangerous the drop-off locations were. All he cared about was getting his money. Nyla was going to make sure he got exactly what was coming to him.

Finally, she saw the white SUV slowly approach. What she didn't see was one of the passengers get out half a block away and make his way to the other side of the house.

Nyla moved swiftly toward the car. As she approached, she held the package low, tightly pressed against her right thigh.

"Yo. What's up?" The driver spoke with a tilt

of his head. Nyla was taken aback. Usually a quick nod, delivery, receipt of the goods and end of transaction was all there was. Salutations of any kind were not forbidden but were rarely spoken. She slowed her pace and peered further into the car. Sitting right beside the driver was the infamous G-Riley.

He gradually lowered his sunglasses and the strain in his dark, angry eyes penetrated her own. Nyla could feel her pulse racing and knew immediately that she was in trouble. She halted in the middle of the street, and contemplated how to make a quick exit. What happened next seemed to move at the speed of light.

Nyla made a quick turn to her left, picked up speed and attempted to put as much distance between her and the SUV as possible. She heard the car doors opening as the driver and the rest of G-Riley's crew jumped out. The chase was on. Fear was the only thing that kept her legs moving.

"Get her!" she heard one of the thugs command. Nyla's heart raced so fast that the rhythmic, pulsating beat in her ears was almost deafening.

"There she is!" she heard another voice yell out in the gray haze of the evening. Two blocks down she cut through the small back yards of the single, red brick houses in her attempt to escape. As she ducked and hid along the side of the houses, she could hear neighborhood dogs barking and a few flat screen televisions blasting from the living rooms. She crept through the yards and saw the shadows as they ran between the houses, scurrying, in their determination to apprehend her. Nyla wedged her body in the corner of an old wooden fence, trying to disappear. When she thought she heard the last of the footsteps pass and voices head in the opposite direction, she made a run for it. Before she could gain any speed, she was blindsided and tackled to the ground.

The weight of her attacker crashed into her like a wrecking ball and knocked the wind out of her. Nyla struggled to catch her breath as she was pulled to her feet and slammed against the side of a brick house.

"What's yo' hurry, punk? We just want to talk to ya for a minute. I think you got somethin' that belongs to my man, G." Nyla turned her head to the side as her attacker pressed his weight against hers, making it almost impossible for her to breathe.

"Well, well, well. What do we have here?" A tall, reddish colored man slowly approached and retrieved Nyla's backpack from the ground. He opened the bag, looked down in it and pulled out one of the bags of white powder. Nyla noticed the wide gap in his teeth when he spoke. "Looks like we got ourselves a rogue, Jerome."

"I'm not..." Nyla's voice was a raspy and strained whisper.

"Did you hear somethin', Jerome?" G held his hand up to his ear.

"Nah, boss, I ain't hear nothin'," Jerome responded, as he pressed Nyla's body even harder against the side of the house. Nyla grimaced as breathing became more difficult. She pulled at Jerome's large arm, as he applied more pressure underneath her chin. Nyla felt light headed, as though she was about to pass out.

"All I know is that somebody been messin' with my stuff and I do believe I've found the fool who thought he could get away with it." Jerome jerked the hoodie off of Nyla's head. The baseball cap fell to the ground and a few golden curls tumbled forward.

"Well, look a here. We got us a prom queen. Too bad I'm gone hafta' mess up that pretty face of yours, prom queen. You see… you done messed with the wrong somebody."

"I ain't messed with nothin'. Tyrone told me to take the stuff to another house before I made the drop." Nyla continued to struggle as she fought to fill her lungs with the precious little air Jerome allowed in. G stood, staring for a moment. Then he signaled Jerome to let up a little bit. As soon as Jerome dropped his arm Nyla began coughing profusely as she grabbed her neck and took several deep breaths.

"You telling me that that *fool* Tyrone is tryin' to play *me*?" Because it was difficult for her to speak, Nyla shook her head, vigorously.

"I… I don't know. I just do what I'm told. I pick the stuff up from one place, take it to another house and wait outside. After that, I take it to the drop." She could see them both contemplating whether or not to believe her.

"Boss, you think he's watering it down?"

"There's only one way to find out." G opened the bag and he knew instinctively that it had been tampered with. He tasted it and threw it to the ground. He was enraged. G pushed Jerome away from Nyla and put a knife to the side of her face. Nyla could see a slither of the deep orange glow from the streetlight reflected against the blade. She trembled as she felt the cool, sharp edge of the blade press against her cheek.

"Now exactly where is this place and when is the next drop scheduled?"

"Uh, I...I'm not sure..." G pressed the knife further into her cheek and Nyla could feel it start to penetrate her skin. She squeezed her eyes shut. She knew she had to think fast.

"Okay. Wait a minute." She held up both hands. "The house is on Crescent Drive in College Park. The next drop is Friday."

"You forgettin' somethin' ain't chu?" Nyla went blank and G was losing patience.

"*Which* house on Crescent Drive?!"

"516. Yeah, that's it, 516 Crescent Drive."

Suddenly, the back yard was flooded with light as someone opened their back door. A dog leapt from the back porch and attacked Jerome's backside. Nyla turned to run, but G grabbed her ponytail. She turned quickly and in one swift move, she floored him with a masterful kick to the groin. The release of the ponytail was immediate. Jerome shot the dog and with the ringing from the gunshot still in her ears, Nyla ran. Her long legs moved like a gazelle and within minutes she was gone.

Nyla ran six blocks before she jumped onto a bus, headed for suburbia. Her entire body was shaking as beads of sweat poured down her face and neck as she presented her pass card to the bus driver.

"You all right?" The bus driver asked. His expression was one of concern for the young girl. Nyla couldn't speak. She simply nodded and moved quickly to the very back of the bus where she desperately tried to become one with the seat. Nyla had set her plan into motion. G was not the top man, but he could be one of the most vicious. Now, he was out for her blood as well as Tyrone's and Friday night would be the moment of truth.

As the bus made its way through the city, Nyla realized she was much too vulnerable. She needed her own protection, just in case things didn't go as she had planned.

≈≈≈≈

Two days later, Nyla walked out of her school and slid into the passenger seat of a beat up 1965 Ford Mustang.

"What's up?" Nate asked, acknowledging her with a slight tilt of the head. When Nyla didn't answer, Nate shook his head as he slowly pulled the car out of the parking lot. He maneuvered around the school buses that were ready to transport the onslaught of children about to rush out of school.

"Did you get it?" she asked anxiously while peering out of the side review mirror.

"Chill, okay? Of course I got it."

"I just need to make this as quick as possible." Nyla looked back over her shoulder. "My brother is going to wonder why I'm not on the bus and I don't want—"

"Like I said, chill. I got what you asked for. Just let me find somewhere to park and we'll take care of it."

The Mustang's loud muffler rumbled as Nate carefully pulled into a nearby half-empty parking lot and turned off the engine.

"Okay." He propped one arm on the back of his seat as he turned to face Nyla. "Whatchu' got for me?" Nate's tone was almost hostile. He was small in stature but stocky and he wore his coarse, black hair in an uncombed, uneven, afro. He was only seventeen but he looked much older. Nyla could see past his tough guy facade but she knew the game.

She placed her hand inside her satchel and wrapped her clammy palm around the envelope. She knew better than to pull it out before she saw the merchandise. "I got the cash, but let me see it first."

Nate watched Nyla closely. He would have never expected someone who looked like her to be buying a gun. With her white polo shirt, skinny jeans and red Converses. Her hair looked like a halo around her head. He thought she looked like she should've been a cheerleader or something but here she was, sitting across from him, buying a gun. *Just goes to show,* he thought, *the package don't always reveal the contents.*

Nate looked around to make sure he wasn't being watched. He leaned forward and pulled a small, brown paper bag from underneath the driver's seat. Still holding it toward the floor, Nate slid the small, silver revolver out of the bag so she could see it. Then, just as quickly, he pushed it back into the bag and under the seat.

"You got the bullets?" she asked with wide-eyed anticipation.

"Open the glove compartment," he instructed. She did as she was told and there inside was a small box of ammo. She grabbed it and put it inside her satchel.

"Okay. Now, where's my money?"

Nyla's hands trembled as she removed the envelope and slid it across the seat. Nate grabbed the cash, counted out two hundred dollars and then handed her the brown bag. She quickly stuffed the bag inside of the satchel and stole another look around the outside of the car.

"You sure you know how to use that, half-pint?"

"You want to try me?" Nate held both hands in the air.

"Hey, don't get all gangsta on me. I thought we was friends."

"Sorry. I ain't got a lot of those." Nyla felt bad. "Listen, thanks for helping me out but I gotta go. I'll see ya around, okay?" She reached for the door handle, but before she could go Nate tugged on her elbow.

"Hey, be careful, a'ight?" He couldn't lie; he was worried.

"Thanks, Nate. That's what I'm trying to do, be more careful." Moments later Nyla was out of the car and across the street, headed for the bus that would take her home.

"I certainly hope so," Nate said under his breath as he watched that golden puff of hair bounce across the street. He had mixed feelings about selling her the gun, but he thought, *At least now she can protect herself.*

# TWENTY-SEVEN

## *LET THERE BE LIGHT*

---

**A**nother week had come to an end and although Raina's head felt as though she were in a fog, she moved through the house expertly from habit. She did her best to make a mental checklist as she maneuvered from one room to the next. She thought about the difficult client she'd been working with. For weeks Raina had tried to find him the perfect house. It would be a cash deal and she could really use the money, but she wasn't sure if even *he* knew what he wanted. All the while she did her best to keep up with Quincy's basketball schedule, Matthew's soccer games and Nyla's track meets. Raina was in a constant state of motion. Even now, as she made her way to the kids' rooms to drop off clean clothes, she tried to mentally arrange her to do list before they got home from school.

Raina exited Quincy's room and made a mental note to have him clean it thoroughly or his cell phone was going to go into hibernation. Further down the hall, she slowed her pace as she approached Nyla's room. Raina opened the door and felt a slight twinge of discomfort as she stepped across the threshold. The room was neat, almost too neat. Raina looked around. *It doesn't even look like anyone is living in here.*

The blinds were closed and the darkness casted a heaviness over the room, which made her even more uncomfortable. Raina walked over to open the blinds, placed a bundle of clothes near the bottom of the bed and reached toward the window. She twisted the thin rod and almost immediately, sunlight flooded the room.

"There, that's better." She looked around and made yet another note to ask Nyla if she wanted to redecorate the room. They could add more of Nyla's own personality and make it look like a teenage girl's room. Pleased with that thought, she reached for the laundry and the pile fell to the floor.

"Great." Raina kneeled down to retrieve the clothes and noticed a sliver of pink, peeking from beneath the bed. She pulled it to her.

"What's this?" she unfolded the bundle.

It was a baby's blanket. Frayed as it was, Raina immediately recognized the patchwork. It looked exactly like the blanket Victoria had made for her as a child. There was what appeared to be a patch of lace from the underlay of Victoria's ivory wedding gown, another from the baby blue shirt her father wore on their first date and a big purple patch from her grandmother's old bedspread. Raina had passed her blanket down to each of her boys, so she was very familiar with the patchwork.

Raina stood, staring at the blanket, completely baffled.

"How in the world does Nyla have a blanket almost identical to mine?"

"What are you doing in here?" Raina jumped at Nyla's sudden appearance.

Nyla stood in the doorway, observing Raina intensely. When her gaze zeroed in on the blanket, she moved quickly and snatched it out of Raina's hands.

"Why are you going through my things?" she asked, suspiciously.

"No. I'm not. I mean... I wasn't. It's just that..."

"I thought you said this was my private space," Nyla said, defiantly, as she held the blanket slightly behind her.

"Of course it is."

"Then why are you going through my stuff?" Her face was flushed. She'd been at track practice and had caught a ride home with Isaias. Her hair was pulled back into a ponytail and she wore over-sized basketball shorts and a sleeveless jersey.

"I'm sorry, Nyla. I promise that it wasn't my intent. I simply brought your laundry in here and when some of it fell to the floor, I saw the blanket and pulled it out. I wasn't going through anything."

"Oh." A few moments of awkward silence followed. Raina finally found the courage to inquire further.

"If I may ask, is that *your* blanket?" Nyla was

uncomfortable with the inquiry. She dropped her book bag to the floor.

"Yeah. It's the only thing I have from my birth mother." Raina was taken aback.

"Oh," she said, a bit startled. "That came from your *birth* mother and not your adopted mother?"

"No. I mean, yeah. What I mean is my mom told me that I was in this blanket when she saw me for the first time. So, I figured it's probably from the woman who gave birth to me."

"Well, I think you're probably right." But how it could be was anything but clear to Raina. Raina moved closer to her and held out her hand. "May I?" She wanted to inspect it further. Nyla hesitantly placed the blanket in Raina's outstretched hand.

"Back in the day, a lot of people made blankets from patches of different material that had special meaning or significance for their newborns. Not so much anymore. But, back then, it was a way to keep the family stories alive and keep that connection, you know?"

Nyla shrugged her shoulders. "I wouldn't know much about that."

"People don't have time to do things like this now-a-days. It takes a great deal of patience," Raina added.

"So... what, you think she made it?" Nyla asked, her voice filled with longing. Silently, she watched as Raina inspected the blanket. Nyla felt her body temperature rise. She pulled at the front of her shirt.

"It's possible," Raina said, and handed it back to her. When Nyla turned around and placed the blanket in her top dresser drawer, Raina noticed the tiny, half-moon-shaped birthmark at the base of her neck. Raina caught her breath and took a couple of steps backward. Now, it was *her* face that became flushed. Beads of perspiration suddenly appeared on her forehead. Raina looked as if she'd seen a ghost.

"What's wrong?" Nyla asked. "Are you okay? You don't look too good."

Raina was speechless. All she could do was nod and stare. She tried to find her tongue and regain her composure but seeing that birthmark, the same birthmark that she'd only seen twice in her life had rocked her to her core. And now, here, the exact same mark was on this girl, a virtual stranger. *Who is she? Where did she come from and why does it seem like she has some kind of connection to my family. She's Keenan's child. How could any of this be possible?* Questions circled her head like a swarm of bees.

"Surprise!" Matthew came up from behind and hugged Raina as tightly as he could.

"Um, yes. Sure. I'm fine," Raina said, a delayed response to Nyla's question. She then turned her attention to Matthew, who had begun talking a mile a minute.

"Slow down, Matthew. What are you asking me?"

"Can I go to the basketball game tonight, *please*? We're playing our rival and since I don't have soccer practice, I really want to go to the game. Please, Mom." Matthew petitioned his mother with both hands clasped together, as if praying to a higher power.

Nyla saw her opportunity to get out of the house

without having to make up another lie. She'd made three deliveries for Tyrone but had decided that tonight would be her last one. She had told Gabby after the last delivery she wasn't going to allow Tyrone to be a threat to her or her family any longer.

"Raina, if you have something else to do, I'll take the squirt to the game."

"Who you calling squirt, girl? I'll have you know, I'm the king!"

"Yeah, whatever, squirt," Nyla swatted him with one of her t-shirts.

"Well the *king* can't go anywhere until he finishes his homework, so you better get to it, okay?" Raina added.

Matthew smiled. "But of course. I finished half of it at school, so that'll be no problem." Just then, they all heard Quincy come in through the garage door.

"Hey, Ma, we're hungry! Matthew ran off to tell Quincy about going to the game. Raina cut her eyes nervously at Nyla.

"Thanks, Nyla. That will really help me out. I would ask Lola but she definitely seems to have her own agenda these days."

"It's no problem. I like being able to help out. You guys have done so much for me. This is nothing compared to..." Her voice trailed off.

"I just appreciate everything, you know?"

"Ma! Where are the chicken nuggets?!"

"Check the freezer, Q!"

"I did. They're not in there!"

The pulse of the house had come to life, but

Raina's brain was still racked with questions regarding Nyla. She knew of only one person who may have the answers and that would be her next move.

Raina walked into the kitchen with Nyla not far behind. They both stared at Quincy, Matthew and Isaias, rummaging through the fridge like raccoons.

"You guys act like you're about to die of starvation," Nyla said, as she walked around Raina into the kitchen.

"We are!" Quincy replied, and removed bacon from the microwave.

"Q's gonna make us his famous BLT," Matthew added.

"And what makes it so famous?" Raina heard Nyla ask as their voices trailed off. Her mind was a hundred miles away as an unsettling current formed in the pit of her stomach. Whatever laid in wait, she prayed to God that she and her family would still be intact when all her questions were answered.

# TWENTY-EIGHT

## THE DOCTOR COMES CLEAN

Lola glided across the hotel lobby of the Four Seasons with her head held high. Not once did she feel her feet touch the ground.

William, an old flame, had called her saying that he was in town for a conference and would love to get together. Her knees grew weak as she made her way toward the restaurant.

She'd always loved the grandness of the Four Seasons, especially the oversized crystal chandeliers hanging from the magnificent, elaborately painted ceiling. Her Jimmy Choos clicked on the marble floor as she strolled through the lobby toward the already bustling French restaurant. The food there was superb but Lola was not there for the food. She had come because of William Edwards. At one point in her life, William was her ideal man. He was larger than life and had a presence that always commanded attention. A successful entrepreneur whose only rule was, there were no rules, especially when he saw something that he wanted. They'd met while he was traveling on business. William had done everything in his power to make sure that Lola was not an exception to the rule. Mr. Goodman had warned her that her involvement with William could be destructive to her road to recovery. William, like most of the men in her life, was unavailable because he was married. All Lola knew was, at that moment, she needed William. She needed him to take her mind off of another unavailable man.

For weeks, Lola had attempted to distance herself from Jeremiah. It was becoming increasingly difficult for her to ignore her attraction to him. Lola knew she wasn't strong enough to resist her own desires, even if it meant him possibly losing his license. She decided to be the bigger person and call and have her file transferred. Needless to say, she was floored when she found out her file had already been transferred. Lola was mortified. How could he have done that without talking to her first? She resolved that she was indeed, damaged goods and there would probably never be a happily ever after for someone like her. So tonight it was William. She would deal with the other lonely nights like she was learning to deal with everything else in her life—one day at a time.

Although Jeremiah had phoned several times, Lola felt like kryptonite. As much as she would love to have a healthy relationship with him, she knew it would only and always be just a dream.

*This is better,* Lola thought. *William Edwards is just the distraction I need to take my mind off of my stupid fantasies.* Lola needed William to help her get in touch with a much-needed reality. Besides, she couldn't stand the idea of Dr. Eli finding out about her, Keenan, Nyla and the whole mess. *Yes, this is for the best, s*he reasoned. William was just what the doctor ordered.

"Hi. Lola Devereux to meet Mr. Edwards," she said to the maître d' as she leaned in toward the podium.

"Yes, mademoiselle. Mr. Edwards has already arrived." The maître d' retrieved a menu and escorted Lola to her table.

When they reached the table the maître d' pulled out the chair for Lola. Before she could be seated, William, in grand fashion, stood and embraced her. The scent of his very expensive cologne tickled her nose. He was six-two, with a cafe-au-lait complexion. His salt and pepper hair gave him a look of distinction. Although he was fifteen years her senior, he didn't look a day over forty-five.

"Ah Lola, my love. You are a breath of fresh air," he said, as his eyes embraced every inch of her.

She wore the Chanel dress he'd purchased for her on their last trip to Paris. It fit her like a glove. The ivory color complemented her skin and the exquisitely thin alligator belt accented her small waist. As usual, Lola's make-up was impeccable. However, if anyone took the time to look closely, they would see the cracks. They were barely hidden underneath all the wrapping, but they were surely there. No one would ever suspect the volcanic eruption that was her reality. The only other person in the room who knew the truth was Dr. Eli, who sat only a few tables away.

Jeremiah noticed her as soon as she had entered the restaurant. It was as if he had sensed her presence. She was undeniably breathtaking and so much of a distraction that he couldn't, for the life of him, focus on the conversation at his own table.

"So, my dear, how have you been? You disappeared from my life and broke my heart."

"I see you're still the charmer, William," Lola replied, in a sultry, flirty voice.

"Oh, but for you, my flower, it is the truth." He smiled and sipped his champagne. Lola smiled and leaned forward like a fish being reeled in. He'd always had that effect on her.

"Have you traded your love for our California beaches for this metropolis of humidity?" William asked, teasing her with his sexy smile.

"Not exactly. I have some things that need my attention here, so...."

"So does that mean you haven't left me?"

"What?" Lola was confused. "What are you talking about?"

William grabbed her hand. "I've been looking for you everywhere. Why didn't you tell me you were in trouble? When I went by your condo and saw the eviction notice, I almost lost my mind. You should've come to me."

"Well, William, I made several attempts to contact you, remember? Your wife intercepted my call and threatened my *life*. I do believe that's when you took *her* on a little trip. I think it was to Italy, wasn't it?" Lola could feel regret creeping up her spine. She didn't want to remember the dynamics of her relationship with William. All she wanted was to be held and to forget the shambles of her present situation. But the more he talked, the more memories of her darkest days came barreling back.

"Yes, well I needed a little time to smooth things over, but I had no idea that you would completely disappear."

"Listen William, let's not do this okay? We're here to have a good time and that's all I can deal with right now."

"Okay," William agreed. "You're right." He held his glass up for a toast. "To making new memories." Lola eyes became fixated on the light, golden liquid floating in the glass. Her mouth felt like cotton. She grabbed the glass of water and drank the entire glass before returning it to the table.

"What's wrong? You're not joining me?" Lola gave him a tense smile.

"No, I uh, actually I've quit." She looked around the restaurant as if waiting for someone to call her a liar. Lola was beginning to realize that coming here was a mistake. Her phone buzzed and she saw a message from Raina. *Important. Please call.*

"Would you please excuse me? I need to go to the ladies room." Lola grabbed her purse and made her exit before William could object. She quickly walked across the restaurant, her attention buried deep inside her purse as she tried to locate a tissue to wipe away the perspiration from her top lip. As she rounded the corner, she was suddenly yanked into a private alcove near the elevators.

"What are you doing here?" It was Jeremiah, towering over her with a scowl.

"What the...?" Lola stopped as she looked up into his piercing black eyes. The close proximity of his body to hers almost took her breath away. Her heart leapt but the excitement was brief.

"Good evening, Dr. Eli. Is this a new side gig of yours, accosting woman in public places?" Lola stole a glance around to make sure William couldn't see them.

"I'm here with a few colleagues, but I couldn't help but notice you dining with your very-married dinner companion. It is just *dinner*, right?" Lola was embarrassed but slowly the embarrassment turned to anger.

"How dare you! Who died and made you the moral gatekeeper?!" she whispered angrily. Her nostrils flared as she glared at him. "You're not my keeper, my doctor or my anything! And I don't have to answer to you or anyone else about who I choose to have dinner with. Now, if you'll excuse me."

Jeremiah wouldn't allow her to pass. Lola looked back up at him. She was stunned.

"You're making a scene," Lola said, as she looked around again, with a nervous smile.

"I don't care. Why haven't you returned my calls?" Lola was at a loss for words. She knew the answer but she dare not admit her reasons to him.

"I've been busy."

"This kind of busy?" Jeremiah tilted his head

back in Williams' direction.

"Wait a minute." She took a step back. "You're out of line." Lola couldn't believe his audacity.

"Yes, well, I just may be, but I thought you wanted better for yourself, to improve your life."

"What are you talking about? How do you know what's best for me?"

"I'm talking about you selling yourself short by being here with that man who's probably old enough to be your father."

"First of all, what I shared with you as my doctor—in confidence I might add—does *not* give you the right to dictate who I see or what I do." Lola spoke through clenched teeth. "Second, if anyone would know about selling themselves short it would be you!"

Now it was Jeremiah's turn to be surprised.

"Excuse me? You've no idea what you're talking about."

"You know, you may have a doctorate in psychology but I've been around long enough to recognize someone who's perpetrating. You're afraid of something."

"And on what authority do you know that?"

"I know because you keep yourself so pinned up. I see the way you keep everyone at a distance. You have this need for everything to be neat and orderly, but that's not realistic, Jeremiah. That's why you focus on everyone else's problems, to keep from dealing with your own. I don't know exactly what happened to you, but I know something did. Either way, that doesn't give you the right to come down on me for wanting to have a little fun."

"Fun?! Is that what you call it? And when he's through using you, are you still going to be having fun?" Before she could stop herself, Lola slapped him as hard as she could. Afterward, they both stood motionless, shocked into silence. Her entire body trembled as she turned to leave, Jeremiah reached out and gently took hold of her wrist.

"Please. Don't go."

"I can't do this right now. I didn't mean to..."

"No. Listen. You were right. I was way out of line but..." Jeremiah ran his large hands down his face.

"Seeing you with him... I don't know." He chuckled with embarrassment. "It was making me crazy."

"Stop. You don't know what you're saying."

"I know exactly what I'm saying, Lola. It's not professional, I know. But you deserve better than that."

"Better than what?"

"Than sitting over there having some jackass undress you every time he looks at you. You need someone who genuinely cares about you. Someone who wants to be that solid foundation for you to brace yourself against." Lola was speechless. She knew from the first day she saw him in his office she wanted something more from him. She had no idea that he felt the same way.

"I... I don't get it," she finally said.

"Can you get that I have feelings for you? That's why I had your file transferred." Relief flooded her entire body.

"Wow."

"The last thing I want to do is risk a healthy recovery but I can't help the way I feel. I want to be a part of your life in a way that I cannot as your doctor."

"I don't know what to say."

"Say yes. Say—"

"Is everything all right, Lola?" It was William. Lola peeked around Jeremiah and saw William standing in his shadow. He was clearly frustrated.

"Oh, yes. Everything's fine," Lola moved around Jeremiah and stood between the two men. "This is Dr. Jeremiah Eli and Dr. this is..."

"Ah, yes. I've read your latest book, Dr. Eli. I'm quite familiar with your work."

"I'm sorry, I can't say the same about you." Each man stood for a moment and evaluated the competition.

"Well, as I was about to say, this is William Edwards. He and I are old friends." The two men shook hands.

"A pleasure to meet you, Dr. Eli, but Ms. Devereux and I have actually decided to order room service where we can have a little more privacy." William wrapped his arm around Lola's waist and drew her closer.

Jeremiah could feel his jaw muscles tighten as he clenched his teeth. Lola became even more uncomfortable as she looked up at Jeremiah. She couldn't bear the angst she saw on his face.

"William? Actually, I think I'm going to take a rain check on dinner tonight," Lola said, turning to face him.

"Oh no. I have something very special I want to

share with you, my sweet," he added, drawing her even closer. Lola leaned back giving him the signal that she could not be persuaded.

"Yes. Well I appreciate that, but I just had a call from my sister and I need to be going." She saw William's disappointment and was thankful when he finally released her.

"I'll call you tomorrow, okay? It's just that something important has come up and I have to deal with it."

"Yes, by all means. I'll speak with you tomorrow, then. Perhaps you can stop by before I leave for the airport."

"Yes, of course. That sounds like a good idea." The elevator arrived. William stepped in reluctantly, and slowly disappeared behind the large ornate doors. Lola felt Jeremiah's eyes boring into her. Her heart beat so loudly she wondered if he could hear it. She turned to face him.

"Do you know what you're doing?" she asked, unsure if she wanted to hear the answer.

"Well, as you said earlier, I have a tendency to be too careful in my actions. I've never been the kind of man to just go with the flow. However, I've tried everything in my power to ignore my feelings for you but they refuse to be ignored or silenced. So what's a man to do?"

"Well you may need to talk to a good therapist," Lola replied with a wicked smile.

"Ah... perhaps I should. Do you think you could recommend someone?"

"Perhaps," she answered, and allowed his dark eyes to take her hostage. Jeremiah couldn't resist any longer. He stepped closer. Her knees became weak as she inhaled his scent. It was intoxicating. Finally, Jeremiah did what he'd wanted to do from the first time he laid eyes on her. He kissed her. Her lips felt soft against his own. He placed his hand on the small of her back and drew her to him. All the hustle and bustle of the hotel faded into the background. In the minutes that passed, it seemed as if they were the only two people in the room. When it was over, Lola took a step back to gather herself.

"Wow," she responded hoarsely.

"Yes. I would say 'wow' is very appropriate," he said, with a boyish grin. He couldn't take his eyes off of her. "Listen, why don't we get out of here?"

"That sounds great, but first I need to call my sister.

"You can call her from my car and I'll bring you back later to pick up your car."

"Okay. What are we waiting for?" *Whoa girl, slow down. This situation requires a different set of rules. Don't get caught up in the moment.*

Once outside, Lola slid into Jeremiah's midnight blue Mercedes. It only took seconds, but by the time Jeremiah climbed in beside her, Lola was panicked.

"Are you okay? What's wrong?" he asked, noticing her worried expression.

"I... um... I don't know if I can do this right now. There are so many things that are going on."

"Hey. There's no pressure. I simply want to spend time with you." Lola looked at him and felt an overwhelming sense of regret. She wanted this, wanted him. *Why did Mr. Right have to show up now?*

"Okay. But first I need you to take me somewhere. There's something important that I really need to do."

"Right this minute?"

"Yes, Jeremiah. It's something I should've taken care of months ago." Lola looked at him with pleading eyes. "If whatever this is between us is going to stand a chance, I have to do this now." He nodded his head thoughtfully.

"Okay. Are you sure you're ready?"

"As ready as I'll ever be."

Jeremiah pressed the accelerator and guided the car into the street. He hoped wherever they were going would not change the course they had only moments before seemed ready take. He'd held his feelings back for so long. Now that he had finally allowed himself to hope, he prayed that wherever they were headed would not cause them to crash and burn before they even got started.

# TWENTY-NINE

## IT'S A SET-UP

"Gabby! Will you please stop tripping? This will work and it'll take care of Tyrone, Jamal and maybe even G."

"You're playing with fire, Ny." Gabby said, as she sat in the back of Isaias' Jeep. She was dumbfounded by Nyla's so-called plan.

Nyla had felt forced to include Isaias in her meeting with Gabby. He'd agreed to be her alibi after she'd missed curfew a couple of times. However, she hadn't told him everything.

"Okay. Let me get this straight. You're gonna trick Tyrone into showing up at the drop-off sight? Why?" Isaias asked, confused.

"I told you. All drug dealers are paranoid. They always think someone is out to get 'em. I kinda made G think that Tyrone's been watering down his stuff."

"Are you crazy?!" Gabby was near hysteria. "What do you mean you kinda made him think that? What did you do?!"

"I just said that Tyrone told me he needs someone to inspect the stuff before it hits the streets."

"Ny, you're gonna get yourself killed."

"Really, Gabby? You don't think I know how dangerous it is out here? Tyrone got me going into some of the worst neighborhoods in the city. You think he's got my back? Hell, no! He don't care if somebody puts a bullet in my head. All he cares about is his *money*. I'm out there by myself!" Nyla said, as she punctuated the air with her index finger. She was angry and on the verge of tears as she tried to get both Gabby and Isaias to understand her plight.

"Okay, okay. Calm down. I feel you but... you know he never goes near a pick up or a drop. How in the world do you plan to get him over there?"

"He says he's looking to buy a house, right? Well, Raina's assistant is gonna call him and tell him that Raina has a great house for him to look at. When he shows up, G's gonna be there waiting for him."

"Raina's assistant? Who in the world is that?" Gabby asked. Nyla turned and looked at Isaias.

"Him?! He's the assistant?!" Gabby didn't know whether to pass out or get out.

"What? Oh, no, wait a minute. You said you didn't want me to get involved," Isaias replied.

"And *you* said you wanted to help."

"Yeah, *help* but not get killed."

"How you gonna get killed, Isaias? It's just a phone call." Nyla shook her head and rolled her eyes in frustration. She was scared too, but she couldn't let them know that.

"Okay, what's gonna happen when he finds out he's been duped?" Isaias asked.

"By the time he suspects anything it'll be too late. G will be at the location tomorrow night, looking for Tyrone.

"And how do you know that?"

"Because I told him that's where he'd be."

Gabby held up her hand. "I don't even want to know how you came face to face with G. What's even crazier is how you got him to *believe* you."

"Yeah, you don't want to hear all the details and I don't want to relive it."

"So now what?" Isaias asked.

"G's gonna be mad 'cause he thinks Tyrone is putting the word out on the street that his stuff is bad. We all know that's bad for business, so right away things are gonna be hot."

"Okay, maybe I'm slow," Isaias interjected, "but tell me again, how is getting G mad at Tyrone going to get you out of having to make drops for Tyrone?" Now it was Gabby's turn to roll her eyes.

"Isaias, have you ever heard the expression, mad enough to kill? There's already bad blood between G and Tyrone and when it comes to drugs and money, all bets are off."

"And to make sure they don't make nice and make up, I got this." Nyla pulled out the gun.

"Oh my God! Nyla! Have you lost your mind?!"

"Calm down, girl!"

"Whoa... where did you get that?" Isaias asked, in shock.

"Don't worry about that. I got it. All I'm gonna do is shoot it in the air or something. When both of those fools hear gun shots, they're gonna start shooting at each other and I'm gon' make sure Tyrone gets his."

"Ny, I think this thing has really gotten way outta hand," Gabby said.

"Well, you should know. Weren't you the one laid up in the hospital half dead about a month ago? Who did that, Gabby? You think he's ever gonna stop? You think he's gonna leave us alone so we can live happily ever after?" Gabby looked out of the window. She knew Nyla was right about Tyrone, but she still didn't think this was the best way to handle it.

"We need to make sure that he never comes back. What better way than to have G take him out?" Nyla asked. "Listen, Isaias, all you have to do is make the call. Tell him that you're Mrs. Blackman's assistant and she wants him to see a house right away. Tell him it's a steal and it just became available. Just try to get him excited. Then set a time to show him the house. Whatever time he says is good, that's what I'm gonna tell G. That should take care of it."

"When you want to do this?" Isaias asked, looking directly at Nyla. He saw Gabby's head jerk as she stared at him in disbelief.

"The sooner the better. Tomorrow night Q has a basketball game and I know Lola and Raina will probably be there. She usually turns her phone down at the games.

"You're gonna do it?" Gabby asked Isaias, astonished.

"What choice do we have? We gotta end this thing or neither one of you is ever going to be safe." Nyla felt a calm come over her. She was relieved. She knew she couldn't do this by herself. She really felt that this was the only way.

"Cool." Nyla was ready to have Tyrone out of her life for good. Tomorrow felt like light years away.

"Come by the house later tonight and we'll make the call from Raina's office, okay?"

"Okay," Isaias agreed.

"You okay?" Nyla asked her friend, who looked fraught with worry.

"Yeah. But I got another question."

"Shoot," Nyla responded. Isaias and Gabby gave Nyla a look. "Okay, bad choice of words. What's your question?"

"You got a back-up plan?"

"Sure do. I call it, *Smith & Wesson*," Nyla said, as she laid the gun on the seat. "Nobody else will ever lay a hand on me again." The mood was somber.

Well, I gotta go," Gabby said. "Looks like you have it all figured out."

"Yep."

Isaias helped Gabby climb out of the Jeep and up onto the front porch. He jumped back into the Jeep and as they backed out into the street, Gabby couldn't shake the bad feeling she had about Nyla's plan and knew of only one person that could help. For months she'd put Lloyd off by not being totally honest for fear that he would learn the truth about Nyla. But now, she knew it was time to come clean.

# THIRTY

## THIRST NO MORE

<hr>

Lloyd closed the door to his twin sons' bedroom and let out a sigh of relief. He padded down the hall and into his office where he slid behind his desk for the third time that evening.

"Finally. Now maybe I can get some work done."

He slid his glasses back on and focused his attention on the computer screen.

"Now, let's see. How do I get out of email jail?" He began pecking at the keyboard. Lloyd had only deleted a couple of emails when the doorbell rang.

"Who in the..." He hadn't been expecting anyone and Jess was asleep. Lloyd checked his watch as he made his way toward the front door.

"Who could this be?" he mumbled as he moved quickly, hoping the doorbell hadn't awakened Jess

or the children. Lloyd peeked through the peephole
and was surprised. He flung the door open and there
she stood. With eyes filled with pools of water, the
golden glow from the porch light danced across her
face, and Lloyd could see the turbulent storm
brewing behind Lola's eyes.

"Hey, cousin. You got a minute?" Lola asked,
her voice wavering.

"Yes, yes of course," Lloyd's pulse quickened as
he motioned for Lola to enter. He stepped aside and
opened the door a little wider. Lola entered the
house and almost immediately felt a sense of relief.

"What's wrong? Is everyone okay?" Lloyd could
feel his shoulder muscles begin to tighten.

"Yes. Everyone's fine. That is, everyone but
me." She stared at him with a look of apprehension.

"You look like you're dressed for the Oscars, so
it can't be all that bad," he joked, trying to lighten
the mood. The expression on her face told him she
didn't find him amusing.

"As usual you're exaggerating. I was out on a
date and things got a little heavy, so I asked him to
drop me off here."

"I see." Lloyd nodded. "Well, come on back and
tell me what's going on." They entered Lloyd's
small, but masculine office. It was similar to
Keenan's, with all the plaques, awards and sports
paraphernalia adorning the walls.

Lola looked around the office as they entered.
"Okay. This is definitely all you. A little cozy
but..."

"Hey, don't start," he chuckled. "When you've
got five children, you make sacrifices."

"Funny you should mention that."

"What? Sacrifices?"

"And children."

"Huh?" Lloyd looked confused. Lola felt as though the walls were beginning to close in on her. She'd known this day would come. The day that Lloyd and the rest of her family would find out how much of a coward she really was. She shivered at the thought. *Once he finds out the truth, what will he think?* There was no way to know the outcome.

"Hey, hey, hey... It can't be that bad," Lloyd attempted to console her.

Lola couldn't hold back the tears any longer. They rushed forward like the rapids of a free flowing river.

"Lola, please tell me what's wrong." There was panic in his voice.

"I'm just....I feel so lost," she said through the tears. "I've been lost for so long and I don't know how to find my way back."

Lloyd grabbed her hand. "You fight, Lola."

"That's what I've been trying to do. I've tried and I've tried but every time," she threw her head back and looked at the ceiling. "Every, single, time I feel like I'm sinking in quick sand. I feel like a hypocrite because of how I've been living and how I was raised but...."

"But what? Did you actually think that just because the Reverend taught you the Word that everything would be perfect? Life is messy and we're not perfect. But what's perfect is God's mercy and grace."

"I know. But... I'm just having a hard time."

"Listen, have you asked God for forgiveness? I mean, have you truly given everything over to Him and allowed God to move without any interference?" Lola pondered his question.

"You're human, Lola. You're no different from the rest of us." Lola shook her head adamantly and a moment of silence passed before she spoke again. She searched her cousin's face with an expression of panic.

"What I've done is unforgivable." Lloyd pulled Lola up from the chair.

"Lola, there is no such thing. God is not a man that He would lie. And there is no sin so great that He will not forgive."

"Not this... Not this lie that..." Lloyd tightened his grip to get her attention.

"Lola. Ask Him. Repent and ask for forgiveness."

"I've tried, but it won't go away! It's with me every morning when I open my eyes. It sits with me all throughout the day, when I'm at work or eating lunch. When I go to sleep at night, it's in my dreams."

"That's not God, Lola, that's an unforgiving spirit. The God I serve is a forgiving God. The Word of God says "Do not be anxious about anything, but in every situation, by prayer and petition, with thanksgiving, present your requests to God." **Philippians 4:6.** "And when you ask, Lola, do so *believing*, and it shall given. He loves us and He wants to give us His mercy. It sounds like you haven't forgiven yourself."

"How can I?"

"First, stop trying to do it alone. You must learn to lean and rely on every living word of God. If you've asked God for forgiveness, know that He's given that to you. Maybe what you need to ask is for Him to help you forgive *yourself*." Lloyd clutched her hands. They stood in the middle of the room. "Will you allow me to do that with you?"

"But you don't know what I've done. I need to tell you what..."

"No. You don't need to tell me. *He* already knows. Let's pray and ask him to help you to forgive." Lola couldn't speak. They kneeled in the middle of the floor and called upon the name of the Lord, asking for peace in the spirit; asking for a release from the lies and the lifestyle that held her in bondage. Lola bowed her head and they began to pray and ask for forgiveness and for another chance to try Him again.

"Lord, with bowed heads and open hearts, we pray in the mighty, magnificent and marvelous name of Jesus the Christ." The richness of Lloyd's strong voice wrapped around her like a cocoon. "We ask that you would please forgive us for all the wrong that we've done and for pain we've caused. We know you're a kind and forgiving God and one of your daughters is seeking you right now, Father. She's thirsty, Lord. She's been in the desert for far too long and she wants to come home. She's *thirsty*, Lord." Lloyd squeezed her hands within his own. "She has tried to leave her pain behind, using alcohol as her refuge. But alcohol could not quench the thirst for truth, for love and for forgiveness. She's still thirsty, Lord. Allow her to drink from the cup that will quench her thirst forever. This may be the second time, the fourth time or maybe even the seventeenth time. But you said in your Word that you would never leave us nor forsake us. And no matter how many times we come back, you'll always be right where we left you, with open arms. So, we pray now, Lord that your will be done, Jesus. Please, let your will be done, Amen."

"Amen." Lola's voice was small as it trailed behind Lloyd's.

They stayed there for a while longer, Lola poured out her soul. She didn't remember how long they stayed there, but for the first time in many years, when she laid down to sleep that night, she felt a sense of peace.

๛ ๛ ๛ ๛

The next morning, Lola drifted in and out of consciousness, on Lloyd's lumpy futon. As she lay with her eyes closed, Lola felt a presence enter the room. She thought perhaps it was one of the kids, so she kept her eyes closed. Whoever it was leaned over her and hovered.

"Go home."

Lola's eyes popped open and she sat up immediately. Looking around the room, she saw no one.

"Lloyd?!" she called out as she scratched her head. There was no answer. "Go home?" she asked, confused. When her eyes fell on the Mickey Mouse clock, Lola was shocked to see that it was well past twelve o'clock. Suddenly, she remembered Raina's text message from last night. She jumped up and began gathering her things. Now she felt a quickening in the center of her stomach. When she located her cell phone, the battery was dead.

With her heels in hand, she headed toward Lloyd's office. The house was uncharacteristically quiet. As Lola entered the kitchen she noticed a note from Jessica on the counter. *Lola, took the kids on a play date and Lloyd had to go into the office for a while. Hope we get to talk soon. Jess.* Lola used Lloyd's office phone to call Raina but there was no answer. She called her mom and got her voicemail. Now the peace she'd had the night before was quickly fading. Lola knew she had to get home and the sooner, the better.

# THIRTY-ONE

## THE DEVEREUX WOMEN

Raina sat on the loveseat in her keeping room. Her entire body shook uncontrollably as she cried openly. Her emotions were spinning like a tornado, threatening to destroy everything in its path. Victoria stood over her daughter and stroked the back of her shoulders with trembling hands. She tried her best to console her, but Raina would not be comforted.

Lola had not returned her text or called her back. Raina had been up half the night, going through her father's old trunk that she kept in the back of her closet. She had not anticipated the horrible truth that confirmed what she had come to suspect but found impossible to believe. "How could all of this be possible?" she whispered as she shook her head. "How?"

"I'm sorry, sweetheart. I'm so, so sorry you had to find out this way," Victoria said, as she wiped away her own tears.

"And you...you, *knew*?" Raina tried desperately to wrap her mind around the absurdity of it all. "You've known the entire time and never said anything to me?" Raina's tone was incredulous.

"Raina, honey, I didn't know everything until recently. I swear to you I..."

Raina held up a hand to ward off more lies. "Mom, please. What I need from you right now is the truth. Just tell me the truth!"

"The truth about what?" Lola asked, her expression full of questions as she came through the door. "Mom, what's going on?" Lola asked, alarmed.

No one spoke. Lola's heart began beating faster and she could feel it pulsating in her neck. Raina stood and turned to face her sister. She was distraught. Her eyes were red and swollen and her hair was a disheveled mess.

"My God, Raina. What wrong? Are the boys all right? Where are they?"

"The boys are fine." Victoria answered. Raina still had not spoken. Now Lola was puzzled. As she moved closer she caught a glimpse of the photos. Raina held them loosely in her hand and there were others on the table nearby. Raina held a photo out toward Lola.

"Whose baby are you holding in the picture, Lola?" she asked, her voice sounding weak. It was a photo of Lola, at seventeen, holding a small bundle, wrapped in a homemade, quilted blanket. Lola felt her mouth go dry and her knees weakened, but she remained standing. Cautiously, Lola took the photograph from Raina and tried to answer, but the words simply would not come. Raina asked her again.

"Is that your baby, Lola?" she asked with a pained expression.

"Raina, she's uh... she's in shock. Why don't we—" Victoria tried to interject.

"I'm talking to Lola!" The volume of her voice startled them.

Lola jumped and then slowly she nodded. "Yes," she answered in barely a whisper. Quickly she wiped away the small line of perspiration that broke out above her lip.

"Okay." Raina moved her hand down her face in an attempt to wipe away the flood of tears.

"And this one, here. This is you and Keenan, right?" Raina held a second photo out toward Lola. Lola's fingers trembled, as she took the second photograph.

It had been taken three weeks after they'd met. Instantly time rolled back and Lola saw herself tearing her bedroom to shreds, as she looked for that very photo. The memory came barreling at her like a roller coaster. It had been the only photo she'd had of her unborn child's father. She never found it.

A small sound escaped past her lips before she quickly covered her mouth. The air in the room felt as if it had evaporated. Lola's tears came so fast she was almost blinded.

"Lola?" Raina spoke with an unsettling calmness. "Is Nyla your daughter? Is she yours...

and Keenan's?" Raina's eyes pleaded with Lola. And as much as she wanted to wipe the pain from her sister's face, Lola knew it was time to tell the truth. Her heart felt like a stone in her chest.

"Please, Raina. I didn't know that... he was *your* Keenan. When I realized, well... how could I tell you? How could I tell *anyone*?" Raina shook her head vigorously. She heard the words but couldn't believe it.

"Wait a minute. You had to tell Mom. How could you not have known about the baby?" Raina turned to Victoria.

"Well, I... I knew about the baby, Raina. I was the one who arranged the adoption, but I had no idea who the father was."

Raina's fingers combed through her hair. "This is insane!"

"Keenan knew he had a child with *you* and he still married me! That's *not* the man I married."

"Keenan didn't know about the baby." Raina became still and watched her sister in utter amazement. "Raina? Did you hear me? Keenan did. not. know. No one knew! We met while I was a freshman at Wesley. We were only together for a short time. When I went back to school he didn't return. Afterwards I realized that I was pregnant and I never went back to Wesley. Mom and the Reverend arranged for the adoption."

"That's what you were arguing about that night he had the heart attack?"

"Yes. I had changed my mind and I wanted to find her. I never saw Keenan again until the night of your rehearsal dinner."

"Did he... remember? I mean... did he still have feelings for you?"

"No. He was in love with the woman he was about to marry. He never knew about Nyla."

"My god, this is crazy. I can't believe you've been living here, right *here* with her *all* of this time and not *once*, not once did you..."

"What did you expect me to do, Raina?! I didn't know what to do. I've been trying to get straight, to get myself clean so I could..."

"To tell the truth! That's what I would've expected."

"Well let me ask you, if you had known, would you have still married him? If you had known everything, would you still have walked down the aisle?"

"I... I don't... I..."

"I know you. You would've done the *right* thing." Lola put up invisible quotation marks. "You would've denied yourself the love of your life and for what? For a fling we had when we were kids? Before either one of us really knew what love was all about? You would've done that and regretted it for the rest of your life."

"So what? You just continued the lie?"

"I didn't know how to tell you, okay?! All of these years I've walked around, trying like hell to keep this... this thing buried. Some days it felt like I was fighting to keep an elephant from breaking through a door. It consumed every minute of every day, so I did everything I could to stay numb." Lola began pacing the floor. "All I've known is how to try and hold it in. When I couldn't do it on my own,

I used anything I thought would help me: men, drugs, alcohol, you name it. So when Nyla showed up, I couldn't face her. I... I went out to clear my head and try to figure out what to do, but I wound up drunk, instead."

Raina snorted. "How could you do that to her? You should be ashamed of yourself."

Lola stopped pacing and drew closer to her sister. "You're right, Raina. We all can't be perfect like you! So *godly*."

"Don't you dare try to turn this on me. You're the one who's been living in deception."

"Girls, please," Victoria begged. "Don't do this."

"Do you actually think I planned this? Dammit, Raina! I've made some mistakes, but I've paid dearly for them." The two sisters were at a standoff. Victoria stood in the middle of the room between them.

"You have no idea that *every single morning*, I've opened my eyes and remembered the look on Dad's face as he fell to the floor. I know that Nyla has spent most of her life in and out of foster homes, because I was too much of a coward. I've carried this guilt like a stone around my neck for years and I'm tired. And yes, Raina, I'm ashamed." Lola collapsed into a chair and wept.

"I... didn't... I had no idea," Raina whispered.

"Raina, she was only trying to protect you."

"Mom, please," Raina said, as she glared at her mother. "How could you let this happen?" Raina's words felt like daggers in her chest.

"I... I was just... God, I don't know." Victoria was not proud of what she'd done. She was not proud of the pain she'd caused her family.

"I wanted the best for you girls. All I tried to do was make it perfect. I'm sorry. Please. I hope you both can find it in your hearts to forgive me."

For a moment, all three Devereux women allowed the magnitude of their words to marinate the air around them. Then out of nowhere, the sound of shattering glass crashing around them was deafening. Each of them almost jumped out of their skin as they ducked to avoid the pellets of sharp glass flying through the air. When it was over they looked up into Nyla's tormented face. She'd thrown the trophy she'd won only hours earlier into the china cabinet.

No one saw her standing nearby, listening to the entire story. Before anyone could say anything Nyla turned and ran back out of the door.

"Oh my God. Nyla!" Lola stepped hurriedly through the shattered glass to try and stop her. Nyla dashed through the back door and sprinted out into the yard. Just as she was heading toward the street, gunshots rang out and everything afterward seemed to move in slow motion.

Lola dashed out of the door just in time to see Tyrone's distorted face as he aimed a gun at Nyla. He pulled the trigger and Lola saw the mist of smoke at the tip of the gun as the bullet pierced the air and landed in the middle of Nyla's chest. Nyla's body was pushed backward by the force of the bullet. Her limp body floated through the air and landed on the front lawn.

"No!" Lola screamed. "No! God, please... no..." she pleaded.

Her feet felt like lead as she tried to run toward Nyla. More shots rang out. Lola fell to the ground but continued to crawl. The sound of screeching tires penetrated the air as the SUV sped off. Isaias ran from across the street toward Lola and as he drew closer and saw Nyla's outstretched body, his knees buckled.

"Nyla!" His voice sounded foreign to his own ears. Raina and Victoria rushed out of the house and when they saw what had happened they collapsed into each other's arms. Nothing could have prepared them for this.

"Call an ambulance!" Lola yelled. "Call for help!" Raina ran back into the house. Within seconds, sirens could be heard on the street. Police cars encircled Tyrone's SUV half a block away, as Lloyd's unmarked car and an ambulance came to an abrupt stop in front of the house.

Lola was crying uncontrollably and screaming at the EMTs as they ran forward. "Help her! Help her, please!

Lloyd pulled Lola to her feet and away so that the EMTs could do what was necessary in an attempt to save Nyla's life.

"No! No, Lloyd. I have to stay with her. Please... God, don't do this... please!" The EMTs moved rapidly. The first one tore open Nyla's shirt and as her partner readied the equipment, suddenly they stopped.

"Oh, my, sweet mother of Jesus," said the EMT. She made the sign of the cross over her chest. Then, all sets of eyes peered down at Nyla. There, right near her heart, the bullet was lodged in her father's championship medal. The medal she'd worn every day since Raina had given it to her. It had made Nyla feel that she had Keenan close, protecting her.

The EMT retrieved the medal and placed it in Lloyd's hand. Lola's and Isaias' eyes were stretched wide in astonishment. They waved smelling salt under her nose. Nyla moaned.

"He... he shot me."

Lloyd kneeled down. "Nyla, you're okay. Look." He held up the medal. She could see the impression that the bullet had left behind. Her chest throbbed as tears streamed down the sides of her face. "He protected me."

"Yes, Nyla. He did." Lloyd placed the medal in Nyla's palm. "He certainly did."

# THIRTY-TWO

## FORGING AHEAD

---

**A**t the hospital, the Devereux women, Lloyd, Jessica, Quincy, Matthew, Isaias and Naomi all waited for a chance to see Nyla. Even Jeremiah stopped by to support Lola and assure her that he was available whenever she needed him.

Gabby was the only one Nyla had agreed to see. Lola sat, tense with emotion, wondering if she would have the opportunity to explain everything to Nyla.

Gabby exited Nyla's room and made her way down the corridor to the small waiting room.

"Lola. Nyla would like to see you."

Lola's heart skipped as she shot out of the chair. Before she could take another step, Gabby gently touched her arm. "I'm telling you this because she's my only true friend and I don't want to see her hurt any more than she's already been. She didn't want to see you. I told her that she owes it to herself to hear everything about *everything.* You feel me?" Lola nodded her head like a second grader who'd been reprimanded. She took a deep breath and moved apprehensively, through the large doors and down the hall.

The door squeaked a bit, as Lola pushed it open. Nyla's legs hung over the side of the bed. She sat with her arm in a sling.

"Hey," Lola greeted her, as she cautiously entered the room. She wiped her sweaty palms on the back of her jeans. Nyla didn't respond.

"I'm glad you wanted to talk. I really..."

"Why did you do it, Lola?" The tightness in her voice stopped Lola cold. "How could you?" Nyla asked, as she raised her gaze from the floor and bore her eyes into Lola's. There was so much anger behind her hazel eyes, Lola wanted to disappear.

"Nyla. I'm..." Lola scratched her head and tried to gather her thoughts. She attempted to replay everything she'd rehearsed and couldn't remember any of it. "You know, you probably don't know this, but Nyla is your birth name. It means, queen warrior. I knew you were strong. You used to kick me so hard and....

"Stop it! You ruined my *life!*" Lola's throat constricted and her body began to tremble. It was exactly as she had feared.

"Please... don't say that. I was young and Mother said it was for the best. I..."

"But what about now, huh? What about *every day* and every night for the past few months? We've been living under the same roof, sitting at the same table and you never *once* said anything! How can you even *stand* yourself?" Lola was speechless. The density of tension in the room made it difficult to breathe.

"I'm... I can't explain why, except to say that I was scared."

"Scared? Scared of what?!" Nyla screamed. Lola's heart was racing. She knew she had to be truthful with Nyla.

"The truth is... that um... I'm an alcoholic," Lola's voice croaked out.

"What?" Nyla could barely hear her. Lola took another deep breath and looked her daughter in the face.

"I said, I am an alcoholic. One who has fallen off the wagon more times than I can count."

Nyla was stunned.

"Yep. That's the only way I found that I could actually stand myself. I've thought about you every day since the day you were given away. And when I first learned who you were, my knee-jerk reaction was to have a drink. That's really the only way I've been able to cope with everything." Lola moved over and sat in the chair near Nyla's bed. "But listen, I've been fighting to stay sober. I wanted to be a better me for you. I didn't want to be like this." Lola began talking with her hands. "I wanted it to be one less disappointment for you to deal with when you found out the truth."

"All of you are just a bunch of liars."

"Not all. Just me. And I know there's no justification for what I did, but... have you ever lied to protect someone you loved? I thought what I was doing was noble, you know? I had no idea that it was just a slow death. Every time I took a drink to forget, I sunk further and further into an abyss of nothingness. I didn't care because no matter how far I fell, my mind never let me forget. So I would start over again."

"You're pathetic." The words were meant to hurt, to cripple any hope for a happily ever after.

"Maybe you're right, but I want you to know that I wanted you. I... I just didn't know how to fight for you." Nyla said nothing, seemingly unmoved. "After you were gone and the Reverend died, I had to get out of here. So I applied to a college as far away from here as possible. That's how I got out to California and that's where I've stayed."

"You live in California?"

"Yes." Lola felt hopeful at Nyla's response.

"Nyla, I'm not perfect by any stretch of the imagination, but I'm begging you for a chance to be a part of your life. To try and make up for..."

"You can't. You can never make up for what you've done or what I've lost."

"Well, what about your future? Will you allow her to try to make a better future for the both of you?" Raina asked, as she and Victoria entered the small room. Lola felt a wave of relief.

"Nyla, no one can change the past, but we can learn from it. We can choose not to let our past mistakes keep us from moving forward," Raina added. Victoria moved closer to Nyla and sat stiffly on the bed.

"Nyla, if you want to blame someone, blame me.

Everything that occurred happened because *I* was selfish. When you were born, I thought your birth would be the downfall of everything I had worked for. I thought more about what other people would think than what my own child needed. I can't put into words how much I regret the pain I've caused. But what I've come to realize is that if you could find it in your heart to forgive me, I will spend the rest of my days trying to make amends. You're the blessing that this family needs."

Nyla sat quietly and tried to wrap her brain around everything that was being said. She stared down at the medal, and turned it over in her hands. She thought about how it had saved her life. Now here she sat in a room with the women responsible for giving her life—her mother, grandmother and aunt. *This* was her family. They all had the same blood running through their veins.

"Nyla, I hope that someday you can find it in your heart to forgive me." Lola's voice shook for fear of rejection. Nyla looked up into Lola's face and for the first time in her entire life, she saw her own reflection. Tears filled the corners of her eyes and Nyla nodded.

"I can try," she replied, hoarsely. Those words were like music floating through the air. Lola closed her eyes. She could feel the weight being lifted from her shoulders. Raina smiled and took a deep breath. "Well, the doctor has already signed the release so... what do you say we get out of here?" They looked at each other, tensely. Nyla grimaced as Lola and Raina helped her off of the bed and into the waiting wheel chair. The four of them cautiously made their way down the hall.

Nyla was completely surprised to see everyone when they entered the waiting area. Even Mrs. Pearl and her husband had stopped by. They all circled her, hugged and kissed her with tears of joy streaming down their faces. Finally, she belonged. She had people who cared about her, a family that wanted to protect her and a mother who wanted her. They knew they had a long way to go, but they each gave thanks, for the spirit of hope had been restored.

## ROMANS 5:3-5

We rejoice in our suffering, knowing that suffering produces endurance, and endurance produces character, and character produces hope, and hope does not put us to shame..."

<<<< >>>>

"When I say I am a Christian" — by Carol Wimmer

When I say … "I am a Christian"
I'm not shouting "I'm clean livin'."
I'm whispering "I was lost,
Now I'm found and forgiven."

When I say … "I am a Christian"
I don't speak of this with pride.
I'm confessing that I stumble
and need Christ to be my guide.

When I say … "I am a Christian"
I'm not trying to be strong.
I'm professing that I'm weak
And need His strength to carry on.

When I say … "I am a Christian"
I'm not bragging of success.
I'm admitting I have failed
And need God to clean my mess.

When I say … "I am a Christian"
I'm not claiming to be perfect,
My flaws are far too visible
But, God believes I am worth it.

When I say … "I am a Christian"
I still feel the sting of pain.
I have my share of heartaches
So I call upon His name.

When I say ... "I am a Christian"
I'm not holier than thou,
I'm just a simple sinner
Who received God's good grace,somehow."